DOUBLE VISION

COLBY MARSHALL

D0111820

BERKLEY BOOKS, NEW YORK

LONGWOOD PUBLIC LIBRARY

THE BERKLEY PUBLISHING GROUP
Published by the Penguin Group
Penguin Group (USA) LLC
375 Hudson Street, New York, New York 10014

USA • Canada • UK • Ireland • Australia • New Zealand • India • South Africa • China

penguin.com

A Penguin Random House Company

This book is an original publication of The Berkley Publishing Group.

Copyright © 2015 by Colby Marshall.
Penguin supports copyright. Copyright fuels creativity, encourages diverse voices,
promotes free speech, and creates a vibrant culture. Thank you for buying an authorized
edition of this book and for complying with copyright laws by not reproducing, scanning,
or distributing any part of it in any form without permission. You are supporting writers
and allowing Penguin to continue to publish books for every reader.

BERKLEY® is a registered trademark of Penguin Group (USA) LLC.
The "B" design is a trademark of Penguin Group (USA) LLC.

Library of Congress Cataloging-in-Publication Data

Marshall, Colby.
Double vision / by Colby Marshall.
pages ; cm.—(A Dr. Jenna Ramey novel)
ISBN 978-0-425-27652-5 (trade)
1. Synesthesia—Fiction.   2. Serial murderers—Fiction.   3. Psychological fiction.   I. Title.
PS3613.A7726D68 2015
813'.6—dc23
2014045842

PUBLISHING HISTORY
Berkley trade paperback edition / April 2015

PRINTED IN THE UNITED STATES OF AMERICA

10   9   8   7   6   5   4   3   2   1

Cover design by Jason Gill.

This is a work of fiction. Names, characters, places, and incidents either are the product
of the author's imagination or are used fictitiously, and any resemblance to actual persons,
living or dead, business establishments, events, or locales is entirely coincidental.

"Every investigation is about ways of seeing, and Colby Marshall explores this idea to compelling effect in the propulsive *Double Vision*." —Andrew Pyper, author of *The Demonologist* and *The Damned*

PRAISE FOR
COLOR BLIND

"Stellar . . . Marshall's style is clipped and spare, her main character and her powerful perceptions an intriguing hero."
—*Milwaukee Journal Sentinel*

"Colby Marshall's wondrous *Color Blind* features one of the most original heroines to grace the pages of thriller fiction in years . . . T. Jefferson Parker mined similar material to great use in *The Fallen*, but Marshall proves herself every bit his equal in this rivetingly effective tale that will stoke memories of early James Patterson at his best." —*Providence Journal*

"High stakes and frequent setbacks keep the action taut and demonstrate Jenna's human frailties. Readers will eagerly await Jenna's next adventure." —*Shelf Awareness*

PRAISE FOR THE NOVELS OF
COLBY MARSHALL

"Colby Marshall has written a book that deserves to be called *thriller*."
—R. L. Stine, *New York Times* bestselling author
of the Goosebumps series

"An intricate puzzle that will keep you guessing until the very end!"
—C. J. Lyons, *New York Times* bestselling author of *Watched*

"Colby Marshall's sterling debut may transpire over more than six or seven days, but like me you'll probably finish it in a single night, racing the dawn to flip the last page. A classic concept updated to fit our politics-wary world." —Jon Land, bestselling author of *Black Scorpion*

Berkley Books by Colby Marshall

COLOR BLIND

DOUBLE VISION

For Olivia and Isaac,
the real double vision responsible for this series

"Nine-one-one, what is your emergency?"

"I'm at the grocery store, and someone is shooting people," Molly said. She had no trouble remembering the number for 911. It was the date they went to the memorial in the city. The highest single digit and the lowest single digit twice. Her birthday.

"Honey, how old are you?"

"Six," Molly answered. *The number of strings on a guitar. Points in a football touchdown. One away from seven.*

Molly pocketed the phone, climbed into the bin of refrigerated meats, and slipped into the other side, the side where the butcher cut them. She'd seen the hole where he could stick the meat through to refill the refrigerator once before. She ducked down behind the bin.

POP. POP. POP.

"I'm back," she said as she held the phone to her ear again.

"What grocery store? Can you tell me where?"

"Lowman's Wholesale," Molly answered. She and Mommy never came here. Mommy said the crowds drove her batty, whatever that meant. G-Ma liked to save money, though. She told Molly a penny saved doesn't do much good, but a hundred pennies is a dollar.

"What's your name, hon?"

G-Ma also said don't give your name to strangers, but this was the person on the other end of 911. He didn't count.

"Molly Keegan."

"Help is coming, Molly. Stay on the phone, okay? Did you see the person who's hurting people?"

POP.

"Sort of," she answered.

"Is it a man or a woman?"

"Don't know," Molly whispered. Masks weren't good for that kind of thing.

Quiet. Finally quiet.

"They might be gone," she said.

"Where are you, Molly?" the 911 operator asked.

"Hiding."

"Stay put, okay?"

But Molly couldn't stay put. She had to see. *G-Ma.*

She peered up from behind the bin, peeked out. No one there. She stood, climbed out. People lay still in an aisle, and red slicked the floors. *Don't look at the red.*

On tiptoes, she crept to the cereal row where she'd last seen G-Ma. A dazed man, probably about her Pop-Pop's age, sat slumped against the shelves. Another man was closer to the far end of the aisle on the left side. The one close to Pop-Pop's age wasn't bleeding. He just looked scared.

"Have you seen my G-Ma?" Molly whispered.

Then, sirens wailing. Footsteps running. The person with the gun appeared at the far end of the cereal aisle, glanced toward the grocery store doors where the police sirens sounded in the distance.

The man closer to the far end of the cereal aisle yelled as the gun came up.

Molly dove under the half-filled bottom shelf, tucking her feet. Boxes crashed around her, and her head burned as it hit the back of the metal.

POP.

. . .

"Molly? Molly! Are you there?" Twenty-five-year-old Yancy Vogul yelled into the phone. Dispatchers were supposed to be calm under pressure, keep the callers calm, but this was a child. He wasn't ready for this.

Ragged panting met his ears. "I'm here," the little voice said.

Shit pickle. Thank you, God.

"Help is coming," Yancy relayed again. He'd done his job, so the cops would know what they were walking into. They depended on him to get the information right, to make sure they knew enough so they wouldn't be blindsided. Enough that they could go home to their families that night.

But damn if he wasn't just happy right now to hear the six-year-old say she was alive.

"Are you hurt?"

"No," she answered. "They ran away."

"The shooter?" Yancy asked.

"Yes."

He wanted to ask which way the gunman had gone, what the child had seen, but for all he knew, if he asked her, she'd go gallivanting around the store trying to find out. Better to sit here, talk to her. Wait for reinforcements.

He entered the child's latest update into his log, hoped it would be enough.

"Seven," Molly's voice said in his ear.

Yancy hadn't asked anything. "Seven?"

"Mm-hm," she said. "Seven shots."

"How do you know?" he asked.

He heard Molly's sigh on the other end of the phone. When she spoke again, she sounded confused, frustrated at his stupidity. "Because I counted."

J enna Ramey thrust a set of keys into her brother's hand.

"And don't forget to lock *both* the front door set and the side door set when you *and* Dad are in the house, and if you go out, leave the side set open. I reset the password today on the alarm, and it's—"

"Sri Lanka 49 Captain C 2. I know, I know. You told me," Charley grumbled, plucking Ayana from Jenna's arms. "I thought you going back to the BAU meant you'd decided Dad and I could be trusted with the fortress. You did uproot us all and drag us to Virginia for this gig, after all. And we *did* do this for years."

That was before. "I know, I know. Chalk it up to me being the nervous mother of a toddler, okay?"

The fact that her daughter happened to be a toddler had nothing to do with it, of course. When her dad and Charley had kept Ayana before, Claudia was safely locked away in a mental institution. Last year, her mother had managed to weasel her way out of the system, and now she roamed the streets unchecked.

Charley plopped Ayana onto the floor in front of the TV, pressed PLAY on the DVD player. Ayana, pacifier still firmly attached to her lips at age three, clapped her hands as *Finding Nemo*'s opening graphics appeared on the screen.

Charley fast-forwarded until the scary part with the barracuda had passed, just like he always did. "Rain Man, I know *why* you do what you do, I'm just reminding you that we've already talked about it, I've consented to implement the iron will that is your weird key system, and we even took a home safety course designed by someone more paranoid than *you*. Now that's saying something. This house is better protected from home invasion than that guy down the road who took the *Halloween* movies way too seriously. Now get *out*!"

Jenna kissed Ayana on top of her fine blond hair, but the little girl didn't notice. On the TV, Marlin instructed Nemo to swim into the anemone, out of the anemone.

"Love you!" Jenna whispered in her ear.

At this, Ayana unplugged her mouth. "Wuv oo!"

Then, the paci went back in, and Ayana's eyes were back to the TV.

Charley shrugged. "Disney waits for no one."

"Come lock me out," Jenna said.

She waited patiently as Charley unbolted each lock. The key system was straightforward if you knew it well enough, but the instructions weren't written anywhere. Each key was color coded, but the key colors didn't match the colors of the locks. In order to know which key went with each lock, you had to have the combination memorized. Red key to green lock, orange key to light blue lock, yellow key to purple lock. In order to open them all, you had to open them in that order, too. Otherwise the bolts of the others would get in the way of the first, causing the door to remain locked. Only one set of the right keys existed and they were kept *on* the "lead person" in the house at all times. The set of keys could not be taken apart or copied, and it was attached to a tracking device.

The passwords were never written down, either, and Jenna changed them daily. That was why she went over them so many times before she left: her dad and brother had to remember them.

They were explicitly forbidden from sending them over text, e-mail, or any other channel. The only way they should be passed was verbally and in person.

"I'll pass along the message to Dad when he wakes up from his nap. Would you like me to perform a urine analysis to make sure he is *actually* Dad before I do so?"

"No, thank you, smart-ass. The blood test is plenty. See you in a few hours," Jenna replied.

The door closed behind her, four clicks. And just like that, she was back in the game.

When Jenna reached the office at Quantico, she seemed to be the last team member of the Behavioral Analysis Unit in the door. The long conference table inside the glassed-in walls was already full. A few curious eyes glanced over as she closed the door and the buzz of the cubicles below them died, but no one said anything. They all looked so young, fresh out of the gate. A frat boy in a ball cap, a girl Charley's age who looked like she could play linebacker for the Dolphins. This would be interesting.

Jenna sat in a chair by the wall, already an outsider.

Saleda Ovarez, special agent in charge and the only person in the room Jenna had worked with besides technical analyst Irv, tacked pictures to the giant whiteboard at the front. The dark-skinned woman glanced at her watch. "I wanted to wait for Agent Dodd before we continued, but it's two after. We need to get started," she said, her Boston accent thick.

So Jenna *wasn't* the last one here. She filed away her superior's jab about being two minutes late as a warning. Next time, she'd brief her dad and brother first thing in the morning, before a call had the chance to come in.

"Shooter came into the Lowman's Wholesale on Grady, opened fire, and escaped on foot. Seven victims, but one in particular," Saleda said, and she tapped the photo at the top left corner. "Miriam Holman, fifty-two."

"As in Virginia *Governor* Miriam Holman?" the kid in the ball cap asked.

"One and the same." Saleda nodded.

"Democrat, strong left. Shocked the hell out of everyone when she was elected. Shooter a card-carrying NRA member, perhaps?" the kid asked. He had to have just started shaving yesterday. How could he have possibly made it to the BAU already?

Rookie.

Saleda beat Jenna to the punch. "Seems likely, even probable that this was politically motivated since the governor was scheduled to speak next door at the public library in the next hour, but it's too soon to assume."

Jenna glanced across the board at the other six victims. All different ethnicities, sexes. "Other victims?"

"Their profiles are included in your briefs," Saleda replied, and she handed a stack of folders to the kid in the ball cap.

He took one and passed the pile of case reports to his right. "Other high profiles?"

Saleda nodded, gestured to the picture next to the photo of the governor. "Frank Kuncaitis, mayor of Falls Church, came to show his support for the governor."

"This couldn't be about him?" the brutish girl with the long, hooked nose asked.

"Doubtful. He wasn't well known or controversial. The rest are unknowns."

"Witnesses?" the girl linebacker asked.

Saleda yanked the clip out of her hair, shook out her dark brown locks. She looked like she'd already had the longest day of her life. "As luck would have it, it was senior citizen's day at Lowman's. We have several witnesses, but most of 'em can barely remember what day it is, much less any important shooting details."

"How many shots?" Jenna asked.

"We think seven," Saleda said.

Seven up, seven down, huh? It spoke volumes. This guy wasn't firing rapidly, hoping to hit any moving target. The shots were specific to a degree.

Jenna nodded to the governor's picture. "Was Miriam Holman the first victim?"

Sure, she was tacked in the first spot, but it *could* be because of her stature.

"No," Saleda replied. "Fourth. Kuncaitis was fifth."

Fourth and fifth. Right in the middle. Jenna thought of Charley at home with Ayana, probably just now watching the part where Marlin meets the sea turtle. Why had she taken this position back again?

"How soon do we leave?"

On the way to the scene, Saleda finally took the time to introduce Jenna to the team, if only because they couldn't do much else until they arrived at Lowman's Wholesale anyway. Both the brutish Teva and Porter, the frat boy, gasped at Jenna's name as though Saleda had sprouted tentacles when she said it.

"Sorry," Saleda muttered from the driver's seat of the black SUV.

"No worries. I get that all the time," Jenna answered truthfully. Her name had been in psychiatry journals across the country for articles she'd published, but everyone in the field knew her more from stories of her teenage years that had made her a national legend. She'd used her unique skill set of associating days, numbers, even people and gut feelings, with colors in order to help the police catch a black widow killer—her mother, Claudia. Grapheme–color synesthesia had made Jenna famous, put her on the path to her career, and influenced countless cases since then. Either she embraced it or shunned it, and only one of the two would do her any good in life.

"Where's Dodd, by the way?" Jenna ventured. Whoever the remaining team member was, he'd be due for a thwacking when he did show.

"No idea. And it's his first day, too, if you can believe it," Saleda said, a hint of disdain in her voice. "Rebuilding's a bitch."

Jenna's cell phone vibrated in her pocket. She reached in and removed her Droid. Yancy. She'd texted to let him know she was en route to a scene, not to count on her for lunch, dinner, or any subsequent meals today because this one sounded huge.

Now she glanced at his message.

I know I'm not allowed to ask, but I'm gonna. Is it what I think it is?

With anyone but him, she'd doubt it, but given their history of being on the same page for random, inexplicable reasons, no telling. Besides, she'd dated him long enough and through enough investigations to know she could trust him with a detail or two.

She texted back:

Tell me the store thing hasn't hit the news already.

His reply came back in less than twenty seconds.

Yes, it's already on the news, but that's not how I knew about it. I took the call.

Shit. Jenna typed back:

Anything worth knowing?

Definitely. Find a kid named Molly.

Jenna relayed Yancy's information to Saleda as she flashed her credentials at the barrier set up by the local cops in front of the Lowman's parking lot. One of the cops manning the blockade nodded, scooted the sawhorse aside for Saleda to drive through. Normally a massacre like this would be a case for the locals, but when two elected government officials were shot, it got high priority. Technically, this was still a local case, but the BAU had already been called in for a consult.

"We didn't know the nine-one-one call came from a kid?" Jenna asked.

Saleda shook her head. "Still processing all the nine-one-one calls. They apparently got upward of a dozen from cell phones in the store. Why find the kid?"

Jenna shrugged. If Yancy thought she should talk to this kid, he must have a good reason. He knew the game—and how Jenna worked—well enough to know what she'd find useful. "We'll see, I guess."

Most of the cop cars in the city seemed to be in this parking lot, which meant the manhunt for the shooter couldn't be high on the priority list.

Are the locals not used to dealing with this much blood, or do they have reason to think this shooter isn't a danger? A dead suspect? One in custody? Jenna hopped out of the SUV and followed Saleda toward the store's entrance.

"Special Agent in Charge Saleda Ovarez. This is Dr. Jenna Ramey, Special Agent Teva Williams, Special Agent Porter Jameson," Saleda said to the cop who greeted them out front.

The reed of a man shook her hand.

"Lieutenant Daly, DCPD. Thanks for coming. S.A. Dodd is already inside."

Uh-oh.

"What?" Saleda said, half question, half exclamation.

"He's walking the grid," Officer Daly replied, confused.

"Aha," Saleda answered, and Jenna detected the way Saleda forced the anger back down in her throat. Already this Dodd character was a piece of work.

"Walk us through?" Saleda asked.

"Sure thing," Daly replied. The team followed him into the store.

As Jenna entered the grocery store, the scene that met her eyes seared into her brain, keeping company with all of the other horrific crime scenes she'd taken in over the years. Smears of blood across the floor, footprints. *Please let the CSIs have gotten to all this before the locals contaminated it to hell and back.*

The first three victims were in the produce section of the store. The first two were close together in front of the apple and orange display, victim one's head apparently at victim two's feet.

"One and two, Clovis Carter and Lily Ross. Both female, fifty-eight and fifty-five, respectively," Saleda recapped for the team.

The shooter had to have come in, turned right, and killed the first people he saw. Unafraid to shoot or *so* afraid that if he didn't go ahead, he might not? Excited? In a rage?

"Cold," Porter mumbled. "Ordered hit?"

"Too soon to say, I think," Saleda replied.

Nearer to the back of the produce section lay victim three, Sherman Frost. The sixty-seven-year-old had originally been found draped over the summer squash, but someone had moved him to try to get him to safety. The bullet in his back made him bleed out before help arrived.

Next the shooter had hit the canned goods aisle, which Jenna now traveled quietly behind Officer Daly like it was a strange tourist attraction and he her tour guide. From the blood-spray angles of the shot to Miriam Holman's face, the shooter had taken the shot from the end of the aisle. Her face was clipped on the left side, and the blood had shot over her left shoulder into a shelf of ramen noodles. Weird.

"From the shot to the third victim, the shooter seemed shorter," Teva commented.

Seemed.

The shooter had also fired at the first two victims at an angle consistent with a right-handed shooter. This shot, however, listed to the left. If he'd come here to kill this specific target—the governor— he sure did take a bad shot to do it. The job was done, but still . . .

"If you were the shooter, wouldn't you be more precise with someone you showed up to pop?" Jenna asked.

"Where's your head at?" Saleda asked.

Jenna bit her lip. "He's not taller than the shot at the third victim made him seem. This one's just different. He took out the first three victims with the gun in front of him. This almost looks like . . ." Her voice trailed off.

"He shot it over his shoulder," Porter filled in.

Jenna nodded. "Almost like an afterthought."

"Could he have not seen her at first? Was afraid she'd get away?"

"Hm. Maybe," Jenna replied. If he *had* seen her and didn't want her to get away, it lent credibility to the idea that he was afraid of the shooting, lacked confidence. That told a different story from a killer who enjoyed the rampage. And yet . . .

Jenna didn't attempt to pull up the colors trying to rise in her brain. She had feelings, but she'd wait for them to solidify.

"Next," Saleda instructed.

Officer Daly led them to the right, past the cereal, baking, and cookie aisles. At the deli toward the end of the store, opposite the produce section, lay the body of victim five, Mayor Frank Kuncaitis.

"He was shot point-blank in the face," Officer Daly reminded them.

"And we're *positive* the mayor couldn't be a target?" Teva asked.

"Never say never," Jenna mumbled. Something about all this was so off. She forced herself to ignore the royal blue tones that tried to crash in. No analyzing colors until she'd had time to process.

Victim six was back toward the checkout line, a bullet between her shoulder blades that came from behind. Rita Keegan had landed facedown on the tile, though her blood had clearly been run through and dragged all over the front of the store by panicked customers, maybe even the shooter.

"Why head back toward the exit?" Porter asked. "His pattern of movement makes no sense."

Saleda's eyes trailed from victim six to the door. "And where's victim seven?"

Officer Daly pointed toward the cereal aisle, which they'd passed earlier. "Back that way."

"Paranoid that his shot at the governor didn't do the job? Was going back to make sure?" Porter ventured.

Teva shook her head. "But why keep moving *deeper* into the store for the mayor and *then* come back for her? If she was your target, walk up to her, put one between her eyes, and leave."

"For that matter, why not wait and shoot her while she's talking in the library. She'd be a sitting duck," Jenna mumbled. "Sure, there'd be a security team, but for a planned hit, it's easier. Predictable. If the security was an issue there but not here, for that matter, wait until she's walking into the library. You know she's going in."

"Maybe it's more to do with the mayor than we thought," Saleda said, standing up from where she'd been kneeling beside Rita Keegan, examining the angle of the blood spray. "Onward."

In aisle seven, body number seven, Blake Spiegel, had been shot straight on, too, only he seemed to have been facing the shooter. He fell backward from the bullet to his chest, which had gone directly through him and lodged into a wall at the back of the store.

Some shots to backs, chests. Others hit faces, but not cleanly. "Training seems minimal. He hits seven for seven shots, but none of them executed perfectly. I'd say military background is doubtful."

"The angle of the bullet that went through Spiegel was odd, too. It went through him, but entry point was a bit left of exit point. He seems to have shot him from a bit to the side the same way he did the governor," Porter said.

The inconsistency of the shots, the victim order. Something about this whole thing didn't mesh. Jenna wasn't ready for colors to show so strong yet. In the past, crime-associated colors burned in her mind based on gut feelings, but only when she had enough information to resolve those feelings. This time, though, purple surrounded the shooting in the cereal aisle before she had seen or heard enough to trust it. An entirely different color from the blue that permeated the rest of the scene.

"This is the only *young* guy," Teva pointed out. "The others were all over fifty."

"Well, it *is* senior citizens' day," Officer Daly said.

Good point. But that didn't mean this victim's age should be discounted. In fact, the more Jenna looked at this scene, the more she wondered if the initial idea of the governor being the motive for the shooting wasn't way off base. The first or last victims should be looked at harder, for sure. Chronological order was important to victim profiling, even if one of the victims *was* in political office. The vics could be random, but they could *not* be random, too.

Saleda was on her phone. "Irv, we need workups on the victims, more in depth than what we currently have. Backgrounds, family, friends. We'll call with more specifics, but for now take the names and break down the usual on each—military, financial, occupation, stressors, etc."

She hung up with the technical analyst, turned to the team. "Teva, you start with the witnesses in the parking lot. Porter, see what CSI has that might be of interest. Jenna and I will break down the witnesses who actually saw the shooter."

"Any recommendations for my team as far as the manhunt?" Daly asked.

Saleda glanced at Jenna.

"Not yet. Keep looking, but proceed with caution. Suspect is armed and dangerous," Jenna replied. She glanced at the seventh victim on the floor, pictured the bullet sailing through his chest at a strange angle toward the back of the store. As an afterthought, she added, "Armed, dangerous, and possibly unstable."

Eldred sat in the parking lot of the grocery store, confused. The police told him he had to stay, but he didn't understand why. Had he done something wrong? Was he being arrested?

More and more had changed for him lately. First, Nancy told him he couldn't stay at home alone anymore, and she'd brought in a nice lady nurse to stay with him on evenings when she couldn't be there. Then his daughter had changed his living arrangements a second time. She said it wouldn't work, staying home with the nurse. He would have to live in a group home, that it was for his own safety.

Pish. His own safety. He knew how to keep himself safe, for crying out loud. He wasn't a baby, after all! He'd been on this earth taking care of himself for over seventy years, dang it! He knew darn well how to take care of himself!

And yet . . . he was at a *grocery store*. How had he gotten to the grocery store? Lately, his days were fuzzy, distorted like the reflection in a funhouse mirror.

"Sir?" a tall, brown-haired girl said, touching him on the shoulder.

"Who are you?"

"Sir, my name is Special Agent Teva Williams. I'm with the FBI. Can you tell me your name?"

Of course he could tell her his name! Eldred. Eldred. Oh, drat it. Eldred . . . "Eldred Beasley."

"Thank you, Mr. Beasley," she replied, and she jotted his name down in a notebook. My, she looked a lot like Nancy. In her twenties, surely. Maybe thirties, that long hair swishing in the wind. "Mr. Beasley, can you tell me where you were in the store when you heard or saw that something was wrong?"

Wrong?

Concentrate.

"What do you mean?" he asked.

"Sir, where were you when the shots were fired? Can you re-member?"

Of course I can remember! "Shots?"

"Dad!"

Eldred turned to see his daughter behind an orange and white sawhorse, jumping up and down and waving to him, frantic. She talked heatedly with the officer in front, though Eldred couldn't make out what she was saying.

"Mr. Beasley?" the girl in front of him said again.

"Yes?"

"Mr. Beasley, when the shots sounded, which part of the store were you in?"

He stared at this girl, who might be crazy. Shots. There weren't any shots. "I . . . I don't know what you're asking . . ."

A moment later, a cop sidled up to the girl. "That's this guy's daughter at the barricade. Says her father has Alzheimer's disease, that he might not be aware of where or who he is. She'd like to come through . . ."

The girl glanced at Eldred, then back toward Nancy. "Let her in."

Alzheimer's disease? That was the most ridiculous thing he'd ever heard! He was perfectly fine!

Nancy closed the gap between the two of them, ran toward him. Hugged him. "Oh, thank God you're all right!"

"What are you doing here, Nan?" He pulled back from her to look in her eyes. Her face was . . . different somehow. "Have you done something new with your makeup?"

Nancy's eyes clouded over; her face dropped. "No, Dad, I . . ." She stopped, turned to the girl. "Nancy. I'm Eldred's daughter."

"Nice to meet you. S.A. Teva Williams," the girl said. She shook Nancy's hand.

Now that he could see them up close, it was obvious to Eldred that Nancy and this girl looked nothing alike. This girl was much younger, Nancy more mature than he was thinking. Maybe that was the way of fathers. You always held only the most flattering mental picture of your child in mind.

"May I speak with you for a moment?" Nancy asked the girl.

"Sure," the girl replied.

They stepped to the side, and Eldred watched as Nancy and the girl exchanged quick, hushed words. He looked around, the parking lot seeming to come into view for the first time. Police cars everywhere, other people sitting with blankets wrapped around them, hugging. Crying.

A thought niggled the back of Eldred's mind. What was happening?

Then, the next moment, Nancy was beside him, her hand on his arm. "I'm going to sit here with you, Dad. We have to wait a little longer. Then you're going to come back home with me for a while. How would that be?"

"What for?" *Please explain all this.*

Nancy squeezed his shoulder. "I just don't want you away from me right now because I can't . . . Dad, do you remember what happened inside?"

Heat climbed up Eldred's face. "Remember? Of course I remember! I was just . . ."

Then, before he could say anything else, the tears stung his eyes. He bit his lip hard, trying to stifle them, but Nancy's frown told him she'd already seen.

"Oh, Dad," she said, pulling him into a tight hug.

He watched a few tears dribble onto his daughter's neck before squeezing his eyes shut. With them closed, she felt like Sarah. Smelled like her. His wife was one of the few things he could remember distinctly, even if it had been years since she passed on somewhere he couldn't follow.

God help him if he ever lost her. He could lose everything else and still make it, but if he lost Sarah . . .

He couldn't lose her. Not again.

Blood. Gunshots. Running. A monster.

Eldred pulled away from his daughter, looked into Nancy's eyes. "There was blood."

Nancy blinked. "Did you see anything, Dad? Did you see the shooter?"

What was she talking about? "What shooter?"

She sighed, shook her head. "Never mind."

And she hugged him again.

Officer Daly led Jenna and Saleda to the back warehouse where the witnesses who said they'd actually *seen* the shooter had been sequestered. Sniffles permeated the air, soft muttering as some of the less traumatized of the group whispered among themselves.

"I'll be out front if you need me," Daly said.

As soon as he was out of earshot, Jenna leaned in to Saleda. "You find Dodd, I find Molly?"

"Sounds good to me," Saleda answered.

Jenna scanned the crowded room, looking for the littlest witness. She'd have asked Daly about her, only technically, this wasn't the FBI's case yet, and Jenna didn't want the locals homing in on the girl if it wasn't necessary. She knew how she'd feel if it was Ayana in this room and there weren't any parents here to look out for her.

She wove through the crowd of people, and finally she spotted the pint-sized brunette sitting in a corner, arms wrapped around her knees. She wasn't alone.

The man crouched across from her looked to be in his late fifties. He gestured with his age-spotted hands as he spoke, the wisps of his tawny hair thicker at the sides of his oval-shaped head than on top.

As Jenna approached, she could hear what he was saying to the little girl.

"And what happened after you hid behind the meat bin?"

She folded her lips, appearing deep in thought. "I talked to the man on the nine-one-one call. I told him the gunshots had stopped. I crawled out to see if the shooter guy was gone. To check on G-Ma."

The kid's composure made her sound about thirty. Totally calm. Poised even.

"Was he gone?" the man in plainclothes across from Molly asked.

Who is *this guy?*

"Excuse me," Jenna said, inserting herself into the conversation. "Could I have a word?"

As he turned to look at her, Jenna realized that not only was the guy about her dad's age, but about his height, too.

He glanced back at Molly. "Back in a jiff," he said, winking. He stood and straightened the tan jacket over his black mock turtleneck. When they were a few steps away from the child, he cleared his throat. "May I ask—"

"Dr. Jenna Ramey, BAU," Jenna said.

"Ah. Dr. Ramey. It's a pleasure," he said. "Gabriel Dodd."

Jenna flinched. Too bad she and Saleda hadn't stuck together. No need for Saleda to waste time looking for him anymore, but no way Jenna was about to leave him with this kid without her for another minute. He'd already broken protocol by skipping the team briefing. How did she know he wouldn't compromise a child witness, too?

"S.A. Dodd. Nice to know you. And who's your friend?"

Dodd smiled a warm, grandfatherly smile, and a smattering of contours like dents of wood grain branched from his eyes. "You know who she is, or you wouldn't have been so keen on finding her. Remember, Doc, we're on the same team."

All I know is she's the kid Yancy talked to on the phone.

"Kid made a nine-one-one call is my only lead, actually," Jenna said. "What do *you* know about her?"

He shook his head. "Well, *now* I know that her grandmother was actually one of the victims, one Rita Keegan, and for a kid so young who just lost a grandparent in front of her eyes, she's calm and composed. Not as surprising to me as it might be to some, I guess. I've found some kids deal with death better than most adults just because they aren't all taught to fear it. But at first I only came over because she *is* a kid, and kids *are* different. Kids are honest, notice things some people don't. She has a unique point of view."

Is that why Yancy thought I should find this kid? Surely there's more to it than that.

"Right. Anything good so far?"

Dodd shrugged. "Haven't had time to ask much. Join me if you like."

With that, he turned back to his interview, squatted next to Molly.

If you can't beat 'em, join 'em.

Jenna sat down cross-legged across from Molly, next to S.A. Dodd.

"Did you notice anything about how the man with the gun looked, Molly?" Jenna asked. It would be nice to be able to ask clarifying questions like whether he was tall or short or fat, but unfortunately, those were considered leading questions. With a child, it was the kind of thing that would get anything Molly said thrown out of court in a heartbeat, if they ever found the guy.

The dark-haired little girl nodded. "Yes. He had on a mask. But do you need to know more about what he looked like when I saw him or more about what he was doing before that?"

Ominous. "Is there something you want to tell us about what you noticed?"

Now Molly looked at the ceiling like she was trying to figure out a really hard math problem. "I know how many steps he took from when I started to count. Eight, like on the fortune-teller ball my friend Jana has. He tapped, too."

"Tapped?" Dodd echoed.

She bobbed her head. "Yes. He tapped his gun with his hand."

Jenna squinted, searched the girl's eyes. This kid was sharp. Observant. No wonder Yancy had thought she ought to talk to her. "How so, Molly?"

Molly brought her hand to her knee. She slapped it three times.

Jenna felt her eyebrows lift. "When did you notice that?"

"Just once. When I saw him coming toward the aisle where I was."

"Can you do that for me again?" Consistency was key here. So important.

Tap, tap, tap.

Again, it was three.

Green burst forth, the color Jenna always associated with the number three. Three taps. A thought she couldn't fully identify tickled at her mind.

"Oh, thank God!"

Jenna whirled around to face the direction from where the voice had come, but the man was already to Molly, scooping her up and hugging her to him. He held her face hard to his chest, closed his eyes as he bowed his head toward her.

"Sorry to interrupt," Saleda said, laying a hand on Jenna's shoulder. "Dr. Jenna Ramey, this is Liam Tyler. Miss Molly's stepdad."

Jenna blanked her face to keep from tearing up at the man's obvious relief over seeing Molly in one piece. Hank would've done the same with Ayana had the situation arisen. As much as Yancy loved A, and as great as he was with her, she'd wondered so many times if a man who wasn't Ayana's real father could be there for her, love her as much as a dad now that Hank was gone. Watching Liam Tyler overcome with emotion at finding Molly tugged her heartstrings. Maybe it was possible.

Jenna stretched out her hand. "Nice to meet you. We were just chatting with Molly a bit about what she saw today."

Liam Tyler's eyes went wide, seemingly at the thought of Molly having seen something so gruesome, but then he pulled back from Molly to look at her face. He smiled wide. "And are you being helpful?" he asked Molly.

Thank ya, Jesus. Not one of those parents who plants thoughts in the kid's head by freaking out over the shooting. Makes things a lot easier.

"Of course," the precocious little girl said, sighing heavily as though it were the silliest question in the world. "I told them the number of steps the bad man took, the number of times he tapped. I was about to tell them about what time it was, but I didn't have a chan—"

Liam looked away from Molly and toward S.A. Dodd. "I'm so sorry. She does this sometimes. We're working on it, but it's unfortunately still kind of a preoccupation."

Jenna cocked her head. "Pardon me? What is it you're working on?"

Liam put Molly down and straightened her coat as he looked over her head at Jenna. "The numbers thing. She'll tell you everything you want to know about every number she counts, but I doubt it'll help you—"

"Oh, no," Jenna cut in quickly. Better to interrupt him and seem rude than give him the chance to plant thoughts in Molly's mind that there was any sort of information she should hold back because it wouldn't be helpful. Parents always meant well, but they never did understand that even the slightest cues given to kids could mean the difference between answers and a missing puzzle piece. She looked at Molly, who was exasperatedly trying to wiggle away from her stepdad's attempts to tidy her up, and smiled. "The numbers are super helpful, Molly. As is anything you remember. What time was it?"

Molly looked up at her and grinned, clearly proud of herself. "Three forty-five. I remember it because it lined up. Three-four-five."

You'd have remembered it if it hadn't. Jenna could practically see the wheels spinning in Molly's head, latching numbers onto events, people, words. She wasn't so different from Jenna at all.

"That was when I looked at my watch, but I'm not sure what time it was when the popping first started," Molly said. As she did, she glanced up toward Liam Tyler.

Subtly seeking parent's approval. Check. This interview would serve them better if they got Molly to a place where they could question her without the parent there to offer even the most well-meant nods of encouragement.

Jenna squatted in front of her. "We'll probably have some more questions for you later, but in the meantime, you tell Mom or Stepdad if you think of anything else that might be important, okay?"

Molly nodded in earnest. "I will think about it hard."

Jenna didn't doubt it.

"Can I take her home now?" Liam Tyler asked, holding Molly's hand. He wore a desperate frown, an expression as worn as his nerves must've been.

Saleda smiled. "Sure. Here's my card. Please call if anything comes up. We'll be in touch, probably arrange another interview down at the station within the next day or two."

Liam nodded. "Thank you."

As they walked away from Molly and her stepfather, Jenna nodded toward S.A. Dodd. "Saleda, this is S.A. Dodd."

Saleda didn't break stride, but Jenna could feel her tense beside her. "Nice to meet you, Special Agent. Tell me, is it standard practice for you to arrive first at your team's crime scene? Are you just incredibly prompt, or is there some sort of early-bird prize the rest of us don't know about?"

Dodd chuckled. "More that I was in the neighborhood."

Saleda stopped walking. "Well, from now on, understand we attend briefings as a team and report in as such, even if you *are* Mr. Rogers."

Ouch.

"Duly noted," Dodd replied, not a hint of animosity in his tone.

You damn sure took that better than I would've.

"What have we learned?" Dodd asked.

I also wouldn't overstep my bounds right this second, either.

Saleda's eyes narrowed, but she faced forward and started walking again. "Not much, considering most of the witnesses are senile, confused, and traumatized."

"The workers?" Jenna asked.

"Most didn't see a thing. They either didn't have sight lines, or they heard shots and ducked under counters for protection, scared shitless. What about the kid?" Saleda asked.

Tapping. "She mentioned a few things. She did actually *see* the guy, but no description, really."

"Could she work with a sketch artist?" Saleda asked.

"Doubtful. She didn't notice enough of those kinds of details." *Tapping. Three taps. What is it about that?*

"Kid's bright, though. She noticed more than most people around her," Dodd chimed in.

"Yeah, I definitely think we'll want to talk to her again," Jenna mumbled. She made a mental note to jot down some ideas later, think about how she might be able to relate looks to numbers when she interviewed Molly again.

"Local cops are setting up roadblocks with a sixty-mile radius. He couldn't have gotten much farther than that, but unfortunately we have virtually nothing to go on. No clue whether he left in a vehicle, on foot, or anything in between. He could've ridden a goddamned Clydesdale horse for all we know," Saleda said.

"We should also check with local psychiatric hospitals for any recently released inpatients. This thing reeks of someone with voices in their head telling them Governor Holman was about to let aliens rule Virginia," Dodd said.

Jenna caught herself nodding. She wasn't sure about the governor and the aliens, but from the moment she'd walked in, the lack of training in the shooter combined with the obvious planning of the event had brought the color blue to her mind. She associated the particular royal shade with a variety of things, but in this case, her gut said whatever its other implications might be, it indicated submission. She usually associated reds with power, blues with submission. One of her most high-profile cases last year had been a classic example, one in which two shooters came together, one red and one blue in her mind—the dominant and the submissive, respectively. In this single-shooter situation though, she had a feeling the submissive blue meant the perpetrator was submitting to some urge he couldn't control. Mental illness, be it schizophrenia or not, was a likely explanation for such a compulsion. True psychopaths, unlike the kind the media portrayed, were scarily *sane*, and usually displayed a great deal of control over their actions. The problem was they didn't have consciences, so they just didn't care about right or wrong.

Jenna's phone vibrated in her pocket. She reached for it reflexively, her heart leaping into her throat. Every time that phone rang, the worst possibilities flashed in. She could practically hear Claudia's voice on the other line, taunting that she had gotten Ayana somehow. With Ayana at home, away from her after everything that had happened last year, Jenna would just as soon turn herself in as the grocery store shooter than not answer that phone.

"Sorry, have to take this," she said with no further explanation. She'd already told Saleda one of her conditions for returning to the team would be that she would have her phone on her at all times for this very reason. Saleda hadn't had enough better options to argue.

When she was a few steps away from Saleda and Dodd, Jenna answered the phone. It wasn't Claudia, nor was it her brother or her dad telling her there was any kind of problem with Ayana.

It was Gerald Fitz, her ex's attorney.

"Dr. Ramey, I'm so sorry to bother you, but I need to have you come down to sign a few papers in the morning so I can file them," he said.

Not more of this. As if the horror of Hank being murdered wasn't enough, she'd found out in the days following his death that he'd named her executor of his will. She'd also learned that when a cop takes out enough life insurance to cover his daughter's entire future in case of what, compared to other professions, could be thought of as a very likely job-related incident, family members he hadn't spoken to in years would somehow assume his will contained equally as much to take care of his loved ones. Even though in reality the only assets he'd had to his name to leave were the fixer-upper he'd bought as a foreclosure and a plot of land near his childhood home he'd inherited when his dad passed. But the insurance money made those long-lost relatives come out of the woodwork, sniffing around and subsequently finding out that the plot of land Daddy Dearest had left him was worth a great deal more than they'd have ever known or cared about otherwise. They'd claim it was rightfully theirs, and unlike the insurance money, the will left more room to be contested. After all, Hank named Ayana alone on his insurance policies. And while he'd named her in his will, too, that will hadn't listed her until a year after she was born. Whoever used to be on it could argue they were still supposed to be. After all, the person running the show was someone who—in their eyes, anyway—stood to gain from them being missing from it.

"I'm at work right now, Mr. Fitz. It'll have to wait until tomorrow—"

"Can't," he said. "Have to get this in by the fifth of the month, Dr. Ramey."

"Well, then tomorrow will be fine. It's only the third," Jenna said.

Her breath caught. *Three taps. March the third. Third month, third day.* A recent crime scene she'd seen in the news flashed in. "Son of a bitch."

"I beg your pardon?" Fitz replied.

"Oh, sorry," Jenna mumbled. "Not you. I need to go. I'll call you shortly."

She hung up, striding toward Saleda and Dodd. No wonder this crime scene hadn't felt politically motivated to her. It wasn't. At least not the way it might seem.

Three. Time was of the essence right now.

She reached Saleda and Dodd just as Saleda was giving instructions to Sergeant Daly on what to release at the press conference based on the shooter's current profile.

"Don't do that," Jenna said, interrupting her supervisory agent. Sometimes insubordination was called for, damn it. "This isn't a random shooter. We've seen him before."

When Jenna, Saleda, and Porter returned to Quantico, Irv had the files and photos they'd requested pulled and ready for them. Dodd had insisted on hanging back at Lowman's to poke around, and Saleda had been so irritated with him, Jenna doubted she wanted him close by anyway. She'd agreed he could stay at the site and interview witnesses as long as Teva stayed to help—or babysit.

Now Porter approached the cherrywood table and lifted one of the photos by its corner. "If the Triple Shooter is the person who shot up Lowman's, why didn't he shoot each of the victims three times?"

As soon as Jenna realized the grocery store shooting had taken place on March the third around 3:33 p.m., Molly's statement about the shooter tapping three times had clicked into place. Until about six weeks ago, the Triple Shooter had kept the Southeast both terrorized and captivated for two months. Still at large, the killer shot his victims only after somehow, in his vision, they lined up with a series of the number three. He had been inactive for a good three fortnights as far as they knew. Either that, or they had missed a few bodies.

As to why the killer had abandoned his MO of shooting each

victim three times, Jenna wasn't even ready to venture a guess. It didn't make sense to her, either. But this was him. It had to be.

"All I can think right now is that the Triple Shooter is still young, kill-wise. He only has three victims, barely enough to qualify as a serial. Serials grow, develop. They experiment and figure out what works and doesn't. The Triple kills because of bizarre coincidences, which definitely supports the theory that he's obsessive-compulsive, maybe schizophrenic. But if he is schizophrenic, just because he kills because voices tell him to doesn't mean he can't learn and adapt," she replied.

She glanced at the photo of victim one in Porter's hand. Twenty-six-year-old Wendy Ulrich had been found in the parking garage outside of her apartment complex in Fairfax. The brunette was shot three times in the chest. A receipt from Demetri's Diner takeout shop was found with her. It had been ripped in half, one half placed over each eyelid. She had been customer number three hundred and thirty-three.

Porter handed Jenna the picture of the second victim, Maitlyn O'Meara. The middle-aged woman had been killed at a rest stop off of exit 9B, just a town over from the site of the first victim's murder. She, too, had been shot three times. From the wounds, the ME had determined that the killer most likely approached the victim on foot and shot her in the back when she ran. Blood smears indicated that she had rolled over, where he then shot her in the chest from a distance, then once in the head at point-blank range. He'd cut her driver's license in half and left one piece over each closed eyelid.

"You think the eye thing has to do with self-loathing? He doesn't want the victims to see him, so he covers their eyes?" Porter said, now studying the third and last confirmed victim's picture.

"Could be," Jenna answered, but something about the submissive blue she associated with this killer tugged at her. She pushed it away. That could be examined later. "But their eyes are closed under the pieces left on top of the lids. I seriously doubt all three victims died from gunshot wounds with their eyes already closed. He has to be closing them."

"That's another difference from the Lowman's shooting, then," Saleda remarked.

Porter held up a hand. "Wait, but if he's closing their eyes to keep them from seeing him, why the pieces over the eyes? Could he hate himself so much he needs a double layer?"

"Doubtful. It's more likely he's using the pieces as a calling card. After all, they do always point us to his motivation for the kill," Saleda said. "The receipt for order number 333. Maitlyn O'Meara's driver's license, when he obviously targeted her because her license plate number was 33 3RBC. The keys on victim three."

Jenna's gaze flitted to the photo Porter held of the third victim, Ainsley Nickerson. Her ex-husband had found her inside her apartment, 333J, where he'd come by after she didn't answer his phone calls about picking up their eight-year-old daughter from her weekend visit. She'd been shot in her bathtub, and two keys were placed over her closed eyes. One was her apartment key, the other a key to her mother's home. Both had been removed from her own key ring.

Jenna imagined a faceless shooter bending over this woman he'd just shot thrice in the torso to ease her eyelids shut, almost as though she were sleeping. The gesture was intimate. Tender, even. The act of closing someone's eyes after death made blue burn even brighter in Jenna's mind.

"The pieces might be calling cards, but closing the eyes of the dead is something someone does as a gesture of reverence, of sorrow," Jenna said. She tried to force her mind to see the crimes in the carmine shade her brain reserved for the needless, horrific acts of violence often committed by psychopaths with no driving force other than to derive shock value, but the cool blue kept creeping in and washing over it. "This guy isn't trying to draw attention to himself or taunt us. He's remorseful."

Saleda shrugged. "It could fit. If he's schizophrenic, he wouldn't necessarily have complete control. Maybe he realizes what he's done after the fact."

"So him not closing people's eyes at the grocery store makes even less sense . . ." Porter said.

"Except the time and date still point to him as our UNSUB," Saleda replied.

"But what would make him deviate so drastically from the current MO? Why seven people and not just one person who happened to be checking out at Lowman's at 3:33 or whatever?" Porter asked.

"Good damned question," Jenna mumbled, taking the picture of Ainsley Nickerson from him. The redhead had two bullets in her chest, one in her right shoulder. If the shooter was facing her, that was consistent with the thinking that the Lowman's shooter was right-handed. "If the shooter fired at Ainsley Nickerson standing about six feet away from the bathtub, he must've fired in rapid succession. That's about the only way to explain the shoulder shot. Recoil. Someone military-trained—hell, even a redneck who spent every evening growing up in his backyard shooting—would probably hit closer to the same mark on all three shots, right?"

"Unless he trained with a military that spends all their time playing Xbox instead of at target practice," Porter answered.

"More evidence this guy isn't trained. Check," Jenna said.

"So what now?" Porter asked, looking to Saleda.

Saleda let the folder she'd been skimming drop to the table. She removed her black frames from her eyes and rubbed the bridge of her nose. "Locals still have roadblocks set up to cover a sixty-mile radius. I've got Irv cross-referencing the Triple Shooter's known victims with the grocery store victims just in case we get lucky. I'm not really expecting a connection, but it'd be nice. In the meantime, Porter, you and I are going to comb these witness testimonies from Lowman's and see if there's anything we can hone in on that's worth a follow-up. Teva and Dodd will keep poking around the crime scene a little more. Jenna, I want you to look over the Triple Shooter case file tonight, see if anything gives further insight into what might have caused his MO to change. Warning signs of escalation, patterns or cycles we've missed until now . . . anything."

Jenna gave her superior a nod. In other words, until something dislodged, it was up to them to pull leads out of thin air. The greatest kinds of cases.

"It'd be nice if he just left us his address, phone number, and copies of all major credit cards," Porter said, leaning back.

"Now, where's the fun in that? Where's your sense of adventure, Porter?" Jenna laughed. She tucked the case file under her arm and made for the door.

Porter sat up and watched over his shoulder as she walked away. "Hey, I didn't say it couldn't be fun! He could leave the phone number scrambled. Or hey! His address could be spelled in answers in a cross-word puzzle."

Jenna opened the door. "So in other words, you'd like our next serial killer to be the Riddler from Batman?"

Porter lifted both hands. "Perfect. Would that be too much to ask?"

Jenna glanced at Saleda, and they shared an eye roll. Then she looked back at Porter. "I personally like my villains a little more Wicked Witch of the West. Easier to get rid of." She shrugged. "See you guys later."

She let the door close behind her. At least this way, she might get to read Ayana a story before bath time, even if her brain *was* filled with images of dead bodies draped over produce bins and blood-smeared floors.

Besides, she was dying to ask Yancy what his thought process was when he'd told her to find Molly Keegan. They were planning to go to dinner, so she'd have a good chance then.

Murder, pictures of dead people's faces, and drippy, romantic candles. All in a day.

H e clawed at his head, but his fingernails were chewed so low that he could only feel his stubby fingers raking against his scalp. Itching, itching. Always itching!

Focus!

He sat on his hands on the bleachers. They wouldn't find him here. Couldn't get to him here. He was safe.

But then, on the basketball court, there they were: the numbers.

Oh, no. Not again! You swore they would stay away!

He closed his eyes as tight as he could, shook his head. But no matter what he did, the numbers burned in front of him like they were branded onto the backs of his eyelids. He would have to follow her now. Just like always.

No! He mustn't! The police would find him if he did now!

But if he didn't follow her, *they* would find him, and *they* were far worse than others. He was their Hand of Justice, and he had to remain so.

Maybe she'd done nothing. Maybe it was a false alarm, and there would be no reason for him to punish her. He would follow just in case, then go home safe and sound, sure they would have no reason to chase him.

. . .

Yancy jogged around Jenna's Blazer and opened the driver's side door. Just because a woman drove was no reason not to be a gentleman.

He grabbed the door and yanked it wider just as she cracked it open. "Madame," he said, giving a little bow.

"You really don't have to do that, you know. We've been dating, in some capacity, since last summer and sleeping together since Christmas Eve. I'm pretty sure the courting stage is over," Jenna said.

Yancy slammed her door, then reached for the duct-taped side mirror. He pressed down the end of the tape-job that was quickly losing its stickiness. "In that case, if you won't let me pick up the check for dinner, at least let me take you to the hardware store and buy some Krazy Glue for this thing."

"Hey. Don't insult the duct tape," she replied, grinning as she gave him a playful smack on the arm. "It might not be perfect, but it gets the job done. Plus it's made in silver for a reason. Silver is a classy color. Matches everything."

He grabbed her hand and pulled her into him for a quick hug. Damn, how had a gimp like him gotten lucky enough to end up with a girl like Jenna? Proof that the world works in mysterious ways. Some white-collar chump out there was sitting in his billion-dollar mansion, wondering why he was all alone, and it was really just because he was too busy making heaps of money to be at a theme park in the middle of the workweek when some deranged psycho decided to shoot up the place.

Now if only Yancy could talk her into marrying him one of these days.

She pulled back from him, but grabbed his hand and twined her fingers in his. "Come on. I'm starved."

Once they were inside the little Italian place and seated at a table in the far right corner of the hole-in-the-wall establishment, Jenna groaned her typical end-of-a-long-work-day sigh.

"How was your day?" she asked.

He sat back, gnawed on a breadstick. "Eh, typical. A couple of kids playing with the phone who got a nasty surprise when police officers showed up at their door, another guy who burned his ass trying to light his farts on fire."

"That's typical?" Jenna laughed.

"Nobody ever said the life of an emergency dispatch operator was boring. Got another domestic call from that same house again," Yancy said, his heart plummeting as he remembered it.

It was the third time he'd talked CiCi Winthrop through one of her husband's drunken rages in the past couple of months, but it didn't seem to get any easier. He did what he was trained to do while on the phone with her: take her information, get her to a safe place in the home if she couldn't leave, and try his best to distract her while she waited for help.

Unfortunately, that meant that over the course of three phone calls, he'd learned that when she was five, she'd wanted to catch a snail for show and tell, but her mother said they only came out at night. She spent the next couple of years unable to sleep in the dark because she was afraid giant slugs came into her room at night. He'd found out she was allergic to strawberries and that the only time she'd been to the beach was when she was ten. He now knew that even before he'd taken any of her emergency calls, she'd been in the hospital twice because her husband had beat her up, and the second time, she'd been nine weeks pregnant and was discharged after losing her unborn baby. Unfortunately, both of those occurrences hadn't involved 911 calls. Just visits to the ER following bizarre "accidents" that no one could do anything about since the victim had, at the time, stuck to her stories of falling down stairs and bumping into shelves in the dark.

"Oh, no," Jenna said, frowning. "Not again. Did they arrest him this time?"

Yancy shook his head, closed his eyes. "I don't know. I hung up with her when the cops checked in at the scene, but I doubt it. The last two times there was no visible evidence of physical abuse, no children to check, thank God." A lump grew in Yancy's throat at this statement. CiCi wished there were. "No property harm at other calls, either. On the one hand, I'm glad he hasn't hurt her again, but on the other, sometimes I wish he'd give her a good smack across the cheek so when they came, they'd have to see it and she wouldn't try to tell them it was a false alarm."

Jenna tore a breadstick in half. "Has she ever tried for a restraining order?"

Yancy raised his eyebrows. "This girl is the poster child for battered person's syndrome, Jenna. She thinks the second she did that, her husband would be right there, know what she'd done, and kill her as soon as he could get his hands on her."

Jenna blew out a long breath. "I'll probably work in psychiatry my whole life and never completely understand learned helplessness."

That's because you have the opposite response to being a victim. When Jenna was barely a teenager, she had helped police catch her mother, Claudia, for killing multiple husbands. Before the cops arrested Claudia, though, Jenna's intervention had culminated in a rampage during which Claudia stabbed Jenna's brother, and she'd fought her mother off long enough for the police to show up. Then just last year, when Claudia had tried to kill Jenna and her dad again, Yancy had seen with his own eyes how Jenna had responded to her mother's freakish tactics. Claudia had held Jenna's daughter as bait, designed a twisted ploy so that the only way Jenna's dad could live was if Jenna gave up the advantage of having Yancy in the cabin—which was supposed to have been a safe house—to fight. But Jenna hadn't broken. Instead, she'd drawn herself up to her full height, her voice steady and calm as she'd said the two words he could still hear so clearly: "Yancy, go." He'd carried Vern out of the cabin, and she'd faced Claudia alone.

"Easy in concept, impossible to understand. Agreed," he replied. "So, yeah. Call from that domestic, a couple of other simple fender benders. Oh, and some call from a kid . . ."

Jenna rolled her eyes then looked at the table. She transferred the uneaten half of the breadstick from one hand to the other.

"I'd ask you what went on today, but since I took the call, I probably shouldn't," Yancy said.

She dropped the breadstick, bowed her head, and rubbed her neck with her right hand. She glanced upward at him. "Since when does knowing you shouldn't do something ever stop you from doing it?"

He smiled. "Never. I just wanted the invitation. So, tell me about it."

Jenna gave him the quick synopsis of what she'd seen at the scene, the conclusion that it had to be the Triple Shooter, and their subsequent findings from there. She shrugged. "And we have no clue where to go next. We obviously didn't find him before, so what makes this time any different other than we have more than double the body count and a set of circumstances that make no sense at all?"

"So we've got an untrained, redneck schizophrenic obsessed with the number three out there shooting people. What's the problem?"

"You have a sick sense of humor, Yance. You know that? Besides, I just said he's probably untrained and possibly schizophrenic. I deliberately said he's probably *not* a redneck. Try and pay attention to the details."

"Right, right. If he grew up shooting in his backyard, that would mean he'd be able to put fifteen bullets right between a possum's eyes while he's hanging upside down on the old tire swing, and all that. I listen, I just creatively interpret sometimes," he said, smiling even though his thoughts trailed in their own direction at the mention of bullets. He could still hear little Molly's voice as she told him about the shots fired. "I'm serious, Jenna. You need to know where to start looking for a guy who kills in threes. So you have to ask what might cause a crazy to latch onto the number three. Best place to go to think of reasons someone might be preoccupied with a number is to the person involved in this case who's fixated on numbers, too."

"He seemed less than thrilled to hear from me," Dodd said as Jenna coasted the Blazer onto the freeway toward the house where Molly Keegan lived with her mother and stepfather. When Jenna had told Saleda she planned to interview Molly a second time, Dodd insisted on coming with her. He'd found Molly at the crime scene, too, and since then, he'd seemed practically territorial regarding her. Whether or not the old codger was afraid Jenna might figure out the Triple Shooter before him, though, was irrelevant. As far as Jenna was concerned, they both wanted the same ending to this saga, so he could tag along all he wanted as long as he didn't hinder her process.

Now Liam Tyler's concerned face filled Jenna's mind, and an amber color flashed in. She pushed it back. No way she was going to try to interpret it at this point. It could mean just about anything in the color dictionary that was her brain, or it could imply something entirely new altogether. Intelligence, denial, caution, deceit, goofiness: all were represented by various shades of orange to Jenna, so what Liam Tyler's orange said about him was anyone's guess. At this point, the only association she made with him was his protectiveness of Molly, and for that she couldn't blame him.

"How'd you manage to get him to let us come by, then?" she asked.

"I didn't. He said a couple of choice phrases to me before the mom took the phone from him and told me to come on over. Said they'd do anything they could to help us catch the person who did this."

Rita Keegan's limp form crossed Jenna's mind. Molly's grandmother had lain facedown in her own blood near the checkout line, the Triple Shooter's unlucky sixth victim. Regardless of whether or not Molly's mom wanted to keep Molly out of the mix, losing a parent was impetus enough to shoo away any misgivings you might have about letting your daughter talk more with police. Jenna should know. It was the same way she'd felt about police interviewing Ayana after Claudia had tried to kill her father last year.

"He's worried," Jenna said.

"He's an ass," Dodd replied.

"Nobody ever said you can't be both. But try to play nice until we get what we need from them."

"He's some kind of priest or something, isn't he? He has to be polite."

Jenna laughed. "I don't think working with a church youth group is quite the same as being a priest. And if you think the church crowd has to be polite, you haven't been to the same churches I have. Like I said, just be on your best behavior, like you should be with anyone, church worker or not. He can make this easier for us or harder."

"I know that, Witch Doctor. Don't worry. This ain't my first rodeo."

"Witch doctor, huh? That's a new one," Jenna said.

"Oh, yeah?"

"Definitely. I usually only get Shrink or Quackerjack. Stuff like that."

Dodd shrugged. "What can I say? I'm an original. Besides, you have that whole magical color thing going on, so you aren't entirely of the medical persuasion alone."

Too right you are.

She pulled into the driveway of the Tudor revival-style home at 1615 Adrianne Circle. Seemed a huge place for only three people, but maybe they'd bought the house with a bigger family in mind. Heck, maybe one of the two owned it before they got married, then the other moved in after.

"Nice digs," Dodd mumbled, his sharp eyes scanning the length of the property. "Shall we go have a little number chat, then?"

"Let's do this."

Jenna led the way up the winding sidewalk lined with liriope and hydrangeas. She rang the doorbell, noted no barking dog followed. Neither did voices or scurrying.

After about thirty seconds, the door creaked open and Jenna stood face-to-face with a woman of about thirty-five, her fine mousy brown hair situated in a stringy ponytail. This had to be Molly's mother.

"Hi, there. I'm Dr. Jenna Ramey with the Behavioral Analysis Unit of the FBI. This is Special Agent Gabriel Dodd. May we come in?"

The frail woman said nothing, only fingered the charm on the gold necklace at her throat as she nodded and stepped to the side. Jenna gave her a close-lipped, sympathetic smile, then walked past her into her home.

The entrance led right into a spacious combination living and dining room. Directly ahead was a large wooden table that sat way more than the family of three, and off to the left, a gargantuan beige sectional sofa set dominated the room.

This was where Molly sat with Liam Tyler, singsonging a rhyme as they played a clapping game. Both seemed oblivious that Jenna and Dodd had entered. "Miss Mary Mack, Mack, Mack. All dressed in black, black, black. With silver buttons, buttons, buttons, all down her back, back, back."

Liam beamed at the little girl, doing a good job of keeping up with Molly's hands, which moved faster and faster the further she got into the rhyme. She smiled a toothy grin, her brown pigtails bobbing with her hand movements.

"They climbed so high, high, high. They touched the sky, sky, sky. And they never came back, back, back, 'til the Fourth of July, ly. Ly, ly!"

Molly squealed and fell backward giggling.

Liam brushed fake sweat off his forehead. "You've practiced this more than me! It's not fair!"

"Aw, you looked like you were holding your own," Jenna interjected.

At this, both Liam's and Molly's heads snapped toward Jenna, and Jenna caught the glance Liam shot at his wife before returning his eyes back to Jenna.

"I'm sorry. I didn't know we had company," he said, his mouth now set in a serious line. He stood up from the couch, straightened his polo shirt, and took a few steps toward Jenna, extending a hand. "Nice to see you again, Dr. Ramey." He gave Dodd a curt nod. "And you as well, Special Agent."

The half grunt, half laugh behind her told Jenna that Dodd was smirking, and she silently willed him to keep his mouth shut. Now wasn't the time.

"Thank you for seeing us on short notice," Jenna replied. She leaned to her right to peer around Liam. "Hi, Molly."

"Hi," the little girl said. She sat up on the couch like she knew how to behave in front of visitors, but her feet swung back and forth with the excited energy remaining after her giggle-fest.

Liam cleared his throat, seemingly to regain Jenna's attention. She looked back at him, and he gestured toward Molly's mother. "I don't think you've met my wife, Raine."

No, I haven't, despite the fact that she answered the door. Jenna turned to Raine, who was still fiddling with her necklace. "It's nice to meet you, Raine. I'm so terribly sorry for your loss."

Raine's eyes filled with tears, and she folded her lips, sucking them inward for a moment. Then she blew out a slow breath. "Thank you," she whispered.

Liam clapped his hands together then held them in front of his chest. "So Special Agent Dodd seems to be of the opinion that Molly may be of some assistance."

Jenna nodded. "Yes. I'd like to ask Molly a few questions."

"I understand, Dr. Ramey, but Molly has told me she has filled you in on everything she remembers about the store that day." He leaned in and lowered his voice, though Jenna was sure Molly could easily still hear him. "She's already having trouble with nightmares, as you can imagine. I'm trying to keep it off her mind as much as I can. We said we'd call if she had anything further to impart."

Dodd coughed.

Jenna held up a hand to Dodd behind her back to silence him. "That may be, but I'd still like to talk with her." Jenna again leaned forward toward the girl. "If that's okay with you, Molly?"

Molly nodded. "I guess so. Is it okay, Mommy?"

Raine nodded.

Liam held his palms out. "Well, I guess that's that then. Ask away."

Tricky. "Actually, Mr. Tyler—"

"Liam, please."

"Right. Liam. Actually, I'd prefer to question Molly by herself, if that's okay. Sometimes adults can influence a child's answers unintentionally just by giving encouraging nods or furrowing their eyebrows in concern. Sometimes it's easier if just us girls talk," Jenna said, giving Molly a wink.

Molly grinned.

"Oh, I don't know if that's a good idea," Liam said, hesitation in his voice.

A protective grayish hue flashed in Jenna's mind for a couple of seconds.

In the moment the color distracted her, Dodd let out a little laugh. "I suspect the things you don't know might fill volumes."

Liam's head snapped toward Dodd. "Excuse me?"

Christ alive. Had Dodd never heard of interpersonal skills, or was he seriously working against her?

"Sir, we're professionals. We do this every day. I think we know the best process for—

"What S.A. Dodd is trying to say is that while we prefer to question Molly on our own, we will of course defer to her parents' judgment," Jenna cut in, whipping around to glare at Dodd.

He pursed his lips and blinked, clearly annoyed she'd interrupted him. Too bad. His lack of tact wasn't exactly thrilling for her, either.

"I think it would be fine," a small voice said from Jenna's side. Raine looked at the ground, and a single tear dripped from her face onto the carpet.

"Okay," Liam agreed, unable to argue with Molly's mother's wishes. He outstretched his hand toward the rest of the house. "Be my guest."

Molly leapt off the sofa. "Come on! I'll take you on a tour."

She clasped Jenna's fingers in hers and tugged her toward the staircase leading to the second level. Dodd trudged behind, but stopped short, fishing in the pocket of his black trousers.

"One sec," he said, removing his cell. "Gotta take this one."

He stepped away to answer his phone, and Jenna stood holding hands with Molly, who bounced excitedly, ready to get the tour under way.

"Do you give a lot of tours or am I getting a treat?" Jenna asked.

Molly tossed her head back and forth, weighing. "A few. Two a month, I'd say."

Numbers.

"You're really good at the clapping game, by the way," Jenna said. Making small talk with a six-year-old wasn't the easiest task, but you had to do what you had to do.

"Thanks! Did you know that in the nineteen fifties, for fifty cents like it says in the rhyme, you could buy a pack of ten Gillette razor blades? Or you could get twelve grapefruits. Those were twenty-five cents for six. Or four heads of lettuce! But that's before figuring in sales tax, but obviously you knew that. So you could probably only get three heads of lettuce so you'd have enough for the tax. Now for fifty cents you can only maybe get two gumballs from a machine, or a can of Coke if you're lucky. Most can machines cost over a dollar now."

Holy bologna.

"Wow. You sure do know a lot of numbers, huh?" Autistic savant? No. The kid's depth of knowledge on her random fixation was definitely savant-like in behavior, but her social interactions showed a *heightened* cognitive development, not a hindered one. Parents rarely opted to demand brain scans on a perfectly healthy child, so no way of telling, but the remarkable displays of ability in certain fields like math, music, or memory in savants tended to be the result of some type of sectional brain damage. The brain hemispheres were thrown off-kilter, often limiting function in areas like social skills but resulting in more pronounced performance in other brain activity.

Molly beamed at the compliment. "Thanks. I love to read. G-Ma always said I got that from her, but technically I guess Mommy got it from her, then I got it from Mommy."

Jenna grinned. This child clearly had no social or language deficits. Prodigy? She'd seen many children in her practice who were brought in by overly worried parents that assumed if their nine-year-old begged to practice piano more than to go to a friend's house and could play Nikolai Rimsky-Korsakov's "Flight of the Bumblebee" without missing a note that they must be mentally disturbed. In reality, the kid just happened to be an extremely gifted musical prodigy who happened to like hanging out with the baby grand in the foyer more than other nine-year-olds and their Xboxes. Child prodigies sometimes grew up to be geniuses, but not always. Sometimes they didn't even display higher than average IQs. Only precociousness and serious talent.

Whatever the case, Molly was a neat kid, and that was all the label Jenna needed for her for now.

Dodd hung up and moved back toward them. "Sorry, but I'm going to need to cut out early. I have to sort out some craziness with this case I'm testifying for. They're sending a car for me. You'll be all right?"

"Sure thing," Jenna said. Then she turned to Molly. "Ready, Freddy?" Molly nodded and tugged her toward the stairs.

Yancy yanked Oboe away from the hydrangeas the dachshund was currently considering marking as his own. The dog *could've* peed before they left the yard of their own apartment, but no. He had to wait and attempt to kill the bushes the neighbor had been cultivating for months. "Must you make all of our neighbors hate us?"

The dog didn't look at him but clearly noticed the yank on the leash, away from the bushes. He changed course and waddled on toward the roadside, a familiar path he and Yancy walked almost every day. Some things never changed.

He slowed to let Oboe sniff at a tin can on the curb. No, unfortunately, some things got stuck in neutral, and no matter how much gas you gave them, they'd just keep at that same speed.

Yancy reached into his pocket, clutched the little velvet bag there, the one that contained the perfect diamond ring for Jenna Ramey. Yeah. Too bad it would stay in that velvet bag in his pocket the rest of his life, probably. Every time he'd even come close to trying to show it to her, something had happened to remind him that she was perfectly fine with the way things were between them, and that change, at this point, was about as welcome as a fan club for her mother at Ayana's next birthday party.

Oboe picked up his pace again, and Yancy trudged behind him. Maybe Ayana's birthday party wasn't such a bad idea. Jenna would be off her guard enough that she wouldn't head him off. Dating a profiler sucked. They could always read you, know exactly which unwanted topic you were about to broach. Steer you away.

Yancy kicked a pebble with his metal hook of a foot, but the stone caught the curve of the prosthetic, which sent the rock straight into Oboe's rear end. The dog jumped and did a half turn in the air, looking for the source of attack.

"Sorry, bud. Didn't mean to take my frustration out on you."

Oboe growled halfheartedly, but faced forward and ambled on. Yancy stared at his feet as they made their way up the next block. *Shoe, thunk, shoe, thunk.* If that stupid foot didn't keep him at a desk, maybe he'd be with Jenna now, working the case. Sure, he'd never made it anywhere past his internship at the Florida Bureau of Investigation, but his imagination could station him anywhere he wanted. All the way at Quantico if he liked, damn it. His brain and that imagination were about *all* he could use as much as he wanted.

He squeezed the velvet bag in his pocket, felt the edges of the stone inside it: a little circle that happened to be the same size as Jenna's finger. Over six months, and even *she* admitted the courting stage was over. So what next? A comfortable toothbrush-at-each-other's-home arrangement, and maybe in a few years they'd adopt a little brother for Oboe together?

If I had both feet and was on the job with her, she wouldn't want to say no. Yancy dropped the bag inside his pocket and removed his hand, empty. It was a ridiculous thought, but he couldn't help it. Last year when he'd been with Jenna every step of the case, she'd fallen for him. That was when she first wanted him. Needed him. She'd never exactly be a shrinking violet, and he'd never want her to be. But it'd be nice to have to open a pickle jar or kill a spider every now and then. But who needed a spider-killer when you had a fully loaded Glock on hand and every door in your house was bolted five times over?

At the corner of Potter Road, Oboe wound left, their usual route, but Yancy paused. On the next corner came Finch Place, then Waverly a block after that. From there, it was only a couple more blocks to Crowe. If they went down Crowe and took a right onto Baxter, it was only a hop, skip, and a jump to Peake.

No, dumbass. You know the rules. Getting personally involved with a caller is not only prohibited, it's just a fucking bad idea.

And yet, he had no way of knowing if CiCi Winthrop had walked away from the latest skirmish with her husband without a scratch or if she'd left on a gurney. Not knowing what happened after the calls he took was hard, but not knowing on one like this was the worst. One of these days, CiCi would hang up after a call and he'd never hear from her again. If she was lucky, it would be because she got to a safe house of some kind, disappeared where the lowlife could never find her again.

What harm could it do just to check?

He pulled back on Oboe's leash, stepping straight ahead. "Come on, boy, this way."

Oboe stood stock-still, stubby legs rooted to the spot.

"Look, I *know* it's not where we usually go, but since when do you not like to explore?" Yancy asked, making sure his voice trailed up high at the end, the tone that always got Oboe excited.

The dog's thin tail quivered.

Yancy smirked at him then took his voice up another notch. "Cooome on, Oboe. You know you wanna, big boy!"

Oboe's tail picked up its pace, swishing faster and faster until it seemed to propel him toward Yancy and forward onto the street ahead of them.

"Attaboy," Yancy said, even though his pitch didn't match the sick feeling in his gut. At best, he was going against protocol and using a caller's address inappropriately to get a cheap thrill and be part of a crisis, kind of like he was last year. At worst, he was borderline stalking.

All he wanted to do was check on her, though. He would never go back after this one time. He just had to make sure she was okay, then he could take the normal left at the corner of Potter again.

8

J enna stepped into the small, burgundy-painted room with Molly. The little girl had taken her to see her bedroom, her mother and Liam's room, the playroom, the bathroom, the kitchen, the guest room, and the den, all the while pointing out the little things only a six-year-old would notice: the doggie door exit off the kitchen, a bird's nest in the crook of the back porch roof and its support beam. She showed Jenna the hope chest in her mother's room that was large enough for her to climb into, the perfect hiding spot during a game of hide and seek.

For the entire sightseeing expedition, Jenna had attempted to pick Molly's brain about the grocery store and numbers in general, but the child was so fixated on being the ultimate tour guide, nothing could distract her from her ongoing monologue about the home's furniture, decorations, and the special stories involved with each.

Now, having seen the exercise area of the basement, which was filled with a treadmill, a stair climber, and another strange machine that seemed to Jenna more like a medieval torture device than work-out equipment, all that was left in the downstairs of the house was another small bathroom and Liam Tyler's office.

Molly pointed at her stepfather's oak corner desk. "That desk used to be Liam's father's, and it was *his* dad's before that. So it's in its third generation."

"Wow. That's pretty cool," Jenna muttered, wandering deeper into the room. She ran a fingertip along the roped edge of the well-crafted desk. "So Liam adopted you when he and your mom got married, huh?"

"Yep. My dad's okay, I guess, but he doesn't really act like a dad. Only seen him a couple of times in my life. He doesn't call or want to *be* my dad or anything. Just met me 'cause Mommy thought I should meet him. Not sure why, but she seemed to think it was important. He was nice enough, but I got the idea he didn't really want a kid. Mommy always says he's just a kid himself. Liam asked if he could adopt me, and I said sure." Molly crouched in front of the desk where she was using her pointer finger to trace one of the patterns carved into the wood. "Mommy and Liam were going to change my name to Molly Tyler when he did, but they ended up leaving it."

Jenna examined a piece of abstract brass art atop the desk. "Why's that?"

Molly giggled, her focus still on the desk's intricate etchings as she now traced the scalloped valance that hung down from the front edge. "G-Ma. She made an *awful* fuss about how if they did, she'd be the only Keegan in the house." She laughed again. "They've never found out G-Ma was doing it for me."

"You didn't want to change it?" Jenna asked, now curious. The revelation that G-Ma, Raine's mother, and Molly had the same last name hadn't been a surprise to her. She'd read in the file on Molly that Irv had put together that Raine had been using her maiden name when she gave birth to Molly, so Jenna was already aware Molly's parents had never married.

Molly shrugged. "Tyler's okay, but I like Keegan. I was so used to my name having the number of letters it does . . . it might be silly, but I didn't want my letter number to change. It just would've felt weird. Liam's fun, but he never would've understood."

Jenna looked at her and smiled when she found Molly was staring up at her, eyes hopeful. *Desires validation. Approval.*

"Well, *I* get it. You can like your new stepdad a lot and still want to be you at the same time," Jenna said. She turned to face a wall with some sort of clay or plaster artwork adorning it. Her gaze drifted up the wall and down, skimming the rows of circular plates, each with the impression of something in the middle, the entire plate painted to its own theme. They looked almost like some kind of fossils.

Molly joined her in front of the display. "Aren't they pretty?"

"Oh, yes," Jenna replied. "What are they?"

"They're rock molds. Volcanic rock molds, to be exact," Molly said, taking a step toward them. She lifted her finger and, without touching the mold right in front of her, traced the line of its impression. "See how in this one, there's a gap in the print here? That's because these kinds of rocks are formed when magma is erupted from a volcano and becomes lava or gets trapped in a pocket inside the earth. Either way, it cools and solidifies, but sometimes gas bubbles get trapped inside. They leave spaces in the rock, like this one." She grinned at Jenna, clearly proud of knowing so much about something Liam had taught her.

"Your stepdad has a bunch, huh?"

She nodded, eager. "Oh, yeah. He's an enthusiast. Makes imprints of his favorites."

Jenna smiled, but on the inside, she was cringing. Sure, everyone had their own thing, but how boring could you get? Rocks as a hobby? Stamps were about as close as anyone she knew had come, and at least *they* were compact enough that you could confine your dull-as-dishwater pastime in a scrapbook or two instead of needing to take up entire shelves and walls.

"So Liam's a rock collector, then?" Jenna asked.

"Well, not to get too technical, but I'm more of a mineral collector than a rock collector."

Jenna whirled around to see Liam Tyler standing in the office doorway.

"How interesting," Jenna said. She turned away from the wall of rock imprints toward the large print of Da Vinci's *The Last Supper* hanging behind Liam's third-generation desk. The colors were much more vivid than in any of the versions of the painting she'd seen.

Molly stepped up beside her, grinning. "It's the restored version. Isn't it cool? I like it because of all the stuff to count."

Liam stepped into the office and put a hand on Molly's shoulder. "Molly, I doubt Dr. Ramey has spent nearly as much time counting the apostles' dishes as you have, hon."

"The feet don't add up, did you notice? Not as many feet as people in the picture," Molly said.

The little girl stepped toward the canvas and gestured to each visible foot with her pointer finger, counting them as she went. "Sixteen. But there are thirteen *people*, so there ought to be twenty-six feet. You can see Jesus's easily, though. If you don't count his, you can only see fourteen feet, not twenty-four. And the cups. Eleven cups, twelve men. Other than Jesus, I mean. Thirteen with him. Have you ever noticed that stuff before, Dr. Ramey?"

Jenna smiled. "No, I haven't, but it *is* fascinating, Molly."

Next to her, Jenna felt Liam stiffen, and she blew out a breath. Contradicting him in front of his stepdaughter didn't make her feel warm and fuzzy inside, but it was in her best interests to make friends with the little girl. And for that to happen, she needed Molly to feel like she was genuinely interested in what she had to say.

"Sorry to disrupt the tour," Liam said. "I just need to grab a file and I'll be on my way."

Liam rounded the corner of the desk, pulled the drawer open, removed a manila folder, and closed the drawer. "Molly, show Dr. Ramey around if you must, but don't be too long, and don't touch. The mineral molds and the artwork are fragile, and fingerprint oil will degrade them over time." He turned to Jenna and smiled. "I'm sorry to be a bit uptight. Expensive hobbies bring out the stickler in a man, I suppose. Let me know if you need me."

With that, Liam left, and Jenna and Molly were alone again in Liam's office.

"He's protective of his rock imprints," Molly said matter-of-factly.

Jenna nodded, glancing back to the painting of *The Last Supper*.

"Do you know about the book *The Da Vinci Code*, Molly?" Jenna asked.

Molly frowned and sighed. "Mom won't let me read it until I'm older. But I did watch part of the movie on one of the paid channels," she admitted sheepishly.

Jenna smiled, thinking of how the number of cups in the painting contributed to the plot. "You're really going to like that book one day." Now to tempt her to talk about numbers in *this* case. "What other things have you counted in the painting?"

Molly's toothy smile came out again. The little girl was clearly eager to be asked about her favorite subject. "Well, five people are wearing something blue, and you can only see twenty-five hands, but there should be twenty-six." She gestured toward the right-hand side of the painting at a man who appeared to be holding up a number one. "He's the only guy who doesn't have two hands."

The little girl seemed to be right. The figure's left hand didn't show. "What's that one about, do you suppose?"

"The finger?" Molly asked.

"Mm-hm," Jenna said, examining the painting herself. For everything she knew in the world, the six-year-old had one-upped her this time. Jenna was no art historian.

"It's doubting Thomas, so probably to do with the finger he poked in Jesus's nail holes to test the evidence. That's what Liam thinks, anyway."

"You and Liam talk about the painting a good bit?"

"Eh, not that much. I've told him stuff I've noticed before. Like the dishes. There are eighteen flat dishes, but only three big ones. So that means fifteen small ones even though only thirteen people. Then there's the one big empty dish in front of Jesus, and the two with food on the sides. Three big dishes could be for the Holy Trinity maybe."

Purple flashed into Jenna's mind against her will, a royal purple, deep in hue. Strange. She usually associated the number three with an avocado green, not purple. *And yet . . .*

She'd seen purple at the crime scene, and every time she thought about the Triple Shooter's spree at the grocery store, a purple nagged her in addition to the similarly jewel-toned blue she'd seen there. The blue she already felt sure was submission to an uncontrollable urge. But the purple . . . That purple was close to the color of impulse or narcissism, but the shade was a bit different.

No matter. She could come back to the color association later. Now that she'd finally gotten Molly on not just numbers, but the number three, no way she was about to waste the opportunity. "Any other theories about the three?"

Molly shrugged. "Threes are used all the time in religious stuff. Father, Son, and Holy Ghost are one thing, but then Jesus took three days to rise from the grave, too. In fact, the number three is used four hundred and sixty-seven times in the Bible."

Jenna bit her lip to hold back the laugh. "Did you count those?"

"Googled it," Molly answered. "Three gets used a lot. Three virtues of Christ, that kind of thing, but that's normal. It's used any time deities come into play in all kinds of religions. Hindu, Buddha, Wicca, everything."

At this Jenna snorted a little.

"What?" Molly asked, wheeling around to face her.

Jenna shook her head. "It's just that I've never met a six-year-old who knows as much as you do about world religions, that's all."

Molly flashed her smile again, proud of herself. "Thanks!"

"Don't mention it. So you're saying *The Last Supper* could just as likely be a Wiccan painting as a Christian one?" Jenna asked. The Triple Shooter was obsessed with threes for a reason, and when obsessions took root, religion could very well be the source of them. People tended to fixate on ideas entrenched in something they already had strong ties to, a broader subject they themselves held dear. Politics, sports, religion. All three were big. Even if a person displayed a compulsion such as hand washing, the behavior and the reasons for it often stemmed from beliefs about another core life principle.

Purple flashed in again. Royalty. A color association even people without grapheme–color synesthesia had.

"I doubt it's *likely*," Molly answered, her voice a bit annoyed. "After all, it *does* have Jesus in it."

Stupid question. She'd phrase it better this time, because the more she thought about it, the more she was sure the purple she kept associating, side by side, with the royal blue she saw in conjunction with the Triple Shooter matched the shade she associated with royalty. The jump from royalty to deity wasn't hard to make. "Right. But let's say you saw a painting with threes in it. A new painting you've never seen. Let's pretend you knew the painting was religious but didn't know which religion. What might you think?"

"Could be anything," Molly said. "Depends on what else was in the painting."

Duh, Jenna. The crime scenes of the Triple Shooter's victims flashed in, one by one. This was either a really good idea or a really bad one.

"Just for argument's sake, let's say the painting had the number three involved, then there were women," Jenna said.

"How many?"

Several. But no. The Triple Shooter, until now, had killed one at a time.

"Just one, maybe. Let's say there's more than one painting, but they're each of a different woman."

"Okay. What are they doing?"

Resting in peace? "Sleeping," Jenna blurted.

"Okay. Sleeping women, one in each painting. What else is in the paintings?"

What could she tell this kid without giving away important case facts they'd withheld? "How about . . ." The case details flitted through her mind. Each of the Triple Shooter's first three victims had at least one chest wound. "They all have a circle right here." Jenna indicated the middle of her breastbone.

Molly scrunched her eyebrows, deep in thought. "Geez, Dr. Ramey. I'm not sure I know. Once you take out the numbers, I'm kind of out of it. I mean, there are the Triple Goddesses in Wicca. That's what I thought of first when you said more than one woman, I guess. They correspond to the three phases of the moon, I think. Full, waxing, and waning, but even then some people say there's a fourth unseen goddess. The Celts had three goddesses. Maid, mother, crone. What paintings are these? How many of them are there?"

Ten. "Oh, never mind, Molly. I was just speculating. We should probably get back upstairs, yeah?"

Molly nodded. "Yeah, I guess so."

Jenna followed Molly back upstairs to the living room, where they found Liam and Raine sitting at the coffee table, looking through papers from the file folder Liam had retrieved from the office. When Liam noticed them, he stood.

"Going through Rita's lease at the apartment she rented to figure out what we're responsible for after the incident," he said. Then, he frowned at Molly, who had blanched at the mention of her grandmother. "Sorry, Molls. Hey! I bet you didn't think to show Dr. Ramey your new invention, did you? I'm guessing not, since you left it on my nightstand last night. Run up and get it, huh? I bet she'd like it."

Molly's eyes lit up again. "Yeah!"

She dashed away up the stairs, taking them two at a time.

"Sorry about that. I've been trying my best to get Raine through the logistics of Rita's passing, and Molly through having maybe seen her grandmother's shooter while she was with her at the grocery store, but those two things don't always align in a simple way."

"Molly'll be okay," Jenna replied. "Kids are resilient. Do let me know if you need me to recommend a good child psychologist, though. I'd be happy to give you some names."

Liam Tyler smiled warmly, but he shook his head. "I doubt that'll be necessary, Dr. Ramey. Even if we're stretched a bit thin, Molly has a good support system here at home, and anything else she needs, we've got a counselor at the church she can talk to."

Molly came thundering down the stairs, holding a Rubik's Cube in her hand. Each of the colored squares on the cube had been numbered in Sharpie marker. Molly began to twist furiously, causing the block to become a mix of different numbers and colors.

"I can't do it by the colors, but once I numbered the blocks . . ."

She held up the cube to show Jenna the colors were sufficiently scrambled, then began to work the tiers of the toy, turning them row by row into place. "I can do it, see?"

She held the cube back up, two neat rows of green already aligned so quickly that Jenna could tell the six-year-old would have all the colors back into place within minutes. "That's awesome, Molly."

"Thanks. I thought it was pretty cool."

Liam put his hands on Molly's shoulders in front of him. "Anything else we can help you with today, Dr. Ramey?"

The Last Supper painting drifted through her mind, the talk about numbers and gods and divinity still fresh. There was something to be tapped there. She just didn't know what yet.

"No, thank you," Jenna replied. "That's all for now."

9

The man who called himself Justice had followed the brunette with the swishy ponytail ever since the basketball game last night. Now he walked about ten feet behind her, toward the Student Life Center at Woodsbridge Community College. Her gray sweatshirt bearing a blue cougar seemed heavy for the springtime air, the girl's waif-like frame lost in its billows. She went to the high school, the one with the blue cougar. It was where he'd seen her play basketball. Maybe she was taking an advanced course here. That would mean she was smart. Maybe he was following her for no reason.

But the threes.

Itching. Always the itching.

She trotted up the short flight of stairs to the pavilion in front of the Student Life Center, cut down its middle toward the set of four stairs on the other side that led inside. He wouldn't be able to follow her much farther without an ID. He'd have to sit here, wait until she came out.

He reached the end of the pavilion as she scanned her access card against the rubber mat beside the door. In she went, away from his sight.

His feet slowed of their own accord, and for a moment, he stared at the closed glass door where she'd stood only moments before, her long, swishy ponytail whipping behind her as she stepped inside. Then, suddenly, his neck burned. He glanced around, sure people had noticed him, were watching him.

Other students walked in twos and threes around the pavilion and the grassy knoll nearby, laughing, chatting. Some hurried with armfuls of books, eyes only on destinations. On the grounds to the left, a girl and a boy lay together on an orange-striped beach towel, the boy on his stomach reading a campus newspaper, the girl on her back, eyes closed and using his back as a pillow.

No one had noticed him. They wouldn't. It was *them* he had to worry about. Not these people.

He glanced around, saw an empty spot at one of the umbrella tables to the right of the pavilion. Settling down in the chair and angling it for a good view of the Student Life Center's glass door, he couldn't help but wish he'd thought to bring a book, a newspaper, a crossword puzzle. Anything to look a little more like he belonged here.

But she's done nothing wrong.

The man who called himself Justice exhaled the deep breath he'd been holding. It probably wouldn't matter if anyone saw him here or not, because so far, he'd followed the numbers and cleared them. They did not ring true. A little longer to watch, of course. To be sure. But at the moment, it looked like he would get to go home tonight without worrying.

Out of the corner of his eye, he noticed another man, the only other on the pavilion rooted to a spot. The white-bearded fellow with waxy, wrinkled skin leaned next to the low wall that set the pavilion's border. He, too, wore clothing uncharacteristically warm for the season in the form of an old, tattered green army jacket. His hands were neatly folded over his stomach, a lidless shoe box at his side.

The man who called himself Justice pulled the ball cap's visor lower over his eyes to block the sun, aware of the glass door in case the brunette with the swishy ponytail came back out, but his gaze lingered on the homeless man with the shoe box across the way. Students entering the pavilion passed him, mostly paying him no mind, ignoring his requests for change as though they couldn't hear them. Standard. As the man who called himself Justice watched them, he seethed quietly. These people had committed no crimes, but to observe people ignoring another human being, even if that man *was* a beggar, brought a metallic taste to his mouth.

Occasionally a guy or girl would smile at the old man and politely explain that they didn't have any spare money. Once or twice, he even saw someone toss a few coins into the cardboard box. Some decency, perhaps. Something to be grateful for.

He glanced at his wristwatch, a cheap plastic thing he bought at the Dollar Roundup for a buck. The brunette with the swishy ponytail had only been inside ten minutes. Why was he so antsy for her to come out?

Across the way, next to where the bearded man sat, a horde of students spilled into the pavilion, no doubt in the fray of time between class periods. The old codger put his shoe box on the wall, then held on to the edge of the low wall, bent one knee, and used the stone slab to push himself to his feet. Just as he reached for his shoe box, however, a hand knocked into it.

For a moment, the old man stared at the ground, the meager contents of his receptacle strewn across the pavilion stone. Then he turned in the direction from where the hand had come. His face looked sunken, confused.

But the man who called himself Justice had already seen what the beggar was now spotting for the first time. Two students. Females. One girl with a pencil-thin neck and bony cheeks stood a foot away from another girl with wild, frizzy red curls. The bony-cheek girl lingered but hid most of her face behind the book she was holding, embarrassed. But the other? The red-haired girl faced the old man, shoulders squared, cackling. She smirked as her laughter waned. The old man put his hands to his knees as he bent ever so slowly at the waist, reaching for a dollar that had been flung from his shoe box. Just as his fingers brushed it, the pointy toe of a black high-heeled boot clamped over its end.

The scrawny beggar looked up at the redhead from his crouch

and shook his head. "Why are you doing this? I just want to pick up my dollar bill here, young lady. No reason to be nasty about it."

The redhead gave the old man a fake smile, marinated in contempt. "*Your* dollar? Don't you mean the dollar of some bleeding heart kid? One who gave you pocket change you're too lazy to earn, because all you do is sit around a college campus all day asking for handouts?"

She slid the dollar under her boot toward her, then bent and lifted it, held it directly in front of the old man's face. "This dollar? It was never yours, and it's not going to be now, either."

She ripped the single bill in two, then crumpled the pieces in her hand, tossed them to the ground by the old man's shoe box, which lay on its side. "Come on, Diana let's go," she said. The redhead whipped around and headed for one of the iron tables adorned with umbrellas, like the one the man who called himself Justice was sitting at now. Her friend, however, stayed behind just long enough to mouth, "I'm sorry," to the shaky old man.

And that's when the man who called himself Justice saw it. The book the friend carried, the one she had used to hide her face. The screened print on the front said very clearly Latin III. That was one three, and the spine of the book she held under it at her side provided the final two threes: Biology 3300. Three threes.

The man who called himself Justice forgot about the glass door of the Student Life Center and the swishy ponytail of the girl inside it as he slowly turned his head a fraction to catch a better glimpse of the girl with the bush of tousled red curls atop her head. She sat in the black wrought-iron chair, dipping a French fry into ketchup. Diana caught up, pulled up a seat, and stared at the table the entire time the redhead yammered on and sniggered to her.

Today wasn't a waste after all. *They* did *lead me here, it just wasn't about who I thought.*

As he watched, the red-haired girl gestured animatedly to her friend, coughing as she nearly choked on a bite of her sandwich, she was laughing so hard.

That's right, little girl. Live it up. After all, it's time to die.

10

Jenna brushed through the gaggle of reporters camped out at the local police department, not even venturing a "No comment" to the questions they yelled at her. It was the unfortunate part of having a known face in this job. But she wasn't prepared to say anything to the press. Not until she knew more about what they were dealing with. After all, the grocery store murders deviated strongly from the Triple Shooter's other killings, and she didn't know why. All she did know was that it sure as hell didn't mean he was stable.

When she reached the conference room, Saleda and Teva were already waiting, flipping through pages and pages of Triple Shooter case notes. She'd called them as soon as she'd left the Tyler house to tell them to pull the files and meet her, that she thought she had a lead. Normally she'd never have overstepped Saleda and instructed the team to do *anything*, but in this case, any information about the Triple Shooter's profile was vital. His *old* crimes were where they would catch him. More consistency, more to go on. The grocery store massacre trail was hot, but the pattern was so off that the only way to use it to find him was to figure out where his old style and these new killings converged.

Saleda glanced at her watch when she saw Jenna come in. "About time."

"Traffic," Jenna muttered.

"Probably the dozens of roadblocks the locals have set up on every street from here to Saskatchewan, which is cute, ya know. Stopping people to check if they're someone you don't know you're looking for. We have no physical description, getaway vehicle, nothing, but these heroes would rather employ martial law to find a phantom than work with what we have, which is a profile."

Jenna smirked as she pulled out a chair next to Teva. "Aw, come on, Saleda. Everyone knows the 'real' cops shouldn't listen to our voodoo shenanigans. 'Behavioral Science,'" she said, miming scare quotes. She flicked her hand, dismissing the thought. "What a crock."

Saleda chuckled, shook her head. "For what it's worth, I stationed Porter and Dodd with the head of the local task force so they can at least help vet any suspicious characters stopped for no good reason."

"Dodd's back already?" Jenna asked.

Saleda waved away the question. "Yeah, they called him in about something regarding the Cobbler case."

"Wow. I had no idea he worked that one," Jenna answered. The case was one of the more famous these days. A while back, a killer had murdered twelve people in the Chicago area. The police arrested the alleged murderer after an anonymous tip call sent them straight to the bastard's door. They found ten feet in the guy's freezer. There were twelve victims.

"Yeah, unfortunately for him. It's a dilly. The defense appealed the court's ruling that the defendant is competent to stand trial, citing new psychiatric evaluations suggesting the perp is criminally insane and needs institution, not jail. Dodd went down there to try to stop a reversal. He worked his ass off for that case, and between us, it was the one that almost broke him. He'll die before he sees that psycho let loose. But yeah, he got to say his piece, and then he joined Porter with the local task force leader here. Now we pursue your gut feeling, Jenna. Just don't make me regret it."

"Oh, you won't," she said. She opened the Triple Shooter case files in front of them, gingerly laying out pictures of the three early victims in a neat line across the table. "The grocery store killings are the exception, not the rule. The older victims are how we'll find him, by smoking out a pattern. Every kill he commits, he gives us another clue, and sometimes he gives us a retroactive one without realizing it."

"We've already established that the Triple Shooter kills compulsively. He isn't searching for fame or notoriety. He *is* doing it to *stop* something from happening, i.e, he's paranoid. Paranoia makes him dangerous, unstable. If spooked, he might run farther, hurt someone, take hostages. His pathology would escalate, maybe trigger a spree."

Teva leaned her elbows on the table, propped her chin on her fists. "Isn't it safe to say he's already *on* a spree?"

"Not anything compared to what'll happen if he gets scared and angry," Jenna replied.

"Okay, so paranoid, dangerous nut job who may or may not see threes that cause him to kill people. What's up with the religious connection you mentioned on the phone?"

Jenna stood and went for the coffeepot. She poured herself a paper cup, dumped in two sugars, then stirred as she sat back at the table. "I talked to the little girl who was a witness at the grocery store. Kid has a sharp eye, notices things others don't. She's also obsessed with numbers, so I thought maybe I could get a childlike perspective on what the numbers might mean."

"Anything good?"

"More than I bargained for," Jenna said. She swallowed the hot coffee hard, the liquid leaving her throat searing.

Jenna took another gulp to stall even as she willed herself to continue. Her suspicion that Molly was pointing her in the right direction might not be seen as valid by most. "We spent time looking at a print of the restored version of *The Last Supper* in her stepfather's study, and she ended up telling me tons about numbers and deities, symbolism. Call me crazy, but I think we should take a harder look at the religion aspect."

"Why do you say that?" Saleda coaxed.

Jenna stood and continued to sip her coffee, pacing the burgundy carpet. "When someone kills another person, they can have a variety of motivations. Passion, financial gain, revenge, political agenda, self-defense, religious fanaticism—that sort of thing. But this guy, he kills because something sets off his compulsions, typically repetition of the number three."

"So the threes align, his sensibilities are, what, offended? So he strikes?" Teva asked.

"Not exactly," Saleda interjected. "Something about the threes lining up has to threaten him or otherwise set off his compulsion. The compulsion isn't the number three alone. Robbery and revenge can be and often are motives, just like Jenna said, but in the case of OCD or schizophrenia, you'd be killing someone because the repetition of the numbers was somehow threatening to you—or because someone told you it was."

Teva nodded. "Okay. So the threes align, the Triple Shooter gets spooked, annihilates the threat before it can annihilate him. So what about the threes freaks him out?"

"Could be anything," Jenna said, pacing the room some more. "Molly talked about deities—for all we know the Triple Shooter could think God is pointing an enemy out for him to kill by showing threes near that person."

Teva strolled slowly past the victim photographs. "We're assuming the deity is the Christian God. Plenty of other religions use threes in conjunction with holiness. Are there any other 'pious' aspects to this case?"

"Besides the remorse of shutting the eyes, you mean?" Saleda asked.

"I'd call that reverence, not piousness," Teva countered.

Jenna, however, stood still, looking at her feet as colors flashed in her mind. Eyes, closed. Pieces of evidence over them. Remorse. Eyes closed in remorse. Religion.

Gold solidified in her mind.

"The eyes were covered. Coins. Greeks put coins over the eyes of the dead. It was a tradition, a fare to pay the boatman to take them across the river to the land of the dead," Jenna whispered.

Both women stared at her, suddenly quiet.

"What?" Teva asked.

"He's not only remorseful for killing them, but he's even willing to pay their passage into the Underworld. The question is, what the heck does this have to do with the threes setting him off?"

Teva chortled. "So this guy thinks Zeus is telling him to smite down anyone attached to the number three?"

Jenna grabbed her satchel and the stack of case folders, and headed for the door. "I haven't gotten that far, but I think it's worth pursuing. We need to find out what all in Greek mythology was associated with the number three. Then maybe we can figure out what's triggering his attacks. I'm going to the community college to talk to the history professor. I'll check in soon."

And with that, Jenna was out the door.

Yancy plopped down into his desk chair, jammed his headphones on. Time to save the world again—or at least save little boys from closet monsters and stupid teenagers who thought 911 existed so they could call and ask for directions when they were lost.

Before he hit his ready button to signify he was in place and prepared to take an emergency call, though, his cell phone lit up. He'd already turned it on silent, which was standard when he was on duty, but seeing the number glowing on the face, he couldn't help but take one more minute off work to answer this one.

"Hey, beautiful lady," he said.

"Hi, yourself," Jenna replied flatly, but Yancy could tell by the sound of her voice that she was smiling. "Listen, I'm on my way to interview someone about the case right now, but I just wanted to call and let you know I can have Irv check in on the domestic abuse vic call if you want, just to make sure it all went down without anything crazy happening. If you were worried, I mean. I know we all have cases that get to us, and sometimes closure is best."

This wasn't going to go well. But, like his grandmother had tried so hard to beat into his rear end with a belt, honesty was the best policy. *Go ahead, rock star. Make her day.*

"Um, that won't be necessary. I, uh . . ." Yancy cleared his throat. *Spit it out, moron.* "I went by her house."

"You *what?*" met his ears, the shrill pitch something like what he expected, only a little louder and a little more angry than confused.

"Hey, before you give me the lecture, relax. I just went by on my walk with Oboe to see if I saw anything. The blinds were open, and I saw her vacuuming. I didn't knock on her door, throw pebbles at her window, nothing. She never knew I was there."

Jenna's sigh echoed in his ears through the phone. "Yancy, it's not *about* whether or not she saw you. It's about protocol and professional distance! You can't get so personally involved. It never ends well. Ever. You know better than this . . ."

The back of Yancy's neck burned, the heat creeping up his cheeks. "Whoa, wait a minute—"

"It's easy to get invested in these cases that crop up a lot. I know. But self-control is—"

"Oh, self-control is important, huh? Not overstepping? But you didn't have any problem breaking protocol or having me overstep when it served your purposes last year . . ."

"Yance, that was different. You were part of the investigation . . ."

But Jenna's tone didn't match the words. She wasn't fooling anyone, and the hell if she was going to scold him about professional standards when she'd broken many bigger rules than walking by someone's house.

"Double standards much?"

"Yancy, I'm an FBI agent, okay? You could get fired from your dispatch position for something like this if anyone found out," Jenna said.

The way he could tell the calm, slow cadence of her words was designed to ease the rising conflict just pissed him off worse. "Don't shrink me, *Doctor.* And don't forget, when you broke all the rules, you *weren't* an FBI agent anymore . . . yet . . . whatever the hell the right word is!"

Jenna's breathing had been even, but was he imagining it was getting heavier?

"Yancy, I'm only trying to protect you—"

He couldn't stop the cold laugh that escaped him. "Protect me? Protect me! That's a hot one. The poor one-legged guy needs his big, bad FBI girlfriend for protection. Can't even take care of himself enough to get a *real* law enforcement job instead of one sitting behind a desk answering the phone all day."

"That's not what I mea—"

He cut her off again. "You know, believe it or not, Jenna, I'm capable of taking care of myself *and* other people. I'd have thought you'd know that by now, considering everything I've done to help *your* superhuman FBI agent rear end, but apparently I only get kudos for my past performances based on affirmative action," he snapped.

"I didn't say tha—"

"Don't worry about it. I have to go now. My piddly little job calls. Talk later. G'bye," he spat, ending the call and shoving his phone into his pocket.

He slammed the ready button with the heel of his palm, and his work line signaled immediately.

"Nine-one-one, what is your emergency?"

Heavy breaths, then an inaudible whisper.

"Are you there?" Yancy asked.

No answer, but breathing. *Deliberately rhythmic breathing.*

"If you are on the line and unable to speak, press a button on your phone twice," Yancy said, holding his earpiece closer to try to hear anything in the background. He glanced to the call window. No address attached to the number. Looked like a cell phone.

BEEP. BEEP.

"Okay, you are on the line and can't speak. If you can't speak because of a medical problem, press a button once. If you cannot speak for fear of an intruder, press a button twice."

Silence.

A long ten seconds went by.

BEEP BEEP.

Yancy typed fast:

```
Caller intentionally not speaking for fear of
alerting intruder.
```

He pressed the mute button so the caller wouldn't hear the panic tied to his next request. "I need a location on this cell number," he yelled into the buzzing hub of the dispatch center. He let up on the mute button. "If you know that the phone you're calling from is a Verizon or Sprint serviced phone, press any button."

Nothing.

That would've been too easy. Verizon and Sprint used internal GPS tracking chips inside their wireless phones that activated upon a 911 call. *Damn. Triangulation it is.*

Now, to get as much information as possible from someone who couldn't talk while he waited for tower signals to bounce around until he could isolate the caller's location. "Okay, someone is there. If you're hiding in a locked room, press a button one time. If you're hiding but there's no lock between you and the intruder, press any button twice."

BEEP. BEEP.

Shit.

Yancy typed fast, his thoughts flying. He sent the report to dispatch, though it did no good since they didn't have a location yet. He glanced at the monitor. One tower pinged. He needed information, but he also had to keep this caller safe so when help arrived at the location, the officers would be handling a home invasion rather than a homicide.

"We're tracking your location right now, but I need you to stay on the line with me so we can get someone to help you. Breathe as slowly as you can. In through your nose and out of your mouth." *And don't hyperventilate.* "If it's possible to move to a place where you can put some distance—and preferably a lock—between you and the intruder, do so. If not, stay put. If you're moving, press a button."

Silence. Another tower pinged on the monitor.

"Okay, I need some more information. If the intruder has a weapon, press any button twice."

BEEP BEEP.
Yancy typed:

```
Intruder armed.
```

"If the intruder has a gun, press any button twice."
Nothing.
"If he has a knife, press any button twice."
Still nothing.
"Press two buttons if it is a blunt object."
BEEP BEEP.
Yancy struck keys to let the officer who would head to the residence when the triangulation finished know what kind of weapon the intruder had. He looked to the monitor.

The last tower pinged, and a bubble popped up on the map. A location he recognized met Yancy's eyes.

"CiCi?"

No words.

Yancy's pulse quickened. He'd taken so many of her calls, and she'd survived these disputes with her husband after each. Yet every single time Yancy talked to her, he couldn't help but think how this might be the last call she'd make. Every incident had the potential to be the one when she wouldn't make it.

Yancy called for the dispatch to the familiar Peake Road address. "Hang on, CiCi. Help is on the way."

Please, God, let them get there in time.

After following the balding history professor through the dining hall line and selecting the least offensive of the choices offered, Jenna sat down across from him at the rickety wooden table.

"I *do* love Salisbury steak day," he commented enthusiastically as he cut into the mystery meat on his plate.

Jenna glanced down at her tray, which bore the same meal Dr. Etkin's did. However, she didn't see the lumpy, gravy-covered mess quite the same way he did. She wouldn't have known what it was at all if he hadn't just identified it for her.

Still, better to be casual, so she cut a piece and gingerly bit it off the tip of her fork. All in all, it wasn't as bad as it looked.

"I'm sorry I couldn't talk in my office, but I was famished. Now tell me again what information it was you were looking for," he said, still chewing a mouthful of green beans.

Jenna swallowed and wiped her mouth. "No problem. I do need to ask that you keep our conversation to yourself to preserve the integrity of the investigation . . ."

He waved her off. "Of course, of course."

"Right. I have a case right now that I'm pretty sure is steeped in

Greek mythology. Or rather, the criminal's motives might be. Particularly as Greek mythology relates to the number three and death. What all can you tell me about the significance of the number?"

Dr. Etkin spooned a heaping bite of mashed potatoes into his mouth. "Hm, let me see. I've taught a Greek mythology course for about thirteen years, but I've never had to think much about all the ways threes could be connected to deaths before. Lots of Greek myth uses the number three. The number three typically symbolizes male gender in Greek mythology. Four is usually symbolic of the feminine, though threes show up in relation to the feminine, too, on occasion. Often certain lesser deities take the form of three separate entities, as in the case of the Fates, for example. The three Fates—Clothos, Lachesis, and Atropos—were in charge of the thread of life. The first spun the thread, the second measured it, and the last cut it to end life. That is one story that mixes threes with death. The three Gorgon sisters Stheno, Euryale, and the most famous, Medusa, had hair made of venomous snakes. Medusa was killed by the hero Perseus, who cut off her head. Any serpentine symbology in these crimes?"

"Not that we've found," Jenna replied. Surely he would say something that would strike a nerve, light a color in her mind that connected. "Please keep throwing out ideas, though. Anything could be significant."

"All right then. Three Harpies—mythical winged monsters. Hesiod mentions a set of three Cyclopes—Brontes, Steropes, and Arges— said in the *Theogony* to have provided the brothers Zeus, Poseidon, and Hades with the thunderbolt, trident, and helmet of invisibility that allowed them to defeat the Titans. However, that this group of three would be so well-known is less likely than some other scenarios. Of Cyclopes, one is more famous than all the others, Polyphemus, due to Homer's stories of Odysseus's encounters with him. Cerberus was the three-headed dog who guarded the gates of the Underworld . . ."

"The Underworld. Hades?" Jenna asked, latching on to the reference to the home of the dead.

"Yes, technically, though most people have a misconception of Hades. Unlike the modern day concept of hell where the 'bad' people go, Hades housed all of the dead, good and bad alike. Some accounts give different sections that kept certain groupings of people. 'Good' people went to the Elysian Fields in Hades, and the damned ended up in Tartarus. Some sources claim Tartarus wasn't a part of Hades at all, but rather, a place far below Hades itself. Either way, by most accounts, all the departed are said to reside in Hades, presided over by the god of the same name. One of Zeus's brothers. I suppose those three main gods are an example of threes in mythology themselves."

"Right," Jenna said, a blazing orange settling in her mind around the concept of Hades, the place. It didn't match any colors she'd seen so far while investigating this case that she could remember, but she filed it away for future reference. Even so, this seemed like a profitable route of inquiry. The sort of thing a paranoid schizophrenic might latch onto. "Any more threes associated with the Underworld?"

Dr. Etkin rubbed his mouth with his napkin. "That's tough. Let me think on it."

"Perhaps you could just tell me more about Hades in general," Jenna prompted.

"All right then. Let's see here. The Greeks believed death wasn't really the end of life, though they did not, I think, consider the dead to make any sort of progress, such as aging, after leaving the earth to go to Hades. The living could enter Hades in certain cases. Persephone, for example, was abducted to be Hades's wife. Different versions of the story quibble over whether what happened next was against Persephone's will or not, but I for one believe that Hades forced her to eat the six pomegranate seeds, which tied her to the Underworld, as this was a fruit linked to Hades. Note that six is the double of three, but I digress. So Persephone . . . she was one. Orpheus traveled to Hades in an attempt to bring his wife Eurydice back to the world of the living. She was bitten by a snake, so that's another serpent reference . . . No?" he said at the shake of Jenna's head.

If the Triple Shooter had been the Double Shooter, then maybe the bullets could be symbolic of fangs, but so far, nothing snakelike about any of these crimes hit her. But this concept of bringing *back* the dead intrigued her. Maybe the Triple Shooter was trying to do that somehow? The submissive shade of blue she'd seen at the grocery store flashed in. She still thought he was submitting to an urge, not missing a loved one who'd passed. The returning-the-dead angle didn't feel right. Still, it was worth a question or two. "Did Orpheus succeed?"

"Good heavens, no. He made it in, all right, though different versions of the tale have him employing different means. But when Hades allowed him to take his wife back to the living world, it was under the condition she walk behind him and he not look back. Before he got past the gates, he disobeyed Hades's order, and Eurydice was ripped from him and back into Hades."

Jenna nodded, forcing away the powder pink of parallels that flashed in. The story had prompted her to think of the parallel biblical story of Lot's wife looking back at Sodom and Gomorrah. The thought was of the sort she always had to sift through in situations like these, to isolate the important associations her mind naturally made from the myriad of insignificant ones. The pink had cropped up because of her own purely anecdotal thought, not due to an impression she had that connected the story with the case. A subtle distinction, but it was a skill she'd honed over time.

"So, Persephone and Orpheus. Anyone else?" Jenna said.

"Odysseus also entered the Underworld alive. Blood offerings were required for the dead to interact, though. A life force offered in exchange for contact. Cerberus was charged with keeping all who entered Hades from leaving, but Odysseus escaped by sailing through an exit of Hades guarded by two monsters. Instead of trying to navigate the water between them, the mistake of most sailors, he stuck close to the tentacled monster, Scylla. He lost men—six—but otherwise he and the rest of his crew escaped. As far as I know, he was the only person who led a ship that sailed into Hades and also sailed out. Now the dead are another story entirely. The Greeks thought that at the moment of death, the soul and corpse separated. The soul assumed the form of a body itself, and that was the part which was taken to Hades."

"By the boatman," Jenna filled in.

"You are correct. Charon, the ferryman, was charged with sailing the shades of the dead to Hades, by some accounts across the river Styx. By others, Acheron, the river of pain."

Jenna cleared her throat. "So there are a lot of discrepancies?"

Etkin nodded. "Depends on whose portrayal you're reading which river was the entrance to the Underworld. Homer said one thing, Euripides another. Everyone else usually something in between. But those are the more popular versions."

"Mm-hm. And Charon was paid two coins over the eyes, correct?" Jenna asked, not mentioning the relevance to the case.

Dr. Etkin nodded. "Sometimes, but not as a rule. Another source of disagreement. Some tales say coins over the eyes, but most if not all instances in literature depict a single coin under the tongue. The eye coins usually appear as the myths are orally passed down as folktales and lose some authenticity."

Jenna let the idea simmer. Apparently, if their killer *did* intend the pieces of evidence to appear as coins, he didn't know his mythology well. An interesting detail, considering their current theory said he was obsessed with it.

"Were coins over the eyes perhaps symbolic of . . . well, anything?" Jenna reached.

Dr. Etkin shook his head. "Not that I know of, young lady. But either way, Charon was a coin taker, and if the dead did not pay, they were condemned to wander the earth as ghosts."

"A bad thing?" Jenna asked, unsure.

"Yes, in that culture. Many thought that reaching the Elysian Fields after death might provide a chance for rebirth. Reincarnation, as it is thought of in traditional society, wasn't on the table back then. There was a very specific set of circumstances the Greeks aspired to in order to have the prospect. And yet, I suppose the possibility comforted them. Ghosts, however, were doomed to a life of seeing but not being part of the world."

"I see," Jenna replied. It *did* sound awful. Seeing Ayana but not being able to talk to her, to touch her. She shook the thought away. "How did Charon land this special little job?"

"Eh, I don't think it's ever really told how the task came to him, though it no doubt happened in the same manner most of the gods acquired charge of their realm: either through being born with the inherent role, or by overthrowing the god or supernatural being who possessed it before them. Some artwork depicts Charon as a decrepit old man, but most portrayals allege he was more something of a demon than a human."

Jenna closed her eyes for a second, swallowing the tepid potatoes in her mouth. Try as she might to force a color to flash in, none would come. Only discerning the colors her mind brought forth was an ability she could master. Grapheme–color synesthesia wasn't a skill or talent, no matter how much she wished it was at times. It simply *was* . . . or, as in this moment, it wasn't.

"You know," Dr. Etkin said, scooping banana pudding into his mouth, "one idea you might consider would be talking to Brody Gallagher. Teaches religion here. He'd be a wealth of knowledge on the numerological implications of the number three. Occurs a ton in Greek mythology surrounding deities, but it's a common integer in many religions. He might be able to give you even more insight than I on the Greeks and the numbers as they relate to deities."

An eggplant purple flashed in as the word religion hit Jenna's ears. She put down her fork. "How can I find him?"

Molly twirled her spaghetti around her fork. She'd had plenty, but Liam always insisted the whole family stay seated at the table until everybody finished. He said it was only polite.

Three witches in Macbeth. *Three books in a trilogy. Three movies in a trilogy. The Three Musketeers. The Three Bears. The Three Little Pigs.*

"There sure are a lot of stories that use it, too," she said, rolling a noodle between her thumb and forefinger.

"Use what, love?" Liam asked.

Molly glanced at her mother. As usual, her mom was quiet, staring at her food like it could help change everything that had happened. She looked back at Liam.

"Three. *Three Blind Mice, Three Billy Goats Gruff. Three Little Kittens Who Lost Their Mittens.*"

Her stepfather looked back to his plate and sawed at his meat. "A lot of books have numbers in their titles, Molly. *A Tale of Two Cities, One Flew Over the Cuckoo's Nest, Around the World in Eighty Days . . .*"

"But those aren't threes," Molly replied as she lifted one noodle at a time to drape over her fork. "Dr. Ramey was most interested in three."

Ever since Dr. Ramey left, Molly had been racking her brain for what she knew about the number three that might help Dr. Ramey. She wasn't really sure what the doctor was looking for, but she understood it was to do with what happened at the grocery store. She could tell that somehow Dr. Ramey needed to peg something special about the number three so she could figure out who had hurt all the people at Lowman's. She wouldn't have asked if she didn't. Molly knew a lot about numbers. She was positive she could help Dr. Ramey, if only she could think of the right three.

"Molly, Dr. Ramey will come and ask you if there's anything else she needs. Stop playing with your food."

Molly dropped the noodle she was holding and lowered her fork to her plate. She bit her lip. Liam was just like all grown-ups who thought kids couldn't really help adults with anything important. Of course he was confident Dr. Ramey didn't need her ideas.

But just because her stepdad was sure didn't mean she had to be.

"May I be excused?" she asked.

"Molly, everyone's not finished yet," Liam said.

Molly let out a sigh and leaned back in her chair. She needed to think harder. She *could* help Dr. Ramey. She sat in silence and watched her stepdad and mother eat. When they'd finally cleared their plates, she tried again.

"May I be excused now?" Molly asked.

"Yes, you may, but go upstairs and take your bath, put on your pj's, and brush your teeth. I'll be up to tuck you in in about an hour and a half. You can play until then."

Molly hopped out of her chair and skipped up the stairs to her room. She closed her door behind her. Then she flopped onto her hot-pink comforter. Finally, some time to think.

Molly pulled the plug up for her bathwater to run out, and she watched the clear soapy liquid swirl toward the drain. Games. Three plays to make in the rock-paper-scissors game. You could make a three-point shot in basketball. Three strikes and a batter was out in baseball. Three bases to touch before running home. Hockey had three twenty-minute time periods. Three strikes in a row in bowling was called a turkey.

She reached for her fluffy pink towel, dried off, then wrapped it around her chest like a dress. Once she was in her bedroom, she pulled on a lavender nightgown with a screen-printed version of Daisy Duck's face on the front, complete with giant pink hair bow. She left the towel on the floor and crawled onto her bed. She pulled back the covers but lay on top of them, still determined to help Dr. Ramey.

She grabbed her pale pink Koosh ball off her nightstand. As she thought, she tossed it up in the air, caught it, and tossed it again. Atoms contained three particles: protons, electrons, and neutrons. The Roman Catholics believed there were three realms in the afterlife: Heaven, Hell, and Purgatory. On some telephone keypads, the number three key was also associated with the letters D, E, and F. Three notes to form a triad, the basic structure of a musical chord. Three was the number of wishes granted in most stories involving genies, wizards, or sorcerers. Three primary colors made all others.

Her door opened, and she looked up, still tossing her Koosh ball into the air and catching it when it came back down.

"Time for little princesses to be in bed," Liam said, catching the Koosh ball in his palm. He set it down on the nightstand, "Yep, in bed . . . with their tootsies under the covers!" Liam smiled just before he dove for Molly's feet.

She squealed and shoved her feet under the sheets, then yanked the blankets up to her chin. She'd made it before he tickled her toes.

"Shucks!" he laughed, shaking his head and snapping the fingers on his right hand once. "Missed getting the feets *again!*"

Molly giggled.

"Next time," he said, leaning down and smoothing her hair back from her face.

Molly narrowed her eyes playfully. "You *hope!*"

Liam chuckled. "Confident, are we? We'll just see tomorrow," he said, giving her a playful punch in the arm. "You brush your teeth?"

"Mm-hm," she said, then gave him the toothiest grin she could manage.

"Sparkly as ever. Wash your face?"

Molly nodded twice.

"Say your prayers?" Liam asked.

"Not yet," she answered.

"Well, come on. I'll help."

"Where's Mommy?" she asked.

Liam frowned. "In bed, puddin'. She's had a hard few days. She needs her rest. Now how about those prayers?"

Molly crawled out, but just before she took her feet out from under the covers, she shot Liam a look. "Are my feet safe from the tickle troll?"

Liam drew an X over his chest. "Cross my heart."

She knelt beside her bed, and Liam crouched and dropped onto both knees next to her. People kneeling and lying down in the grocery store after they were killed. Others sat slumped, trying to take cover. The three taps the shooter made before he fired. Most of the people who were still alive that she'd seen or talked to inside the grocery store had been in that little room where she'd first met Dr. Ramey and Agent Dodd. *Three taps before the shooter fired.*

She'd talked to someone else inside the store. Someone not in that back room. That old man. The one that looked like Pop-Pop.

Molly looked at Liam, who already had his hands folded, his head bowed. "Liam, can I ask you something?"

"Sure, love. Anything," he said, unfolding his hands.

"I remember talking to another man that day on the aisle where the last guy got shot. They kept all the witnesses who might've seen the shooter in the back room to ask us questions. They talked to everyone else who hadn't seen the shooter out in the parking lot. This man I saw, he definitely could've seen the shooter. But he wasn't in the back room with the witnesses."

Liam's eyebrows narrowed. "What're you trying to say here, Molly?"

Molly shook her head. "I don't know," she muttered. "It just might be important . . ."

They said their prayers, then Liam lifted Molly onto her bed and tucked her in. He kissed her on both cheeks and rubbed his nose to hers. "Everything's going to be fine, Molly. Do your best not to worry."

Molly nodded. "I'll try."

Liam left the room, flipping the switch next to the door on his way out and dousing the room in darkness, the only light left cast by the glow-in-the-dark stars on Molly's ceiling. But Molly wasn't sleepy. Not at all. Something in her gut told her that old man she had talked to in the aisle was important. He'd seen something, and maybe she could find out what it was.

Eldred lay back against the plush lavender pillows. What had he been thinking about?

Nancy sat in a kitchen chair next to him, wiping his sweaty forehead with a wet washcloth. "Feeling better, Dad?"

Better? How could he feel better? He couldn't remember what he'd been thinking of. How could anyone be content when they couldn't hold a train of thought? Madness.

"Fuzzy," he replied through thick lips. The man from the truck with the flashing lights had plunged a needle into his arm. What was the word for that truck? Ambrosia? Ambrol? No. That wasn't even a word. Something wet and warm had squished inside his veins, and his bicep had tingled. The room spun, and his head swam. He sat down, his knees suddenly rubbery and jellylike.

The man and Nancy had whispered at the door, then, finally, the man left along with the other people who'd come with him in that ambivalent. Darn it. That wasn't it, either.

"It's all okay. You just lay back and relax. Everything is going to be all right," his daughter said.

All right? What would be all right? What had happened?

Gunfire. Cereal boxes falling, sliding across the floor in front of him. Something niggled at his mind.

"Sarah, what was that cereal you used to like? The ones with the marshmallows?"

The woman beside him squeezed his hand. "Dad, I'm Nancy, remember? Your daughter, Nancy."

He squinted at her and studied her slender nose, her long, wavy brown hair. "What are you playing at, Sarah? I recognize my own wife."

"Dad . . ."

Then he noticed the bags under the eyes. Brown eyes. Not hazel.

"Who are you? What have you done with Sarah?"

The imposter squeezed his hand again, and he tried to wrench it away. His limbs felt heavy, lethargic. "Get away," he mumbled through dry lips.

His eyelids fluttered, and he fought as sleep overcame him. Cereal boxes. Gunshots. Footsteps. A voice . . .

Then Eldred's brain blurred all of the images together, and grapple as he might to hang on, the pictures drifted from his mind.

Brody Gallagher turned out to be younger than Dr. Etkin. His office was plastered with pictures of his young wife and two toddlers that might be twins, all of the photos telling the tale of a perfect nuclear family with a picket fence and a dog named Rover.

Gallagher sat behind his desk, resting his chin on his thumb and forefinger pressed together. His clean-shaven face and curly ginger hair gave him the appearance of a high school kid who'd just gone through puberty rather than a college professor.

"Your case has religious undertones, then?" he asked after Jenna finished filling him in on the reason for her visit.

"Kind of. Maybe. This is more of a theory I'm researching. I'll need everything we say here to remain between us so as not to compromise the investigation."

"As you wish," Gallagher replied. "What exactly would you like to know?"

Isn't that a good question? "Dr. Etkin tells me numbers—particularly the number three—are a common theme in many religions."

"And he did not steer you awry. Threes are especially significant when talking about deities. Many deities are triplicates—that is, depicted as threefold. Studies of various religions are rife with the number three. Christianity portrays the Trinity of the Father, the Son, and the Holy Spirit. The Indo-Europeans depicted the 'spinners of destiny' in much the same way the Greeks did, though their names were different. The three cranes of Arabian folklore, popular trios of gods and goddesses like the Greeks' Zeus, Poseidon, and Hades or the Norns in Norse mythology. Many gods and goddesses were thought to have three heads even, like the Hindu goddess Durga. The list goes on and on. You're sure you can narrow your case down to Greek myth?"

Another worthy question. Jenna closed her eyes, went over the case details again in her mind. The makeshift "coins" over the eyes, the number three . . . what else told her Greek myth played a role here? Nothing. And yet, any time the "coins" over the victims' eyes came to mind, a white color coalesced in Jenna's mind. It could mean anything, but Jenna's gut said it was the same clean, fresh color she associated with ancient Greece.

"I suppose the truth is that I can't be certain. Call it gut feeling," she said, cringing as she waited for yet another negative reaction to her giving the familiar reasoning no one ever seemed to quite understand.

However, Brody Gallagher didn't seem fazed. Instead, he shrugged. "Fair enough. So, let's go with the notion that your guy is obsessed with Greek mythology. Specifically, threes in Greek mythology. Dr. Etkin said he gave you the rundown of some basic concepts like the Underworld, Cerberus, and some of the more popular threes of the Greeks. Let me see if I can give any insight into some other aspects of the number and narrow this down for you."

Jenna nodded. Narrowing things down was what she really needed. "That would be welcome."

Gallagher leaned back in his leather armchair. "All right. First, you need to understand why religions have such a fascination with the integer. There's not really a simple answer as to why the number claims such significance in beliefs of all varieties. A lot of factors lend the number three a special symbolism. For example, three is the number associated with all things solid. Two-dimensional objects are, alas, flat. When physical items have height, width, *and* depth, they are tangible. Time is also represented by three distinct divisions—past, present, future. The most striking of all reasons for the religious attraction to the number, however, is its association with divine perfection."

"How is it considered more perfect than other numbers?" Jenna asked.

"It's the first of the four biblically perfect numbers. Spiritually considered perfect in many different religions, even though this spiritual perfection regarding these four is most often attributed to the Bible. This isn't surprising since many religions contain parallels, no matter how different. Anyway, the four perfect spiritual numbers I speak of: three, seven, ten, and twelve."

The word "seven" jumped out at Jenna. Seven victims of the grocery store shootings. *But the Triple Shooter had no other noted connections to the number seven, and every other time there had only been one victim.*

She pushed the thought away. "Tell me more."

"Those four numbers, considered by many to be spiritually perfect, are each associated with different aspects of society. Twelve, governmental perfection. Ten, ordinal perfection—"

"Ordinal perfection?" Jenna cut in.

"Perfection of spiritual order. Interestingly enough, this does have some mathematical significance even though these four numbers have little to do with the *mathematically* perfect numbers. In counting, ten represents the completion of the cycle of the number one, or the beginning of a new cycle of one. Mathematically, the product of those four numbers—three, seven, ten, and twelve—is 2,520, which happens to be the least common multiple of every single digit of the completion cycle of the number one. To be honest, I'm not sure if that concept makes those biblically special numbers logical or whether the people who believe those numbers are special searched for a mathematical pattern to justify them as important, but either way, ten is valued for its sense of completeness. Children were often considered 'whole' if born with ten toes and ten fingers, for instance. But in spiritual context, we see the number ten many times in association with regulation. Guidelines, if you will. The Ten Commandments, the tithe. The number ten also reduces back to the number one. The light source, the beginning of all things."

"Makes *some* sense," Jenna replied. "And the other spiritually perfect numbers?"

Gallagher unfolded his arms and ticked them off on his fingers. "Seven is associated with *actual* spiritual perfection. It's more of a *magical* sort of number, as far as it is connected to events and ideas in scripture. Tends to denote God's perfection of his own system. Seven days of creation is a good example. Jesus said seven things on the cross. Seven seals, seven trumpets, seven promises to the church. The list continues. Then there's your three." His left fist closed, and he folded his ring finger and pinky down.

Avocado green flashed in as she looked at the three fingers he held up.

"Divine perfection," he said. "Space, time, matter, humanity . . . all come in three forms."

"Humanity?"

Gallagher cocked his head, then smiled. "Ah. Yes, let me clarify. Many describe humans as made of three parts: mind, body, and soul."

Jenna nodded. "Sounds about right."

Gallagher stroked his chin, a gesture which struck Jenna as odd, given his young age, even if she couldn't place why age should matter.

"If Christians are to be believed, three is also indicative of Christ's very existence. He rose three days after his death, he subsists in three time periods: past, present, and future."

"What does all of this have to do with the Greeks?" Jenna asked, mustering patience. As they sat here, the Triple Shooter could be driving states away or, worse, killing another victim.

"A lot of the same principles apply. But simply put, in any religion, the preoccupation with the number three and its association to deities is due to one thing: balance. Two can agree—wrongly—and move forward even if ill-advised or ill-conceived. Two can disagree and precipitate deadlock in rule. Four can be divided evenly with no one to break a tie, and more than four in rule constitutes too many cooks in the kitchen, so to speak. Three represents an ideal division of power, one that is infallible."

Jenna tossed the concept around in her mind. The Triple Shooter killed where threes lined up. An irrational reasoning or a rational one? As rational as a cold-blooded killer could be, anyway. Schizophrenics did often consider the voices they heard to be those of God, so it made sense to think the Triple Shooter could be hearing a god. Rational reasons for threes lining up that would precipitate the need to annihilate someone were slim. Loathing of the god in his head, his belief he was better than the god he heard . . . anger at the god. The god's vengeance. That was a common one. Murdering schizophrenics were famous for killing people because "the voices told them to."

The Triple Shooter believing he was superior didn't ring true to Jenna. The coins over the eyes were remorseful. Not a narcissistic display of power. Anger didn't make a lot of sense, either. Gunshots weren't a very passionate method of killing. Not unheard of for an angry perp to shoot out of ire, but those were usually crimes of passion. Anger took passion, and while the Triple Shooter's remorse might fall in line with the details of some crimes of passion, in serials, it wasn't as common. Stab wounds were much angrier.

Hearing voices seemed the most semi-rational logic the killer might be employing.

Irrational reasoning was a totally different beast entirely. No way to even speculate. Irrational thoughts were just that . . . irrational.

The slate gray she associated with the sense of hearing flashed in, clearly distinct from the Prussian blue she associated with the sense of sight. Hearing seemed right here. No way around it.

But if the Triple Shooter heard the voice of some god telling him to kill someone, who was he hearing?

"Dr. Gallagher, you mentioned the triad of Zeus and his brothers in Greek mythology, and Dr. Etkin told me more about the three Fates. What other deities in Greek mythology presented in triad form or as personifications of three different related concepts like Fate?"

"Oh, plenty. As you say, the Fates represented the three stages of life: birth, life, and death . . ."

Jenna pressed her mind to find a connection. The shooter being the taker of life seemed to make this particular set intriguing, but she simply couldn't find a link. Not yet, anyway. And unfortunately, no color manifested to help her out.

"Nine muses in all, so there's a multiple of three. Three threes. Interestingly enough, originally there were only three muses. Aoide, Melete, and Mneme, the goddesses of song, practice, and memory, respectively. Mneme being the origin of the word mnemonic, of course. A group known as the Hundred-Handed Ones, who were responsible for storms. The Cyclopes were technically gods since they were sons of Poseidon, though most people don't think of them quite that way. There was a set of three of them. Um . . . lots of concepts personified, like Fate. Several lesser known ones, like the spirits of pain and suffering."

"Sounds promising," Jenna quipped, though the Triple Shooter wasn't really the pain and suffering type. Sure, he killed people, but that was more incidental. Torture killers didn't typically feel remorse. It took a certain level of psychopathy to purposely inflict misery on other human beings. Lack of empathy meant lack of remorse . . . always. A torture killer might shoot a victim after he was finished committing whatever sadistic acts his perverted little heart desired, but only as an end to his means, and certainly not because he felt sorry for them. Not sorry during and not sorry after.

Gallagher shrugged again. "I know there are plenty I'm not thinking of. I can get you a comprehensive list from a friend of mine who studies ancient mythological sciences. Uh . . . there were three judges of the dead, I think, but I can't recall details about them . . ."

Gallagher's friend might be most helpful. "That's all right, Doctor. Could you put me in touch with this friend of yours?"

Brody Gallagher nodded, opening a drawer of his desk. "Sure, sure. Calliope is a character, I warn you, but she knows her stuff."

Jenna watched as he scratched a name and phone number on a blank sheet of computer paper with the pen he'd taken from the desk drawer. "Her name is *Calliope*?"

He chuckled, eyes flitting from where his cell phone displayed the contact card to the paper. "Not her *given* name, of course. She changed it several years ago after she took a sabbatical in Turkey in order to read Homer's works in full in the place of his birth. The mythological figure Calliope is widely considered to be Homer's muse, apparently, and what can I say? I guess it struck a chord in my friend."

Jenna smiled, imagining a kooky woman in huge glasses, a raggedy shawl, and large, gypsy-esque earrings. "No pun intended, huh?"

Gallagher laughed again. He passed Jenna the sheet of paper. "She's a fun gal. Smart as a whip. Tell her I said hello, will you?"

"Of course," Jenna replied, thinking that if a hello was warranted, this Calliope might not be as good of a friend as Gallagher intimated. Still, she was worth a try. "Thank you so much, Dr. Gallagher."

"Any time," he replied.

With that, Jenna shook the man's hand and took her leave. *Calliope Jones, ready or not, here I come.*

Yancy sat at the kitchen table at Jenna's house, sipping a bottled water and staring at the newspaper even though he wasn't reading it. He was supposed to have a late dinner with Jenna, but as usual, she was running even later.

Vern and Charley were both in the living room watching cartoons with Ayana, and as much as Yancy loved the three of them, he was probably about as pleasant to be around right now as a Chihuahua during a malfunctioning burglar alarm episode. He'd told them he had to go over the updated training manual for emergency dispatchers, and they'd accepted his reasoning to stay in the kitchen without any questions.

Now he glared at the black-and-white paper in front of him, the words blurring together through the mist of his mind. He'd thought maybe tonight he'd take another shot at mustering the courage to yank the ring out of his pocket, but after their fight this afternoon, that courage had deflated into nonexistence. Hell, he wasn't even sure why he was in Jenna's kitchen right now. Sure, the sheer fact that he was allowed in Jenna's military compound of a house was a compliment in itself, but really, what could he offer her? A magnetic surface where she could pin up pictures of Ayana?

"Hey there, Steampunk. How's the studying going?"

Yancy's train of thought dissipated at the sound of Vern's voice, and he smiled despite how crummy he was feeling. Jenna's dad had given him the nickname when he found out Yancy carried a gun in his prosthetic leg, and it always felt like something of an honor. In this family, you got a nickname when you were family, too.

"Eh, kinda distracted to be honest," Yancy said. What else could he do but be honest? He'd been caught red-handed without a manual in sight. "Decided to save the work for later."

"Hmm," Vern said, nodding knowingly as he stood at the sink and refilled his glass with water. Something in his voice told Yancy he hadn't fooled anyone with his fib in the first place. "Later, as in after that tiny thing weighing down your pocket is out in the open?"

Yancy half laughed. "Something like that."

Vern shut off the faucet and crossed back toward the living room. He stopped in front of Yancy and laid a hand on his shoulder. "I know it didn't work out too well for me, but trust me. Just because my blushing bride turned out to be a psycho killer doesn't mean I don't remember how nauseated I was with that damned diamond burning a hole in my pocket when I was working up the nerve to show it to her. The right time will show itself. You'll see."

Yancy bit his lip and nodded, guilt biting at his gut. Here he was, feeling sorry for himself, and really, compared to the man in front of him, he didn't have any reason to. Vern had been in love with a woman he'd never even really known, and when he'd vowed to care for her forever, she returned the sentiment by trying to kill him. Twice.

And yet, despite everything Vern had been through, he'd not only welcomed Yancy into his life, but he had trusted him enough to give Yancy his blessing to ask Jenna to marry him.

"Thanks, Vern. For everything," Yancy replied.

"Eh, no thanks required. Takes a good man to tame El Tigre. I can't ever seem to get her to remember to take a deep breath and play a little Yahtzee every once in a while, so I figure you're doing me a favor. Speaking of workaholics, since your manual seems to have grown legs and run off, why don't you come on in and hit up the La-Z-Boy while you wait? *SpongeBob* marathon going on in the living room and a chair with your name on it. Whaddaya say?"

Vern gave him too much credit. Yancy hadn't tamed Jenna. Didn't want to. All he cared about was staying in stride right there with her, something he didn't seem capable of at the moment.

"Nah, I think I'll pass tonight. Nerves and nausea and hearing about pineapples under the sea might tip a delicate balance," he said, trying to sound lighthearted.

"Okay," Vern replied, giving him another pat on the shoulder and walking away. "But if you change your mind, we'll even let you have a turn with the volume remote."

And he left, leaving Yancy thinking how much he wished he felt like doing just that. This day didn't seem to be conducive to making any decisions that would be right, though. *Yeah, cool guy. Sit here and sulk. It helps everything.*

CiCi Winthrop popped into his thoughts, the labored breathing on the other end of the phone as he'd promised her help was coming. One of these days, he was going to be wrong.

Locks turned and the doorknob twisted.

A frazzled-looking Jenna appeared, colored keys in hand. "Hey, you."

Yancy stood and jammed his hands in his pockets. He moved toward her, kissed her cheek. His fingers brushed the ring in his pocket. "Hard day?"

"Not over yet, either," she replied. "I might have to postpone dinner . . . again. Trying to get in touch with a source. Some kind of mythology expert."

"Oh, yeah? What does that have to do with anything?"

Jenna opened the fridge, took out a Coke. "Long story short, Triple Shooter's obsession with threes might be motivated by Greek mythology."

"Still thinking the Triple Shooter's the guy even though there were seven victims? That *still* makes no sense."

She leaned against the counter and ran a hand through her chestnut hair. "You're telling me."

Yancy sighed and sat back down at the table. Once upon a time, he'd have gotten a more in-depth answer to that statement, some glimpse into why Jenna still had reason to think what she did. What kind of problems came with whatever she was thinking to bring on the frustrated sigh she let out after she was quiet again, the little shake of her head that said nothing but, *If you only knew.*

"Where's the crew?" Jenna asked.

Yancy cocked his head toward the den. "It's cartoon hour."

"Isn't that every hour?"

"Yeah, but who's counting." *Okay, cool guy. Smooth this over. You're awkward enough without this tension hanging around.* He stood again and stepped around the table. He leaned into her, putting one arm on either side of her on the counter. "So, what do you say I whip us up something here? I'm not a gourmet chef by any means, but I do make a mean BLT."

She smiled, then laughed, the strain between them melting. "I seem to remember you making more than *that* . . ."

His arms drifted from the countertop to around her trim waistline. "Is that an offer, Dr. Ramey?"

"Well, A is occupied, dinner is up in the air, at best . . ." She wrapped her arms around his neck. "Think of it as more of a . . . suggestion."

He leaned in, the smell of her lotion sugary, her breath hot. His lips grazed hers, soft and smooth and so, so sweet.

Her phone rang, and she tensed in his embrace. He pulled back from her.

She frowned. "Sorry."

"No need," he said, letting go of her. After all, as much as he hated what the intense nature of her job did to them, if not for her being what she was, he'd have never found her.

Jenna took her phone from the holster on her belt. Yancy liked to kid her about it, but she always claimed its practical use outweighed the fashion flub.

"Jenna Ramey," she answered.

Yancy paced the kitchen as he listened to Jenna's side of the conversation, and it soon became clear dinner *and* the evening quickie were off the table. She agreed to meet someone in an hour, and it sounded like it was the person she'd been trying, without avail, to get hold of all afternoon.

She dropped the phone from her ear, re-holstered it. "That was Calliope Jones, the mythology expert. Going to meet her at her apartment."

"*Calliope?*"

Jenna smiled. "I said the same thing."

Yancy shrugged. To each his own.

Suddenly his face seared, guilt over the thoughts he was having pummeling his self-worth, heating him from the inside out. He knew it wasn't appropriate, and he knew what she'd say. But still, he couldn't help the burning desire to be back on par with her, part of her life again. The image of the two of them as a team tickled his imagination, and he couldn't stop himself. "Hey, why don't I tag along? Extra ears have been useful in the past . . . maybe I can help you bounce ideas afterward."

As soon as the words left his lips, he regretted them, if only because he knew he'd resent her answer. Even if she was right.

She didn't disappoint. Her lips pursed, a look that said one thing . . . pity.

"Yance, I'd love to have you along. Really, I would—"

"But."

Jenna closed her eyes then opened them again, her gaze meeting his. "You know I can't."

He nodded, turning back toward his unread newspaper.

"Yeah," he said. "I know."

"I think I'll sneak out without venturing into the living room. Much as I want to see A, if I go in just to leave again, it'll be worse than if she didn't know I was back yet." She walked over, kissed the top of his head. "I'll call you later, k?"

Under the table, his fist clenched the ring from outside his pants pocket. "Sounds good."

And Jenna left, the air of what might have been the only thing to keep him company.

Yancy drummed his fingers on the table. God, he missed that sense of place he'd had last year. He'd never wanted that whole episode, but it had felt so good to be useful. After being out of the action for so long and ending up out of commission before ever finishing his state-level FBI training, last year he'd finally gotten his chance to do what he'd always wanted to do. Hell, he'd even found out he had a knack for it.

He could help again someday, right? Surely his destiny wasn't to sit behind a phone and then come home to a horny dachshund whose idea of fun was humping his leg before passing out cold on the kitchen floor with his tongue hanging out.

CiCi Winthrop popped back to mind. His gut had proved right last year . . . What if his intuition telling him to check up on her was right this time? Jenna acted on hunches all the time. Grapheme synesthesia or no grapheme synesthesia, his instincts were just a different brand.

Stop rationalizing, loser. You don't need to do this.

But even as he talked himself down, he was already visualizing the number on his screen, the cell phone he'd triangulated to get her location. Was it hers? Maybe he'd just call. See if she was okay . . . *Don't do it.*

He dialed. A feminine voice he recognized answered the phone. So, she was okay. He could hang up now, and she'd never be the wiser.

Yancy gripped the cell tighter. "CiCi, it's Yancy. From, um, the emergency line. I was just calling to check on you."

After a long pause, she started to spew how nice of him it was to think about her. *Needed.*

"Um, I know this might sound weird, and I know it's late. But how would you feel about grabbing a cup of coffee tomorrow?"

16

Jenna wandered into Calliope Jones's apartment when the expert on Greek mythology held open her door. It was a good thing Jenna had a lot of practice at seeing and hearing the bizarre, because not reacting to the wacky décor of the place was a task all its own.

The living room walls were covered in artwork depicting winged horses, many-headed monsters, and old men in togas. Statuettes of women with snakes for hair and men with the bodies of animals sat on the sofa end tables, and over the couch a hand-embroidered tapestry bearing the words PRINCIPAL GODS FAMILY TREE hung. Jenna stopped in front of a canvas that reminded her vaguely in style of the painting of the Last Supper in Liam Tyler's office. That was, if you could get past the cherubs buzzing overhead and the naked woman smack in the middle of the artwork. Still, Jenna couldn't help but imagine that Molly Keegan would have a great time counting the various people and objects in the painting. Jenna found herself unwittingly counting them herself. *Seven books, two masks . . .*

"Do you like it?" Calliope said from behind her. "It's Nicolas Poussin. *Apollo and the Muses.* Of course, *The Rape of the Sabine Women* is the far more famous of his paintings, but I prefer his more whimsical work."

Jenna turned around and smiled. "Yes, it's beautiful."

Calliope Jones wasn't exactly what Jenna had expected. She didn't have the shawl, nor the huge glasses. Rather, the fifty-something blond woman was dressed in smart black slacks and a short, light black trench coat. If she'd seen her on the street, Jenna probably would've pegged Calliope for a fashion editor or a television anchorwoman, not someone who had made a life of studying Greek mythology. Some profiler she was.

The woman gestured around the room to her paintings. "These are some of my favorites, though I have a larger collection in my office. Couldn't possibly hang every one at home."

"Hardly," Jenna said.

Calliope extended her hand toward the sofa. "Please," she said.

Jenna obliged, and the mythology expert sat down in a tattered armchair beside the couch.

"Thank you for making time to see me, Ms. Jones."

"Oh, Calliope, please. I insist!"

"Yes. Calliope. I have a bit of a puzzle here I'm hoping you can help with."

Calliope leaned back and crossed her legs. "I'm all ears."

Jenna launched into the best explanation she could about the case and what she thought it could possibly have to do with Greek mythology. She'd decided on the way over to be more open with Calliope Jones regarding the details of the case that had brought her here. In a perfect world, she could keep every little sliver of information about the actual crimes to herself to preserve case integrity while still divulging just enough that the mythology expert would be able to pass along any relevant information she might have to add. But Jenna's conversations with the two professors previously had showed her that while they could circle the neighborhood of answers without being abreast of everything weighing in on the issue, a landing spot would be difficult to suss out without full disclosure to allow for honing in on the path to take where the landing spot would become visible.

Jenna stopped a few times to field questions about schizophrenia, profiling techniques, and certain details about the crime she'd decided to share this time.

"So that's where I am. I have a bunch of bodies; a killer who, until now, killed one person at a time only when threes aligned and who may hear the voices of some Greek god; and a lot of things that don't make sense. I need to figure out if this obsession with threes has to do with a Greek god because if I can crack his thought pattern, I have a better chance of figuring out where to start looking for him. And even if I can't figure out what god he's hearing, maybe I can find *some* connection in the crimes to either make the random murdering of seven people, instead of one who aligned with threes, make sense to give me a more accurate profile of the shooter, or to link the victims in some way I haven't seen yet and keep working with the current profile based on similarities of victims instead of focusing on the number of them. I know it's a tall order, but I'd appreciate any thoughts you might give me on triplicate Greek gods, particularly those to do with death, like the Fates," Jenna said.

Calliope cocked her head. "This is a wild thought, but have you considered that the voices may have nothing to do with death?"

Jenna blinked. No, actually she hadn't. Not really, anyway. The possibility always existed, of course, but in murders perpetrated by schizophrenics, voices telling them to kill were a common thread. "Well, I suppose if you have a theory . . ."

Calliope waved her hand. "Oh, no. Not yet anyway. Not about a specific set of gods or goddesses. But with that in mind, if I was you, I would consider that in Greek myth, death was more of an . . . incidental occurrence. The gods and goddesses were mostly concerned with carrying out their whims as they pertained to the *living*."

An auburn color flashed in, though Jenna couldn't yet place it. *Not quite the color of power. Too dark to be aggression . . .*

More information needed. "How so?" Jenna asked.

Calliope folded her hands. Some people talked with their hands; Calliope's speech was oddly devoid of animation. "The Greek gods were vain, easily angered. Religious ideas often depict gods as wise and able to determine their actions based on the good of mankind. People like to think gods are infallible. The truth is, though, gods—particularly the Greek gods—tended to act based on their own interests. Poseidon kept poor Odysseus from returning home for a dreadfully long time because Odysseus blinded his son, Polyphemus." Calliope let out a jovial laugh as though they were sharing an inside joke. "Not unlike the portrayal in the Bible of the God of the modern Christians, Greek gods were wrathful when angered. Only their anger went a step further than simply asking that no gods be worshipped before them, and they were not always considered 'good' overall."

"So there were evil gods?" Jenna asked.

Calliope moved her head from side to side as if weighing her thoughts. "Not exactly. Just selfish ones. Ill-tempered ones. And alas, some charged with jobs that were more unpleasant than others."

"Like what?"

"Well, your example of the Fates was a good one, though their job was perhaps less repulsive than some. I personally don't envy Eileithyia's job, but that's just me."

Jenna took a deep breath as the thistle color of vanity flashed in, quickly followed by the redwood shade Jenna associated with attention seeking. Sure, Calliope probably didn't get a lot of chances to display her vast knowledge to a willing victim, but name-dropping something obscure for the purpose of coercing another to ask for an in-depth explanation had long been a pet peeve of Jenna's in this line of work.

Nevertheless, she bit. "Who was that?"

Calliope grinned, again lapping up the opportunity presented to her like a thirsty Labrador shown a full water dish. "Goddess of childbirth."

"Ah," Jenna replied. *Back to the point.* "Any of these deities with unfavorable tasks come in triad form?"

"Oh, yes. The Judges of the Dead—Rhadamanthys, Minos, and

Aiakos—come to mind. But probably my best answer to that one would be the Erinyes."

This time Jenna didn't ask. Instead, she simply leaned her head forward in a move that clearly said, *Go on . . .*

Calliope unclasped her hands and pointed to a painting on the far wall across from both of them. In it, a tortured-looking, mostly naked man covering his ears stood front and center, and behind him, four willowy figures perpetuated chaos. One was a fainting person draped with a red sheet, a golden dagger protruding from the heart. The other three were set slightly deeper into the painting than the stabbed form, and they were somewhat more ethereal. They looked similar physically, and they all stared at the man, each wearing an expression of ire. One wielded a torch, which was raised as though about to strike.

"Behold, the Erinyes. The three sisters known as the Furies."

S hortly after the dramatic statement, auburn had flashed in. The color of vengeance. Jenna's team pager had gone off, and she'd excused herself. "Calliope, I appreciate you taking the time to go over these things with me. You've been more helpful than you can possibly know. But I'm afraid I have to cut this meeting short. The rest of the Behavioral Analysis Unit needs to meet, share what we've found out, and regroup. But I may have a few more questions later if that's okay."

"Oh, it'll be quite all right. I'll do what I can. You won't mind, of course, if I ask you to see yourself to the door. I have a lot of work to do."

"Not at all," Jenna said, with a sneaking suspicion that she'd hurt the mythology expert's feelings. Ah, well. Duty called.

After all, a theory was forming in her head now. What better way to test a theory than to run it by the best of the best? Not to mention she wouldn't exactly mind knowing what the other team members were up to. Jenna hopped in her Blazer and drove five over the speed limit as she raced across town to Quantico.

The team was already seated around the table, Dodd noticeably missing. All eyes followed Jenna as she slipped into a vacant chair near the door. But when Saleda spoke up, all heads turned to focus on her.

"We've each been working different angles, thinking we could divide and conquer in this case, but I thought it best to call you all back since there's been another murder."

The silence was so thick it was suffocating. Saleda opened her shiny blue folder and removed a glossy black-and-white photo. She pinned the photograph onto the felt board beside her. "Ladies and gents, this is Brooklyn Satterhorne. She was found in a Target parking lot around eight p.m. tonight by another shopper. Shot three times—clipped once in the left forearm, once in the left shoulder, and once in the chest. A penny over each eye."

Jenna stared back at the smiling photo of what looked like a high schooler with wild, curly hair and a bridge of freckles dotting her nose.

"Pennies? Where are the threes?" Jenna asked.

"That's the funny part. Well, if you have a warped sense of humor anyway. No discernable connection to the number three aside from the three gunshots," Saleda replied.

A few colors fought for dominance in Jenna's mind. None of this made any sense. *Relax. Don't force it.*

"And the pennies are different, too," Jenna muttered.

"No threes, nothing related to put over the eyes," Porter piped up from the other side of the table.

Teva frowned. "The pennies have to be related in some way, though."

Nail, meet head. Figure out the relationship of the pennies, the details of this profile might solidify enough that the team might at least know they were on the right track. Either that or they could steer in the direction they needed to go.

"Ballsy," Porter said, crunching the bill of the ball cap on his head. "Shooting her during the store's open hours."

Next to him, Teva's pencil seesawed in between her thumb and forefinger. "He's spiraling, maybe? Making mistakes?"

"I'd say he spiraled way before now, what with the seven dead people in the grocery store," a voice said from the doorway.

Jenna's head whipped around to see Dodd entering the room. No one asked questions about where he'd been as he circled the table. He unbuttoned the top collar button of his navy polo as he parked in the only remaining empty seat. Saleda glared at him.

Despite the dark circles under his eyes, he didn't seem irritated. He smiled a tired but jovial grin, ignoring Saleda's annoyance. "He's a bad shot, too. Clipped her in the left arm?"

Saleda turned away from him and to the table, seemingly to keep herself from screaming. "Shots were fired from at least a few yards away."

The cornflower blue Jenna associated with sloppiness flashed in. Once again, confirmation this killer was disorganized.

"So if we're right that this is the same UNSUB as the one at the grocery store, and our UNSUB is right-handed, the victim was facing him," Porter replied.

"Maybe. We'll have to wait until we have more details to be sure."

Dodd leaned forward. "Speaking of, why are we talking about this here? Why aren't we at the crime scene scrutinizing the evidence and seeing this bastard's inept shooting skills for ourselves?"

Saleda took a deep breath. "Because we were waiting for confirmation this was tied to our case, since until about two minutes ago, it could've been anything. But as of a couple minutes ago, she's in the morgue at Prince William County Hospital. Only when she was pronounced DOA there did the locals run this through as a homicide. Until then, this shooting was nothing more than clatter on the tip line. Wouldn't have mattered if they'd run it through as an attempted homicide before, either, I don't guess. Even if she'd been so badly injured that she couldn't wiggle and disturb the evidence, the paramedics would've destroyed what was left, coins or no coins—"

"What are you muttering about here, boss?" Porter cut in.

"We're here and not in the Target parking lot because I didn't know for sure that this shooting was linked to our case until I got details from the homicide report filed after she was declared at Prince William County Hospital. Prior to that, she was any other shooting to their first responders, even though she was lying on the parking lot cement with a coin over each eye.

"Now that we know, we need to split up again, but in one less group than we would've if Brooklyn Satterhorne was still with us, because then we'd be interviewing her, too. As it is, we've got Target crime scene, potential witnesses, and family. No Brooklyn herself.

"Shame, too," Saleda continued. "When the shopper found her in the parking lot, Brooklyn was still alive. She might've stared right at him as he bent to put the coins on her eyes so they'd be that way when the shopper found her."

"How can he show remorse, put down the coins to pay the ferryman for her crossing, if she wasn't dead yet?" Teva asked.

"Maybe he knew she would be. Didn't care? Maybe his ritual was more important than the act of killing itself—"

Jenna cut Dodd off. "Maybe he was too delusional to stop and check for vitals. Look too hard. If you're so out of it that you think a god or goddess is telling you to kill, you're not going to plug a person with a third gunshot, then wait until after emergency responders arrive and determine if the victim's dead so if he is, you can somehow manage to lay down calling cards and tokens for the cops to find. If a god's telling you to do it, the god's obviously going to make sure it goes to plot. Plus, the rest of the circumstances told him what he wanted to know. His shots—location and number—suggested she would die or was already dead. Brooklyn's own stillness when he laid the coins over her eyes makes it look like she didn't speak to him again or move anymore."

Saleda chimed in. "Question is, did she talk to anyone or move anymore after her shooter was gone? I want to know every shopper who squatted beside her in the parking lot, every medic who took her pulse, and every number her fingers could reach to send a text to before she was pronounced DOA at the hospital. I want to know if by some chance she was trying to get us a message, or if she was just weak, incoherent, and barely even cognizant during her last moments on earth." Saleda turned to Jenna. "And I want you to find the shopper who found her in the parking lot when she was still alive. I want to know if that shopper saw or spoke to anyone anywhere near where she found Brooklyn Satterhorne, and whether or not Brooklyn herself said anything to or so much as grunted at this shopper."

M olly woke with a start. *G-Ma. The people running.* Her heart raced. She blinked into the darkness, and the butterflies hanging from the ceiling fan slowly came into focus as her eyes adjusted.

She wanted to get up, run to Mommy and Liam's room.

No. Mommy is barely sleeping at night anyway. She needs to sleep.

Think about something else.

Else. Four letters. Letters. Seven. Seven. Five letters.

She pushed away the covers and swung her feet off the side of the bed, then padded toward the bathroom. The flower-shaped nightlight glimmered from the wall socket, giving her face an eerie glow in the mirror. She couldn't help it; she needed to walk around. She had to dislodge this thing stuck in her brain she hadn't yet been able to jog loose.

As she'd tried to fall asleep earlier, she'd gone over and over the grocery store in her mind. She knew most kids her age would be afraid, and a lot of adults seemed to be worried about her. She wasn't a scaredy-cat, though. She just wanted to help.

The old man in the aisle had been what she'd tried to remember. Why hadn't he been in the back room with all the other witnesses that day?

He'd had four items in his grocery basket. Two were cereal. The same kind. He'd been in the cereal aisle. What other numbers? *Come on, head.*

He'd been wearing a gold watch, the kind with slash marks instead of numbers. Molly hated those kinds of watches.

She leaned against the sink, closed her eyes tight. His shirt. Two diamonds on the pocket of the T-shirt. They overlapped.

Associations with the number two flew through Molly's mind. *The smallest prime number. The smallest number in a standard deck of cards. Two mountains in the left window of Liam's painting of* The Last Supper. *The number of NASCAR racer Rusty Wallace.*

The diamond image burned in her mind. Two.

Molly blinked. She'd been walking into the store with G-Ma. A short bus had been parked in front of the entrance. Two diamonds, overlapping, were painted on the sign.

She scampered back to bed, climbed in, and pulled the covers all the way to her chin, even though she knew she wouldn't get any more sleep tonight. She was still thinking about those two diamonds. The ones on the short-bus sign.

Under the diamonds had been the words CARMINE MANOR. In small type below that had been ASSISTED LIVING FOR SENIORS.

Once Saleda had assigned Porter to go take a statement from the family, told Teva to accompany her to the crime scene, and stuck Jenna with Dodd, the latter two had left to interview the traumatized shopper who'd found poor Brooklyn Satterhorne. Jenna wondered if maybe she ought to take it as a compliment—the fact that Saleda thought she could handle the rogue—but somehow his pairing with her didn't exactly feel like a medal of honor. If the last interview they'd performed together was any indication, this would go over about as well as that time Ayana thought her goldfish would like to try some of her Kool-Aid.

As they climbed into the FBI-issued SUV, Dodd in the driver's seat, Jenna tried to sound nonchalant. "So, where have you been?"

Dodd sighed heavily, and his shoulders hunched. "Big case I was head investigator on a few years back has been reopened. Defense appealed a competency ruling, more medical and psych evaluations followed. Doing everything I can to keep that bastard on the inside. If ever I wanted to see a killer convicted, it was him. To do what he did to those people took something. Something awful. Inhuman, even."

Jenna nodded, solemn. "Saleda told me about the Cobbler. I hadn't realized until then you'd been on that case."

Dodd's gaze stayed on the road as he turned right out of the Quantico parking lot. "Unfortunately."

Jenna sat in silence, unsure what to say as the particulars of the infamous serial murder case drifted through her head. Every member of the BAU had looked at them, after all. The case was still somewhat of a mystery in the profiling world. Twelve people's throats slashed, and when the FBI's Violent Criminal Apprehension Program assessed the victims for possible connections to known serial murder cases, all twelve fit the ViCAP data for the slayer the media had dubbed the Cobbler due to his MO of cutting off *some* of his victims' feet. An individual with a known history of mental disorder had eventually been implicated in the case, and when his home was raided, investigators found the ten feet that *had* been severed in the guy's freezer. Despite his questionable mental capacity, the killer had been convicted of twelve counts of murder among a slew of other charges and was sentenced to death. However, no one could explain why he chose to remove some of his victims' feet and left others' intact. The acts certainly didn't fit the standard concept of a trophy killer. Some investigators had surmised that he'd simply been interrupted or spooked during the killings where the feet were left alone, but Jenna had never bought it. It didn't make any sense. Some people lost one foot, some two. Others had kept both. Jenna's gut said those discriminations happened for a reason, but what it was she'd probably never know.

"Ridiculous is what it is. That now . . . It's not just that they're tryin' to get him put into psych lockup instead of death row, where he belongs. No. It's worse. Defense is hinting that they've got proof coming out soon that there's no way their client committed the Cobbler murders. Damned out-and-out ridiculous is what it is. Feagin McKye had ten feet in his freezer, for Christ's sake. It takes a lot of balls to dismember someone. Forget *multiple* someones," Dodd muttered.

A pang of pity hit Jenna. No matter what she thought of Dodd, she couldn't help but feel bad for the guy. He'd apparently put this case to bed in his own mind long ago, something everyone in this job knew you couldn't really do with one you were sure you'd solved until the perp was apprehended, the trial and all its appeals over. If you were lucky, sometimes the execution that followed gave closure. Sure, they must have some huge questions to reopen what seemed so cut-and-dry a case, and she was sure Dodd was biased. After all, your gut was all you had in some cases. She couldn't blame Dodd for feeling so sure he had the right man. If Jenna had found a bunch of feet belonging to victims in someone's freezer, she'd consider it a closed case, too.

Which, of course, begged the questions: if the new evidence did turn out to be game-changing and by some chance proved Dodd had been wrong, where the hell was the real killer, and how did those feet get in that guy's freezer?

"What now?" she asked, despite her better judgment.

Dodd put on his blinker. "Well, for now, we find out what we can about Brooklyn Satterhorne."

The sun was creeping over the horizon by the time they arrived at the home of Sheila Maxwell, the unfortunate soul who had stumbled across the disturbing scene that was Brooklyn Satterhorne in the Target parking lot in Fredericksburg. The location told Jenna their killer was within a small radius of Quantico. Scary that the FBI could be based here and yet could be as clueless as they currently were as to who the hell was at the root of all this madness.

The cream-colored, Mediterranean-style home looked more like something Jenna would've expected to find in Boca Raton than Fredericksburg, Virginia. The stucco villa's lawn was just screaming for a palm tree or two. Looked like somewhere Hank would've wanted to live. He'd always said, back when they were together, that one day he wanted to live closer to the beach. She'd been the one to go back to her home in Florida after they broke it off, even though it hadn't been near the waterfront. But back then she'd always thought that one day they'd retire together and move close to the sand.

He'd died there, in her home.

Jenna pushed the thought of Hank's frozen, staring eyes toward a happier image. Ayana's lively, energetic eyes. Copies of Hank's. *God. I miss you, A.*

Dodd knocked on the front door, and Jenna pushed the thoughts of everything from Hank to missing Ayana to the Cobbler out of her head to focus on what she needed to know from Sheila Maxwell.

A brunette of about five-foot-two answered the door.

"Ms. Maxwell?" Dodd asked.

The lady shook her head. "No, I'm her sister. Come in. Sheila's resting on the couch."

Sedated? It wasn't uncommon for doctors to medicate someone who'd seen something like what Sheila had, but Jenna only hoped they hadn't given her something too heavy. Maybe it was cruel, but witnesses could remember a lot more clearly when they were conscious.

Jenna and Dodd followed Sheila Maxwell's sister through the hallway and into the wicker-clad living room. Another brunette, much taller than the sister who'd greeted them, lay on the white wicker couch, her eyes red from tears, her hair mussed. Her legs were curled toward her chest to ensure she fit on the tiny sofa, but the position made her look somewhat like a giant on the type of furniture usually reserved for brief perching as neighbors carried on polite conversations about the weather during patio cookouts.

When she saw Jenna and Dodd, Sheila sat up and wiped her eyes as though she thought they wouldn't be able to tell she was distraught if she had no tears visible.

"Sheila, these are the detectives I told you were coming," her sister said.

"Agents," Dodd corrected.

Jenna shot him a look, then turned back to Sheila. "Ms. Maxwell, I know this is a horrible time for you, and I can't imagine what you're going through . . ." True enough statement. Jenna had seen so many dead bodies, she could no longer remember what it was like to see a scene and be so disturbed she lay on the couch and cried. *Depressing.* "But we do need to ask you some questions."

Sheila nodded quickly, though experience told Jenna it was out of anxiety rather than eagerness. Luckily, the woman didn't seem *very* drugged.

"Ms. Maxwell, what was the first thing you noticed in the parking lot?"

The woman stared at Dodd like he was made of the same wicker as her furniture. She blinked. "A body."

Points for explaining.

"Could you tell us what you noticed about the body specifically, Ms. Maxwell?" Jenna clarified. Dodd apparently hadn't done this in a long time. "Which way it was facing, the physical condition . . . just describe to us exactly what you saw."

The woman nodded again. "Um . . . she was lying on the ground. On her back."

Bullet impact threw her backward. She was facing the shooter.

Sheila Maxwell pulled her knees to her chest now, childlike. "Red soaked her arms and her torso, and her eyes didn't look normal."

Jenna gave an encouraging nod. "What happened next?"

The woman dug her nails into her black trousers. "I screamed. I screamed, but for some reason, I went toward her anyway. I looked down at her as I got closer, and there were coins over her eyes. She wasn't moving."

"Ms. Maxwell, what did you do after you saw the coins?" Jenna asked.

"Nothing. I waited. Some other people ran past me and knelt by her. I heard someone say she was alive. Other people called nine-one-one. I just . . . stood there," she said, sounding ashamed.

"Ms. Maxwell, you went through a terrible experience. You can't fault yourself for being shocked. Your reaction was a very natural one. Your scream alerted help. You did a good job," Dodd said.

Jenna glanced at him, not positive she'd heard him right. Surely that couldn't have been Dodd . . .

She shook off her surprise. Maybe he had one or two good bones in his body after all.

"Do you remember what the victim looked like?" Jenna asked.

Sheila Maxwell bobbled her head. "Red hair. Curly. That's mainly what I remember."

The second redheaded victim. Coincidence? Ainsley Nickerson, who'd been one of the original three victims, had been murdered in her bathtub. Her hair was more auburn, though. Brooklyn's was carrot, ginger. "What else?"

Sheila Maxwell rubbed the invisible goosebumps on her arms. "She had on a blue sweater. No, wait . . . purple." The lady blinked rapidly. "I remember her . . . oh, God. I remember seeing her!"

She choked out a sob as her hand flew to her mouth, but Jenna was too intrigued to worry about Sheila Maxwell's comfort.

"Ms. Maxwell, *where* did you see the victim?" she asked.

"In the store," Sheila whispered. "She was shopping with another girl."

Another girl?

Jenna leaned forward. "This is very important, Ms. Maxwell. Do you remember anything about the other girl?"

Sheila shook her head, but Jenna could tell by the look in her eyes she was searching her brain.

"The friend was wearing blue. Maybe a shirt from the community college," Sheila said. She closed her eyes. "I think she was carrying an iPhone. It had a pink case, maybe? I'm not sure . . ."

Jenna leapt up and left Dodd to continue the questioning. She walked into the hallway, Irv's speed-dial button already pressed.

"How can I help you, my Color-Coded Queen?" Irv answered.

"I need a cross-reference of everyone in Brooklyn Satterhorne's college classes with her phone calls and texts in . . . let's say the past twenty-four hours. Kids shopping together call each other first, right?"

"Oh, for sure. I *always* call my buddies before we hit up the Fashion Bug."

Jenna couldn't hold in the laugh. "The Fashion Bug? They still have those?"

"Claire's?" Irv said.

"Try again . . ."

"Burlington Coat Factory? Rue 21? Aw, screw it. I'll have the cross-reference to you in five."

"Thanks, Irv," Jenna said, smiling in spite of herself.

She hung up and shoved her phone back into the clip. If a girl was with Brooklyn Satterhorne at Target, she was their best bet at finding out why Brooklyn was killed . . . and who might've done this to her.

I t was morning time when Eldred opened his eyes. He was back at his apartment. Carmichael Manor, was it? No. Carmine. Yes, that was right. How had he gotten here?

He staggered through the tiny hallway to the kitchenette. Nancy still sometimes checked him out for trips to her house, and sometimes he slept there in a twin bed next to her bedroom. It was better there than here. Here, it smelled like old people.

Dying people.

Eldred scratched his head, felt a knot there. That was right. He'd hit his head. Somewhere.

He reached for the box of Cocoa Puffs on the counter. He wasn't supposed to eat them, he knew, but the bran cereal Sarah always brought him didn't taste as good.

No. Not Sarah. Sarah was gone.

His heart stung, his chest clenched. His Sarah. Gone. Always gone.

It was Nancy. Nancy brought the bran flakes.

He shook some cereal into the bowl, and again, something tickled his mind. What couldn't he remember? Something someone had told him, maybe? Something about Nancy?

About Sarah?

Unable to help it, his hand holding the box trembled as his sadness became frustration. He gripped the cereal box harder until its edge crinkled under his hand. He yelled and threw it across the room into the little two-person table. Not his table! Not his and Sarah's table!

"The kitchen isn't big enough for that table, Dad," Nancy had said when they'd moved him in. "I got this smaller one for you. Isn't it nice?"

Where was his table? Sarah's table?

He noticed the Cocoa Puffs on the floor. How had those gotten there?

Eldred picked up the dustpan and small brush hanging beside the sink and ambled over to the mess. He crouched down and swept the cereal into the pan. Cereal. Boxes. Loud noises.

He stopped sweeping, tears stinging his eyes. It was on the tip of his tongue, right there. *Remember. Please.*

The phone mounted on the wall rang. Then again, interrupting the ever-so-close memory he'd been grappling to seize. He groaned as he heaved himself off the floor, leaving the dustpan full of cereal where it was. Whoever this was had ruined his chance of remembering! They would hear. They would hear from him . . .

"Hello!" he barked.

"Hi," a tiny voice on the other end of the phone replied. "Um, my name is Molly Keegan. I met you at the grocery store."

Suddenly, the memory he'd been reaching for flew into his waiting hands, slammed them with the weight of a crashing plane.

The little girl who'd dived between the cereal boxes. Why he'd probably hit his head. What he'd seen.

What he knew.

Grown-ups always said you shouldn't talk to strangers, but there were plenty of exceptions to that rule. Teachers on the first day of school, the man behind the ice cream counter when he asked what flavor you wanted. Police who asked questions after something bad happened.

Besides, the old man Molly now knew was called Eldred Beasley wasn't a stranger. Not really. She'd met him before. And people could just as easily be good as bad, right?

After Liam and her mother had left to meet with the funeral people that morning, Molly had pulled out the piece of paper where she'd written down the number for Carmine Manor she'd looked up in the yellow pages book in the kitchen drawer. She asked the nice lady—a stranger—who'd answered the phone about the man in the store, only she didn't tell the nice lady she knew him from the store. She'd told her she'd found something of his she was hoping to return. After all, grown-ups also fibbed. They told people they looked pretty even if they looked silly. Liam told a church member everything would be okay with her husband who had cancer even though he knew it might not be.

Grown-ups said lies were okay as long as they were small and for the right reasons.

The lady had known who the man was as soon as Molly described him. She'd given Molly another name of someone to call about talking to him, saying the man might not understand why she was calling, but Molly called him anyway. Somehow, she knew she had to talk to him and only him. No one else would understand, even if she couldn't explain to anyone—including herself—why.

Now, as she heard the voice on the other end and gripped the phone tighter in her hand, she knew exactly why she'd needed to talk to him herself.

"Molly, you said? You were on the cereal aisle . . ."

His voice sounded hazy, the way hers did when she first woke up from a dream and couldn't tell if it had been real or not.

"Yes, sir," she said. She hadn't really planned what to say to him when she called. She'd spent so much time finding him, it hadn't occurred to her she'd need a plan.

"You . . . right before the last . . ."

Molly nodded hard, feeling more than knowing that this man was realizing something he hadn't before. He hadn't been in the room, and she didn't know why, but right now, it seemed like it was because he had forgotten about the grocery store altogether.

"Yes, sir," she said again. "I was with you right before the last shot."

"Oh, my dear, sweet Lord," Eldred Beasley breathed. "I need to talk to the police."

Yancy put his Prius into park outside the little bungalow on Peake. As much as he dreaded having to explain to CiCi how the modifier worked that allowed him to control the accelerator with his left foot instead of his prosthetic, he'd rather do that than walk to her house only to have her look at him like he was nuts if he thought she was going to walk ten blocks to the coffee shop. Some girls weren't outdoorsy types, and even if this wasn't a date, he could still be a gentleman.

Not a date, huh, jackass? Then what is it?

He wasn't cheating on Jenna. He wasn't. They'd never agreed to be exclusive. Even if he *did* have a ring for her in his pocket, they'd never decided to date only each other, and though this wasn't a date, it was "legal" even so. They'd done and would do nothing sketchy, and even if they had or did, coffee wasn't a lace-teddy-and-chocolate-dipped-strawberries date by any means. Besides, no real date took place before eleven a.m. This didn't even qualify as brunch. The only people who met for coffee before brunch were business associates, mommy play-groups, and acquaintances.

On his way up the walk, he tried to imagine explaining to her why he'd asked her to get coffee, though. Even if this wasn't a date, *she* probably assumed it was. Why else would a man ask a woman out for coffee?

Then again, what kind of married woman would accept without knowing his motivations?

The kind who is desperate, lonely, and abused.

Yancy climbed the three steps of the porch. Just as he raised his hand to knock on the door, though, he heard raised voices coming from inside.

"Where's the *money*, CiCi?" a man's voice growled.

Holy shit.

Yancy eased to the side of the porch, glancing in the big bay window in front. Movement in a room toward the back of the house, but he couldn't see anything else. He rushed down the porch stairs and rounded the right side of the house toward the room in question, yanking his cell phone from his pocket and dialing 911.

"Nine-one-one, can you please hold?"

The stiff air of the hold hit his ears.

"When I find out who took this call, I swear I will get your protocol-ditching ass fired, then boot you out the door with my own metal foot," he muttered.

He turned the corner to see a screened porch in the backyard. He crept in.

The voices were louder now.

"Please, Denny," CiCi's high-pitched voice choked. It sounded like she was being strangled.

Shit.

Yancy headed for the door that led to the house's interior. *Bad idea, buddy. You might not be a cop, but you do have training enough to know you shouldn't be moving in. You don't know the layout, you don't know the situation. Back off and call help.*

The knob turned under his hand. It was unlocked.

Yancy eased it shut again. He reached for his prosthetic, hit the hidden latch custom-built just for him.

In a flash, he held his Ruger .380.

He noiselessly turned the knob, opened the door.

In a crouch, he took the room in, listened closely for the direction of the voices. From the movement he'd seen in the window, they *should* be off to his right.

"CiCi, God help me, if you spent all that money again—"

Right.

"I didn't. I put it . . . somewhere safe."

Yancy crept through the halls, then leaned against the wall next to what seemed like the room where the conversation was taking place. The kitchen.

"You're lying," the man rasped. "And you know what I do to liars . . ."

Yancy swung his left leg around, weapon trained. "Let her go."

The dark-haired man released CiCi Winthrop's throat and spun around. "Who the fuck are you?"

"I'll be your worst goddamn nightmare if you don't walk out of this house right this minute," Yancy said.

Denny smirked, laughed.

Then, before Yancy knew what was happening, Denny's right hand flew to his waistline. A gun barrel appeared.

Yancy pulled the trigger.

CiCi squealed as the bullet caught her husband square in the chest.

Denny blinked for a moment, a confused look on his face. Then his face contorted, and a few strange noises came from his mouth as though he was having trouble getting words out. He fell to his knees and slammed both palms to the floor.

Oh, shit. What did you do?

Yancy's hand holding the gun fell as he stared at Denny on the floor for a long minute.

Denny's arms went limp, and he face-planted into the white tile.

Do something!

Yancy rushed to his side, rolled him over. He touched two fingers to his wrist, then his neck. Nothing.

Oh, holy God help me.

Yancy tilted Denny's chin back. *You better live, you motherfucker.*

He leaned into the man he'd shot and pressed his lips to Denny's. He breathed a slow breath.

A strange wheeze, then a wet spray. Blood had spattered from Denny's chest.

"Do you have plastic wrap?" Yancy said heatedly.

"What?" CiCi squeaked.

"Plastic wrap. Cling wrap. His lung is punctured. Do you have any?"

"Um, maybe," she said, and she started opening cabinets.

Yancy's head fell to his chest. It wouldn't matter even if she found it. One lung collapsed wouldn't have made his pulse disappear. The bullet had to have hit a major artery.

"He's . . . dead," Yancy said softly. "Your husband's . . . dead."

What can you possibly say to a woman whose husband you've just shot, even if you did it to defend her? Oh, God. He had to call someone. Do something.

"He's not my husband," CiCi whispered.

What?

He turned from Denny's fixed stare to look at this woman he'd come here to take out for coffee. Her hair was matted to her face with sweat, tears streaking her cheeks. She held a hand over her mouth, the pink nails chewed to the quicks from nervous nights in this very home. So many times he'd talked to her at the height of panic in moments she wasn't sure she'd live to see another day. It'd been so easy to assume the man cutting off her air supply seconds before was the same phantom of a monster Yancy had come to hate since he'd started taking calls from her. So many times he'd thought about being able to save her, even though he didn't know her. The almost palpable fear in her voice during every call, the sharp, rapid breaths she'd take while staying on the line waiting for help, trying to be quiet so he wouldn't find her hiding place. No one deserved to live that way.

But this wasn't him. Who the hell had he just shot?

"Who . . ."

This man had been asking her for money. Demanding it.

Oh, God, I've killed someone.

As scenarios flew through Yancy's mind of what would happen next, what kind of trouble he might be in in addition to the guilt coursing through him, he shook his head back and forth. This wasn't happening. Couldn't be.

"CiCi, we have to call an ambulance . . . the police . . ."

Yancy stood and pulled out his cell phone again, but a hot, sweaty grip around his wrist stayed his hand.

"We can't! Yancy . . ."

For the first time, her eyes met his. She had to be thinking the same thing he was: "So it's you."

"Yancy," she repeated.

"Um. Hey," he said. Then, he tore his eyes from hers. "As much as I'd love to have met a little more formally, we have to call someone!"

She shook her head furiously. "We can't. You don't understand . . ."

"I understand that we're standing in a kitchen with a dead guy . . . a dead guy you don't particularly seem too concerned about being dead. A guy who was demanding money from you a few seconds ago, but who isn't your abusive husband. What is he? A boyfriend? What?"

None of this made any sense.

"Not exactly," she muttered.

"Look, I don't mean to sound like an insensitive prick or anything, but considering I just shot a guy to save your life, I'm pretty sure I deserve some *fucking* details."

"He's . . . oh, God. Shit. Yancy, he's a . . ."

She stopped and closed her eyes. She looked like she might be about to puke.

"He's a what? A door-to-door encyclopedia salesman? A Sondheim fan? A towel boy for women's volleyball? What?"

She gulped, opened her eyes, and stared at him. "He's a pimp, Yancy."

What the . . .

This nice-looking, all-American girl in front of him in her cozy house with planter boxes out front and a WIPE YOUR PAWS welcome mat in front of the door, a hooker? This just didn't add up.

Then again, desperate times . . . maybe she was trying to score some money her evil husband wouldn't know about to stash into a getaway fund? Or was there even a husband at all? Maybe this was the guy who'd been beating her all along. But if he was, why protect him every time? Why say to 911 dispatch he was her husband?

And if she didn't need to squirrel away cash to escape an abusive home that didn't exist, then why the hell did a woman like her sell her body to random men?

Don't ask. Not right now.

"Okay, so he's a pimp. All the better. No one's going to lose sleep over someone shooting a pimp in self-defense, right? We just call the police, tell them what happened. We can make up a reason you were involved with him. Maybe he just broke in or something . . . we can keep whatever your relationship is to him out of this . . ."

"Yancy, he's a cop!"

"What?"

"Yeah. He's a cop. A group of them are dirty, and they run a . . ." Her voice trailed off.

"A prostitution ring?" Yancy asked, bile rising in his throat. This wasn't good. Not at all. *Oh, Jenna. I need you right now.*

"Exactly." CiCi stared at the tile for a moment, her eyes shifting back and forth. Then she looked at him again. "Why do you think they never do anything about him when the nine-one-one calls happen?"

Yancy took a step back. "Well, I'd assumed it was because you backed off like a lot of women who are in domestic disputes and didn't have him carted off in cuffs, but seeing as how he isn't your husband, my next thought was you didn't want to be hauled off with him on prostitution charges. You mean it's always him? You said it was your husband—"

Do you even have a husband?

Angry tears bit CiCi's eyes. "I know what I said, okay! I lied. There!

I've been lying this whole time. And now . . . oh, God, what are we going to do? They'll kill me. We'll both get killed."

"Oh, damn, oh damn. Okay. It's okay. We can do something. We have options here. We can go to the state cops instead of the locals. I have . . . contacts . . ." Jenna's face drifted through Yancy's mind. What the hell would she say when he told her? How could he possibly even *begin* that conversation? "It's going to be okay."

CiCi wept uncontrollably. She retched, put her hands on her knees. "You don't understand. It goes high up. I know for a fact a judge is involved. These guys—" She retched again, then spat some excess saliva onto the floor. "These guys are brutal, Yancy. A girl I knew—the girl who sent me to them when I was in trouble—she held out on them one too many times. She was found in an alley, beaten and raped. They cut her throat. Made it look like a gang initiation thing. Even planted evidence on some poor black kid in the projects. Only reason I know for sure it was them was because Denny"—she coughed, hacked—"told me if I didn't pay up soon I'd end up just like her."

Oh, Jesus. This is bad. How the fuck do you get yourself into situations like this, cool stuff?

"They have witness protection—"

"We'd be dead before they could hide us away. I know too much about how their operation works, who's involved. They'd cut my throat before I finished answering the cops' questions. Besides, I can't just disappear. I have family to take care of . . ."

Jenna. Vern. Charley. Ayana.

They can come after them, too.

"Okay," Yancy said, steeling himself. Before he'd lost his leg, he'd trained to go after these fuckers. Now he couldn't do anything about them except try with everything he had to think like they did. He could figure out whether or not she ever had a real husband later. Right now, he needed to move fast. "But starting right this second, every single move we make has to be perfect, or else we're as dead as he is."

22

Jenna rode in the passenger's seat of the SUV, quiet, as Dodd navigated them through the roads near the Clairefall Heights neighborhood. So much about this entire situation didn't make sense.

She had paced the hallway outside Sheila Maxwell's living room until her phone vibrated. She'd picked up.

"Buzz, buzz," Irv had said. "I have one name and address of a gal whose phone number crosses with records of students in Brooklyn Satterhorne's college classes. Diana Delmont. Real name, not stripper name."

"Thanks for the qualifier," Jenna had replied.

She had extracted Dodd from his questioning as soon as she could. Sheila wasn't recounting anything else useful anyway. The witness had started telling him her opinions on who might've done this to poor Brooklyn, speculations that ranged from wild to wilder.

Now Jenna glanced out the window, watching the roadside swish beneath them like a conveyor belt. Something wasn't adding up.

"The Triple Shooter—"

"The UNSUB," Dodd said, cutting her off.

Jenna blinked. This thing with his old case must be getting to him. Still, he was probably right. The killer was the Unidentified Subject until they caught his ass, at which point they'd plainly see he was the Triple Shooter. Still, no one else had been a stickler about this rule until now, and Jenna could only assume Dodd's correction was out of an overabundance of caution. Hell, she'd be cautious, too, if she had any hint her prize case might have ended with locking up the wrong guy for years.

"Right. So, the *UNSUB*, who is likely the Triple Shooter, kills seven people in a grocery store. This deviates extremely from every single aspect of the *known* Triple Shooter's MO except for the lining up of the threes. No covering eyes, each body with varying numbers of bullet wounds instead of a characteristic three. What do you make of that?" Jenna asked. She wasn't even really sure she wanted Dodd's answer, but she had to bat ideas with someone. Unfortunately, he was the only option.

He sighed. "A lot of scenarios have crossed my mind. Each is as unlikely as the next."

"Let's hear some."

"If he *is* the Triple Shooter, which I think he probably is, could be he's breaking down. Flying into a rage, unable to control himself as well," Dodd said.

"But the return to the pattern . . . kind of . . ." Jenna replied. The latest murder hadn't been *exactly* like his others, but it was a lot closer to his normal standards. Still, why the difference at all? And how did the grocery store fit?

Not to mention, Brooklyn Satterhorne's murder immediately registered in Jenna's mind as green, the same color she associated with the other Triple Shooter killings. Except the grocery store, that was. Purple.

"Exactly. The pattern, as you said, is 'kind of' back. Plus, even if it is a rage, schizophrenic killers like the Triple Shooter—at least what we have guessed about him—have a sort of method to their madness. They kill because something tells them to, and thus, there's a reason for the pattern. He wouldn't devolve and then spiral back *up*. We're not seeing something we should be," Dodd said.

"You can say that again," Jenna mumbled.

Her phone vibrated, and she pressed the button to open the text. It was from Charley.

Hey, Rain Man, when you get a minute, you should really come watch cartoons with us. Not because we need you or anything, but I think you could do some cool color associations with the characters on Clifford the Big Red Dog.

She breathed in slowly, then out. Ayana wasn't getting any younger. So many of these things she missed out on that her dad and Charley shared with her daughter every day.

And Ayana doesn't have a dad anymore. You're all the parent she has left.

She hit the reply button:

Definitely see Clifford as blue.

The joke about blue—the color she picked at random for that very reason—triggered a color from that family to flash in. Blue—very similar to the cornflower she had earlier associated with the killer's disorganization. His sloppiness. No wonder she hadn't noticed this particular shade before when it had appeared. It was the sky blue she associated with randomness.

"He chose the singular victims very carefully. Each had some reason we haven't found yet, though right now we're assuming Greek mythology plays a big part. The group of seven, though . . ."

"They were at the wrong place at the wrong time," Dodd finished.

Jenna nodded. "Random. The threes of the date and time aligned, but why seven people? If they were like his other victims, the numbers would line up, he'd follow a person to a place where he wouldn't be seen, shoot them three times, then leave pay for the boatman on their eyes in the form of evidence. The seven victims at Lowman's were shot with wild abandon just because they were there. And he showed them no remorse by tipping the ferry to take them away."

"Theories?" Dodd asked.

Not yet. "This last one has thrown me even worse, to be honest."

"The pennies," he said. It was a statement, not a question.

"No trace of threes yet, and the pennies don't point to anything I can fathom yet. But he understands them. That's one thing I'm sure of. To him, they make perfect sense, just like the keys and receipts and all the other little prizes he's left over his victims' eyes," Jenna said. Her conversation with Calliope Jones burned in her mind, and pieces of the bizarre puzzle flitted around like they had minds of their own.

He doesn't know the boatman was always said to have taken payments under the tongue.

Her phone flashed again. She read the text from Charley:

Very funny. But seriously, come home soon. Missing Mommy is one thing duct tape can't fix.

Heat prickled up Jenna's neck, and tears bit the corners of her eyes. Charley didn't mean it to hurt, but damn, did it sting. Then again, maybe that's exactly how he meant it to feel.

She typed back, then hit send.

I've never let you down yet, have I? Home soon. Promise.

Jenna and Dodd rode in silence, and Jenna knew they were both racking their brains for that one detail they hadn't noticed that could break this case wide open. If only it would come before another girl—or seven—were killed.

"That's another thing," Jenna blurted. "All the singular victims were female."

Dodd let out a grunt. "Touché. More proof the grocery store shooting was different. Maybe it wasn't him at all."

Jenna turned away from Dodd to look back out the window. It was him. She knew it. The colors didn't match perfectly—that purple was so odd—but still, she knew it all the same.

Her phone vibrated again.

She looked at the screen, expecting it to be Charley, taking his guilt trip to a new level by calling. However, the number wasn't familiar.

"Dr. Jenna Ramey," she answered.

"Dr. Ramey? My name is Eldred Beasley. I need to tell you some things I remember."

23

J enna gripped the phone tighter, trying to hear the faint voice
on the other end. "Mr. Beasley?"

He coughed. "Call me Eldred. I have to tell you before I
forget. If we lose the connection, call my daughter, Nancy. You can
reach me at the home. I was at the grocery store."

Jenna's heart sped up. She didn't remember reading this witness's
statement. "What is it you remember, Eldred?"

"A couple of things," the man said. His voice was so shaky. "First
is the cereal row. I was in the cereal row, and I saw the shooter coming."

"Eldred, you *saw* the shooter? Is there anything you can tell me
about him—"

"Don't get ahead of me now!" he barked.

Anger. Maybe frustration.

Still, Jenna didn't apologize. Clearly, this man had some kind of
memory issue. He was so worried about forgetting. She made a
mental note to contact the daughter to follow up but was silent, lest
she interrupt his train of thought again.

"The shooter hit the guy he hit, but he didn't mean to," Eldred
Beasley said.

"What do you mean?" Jenna whispered, her blood pulsing through her veins.

"What do you mean, what do I mean? I was as clear as day!"

Again, Jenna went silent, hoping the man would get back on track. The hair on her arms prickled. Something was about to come out. She knew it.

Eldred Beasley coughed again. "Took my pill last night, I think. Might not've taken the medicine this morning, though."

She heard rustling on the other end of the phone, then something rattling, like a canister of pills.

"Gotta get me a glass of water," Eldred said.

His voice sounded different—foggy. Like it was blurred at the edges, more an inner monologue than a telephone conversation.

He's forgotten he's talking to me.

"Mr. Beasley?"

"Wha—who're you? Who is this? Sarah?"

Oh, boy. "Um, no sir, this is Dr. Jenna Ramey. You called me about the grocery store . . ."

"Called you? I didn't call anyone!" Eldred growled.

Uh-oh. Better, maybe, to follow up with the daughter. Maybe if he recalled something once, his clarity would return again. Dementia? Alzheimer's?

"I'm sorry to have bothered you, sir. Good-bye."

When she had hung up the phone, Dodd was stopped in the driveway belonging to the family of Diana Delmont, the friend who'd been shopping with Brooklyn. He was staring at her, but she couldn't get any words to come out.

The shooter hadn't meant to shoot the last victim he had. This insinuated that he *had* been trying to shoot someone else. They'd started out by disproving the idea that the killer had been there to kill a politician, be it the Virginia governor, Miriam Holman, or Frank Kuncaitis, the mayor of the town they'd been in. Maybe he had been there to kill someone else entirely. Maybe the victims *were* important, and the reason no remorse was shown was because he hadn't killed the person he'd intended.

Again, purple crept into Jenna's psyche, but she pushed it away. She couldn't embrace it yet. She didn't have a good enough grasp on its exact shade to rein in the color's meaning. Sure, she could try to delve into everything any purple had ever meant to her and use the process of elimination, but there were so many definitions it seemed futile. *Wait for it.*

"I think we need to do this interview, but tomorrow we start fresh looking at other people in the grocery store at the time of the shootings. I think someone else might be the target."

As Jenna followed Diana Delmont's stout mother through the upstairs hallway toward the room belonging to Brooklyn's friend, she took in what she could about the home, even though profiling the friend wouldn't go a long way toward telling her anything about the killer. After all, the shooter had targeted Brooklyn, not Diana.

The hallway carpet was a deep mud-colored shag straight out of the sixties. Maybe the best thing about it was that it hid any signs of dirt, but dang, was it ugly. The walls were lined with cartoonish paintings of fruit. Apples in a basket, pears on a table. A cut-open kiwi here, oranges in a bowl there.

Mrs. Delmont stopped in front of a closed door. She tapped on it with her knuckles. "Diana, honey? Are you dressed?"

A sniff, a muffled sound like a nose blowing. Another sniff. "Yes. Come in."

If only my mother had been that polite.

Mrs. Delmont opened the door to reveal Diana, a skinny girl in pajamas, lying on her bed and clutching a box of tissues as though it were her teddy bear. Her recent tears were obvious, and unlike Sheila Maxwell, she probably hadn't been sedated *nearly* enough for having found out her friend was murdered right after she left her. Survivor's guilt was a bitch.

"Diana, these are Agents Dodd and Ramey. They need to ask you some questions."

Diana frowned, clearly dreading what was coming, though her eyes were set. Resigned. She glanced back and forth from Jenna to Dodd, skittish, nervous. Man, this was going to suck.

"Hi. I'm Dr. Ramey. I'm with the FBI Behavioral Analysis Unit," Jenna said, stepping forward to offer Diana her hand. In some cases like this, she didn't do that. Sometimes people recently traumatized by something like this didn't want to be touched or were nervous to be approached. But in this instance, the blush pink that rushed forth in Jenna's mind when Diana had looked uneasily back and forth between her and Dodd was the same color Jenna remembered from the time she had sat in the police station to be questioned about the journal she'd kept about her mother. She'd known she hadn't done anything wrong, but at the same time, the anxiety had been intense. And it hadn't been just the guilt of turning her mother over to the police. It had been every bit as much about what the police themselves would think about *her* if her mother was such a monster.

Diana needed to be assured that they didn't hold her at fault in any way. She needed to know they didn't consider her the enemy. And most of all, she needed to realize that no matter what had happened, they didn't view her as horrible, even if right now she was feeling terrible for living when her friend had died.

The girl sat up a little straighter and stretched out her hand. They shook, Diana's hand cold and clammy in Jenna's own.

Jenna resisted the urge to wipe her palm on her trousers when they let go, and instead, she sat on the foot of Diana's bed, putting them on the same level. No one wanted to be looked down at while carrying on a conversation.

"I'm sorry for your loss," Jenna said gently.

The girl sniffled again, then whispered, "Thank you."

Careful to keep any hint of accusation out of her voice, Jenna framed her question. "Diana, you two were at Target together. Why did you decide to leave sooner than Brooklyn did?"

Diana's eyes welled up again, and ash gray flashed into Jenna's mind. The color she associated with guilt.

"I had a Latin exam and needed to study. She wanted to stay and wait around for Kenny to get off work."

"Who's Kenny?" Jenna prodded.

Diana wiped her eye with the back of her hand, then dried it on the patchwork quilt on her bed. "Kenny Ingle. This boy she likes."

Jenna cocked her head. Of the initial interview Porter and Teva had with the family and the background Irv had dug up, this was the first mention she'd heard of any Kenny.

"Were Brooklyn and Kenny dating?"

"Not exactly," Diana said. "I mean, they were talking. That's it."

Jenna hoped she didn't look as dumb as she felt. "What do you mean they were talking?"

Dodd cleared his throat. "It means they were talking on the phone or texting or whatever kids do to get to know each other now. You know, kind of a warm-up to dating."

She shot Dodd a look. How the hell did he know that?

"Wasn't long ago my daughter was in high school," he said, shrugging.

Jenna turned back to Diana. This Kenny person wasn't a likely suspect, but they'd have to follow up with him, just in case. "Diana, did you notice anything strange while the two of you were in Target? Anyone following the both of you or watching you? Anything like that?"

Diana shook her head. "No. Nothing like that."

Of course not. That would've been too easy. "Did Brooklyn talk to anyone that she knew while you were there, or that it *seemed* like she knew or had met before? On the phone, in the store, via text . . . anything?"

"No," Diana said again, shaking.

The girl rubbed her arms and rocked herself a little. Somewhere behind those eyes, Jenna knew she was seeing Brooklyn, imagining what had happened. Thinking she was so glad it wasn't her, but then feeling guilty it hadn't been. She knew the look all too well. She'd felt it before, too, when her mother had stabbed Charley when they were kids.

"It's okay, Diana. It's okay for you to hurt, be scared, grieve, feel relieved and distraught all at the same time. Anything you're feeling is okay. We're here to help Brooklyn. We're here to find who did this to your friend. Just keep talking to us."

The girl curled up, hugged her knees to her chest. She looked down at nothing in particular, but she nodded.

"All right. So Brooklyn wanted to stay and meet up with Kenny, and you decided to leave. Where were you guys when you said good-bye?" Jenna asked.

"In the store," Diana said, monotone.

"Where in the store? What section?"

"Um . . . the bed and bath stuff. Brooklyn wanted to find a new shower curtain. Her old one was gross or something."

Jenna patted Diana's knee. "That's good. Can you tell me everything you remember that you both said or did right before you left?"

Diana closed her eyes. "Yeah. Um . . . I pulled out my phone to check a text and saw what time it was. I told Brooklyn I needed to leave. She . . . wasn't really happy. She said some kind of . . . some rude things to me."

Great. Not only force her to relive her last moments with her friend, but make her relive her last fight with her friend. Still, if Brooklyn had threatened to do anything impulsive in retribution or anything of that nature, they needed to know. "What sorts of things?"

"She said I should live a little. That I was always such a goody-goody that I wouldn't know life if it bit me in the face," Diana whispered, still looking down.

Harsh. A deep plum Jenna had come to associate with rudeness based in hostility rather than ignorance flashed in.

"What happened next?" Jenna asked.

Tears sprung to Diana's eyes as she gripped the quilt and twisted it. "I told her . . . I said she didn't always have to be such a bitch to everyone."

Diana's head collapsed to her knees, her body racked with sobs.

Do no harm. How was it she could be in a profession with an oath requiring her to hurt no one, and yet, in her line of work, it was virtually impossible not to?

"Then what?"

Diana wiped her face with her fingertips. "I left. I walked to my car, drove away. I came home and studied for my Latin test. I didn't even know anything had happened until . . ." She let out a sob. "Until Brooklyn's mom called mine."

Jenna nodded. This girl might remember something else worth knowing, but it wouldn't be tonight. Her head was too cluttered with guilt.

"Diana, we'll let you rest now, but I'll leave my card with your mom. I need you to call me if you remember anything about Target that might be significant. Someone you saw in the store or the parking lot that just gave you a weird feeling for some reason, a friend Brooklyn spoke to, a call she made . . . anything. Nothing is too small. Okay?" Jenna said.

Diana nodded.

"Thank you for talking with us. I can't imagine what you're feeling," Jenna continued. *Never say you understand. You don't. Everyone's reactions are different, even if they were in the exact same situation you'd been in twenty times.* "But you've done a great job recounting what you did. And if you need to talk to someone who isn't your mom or stepdad or a friend, let me know, and I can set you up with someone who is used to helping people talk through times like this. There's nothing shameful about needing someone outside the family to listen to what you're going through. You did nothing wrong."

Diana sniffled. "Thank you."

Jenna stood and made for the door, Dodd trailing her. As interviews went, not the most significant, but she *did* want to follow up with this Kenny person, maybe interview Brooklyn's family and find out more about the girl, who sounded about as pleasant as a tobacco-filled enema. They had never found a personal connection between the Triple Shooter and any of his victims, but that didn't mean Brooklyn was a stranger. Even serial killers were vulnerable to hurting someone in their everyday lives if a person rubbed them wrong, and Brooklyn sounded like a character ripe for making enemies. It wouldn't be the first time a real-life connection turned out to be a serial killer's downfall.

"Jenna, wait," Dodd's voice called from behind.

She turned around, half-annoyed that Dodd was prolonging their visit with Diana Delmont. The girl was clearly out of her mind with misplaced responsibility, and the last thing she needed was some sort of interrogation or argument the likes of which Dodd had provoked Liam Tyler into.

But arguments didn't seem to be what Dodd had on his mind. He was standing in front of the small desk against the left wall of the room. It was strewn with mechanical pencils, notebooks, and Post-it Notes. An open textbook splayed across the middle, one Dodd now closed. He shifted the book so its spine faced Jenna.

LATIN III.

Green flashed in, and Jenna's gaze darted to the other textbooks on the desk. Calculus, Art History, British Literature. Then it came into her vision: *Cellular Biology: Structure and Functioning on a Microscopic Level.* At the bottom of the spine, a bookstore sticker displayed BIOLOGY 3300.

Latin III. Biology 3300. Drop the zeroes from the biology book, and there they were. Three threes.

It could be a coincidence. After all, Diana Delmont was here, safe in her room. Brooklyn was the one in the morgue.

And yet, a puce color pervaded Jenna's psyche, the same one she'd noticed all those times her gut told her that her brother getting sick after eating something her mother cooked wasn't happenstance. It was the color she saw when certain actions of Claudia's corresponded to unpleasant events in the house, like when she washed Dad's clothes after a fight they'd had and the first time he wore something from that laundry load he broke out in hives. Those instances might've been flukes, but their timing and the gut feeling surrounding those things always seemed to have a cause-and-effect relationship. A synchronicity.

But if the threes lined up on Diana's books, either Brooklyn's classes were identical to Diana's, or the two had been together when the killer saw that particular grouping of threes. If the latter was the case, the killer had chosen to take out whatever it was the combination set off in him on Brooklyn instead of Diana.

Jenna nodded at Dodd. For now, they had some more interviews to do and some checking into Brooklyn's class schedule to assign to Irv. She also needed to look into the other patrons in the grocery store at the time of the massacre there, the incident that didn't make any sense with the Triple Shooter's profile.

They thanked Mrs. Delmont, told her they'd be in touch, and climbed into the SUV. Jenna glanced up to the lighted window she now knew to be Diana's. Somehow, she doubted this would be their last visit.

When they were on the road again, Dodd dialed Irv and asked him about Brooklyn's class schedule. Jenna drummed her fingers on the passenger door while she waited anxiously, though somehow, she already knew what they'd find out.

"What? No? Got it. Thanks, Irv," Dodd said, and he hung up. "No Latin III."

"Shock me further," Jenna muttered.

"Yeah, I had the same feeling. But what do you make of it? Diana Delmont had the toxic three lineup, but she isn't dead."

"No, she's definitely not . . ." And if Diana wasn't dead, why? What did the Triple Shooter see in Brooklyn . . . or *not* in Diana? "I just don't know. It doesn't make a lot of sense. Though . . ." Jenna stopped, hesitant. She hated bringing the color thing into it. No one ever understood.

"What?" Dodd prodded.

"Well, I saw puce. With the books, I mean. It's something I associate with synchronicity," she replied. She braced for questions.

"Puce, huh? What do you do? Sit around memorizing crayon names?"

Jenna let out the nervous laugh she'd been holding on to. Maybe she didn't give Dodd enough credit for his ability to be an ass. She'd worried he wouldn't understand the color thing. And yet, even though they'd gotten past that part when he accepted it despite not totally understanding why it made sense to her, he wasn't just going to let it go without antagonizing her. "Yeah. Kind of."

"Then I can only imagine the Crayola creation you have stored up there to equal Beasley," Dodd said.

Jenna contemplated. For the time they'd visited Diana, she'd put Eldred Beasley's call out of her mind, but now, it came rushing back full force. Acting like she hadn't heard the comment about color and only the old man's name, she said, "You're right. We should do some checking into Beasley. I want to look into other patrons, see what threes we can find surrounding them. I still have no clue why so many people instead of just one, but if the shooter didn't hit who he was supposed to, I guess that's why he didn't leave anything over any eyes as evidence. Figuring out who that real target was is as good a next goal as I can think of."

Dodd turned the steering wheel right. "I think it's a worthy plan, but first, I say you go on home and get some rest, give the boyfriend a little hanky-panky, whatever it is you do. I can work up some profiles of the other store patrons to have fresh in the morning."

Jenna glared at him. "Did you just say 'hanky-panky'?"

Never mind that she had no idea what Yancy was up to right now. She hadn't texted him all day, actually. Since their squabble yesterday, he probably needed the space. But maybe she *should* call . . .

"Don't make fun of us old-timers," Dodd said, smiling. "We might have some rust on the genuine works *and* aren't up-to-date with what terms define 'em these days, but we remember what they mean, mind you. You, however, ought to get up to 'em while you have access to more than their definitions, if you're with me."

"Why the sudden interest in my well-being?" Jenna asked.

Dodd smirked, then his smile turned to a frown. "Let's just say you still have a family. The career ate mine a long time ago. I have nothing better to do but go back to Quantico and put together profiles. You still do."

The green of regret washed through Jenna's mind at Dodd's words. He sounded so sad that for a moment she almost forgot her disdain for him.

"Maybe you're right," she said. "I haven't been there to tuck my little girl in, but maybe I could catch a few hours of sleep and still be around to have lunch with her before I head back out. Besides, I have some legal stuff I have to deal with." Hank's face popped to mind. Jenna sighed. Geez. The phone call from the lawyer regarding Hank's estate seemed like it was years ago.

"Good plan," he said. "Can I drop you off?"

Jenna drove her Blazer back to the house. Despite Dodd's generous offer and her eyelids drooping dangerously, she hadn't let him drive her back. Call her paranoid, but nobody could know where she lived who didn't know already. Even people she worked with. It wasn't that she didn't trust them. It was just that anyone who knew could lead someone back to her family whether they intended to or not.

That was why when she pulled into the driveway and saw an unfamiliar vehicle parked in the drive—a white Honda Civic—she leapt out of the Blazer, gun drawn. Around the back of the house, she peeked in the window. No one.

Locks were intact, colors in line. She keyed them one by one, her pulse racing. If the locks were on, her dad, Charley, or Yancy had to have unlocked them *and* locked them back. Had someone forced them? They never had visitors . . .

She pushed into the door, gun trained to the right to sweep.

Charley lifted both his hands off his coffee mug. "Don't shoot, Rain Man. I just borrowed the gum. I was gonna give it back."

Jenna didn't lower her weapon. Instead, she looked toward the black man sitting across from Charley, also holding a steaming cup. "Who the hell are you?"

The man blinked. "Nice to meet you as well."

Jenna took a step toward him, gun still aimed. "Just because my brother is having coffee with you doesn't mean I can't shoot you. Who are you?"

"I'm sorry," he said, also raising both hands. "I didn't mean to offend. I'm Victor. Victor Ellis."

Jenna's arm holding the Glock dropped to her side, and she stared, wide-eyed. Hank's brother.

"Now," Charley said, "aren't you *glad* you didn't kill him?"

She reached down and flipped on the gun's safety, holstered it. "That remains to be seen. And don't think I'm finished deciding I'm not going to yet, either. How did you find this place?"

Victor withdrew the hand he'd extended toward her. "I, um, I'm a cop. You know, with the police force."

"And I'm the Easter Bunny. Neither knows where we are. No one does."

Victor smirked. "With all due respect, miss, someone obviously does."

Jenna forced herself to breathe evenly. Clearly, she hadn't planned something about this hideaway perfectly, but the brother of her ex, who she'd only heard about in theory, sitting in her kitchen, telling her of her oversights, wasn't exactly the way she wanted to find out.

Would you rather it be Claudia?

"Right," she said. "Could you please be more specific about how you obtained this address?"

"I, uh . . ." Victor's smart-assery seemed to suddenly disappear.

Charley slurped a sip of coffee, then slammed his mug down. "Well, I'll tell you if he won't. Hank left word with his brother that if anything ever happened to him in the line of duty—especially anything to do with Claudia after she got out—that he should keep an eye on Ayana."

What? Hank, who had spent so much time telling Jenna she was paranoid about Claudia. Hank, who had underestimated Claudia enough that it had gotten him killed.

"So you . . . what? Followed us? Starting after Hank's death?" Jenna said incredulously.

Now Victor looked her straight in the eye. "Something like that."

Jenna threw her arms up. This guy obviously didn't know what he was dealing with, following her after last year. If she'd seen him once, he'd have been as good as dead.

But she hadn't seen him once.

"You know, a nice, 'Hi, I'm Hank's brother, and he asked me to watch over you,' might've been appropriate," she sneered.

Victor cocked his head. "You're telling me you'd have just accepted my help?"

Jenna balled her fists. "Touché. So why come out of the shadows now?"

Hank's brother frowned. "I wanted to warn you about something."

"And?"

Charley rolled his eyes. "Rain Man, how about you come sit down? Have a cuppa? We can all be friends, talk a bit. You know, not scream at friendly protectors on our side . . . not point guns at them . . ."

She blew out a breath. Her brother, the perpetual optimist. You'd think he'd totally forgotten being stabbed by his mother as a kid, targeted by a nutcase last year, all that good stuff.

"Fine," she said.

Jenna yanked her favorite mug with Ayana's handprint on it out of the cupboard and poured herself coffee. She didn't bother adding cream or sugar, even though it would taste better. She would sit here and hear the guy out, but she didn't have to enjoy it.

"I'm supposed to go down to the lawyer's office to file some paperwork regarding the estate today," she said, as if the information was relevant to the topic at hand. Who cared if it wasn't even close. Hell, it was the only talking point she had.

"That's why I'm here," Victor said. "Sort of."

Jenna looked at him but said nothing.

"I'm afraid my mother isn't exactly going to be, erm, *helpful* there."

"Your mother?" Jenna parroted.

Victor nodded, sipped his dark roast. "I'm not sure how to say this, but she's planning to challenge Ayana as the beneficiary of Hank's will."

"What?" Jenna shouted. She'd never even *met* Hank's mother. They'd never been close, and the woman had never really wanted a relationship with Ayana, either. Jenna had always assumed it was all because Hank and his mother hadn't had much to do with each other anymore.

Victor nodded. "I'm sorry."

"Let me guess," Jenna said. "She wants the money?" People Hank probably hadn't even met in real life had come to chase the invisible money. Why not his mom? If she and Hank didn't speak very much—as Jenna had known to be true in past years, anyway—she had no way of knowing that the only cash money anybody would be getting was the life insurance, and that went to Ayana without question.

"Not exactly," Victor replied.

"Do you ever answer a question with a straight answer?"

Victor's eyes narrowed. "Do you ever *not* bite the hand that feeds you?"

A rose color permeated Jenna's mind. Familial love. He was sincere, wasn't he?

"I apologize," she mumbled.

"It's fine," he said curtly. "It's not that she wants the money. Yes, I said *the* money. I know the land is worth a lot of money, as everyone in the continental US does by now who ever shared the two traits of some obscure blood relation to Hank and enough coins in a jar to roll and afford a two-bit lawyer to contest the will. But I knew what it was worth before all this, for what that matters, and Mama did, too. She thinks *you* want the money."

Jenna shook her head. "That's ridiculous."

"I know. But she's old-fashioned. The two of you weren't married, so she automatically views your relationship a certain way."

"The gold-digging bimbo way?" Jenna asked.

Victor let out a big sigh. "Maybe. Who knows. But I wanted you to be ready, because I know Hank wouldn't want this. She's going to try to prove Ayana isn't his kid."

At this, Jenna stood up and started pacing. "That's just . . . that's crazy."

"You know it, and I know it, but she doesn't think it is."

Jenna whirled around. "Why? Because Ayana looks white?"

Victor looked down at the table. "Something like that."

"Shit," Jenna said.

"My thoughts exactly," said Victor. He stood. "I should probably go. I've brought enough trouble for one day. Just know I'll try to help in any way I can, though I have no idea how that will be yet."

Jenna looked into Hank's brother's eyes and saw Ayana's looking back at her. A rush of affection surged through her, one she resented, given that this man had been following her for months without so much as a peep. Invading her family's privacy. Knowing about a compromise of their safety and never saying anything. He didn't look much like Hank otherwise, but the eyes were uncanny.

"Thank you for coming," she said. This time, she extended her hand.

He stepped forward, shook it. "I'm sorry for the scare."

She nodded. "Just don't call me miss again, okay?"

He smiled. "Yes, ma'am."

"Ma'am, either."

Victor grinned. "Would Hardass suffice?"

For the first time, she smiled back. "I think that would work."

She opened the door for him, one lock at a time, aware of Charley watching her from behind.

"I'll be in touch," he said.

She closed the door and turned to face Charley, ready to give him a thorough dressing down for letting *anyone* inside the house.

He waved her off. "Save it, sister. I know all the reasons I shouldn't ever do it again, but for once, can't you just be glad I'm not as anti-social as you are?"

As much as she hated it, he was right. "What are we going to do?"

Charley gulped the last of his coffee. "I don't know about you, but I'm going to see if Dad and A need an extra Hungry Hungry Hippos player."

He left her standing in the kitchen, wondering what the hell had just happened, and how exactly Charley had a way of insufferably ignoring everything risky in their lives while at the same time making her want to ignore them, too.

She followed him toward A's room. Maybe Hungry Hungry Hippos was exactly what she needed.

Yancy drove and drove and drove, all the while thinking about everything he'd been trained to do before he'd lost his leg. He was going to be an agent, just like Jenna. Well, maybe just like Jenna but on a state and not a federal level, and completely aside from the fact that she had a weird human trick and wouldn't compromise every single ethic she'd ever had for someone she didn't know. *You idiot.*

The car could be traced, he knew, but it was maybe the only point he couldn't control. Not entirely, anyway. Someone—anyone—could've seen his car at CiCi's. He'd had to leave in it, and he couldn't leave with it inside a giant tarp. Not like they'd had one, anyway.

Heat crept up Yancy's neck as he played the scene over and over in his mind, both doing his best to convince himself there'd been no other course of action and yet trying to find a way he could've done things differently all at the same time. A ring of dirty cops running a high-dollar hooker outfit, one of their own dead with Yancy's hand left holding the smoking gun. CiCi would be dead if they found out, but so would he. In the process, he'd put every single person involved with him in jeopardy. They didn't have to worry about the husband coming home and finding the body. In the blur that had been getting the mess cleaned up, Yancy had ascertained through some of CiCi's traumatized muttering that he'd left her months ago. She hadn't said why and hadn't been in any condition for Yancy to interrogate her about it, even if his mind hadn't been preoccupied with the more pressing task at the time. Maybe he'd left her because she was hooking, or maybe she was hooking because she needed money after he left. Who knew? It didn't matter right now. What did matter was that whatever route he took—leaving the body to be found, calling the police—both options led to the same climax. The cops would eventually come, good or bad. And eventually, the dirty cops would hear. He could confess, but then it was only a matter of time before they came after him. If he didn't and the body was discovered, there would be an investigation. Yancy knew way too much about police and evidence to think something in the kitchen wouldn't lead to him. Not to mention CiCi's frequent 911 calls, his car parked in front of her house . . .

The choice was the only one he had.

Right?

CiCi had met him, as he'd told her to. She'd wanted to come with him, but that was out of the question. The less involved she was, the better. She was going to have too many questions to answer as it was. God help him, hopefully everything he'd set in motion for her when the bad guys came calling would hold up. He'd tried so hard to think of everything, but if he'd thought of everything, he wouldn't even be here.

Goddamnit, asshole!

He tried to force his mind to focus on anything but what he was doing, where he was going. Keeping the car at an even forty-five when the speed limit changed to fifty, he recited children's nursery rhymes he'd heard as a kid, turned on the radio, sang three dozen rounds of "I'm Henry the Eighth I Am" and a full, no-holds-barred rendition of "Ninety-Nine Bottles of Beer on the Wall." When that didn't work, he let his mind drift to the one place he *never* allowed if he could manage it: his godforsaken leg crushed in the elevator shaft, and how bad it had hurt. The hospital afterward, the flood of visitors from the Academy at first, then the way they slowed to a trickle. How they stopped completely.

He revisited the humiliation of rehab, of being fitted for his first prosthetic. Of gradually learning to walk again.

Oboe came to mind, that first day at the shelter when he'd considered the dachshund in the cage next to the German shepherd that looked just like Rin Tin Tin. The German shepherd was young, sleek, the perfect dog. Ten minutes later, he'd left with the dachshund.

The dog had turned out to be a pain, but then again, Yancy was probably a pain to him, too. So, they deserved each other somehow.

Oboe might be an asshole, but he deserves better than to have some common criminal-liar-douchebag for an owner.

He'd get home in time to feed him not too late, right? Yeah. He could get home and be just a couple hours late. Oboe wasn't missing many meals by any stretch of the imagination. The wiener would be okay. Still, he'd throw in an extra scoop for the lateness . . . and for being a murdering, lying scum of the earth. Make it two scoops.

Normally, he'd try to get Jenna to go over and feed Oboe if he was going to be really late, but the thought of talking to Jenna right now . . . geez. His first instinct had been to call her, tell her everything. But if she knew, she'd only be in danger. Besides, if she helped him or even knew what he was doing and *wasn't* in danger, her career would be on the line. He wouldn't put her at risk just because he . . .

Shit, dumbass. You've really done it this time.

He made a right-hand turn. Finally, he was there. The big thing would be to do what he had to, then to handle himself once he left.

The break hadn't been long enough, but when Saleda called to say she'd done the impossible and gotten Brooklyn Satterhorne's family to agree to another FBI visit in addition to the one Porter had already paid them—this time accompanied by their own volunteered signed agreement to allow the BAU to perform a second unwarranted search of their home—Jenna couldn't pass it up. She'd kissed Ayana, who had grinned and winked—her newest trick.

"See ya later, alligator!" Ayana had said.

Now Jenna and Saleda padded through the hallway toward Brooklyn's room. The feeling was very different from that of the day before at Diana Delmont's. First of all, this time the mother declined to go with them. Obviously they'd find no daughter inside.

The hall was different from the Delmonts', too. Instead of fruit, it was covered in pictures of Brooklyn. As a baby, a toddler, a six-year-old flashing a toothy smile, an awkward tween with braces and frizzy hair. At graduation with no braces. With friends in bikini bathing suits, her characteristic spiral red curls flat from a recent ocean swim.

The door to the room at the very end of the hall was open, afternoon sunlight streaming inside. A black-and-white floral comforter, satin, covered the four-poster wrought-iron bed, and a matching full-length mirror of black-painted iron stood across from the bed.

"Vanity," Jenna muttered as the familiar thistle color flashed in.

"You're thinking narcissism?" Saleda asked.

"Not yet," Jenna replied. "Simple vanity right now. Maybe narcissism later."

She crossed the room toward the bureau, where a vase of dried roses stood. Jenna had always hated the tradition of drying flowers. Maybe they had sentimental value, but once deprived of their beauty, what was the point?

"Did you ever dry your flowers, Saleda?"

"No. Always thought it was a little creepy. Why?"

Jenna nodded to the vase. "It's always been a certain type of girl I've known to dry bouquets. That's all."

"What kind?" Saleda asked, shifting a notebook from the desk to look at the binder underneath.

Jenna wandered toward the open jewelry box, which was filled with expensive-looking pieces most college-aged students didn't own. Heck, most thirty-year-olds didn't own diamond earrings that big. Jenna sure didn't.

"Usually the kind of girls who've been programmed to think that's what you're supposed to do. The same ones who end up steam-cleaning their wedding dresses and sealing them in a box in the closet, never to be seen again," she replied. "Not a bad thing necessarily, just a type."

Jenna's gaze roamed the pictures on the chest of drawers, all in ornate iron-looking frames. While she'd said it wasn't always a bad thing, this room made her think of all the girls she'd ever known with perfect, just-so clothing, shoes that cost more than Jenna's entire wardrobe. The word "spoiled" came to mind. Based on what Diana had told the team about Brooklyn, that guess probably wasn't too far off.

"I think I've got about the same picture of Brooklyn I expected to have," Jenna said. Porter and Teva had already collected anything and everything of interest from the room, including the computer. They'd found nothing on it so far. "Any word on the boyfriend?"

"Don't you mean 'talking friend'?" Saleda asked.

"Yeah, whatever they call it. Kenny." Though, as she glanced around, the room didn't show any signs of Kenny, if he was involved with her. Or any signs of any other boy involved with her in a way that seemed more than the fleeting, friend-zone type of relationship.

Saleda clicked a button on her phone, read a text. "My sources say he's at work now."

"What are we waiting for?"

Twenty minutes later, Jenna and Saleda sat in the Target break room with Kenny Ingle.

"I want a lawyer," he said for the dozenth time.

Jenna folded her arms as she watched Saleda field the request. Again.

"Kenny, we'll get you a lawyer, but like I said, you are in no way *at all* implicated in Brooklyn's murder. We already have a suspect, and this person was most likely a stranger. You don't fit his profile . . . at all," Saleda replied.

Frankly, you're not smart enough.

"I don't know nothin'!" Kenny said.

Shocking. I believe you.

"Kenny, we need to know more about Brooklyn and what she was like. It might help us learn more about who might've wanted to hurt her," Jenna said. The kid might not be a murderer, but for someone whose maybe-girlfriend had just been killed, distraught he wasn't.

"Look," he said, "I don't know what you've heard, but I don't even know her that well. She wanted to date, but she wasn't really my type."

"Meaning what?"

Kenny laughed. Great reaction to a murder.

"Meaning she was a bitch!"

Whoa.

"But her friend said you two were 'talking,'" Saleda said.

Kenny smirked, leaned back in his chair. "She was talking. I was not listening."

"So she wanted to date, but you told her you weren't interested?" Saleda asked.

"Kinda. She texted me a lot. Bugged the crap out of me."

"How was she 'a bitch'?" Jenna asked, miming air quotes with her pointer and middle fingers on each hand as she repeated his words.

He rolled his eyes. "You name it. She was always doing things just to be bitchy. She'd talk about her friends behind their backs, do stuff like take pictures of them without makeup and send them to me. I think somehow it made her feel good about herself, to point out how bad her friends looked."

Wow. Good insight for a kid exhibiting an amount of mourning equal to that of a bird passing a cat's flattened carcass on the roadside.

"You mean she'd text pictures of friends without their knowledge or consent?" Saleda clarified.

"Not text. She wasn't that dumb. She'd snap them."

"You mean Snapchat?" Jenna asked, unsure if this was the verb form of the term but going with it. Seemed right, and better to stay in the lingo with this kid since he was already acting like they were only one degree of difference from his own parents grilling him about the hygiene habits of his peers.

Kenny nodded, his face conveying the "Duh" that his mouth somehow seemed to hold in.

Saleda looked at Jenna, questioning.

"Snapchat is an app that lets kids send photos or videos that disappear in a few seconds," Jenna said. "Right?"

"Yeah," Kenny answered, sounding annoyed that he was having to tell adults something they should already know.

"And there's no way to access the messages?" Saleda asked.

"You can take a screenshot of the snap, but I think the sender is automatically notified when that happens. Am I right, Kenny?" Jenna asked. She hated that she knew about this at all, but her dad had sent her an article about it as soon as he'd seen it online as a heads-up on a new way people were sending information. He knew anything Claudia could use was important for both of them to be aware of.

"Used to be, but now there's Snap Save," he said.

"Snap Save?" Jenna asked.

"App you can use to save snaps without the sender knowing."

"God, I hate technology," Saleda muttered.

Jenna, however, felt her pulse build. "Did you save any of hers, Kenny? Any of Brooklyn's snaps?"

His eyes narrowed. "Why?"

Jenna sat down across from him and folded her hands. She leaned in toward him. "Oh, I don't know, hotshot. Maybe because someone has been *killed*. Anything we know that could've earned her an enemy could be a lead to help us find her killer. Unless, of course, there's some reason you don't want us to find who did it?"

"Hey! You said I wasn't a suspect!"

She leaned back. "You're not, Kenny. But that doesn't mean you can't help us catch who murdered her. You have a mom? A sister?"

He licked his teeth. "Yeah. Both. What does it matter?"

"This guy who murdered Brooklyn, he's killed several women, Kenny. He's going to kill more. Could be someone else you know. Your family. Think about it."

He stared at the floor for a long minute, his eyes changing from guarded to concerned.

"What do you need?" he asked.

Jenna cocked her head. Who needed the time it took to find a judge to sign off on a search, then perform the thing, when you could have the annoying teenager with a conscience save you all that trouble? "What do you have?"

27

Justice scratched his elbow hard as he stood waiting for the shop owner to retrieve the box of bullets. *Itching. Always the itching.*

"You okay, buddy?" the shop owner asked, laying the bullets on the counter and tapping a few cash register keys.

Justice squinted, scratched harder. "Yeah, yeah. My psoriasis, acting up."

He'd learned long ago psoriasis was a good answer for the itching if anyone asked. Much better than explaining *them.*

His nubby nails dug in, clawed at his flesh. It burned inside. He had to get this done. He couldn't help it. He'd seen it, had to do it. He already knew it needed to happen.

"That'll be twenty-one forty-two," the man said.

Justice dropped his right hand from his left elbow and dug it into his pocket. Two bills, a handful of change. He dumped it on the counter, not wanting to so much as brush the man's hand. Touching other people rarely went well.

Itching. God, the itching!

The shop owner swept it off the counter into his hand, then tipped his ball cap. "Thank you much, sir. Until next time."

Justice took the box and walked out the door into the afternoon sun, dreading the next part. But he had to keep moving. There was no stopping it now.

This time when Jenna and Saleda made it to Diana Delmont's house, Diana was sitting on the screened porch, rocking on a wooden swing slowly, back and forth.

"Diana?" Jenna said, giving warning she was in the vicinity. Diana's mother had told the girl they were coming, she knew, but after a friend's murder, sneaking up on someone wasn't a good idea for more than one reason.

The girl didn't turn. "Do you ever think about waking up one day and realizing everything was all a big joke? Like you're starring in some reality TV show no one told you about, like in that Jim Carrey movie?"

Jenna sat down next to Diana on the swing. "More than you know," she said truthfully.

Diana tapped her white-tennis-shoe-clad toes on the wood planks of the floor. "I feel like I'm gonna find out this was all a big candid-camera thing. Or Brooklyn playing some awful prank on me or something."

Jenna blew out a deep breath. The perfect opening, sadly.

"Actually, Diana, I wanted to ask you about something like that," Jenna said.

The girl didn't respond.

From the large pocket inside her tan peacoat, Jenna produced the printouts of the Snapchats they'd taken from those saved on Kenny Ingle's phone and unfolded the stack of them. Kenny had explained he'd kept them around to send to his friends. The little punk had been doing the same thing to Brooklyn he'd claimed was a bitchy move she pulled on her *own* friends, but then again, after seeing the saved shots, Jenna wasn't sure she blamed him for letting his buddies in on the "crazy" of the girl pursuing him.

She slid the stack of printouts into Diana's lap. "Diana, I need you to tell me if you were with Brooklyn when any of these were taken. If you can try to remember . . ."

Diana glanced down at the top photo: a snap of a test paper belonging to a girl named Effie. Brooklyn had apparently graded it in class during one of those "Pass your paper to the person on your right" exercises.

Jenna had specifically chosen only snaps where the incident shown or talked about in the message could've been seen by others and so had to have taken place somewhat in public at a time when Brooklyn could've been near Diana. The last part was important, since the threes lined up with Diana's books. Brooklyn had to have been with Diana when the Triple Shooter saw her and the alignment of threes.

Diana looked back up quickly. "I didn't see this, no," she said.

"Were you present, or *could you have been* present, when this was taken?" Saleda asked.

The girl glanced at Saleda. "I don't . . . I don't know. Maybe. What difference does it make?"

You don't want to know. The survivor's guilt was bad enough. Just wait until Diana found out that her books were what attracted attention to Brooklyn—or sealed her fate, anyway. Jenna hadn't been looking forward to explaining it, but she'd known all along she'd have to at some point. Now was as good a time as any ever would be.

"Diana, this is going to be tough to hear, but it seems as though the killer may have noticed Brooklyn while the two of you were together," Jenna said slowly.

"What? How could you possibly know something like that?" Diana practically shrieked.

"This killer has a very specific MO, a method of operation so distinct it allows us to qualify that a victim is almost assuredly his victim as opposed to that of another random or even serial shooter. This particular MO always involves the lining up of the number three," Saleda said.

Diana's hand flew to her mouth, then she started shaking her head. "The Triple . . . you were looking at my books! My Latin and . . . oh, God!"

The girl leaned over and vomited all over the wooden porch.

Jenna looked away from the mess but placed her hand on Diana's back and rubbed, just like she would for Ayana when she was ill. Jesus. One day her daughter would be this big. God help her.

"I'll get some water and paper towels," Saleda said.

Jenna heard the porch door close behind her. "I know this is a shock, Diana. But you have to keep remembering this is *not* your fault. This was the doing of a sick, demented individual. That your books were present near that individual was a coincidence. You were doing nothing wrong by having them with you, by carrying them. Nothing."

The girl heaved again, this time spitting out only whatever grossness lingered in her mouth. She coughed, then sobbed. "I know that, but how can I *feel* that?"

I know. Jenna couldn't do anything or say anything, but she could sympathize more than this girl could ever understand. After all, if she'd never figured out what Claudia was, maybe Dad and Charley wouldn't be in danger now. She knew it wasn't rational—Claudia had already been hurting them anyway. But somehow, in her head, she'd caused the trouble. Should've let someone else come to the rescue. In Jenna's mind, if someone else had been the hero she tried to be, maybe last year wouldn't have happened. Hank would still be here, and Victor would still have his brother. Ayana would still have a dad.

"You might always feel it, Diana. I won't lie to you. But the best way to ease that particular pain is to try to help us figure out who did this," Jenna replied. Jesus. She'd just told the girl she wouldn't lie to her, then in the next breath, she'd told the tallest tale in her recent memory. She'd had to do it, because they needed to find this guy to save someone *else* in the future from this same fate Diana was grappling with—and worse—but the truth was, assisting the investigation probably wouldn't save Diana in the slightest.

Saleda returned with Mrs. Delmont, who traded places with Jenna and properly pampered her little girl, wiping her mouth and handing her a cup of fizzy liquid. She laid a damp paper towel on the back of Diana's neck and used another to swipe at her daughter's brow.

"I'm sorry, Mama," Diana said.

"For what, baby?" Mrs. Delmont asked, patting Diana's cheeks and forehead with the cloth.

"For getting sick all over the porch," Diana said weakly.

Mrs. Delmont pulled Diana into a side hug and held her daughter's head to her shoulder with the palm of her hand. "Oh, sweetheart. It's okay. It's nothing a hose won't fix." Mrs. Delmont turned to Jenna. "Maybe we need to finish this another time. I think this might be too much too soon—"

Diana stood up and vigorously shook her head. "No, Mama. I need to do this. Now."

She grabbed up the stack of Snapchat printouts from the porch windowsill, where Jenna had moved them out of harm's way a few moments before, and sifted through them one by one. At about the fourth, she stopped. Her eyes watered, and she bit her lip, fighting more tears.

After a long moment, she handed it to Jenna.

The picture showed a graying man in tattered clothes lying on what looked like some kind of stone pathway. He seemed to be asleep. Next to him sat a yellow shoe box, and a few empty soda cans were strewn on the ground nearby.

"I wasn't there when she took this picture, but . . . I know why she took it," Diana muttered, looking at her feet.

Ash gray flashed in. Guilt.

"Why did she take it?" Jenna asked.

"Well, maybe she didn't take it because of this, but . . ."

"Go ahead, Diana. We're not here to judge you," Saleda pressed.

"Or Brooklyn," Jenna breathed.

Diana glanced at Jenna, then back toward the photo. She wrung her hands. "Earlier that day, Brooklyn had . . ."

Jenna didn't push. She let Diana take her time. Clearly whatever the girl had to say, she wasn't proud of her friend for it.

"Brooklyn had been mean to that guy. He stays there, outside the college pretty much every day. He doesn't bother anyone. He just sits there with his box. Sometimes people will give him a sandwich from inside the dining hall, and some kids even toss their change from buying lunch into his box," Diana said.

"And Brooklyn?" Saleda prodded.

Diana continued to stare at her feet. "Brooklyn knocked over his shoe box that day. On purpose."

Several colors assaulted Jenna's vision in rapid succession as she imagined the living, breathing Brooklyn taking an old homeless man to task just for being where and who he was. The plum she associated with hostility flashed in. It morphed into the orchid of superiority.

Jenna closed her eyes, pictured the photos of Brooklyn taken at the hospital morgue. Auburn, rich and bright, flashed in. Then a flicker of green. That was the Triple Shooter's green three, she knew. But the auburn. She'd seen it somewhere recently . . .

She opened her eyes with a start. *Calliope Jones.*

"Thank you, Diana. That's exactly what we needed to know. I'm sorry to rush off, but we have to go. Now that you've given us this important piece of information, there's someone else I need to talk to."

28

Jenna hit the answer button and turned on speakerphone. "I hope you're about to tell me where Calliope Jones is, because she isn't home."

"Luckily, due to an eight-millimeter DARPA tracking chip her parents had installed in her neck without her knowledge after a failed attempt to run away at age ten, all I had to do was hack into the air force's GPS control segment and lock in on the signal. After accessing their secret databases, I was able to learn she's at a very exclusive, clandestine book signing at Two Fifteen Dradenburg," Irv said.

"Right. Air force GPS segment," Jenna said, throwing the SUV into reverse and backing up to have room to return the way she came. "That or you checked her Twitter feed."

"Hey. Be nice to your friendly FBI technical analyst. Just because this time I was an able body in front of a computer screen who could find out where she might be using Google doesn't mean next time you won't need info only I can obtain without getting arrested because the government happens to pay me to find it."

"You're right, Irv. I'm sorry. Your skills are legendary, and only you could find me a book signing on Twitter quite as *well* as you did," Jenna said, letting out a laugh. She peeled out of the parking lot of

Calliope's apartment building. The woman hadn't answered her cell, either. This would explain it. "But who are you kidding? Even if you weren't FBI, you're way too good to get arrested. Two Fifteen Dradenburg is a thrift-shop bookstore, right?" she asked.

"Ooh. I do love having my ego gently massaged while I do your bidding," Irv said as he pecked a few more keys on his end. "Yeah, looks like a classy joint. I recommend taking a can of Cheez Whiz to go with the wine."

"They can't all be on *Oprah*, Irv."

"Damn right. Can't all make *Psychiatry Today*, either," he replied.

"I was never in that magazine, smart-ass. It doesn't exist. I'll be back in touch in a little while. In the meantime, send anything and everything you can find on the grocery store patrons we have listed to Dodd, Teva, and Porter."

"Already on it," he said.

Jenna hung up, then glanced at Saleda out of the corner of her eye. "The color auburn—the one that I saw at Diana's that made me want to find Calliope—I saw that same color here inside Calliope Jones's place when we were looking at some painting, but I can't remember what it was to save my life. I had to rush out the second we started talking about it that day, because my pager went off about Brooklyn."

"Don't worry. We'll find out," Saleda said.

When they arrived at the tiny hole-in-the-wall bookstore, a bell tinkled to announce their arrival.

The store was practically empty, save for the person behind the counter and Calliope Jones, this time wearing a crisp white button-down shirt and sitting behind a rickety table stacked with many copies of a single book. One was turned up on a small easel, and it bore her name in big pink letters along with the title *Gifts of the Greeks*.

Jenna and Saleda marched straight to the table.

"Ms. Jones, we need to ask you a few more questions," Jenna said.

Calliope's mouth formed a smug, thin-lipped smile that dripped contempt. "Agent Ramey, I'm in the middle of a book signing. If you'd needed to talk to me, we had plenty of time during our prior get-together. If you require something further, we'll have to schedule an appointment at another time."

Jenna glanced around at the empty store. "Yes, I can *tell* you're busy. However, this is a matter of life and death, as I'm sure you can understand. Didn't the Greeks believe in some sort of karma?"

"Not exactly," Saleda piped up.

Jenna shot her a look but quickly turned back to Calliope.

Calliope, however, had glanced interestedly at Saleda. Slowly, she returned her eyes to Jenna as though she'd much rather have this conversation with the woman beside her, who was clearly more intelligent in all things Greek.

"Your colleague is correct. The Greeks were more concerned with fate. Destiny, if you will."

"But didn't they constantly have bad things happening to them if they did something wrong? Look at Ulysses!" Jenna sputtered.

Calliope gave a patronizing laugh. "Odysseus wasn't doomed to not make it home for years because of karma, Agent Ramey. He angered a god. That's a different story entirely. Gods punish those who anger them."

The auburn flashed in again.

"That's exactly what I want to know about. The painting we were looking at when I had to leave your apartment the other day. What was that painting again? Or rather, what were the mythological beings in the painting?"

Calliope sighed, resigned. "The Erinyes. The Furies."

The human-like forms came back full force in Jenna's head: the tortured man, the stabbed figure, the three angry, spirit-like women. One with a torch . . .

"The Furies. Goddesses of vengeance. We need to know more about them," Saleda said.

Saleda knew about Greek mythology?

If only the two of them could've been sharing their two brains—one with color associations, the other with this knowledge—maybe they could've avoided Calliope Jones altogether.

"Very good." Calliope nodded at Saleda. She folded her hands on the table, perfectly manicured nails shining gently in the low light of the store. "The three goddesses of vengeance, sometimes known as the Daughters of Night. The latter is a misnomer, though. They were the children of Mother Earth, or Gaea, and Uranus."

Thank goodness we have their family tree.

"Did they each perform a different function?" Jenna asked, remembering only one holding a torch. She couldn't quite recall the other two. One might've been draped in cloth . . .

"Oh, yes. Quite. Tisiphone was the avenger of murder, Alecto represented constant anger, and Megaera, oh, Megaera," Calliope said, laughing jovially, as though thinking of an old friend. "She was the jealous one."

"Tisiphone avenged murder," Jenna repeated, confused. The other two had been named with traits, but only the one seemed to have a specific purpose.

Calliope nodded. "Specifically matricide and patricide, though technically she avenged all homicide. We'll just call that her pet peeve. She was described in the *Aeneid* as guarding the gates of Tartarus itself wearing a blood-wet dress."

"She was the cloth-draped figure in the painting?" Jenna asked.

"You're thinking of Orestes's mother, my sweet. She is wrapped in red cloth in this particular painting and has a golden dagger protruding from her chest. The three Furies are torturing Orestes. He had killed his mother, you see."

Jenna closed her eyes and found she could recount the painting better than she imagined she could've. The auburn burned through again. The colors lined up, so it was possible these were the voices the Triple Shooter heard in his head. Still, the concept of a homicidal maniac murdering in the name of avengers of homicides sounded either too good to be true or like it had to be stand-up material, especially given that as far as Jenna knew, none of the shooting victims had killed anyone.

"Maybe the victims each had a parent who died, and the Triple

Shooter somehow placed blame on them for their parents' deaths?" Saleda ventured. Saleda seemed to be thinking along the same lines.

"What did the other two avenge?" Jenna asked.

"Megaera, the jealous one, was particularly famous for punishing infidelity," Calliope said.

"Makes sense."

"Alecto's job was to castigate moral crimes, particularly those against other people," Calliope continued.

"Except infidelity?" Saleda asked.

Calliope looked disappointed in her prize pupil. "No, not except infidelity. The Furies each had particular crimes to which they had a *special aversion*, but don't get me wrong. As an entity, they went after those who provoked their ire or those they were called upon to torture. They punished matricide and patricide first and foremost, but they also pursued other criminals and would *never* stop following them."

"What kinds of other criminals besides those committing infidelity? What were the moral crimes you mentioned?" Jenna asked.

Calliope shrugged. "Anyone who broke rules in society, especially those not governed by society. They regulated ethical concerns. Killing mom and pop was big, but disrespecting them was bad, too. A parent calling the curse of the Erinyes on a child wasn't taken lightly. Lack of respect for authority in general, in fact, was something the Furies took up as a cause. Impertinence toward the gods, breaking oaths. That sort of thing. Parents weren't free from punishment, by any means, though. A mother harming her child, for example, would incur the wrath of the Furies. They were known in particular for protecting the defenseless: children, animals, beggars . . ."

Jenna snapped to attention. "Beggars?"

"The down-on-their luck, defenseless ones, yes," Calliope answered.

Jenna and Saleda exchanged a glance. Brooklyn and the homeless man. Someone had to have seen that exchange.

Jenna whipped out her cell phone. "Irv, we need to find out if there are any surveillance cameras outside the Student Life Center at Woodsbridge Community College. I need video from the day

Brooklyn Satterhorne died. That afternoon, from every single possible angle you can get your hands on."

"Oh, if only Google Earth kept continuous video flow," Irv replied.

"One day, Irv," Jenna said.

"You keep promising me that . . ." he said, but she could hear him push back from the table, his yawn giving away his stretching. "On it. Anything else, my liege?"

Jenna thought for a minute. The previous Triple Shooter victims had probably committed some kind of moral sin, as well, but the chances of them learning what those might've been right now were slim. And yet . . .

She stepped away from the table and hopefully out of Calliope Jones's earshot.

"Start thinking now about ways we can find out if the other Triple Shooter victims were, um, amoral."

Irv laughed in her ear. "You want me to see if they went to confession or had any recent purchases of scarlet letters in their receipt bins, or what?"

Jenna shook her head. "I have no idea yet. But I will. Talk soon."

She hung up and stepped back to the table.

Saleda didn't ask about the conversation because she was still engaging Calliope with question after question. "If they never stopped pursuing the criminals they were after, did they eventually kill the criminals they tortured, then?"

"Not literally," Calliope said. "Some committed suicide, but most were simply tortured into madness."

Madness. Schizophrenia.

If the UNSUB believes he's hearing the Furies, does he believe they're torturing him for somehow being dishonorable?

Schizophrenics usually weren't that logical. Still, the idea couldn't be discounted. All the same, the idea of the Furies had to have been planted in the shooter's head at some point. Could've been anywhere at any time, though. Trying to track down sources of mythological learning for someone whose identity they didn't know would be about as fruitful as looking for the next Triple Shooter victim before he killed her.

But the question of who the *real* victim was supposed to be in the grocery store still existed. Now they could look even further into the profiles of the patrons at Lowman's that day to see who it might've been rather than just how they meshed with the number three.

"If our UNSUB feels he's being followed by the Furies—hearing them—well, is there anything in mythology that he might do, anything he might turn to to get away from them?" Jenna asked. Maybe he thought that by avenging their wrongdoings *for* them, like once he'd done a certain number of tasks as such, they'd let him go? They would leave him alone?

Calliope grunted. "If your killer believes the Furies are torturing him, then good luck. That was why so many of those they punished ended up killing themselves. The Erinyes are merciless. The Furies will never stop."

As Jenna and Saleda pulled out of the bookstore's parking lot, Jenna searched for something—*anything*—to tell Irv to look for in the profiles of the people inside the grocery store during the shooting. Something that might give them some idea of who the Triple Shooter was after—chiefly, who collided with some sort of immorality that would've drawn the attention of the Triple Shooter and, in his head, the Furies.

"So what's the plan?" she asked Saleda.

Saleda shook her head slowly as she navigated the SUV through the streets. "I'd say we could take closer looks at the previous Triple Shooter victims prior to the grocery store to see if we could learn what mysterious morality crimes they committed, then follow the trail of those in an effort to link it back to the killer the same way we're hoping the surveillance footage from the college will give us something. But I don't think the old victims are a useful tack. Actually attempting to determine the 'sins'—or whatever caused the Triple to target these girls—this long after the crimes were committed would be nothing more than hoping to get lucky in a guessing game. Unless you have better ideas than I do."

"I wish. I'm on the same page, though. I don't think finding the 'sins' of the previous victims is what we need to focus on," Jenna said. Her comment to Irv from a few minutes before popped into her head. "What we need is some way to look at the so-called 'morality' of the people in the grocery store at the time of the mass shooting. One of them was the target, and figuring out which might be our best shot at tracing how this guy came to be there to off him or her."

"Good luck with that. My ideas were sketchy for that angle on the old Triple Shooter victims. They didn't magically turn into something more worthwhile when we started talking about the grocery store victims. The only thing I can think of is to do more interviews," Saleda replied.

Jenna sighed and leaned back, intentionally banging her head against the seat's headrest. Asking people to confide all the ways in which an objective party might consider them to be immoral and getting useful answers was about as likely as she and Claudia making a party of burying the proverbial hatchet and skipping away from the fresh hole as best buds. Even if the survivors of the grocery store shootings were willing to tell their darkest secrets—which they most likely wouldn't be—if they happened to be anything like Brooklyn and somewhat *subjectively* awful, they wouldn't have the self-awareness to explain that they treated other human beings like crap.

"Okay, so other than interviews, if you were looking into someone's life and a person's actions, what would you use to try to assess their . . . I don't know . . . moral compass?" Jenna asked.

"Shit," Saleda said. "Uh, movie preferences? Maybe Netflix downloads? Music taste?"

The pearl pink color Jenna associated with subjectivity flashed in. "Too individualized to personal taste. The music one person thinks is immoral doesn't faze another. We need something more universal. Something that applies to or at least exists on the same plane as the guidelines Calliope Jones laid out regarding moral crimes the Furies punish."

"All right. So sexual deviances, maybe. Swing groups? Cheating.

How we'd know much of this kind of detail on any one of these people we're talking about is beyond me, though. Maybe there's some giant list of swingers kept on the Internet I don't know about, though I daresay Irv could dig it up . . ."

Jenna laughed. "Yeah. I can just see us arranging stakeouts on thirty people to determine the chances any one of them might be cheating on a spouse. I'm sure the Bureau would be happy to clear that use of manpower."

"Yes. And judges tend to giddily approve search warrants and seizures of victims' property when we can't yet prove any of it directly relates to a suspect at all. 'We know one of these people is immoral' is a little too vague for any judge without a blood alcohol level of point five to grant," Saleda said with her own chuckle.

"Point five if they were even victims," Jenna countered. "They're not, though. They're *potential* victims. Of a *past* crime. So now we don't need a judge who registers point five on a Breathalyzer so much as one with enough whiskey in his bloodstream that he can't take one because he's passed out. We find him, we're covered. One of us holds the paperwork still, and the other moves the pen across it in his hand."

"Even better. Now we just need to know where to go to find sloppy-drunk judges in the middle of the afternoon. Know any favorite watering holes?"

Jenna's phone vibrated, and she laughed as she pulled it out. She'd kind of hoped it would be Yancy, seeing as how they hadn't talked since their spat, but it was Charley, wondering whether or not he should be worried if Ayana ate a bath crayon. Great.

She replied that no, unless Ayana had choked on it, he had nothing to worry about. The things were as nontoxic as they came, which, sadly, she couldn't say for most things in Ayana's life.

Truth was, though, A had no idea her life was at all strange or different from that of any other kid. She didn't know any better than having her grandfather and uncle take care of her every day while Mommy was at work, or that there was something extremely disturbing about living in a house you were locked into with a series of nearly undecipherable locks and passwords that changed *far* more often than Uncle Charley's socks. Funny how kids could have that sort of perspective, whereas adults tended to lose that innocence.

Color burst forth in Jenna's mind. A terra-cotta shade, one she'd seen before. *But where?*

She closed her eyes, concentrated on the hue, tried to hold it there. *Remember.*

Dodd.

The mental images of him flew through her brain: Dodd in Liam Tyler's house just before he'd left; Dodd in the SUV on the way back to Quantico following their last outing, when he'd talked about no longer having a family; Dodd squatting on the floor in front of Molly Keegan that first time Jenna had seen him.

It was the color she'd come to associate with Dodd, but finally she understood why it was flashing in at this very moment. When she'd first met Dodd, he'd been interviewing Molly Keegan without so much as a tip from Yancy to go on.

"I only came over because she is *a kid, and kids* are *different . . . Kids are honest, notice things some people don't,"* he'd said when she had asked him why he was questioning Molly. *"She has a unique point of view."*

How this little girl kept finding her way into the case, Jenna might never know. But one thing seemed for sure right now.

"Saleda, you aren't going to like this, but I think we *do* need to conduct another interview. With Molly Keegan."

Saleda's neck arched back. "What? Why?"

Jenna blew out a breath, already resigning herself to the next sparring match with Liam Tyler at worst, another unpleasant encounter with him at best. Hell, she didn't blame him. If she was the girl's parent—or parental *figure*—she'd want their family to be allowed to move on as well as possible and stop thinking about this whole mess as much as they could, too.

"Because," Jenna said, "she might be the only person who was in that grocery store who could give us some conjecture that might show the good guys from the 'possibly immoral' guys on instinct. It's a talent only children have most of the time, because everyone else knows too much, is too ingrained with social protocol. For most, the norm has become not to look, not to stare. To give people *too much* benefit of the doubt."

"Are you sure this is absolutely necessary? The only way to do whatever it is you think we need to do? This isn't going to make my day or my career any easier. Teva's already been over there once today to talk to Molly about how she found Eldred Beasley's phone number and to take a statement from her about their conversation."

"But you're making my point for me, Saleda. Forget for a minute all the implications of that she *could* find him to contact him based only on her observations. The sole reason she initiated that contact was because she noticed where no one else did that he—a man who'd been as close to the shooter as she had, if not closer—had been missing from the room where the witnesses who saw the shooter were held until statements could be taken. *She* called Beasley because she had noticed he should've been included in the group none of us noticed to put him in," Jenna said.

"I know, I know. It's just . . ." Saleda groaned. "Just be for damned sure this is the right step, Jenna. The only step. Please? For me? My sanity?" Saleda said.

"I *am* sure," Jenna said, Dodd's words haunting her thoughts. "She notices things some people don't."

M olly poked her head through the railings at the top of the stairs. She couldn't see Dr. Ramey, but she could hear her voice. She was with another woman this time. Thank goodness. Liam did *not* like that Agent Dodd from before, even though Molly thought he was a nice enough man. Maybe he'd just had a bad day the other day, the same kind Molly had had the day her friend had kicked her in the shin accidentally while their class was learning how to play soccer at PE. She'd been grumpy all afternoon the day that happened.

"Ladies, I'm trying to be hospitable, but this is getting a bit ridiculous and excessive," Liam's voice echoed from the foyer. "What could a six-year-old possibly know about a crime scene that others couldn't undoubtedly tell you more about?"

Molly resisted the urge to blow a raspberry. Six was a perfectly fine number to have as an age. Sure, it was a devil's number to some people, but it was also the number of geese a-laying in "The Twelve Days of Christmas." Geese were neat birds. It was the number of legs insects were born or hatched with, the number of cans in a regular pack of soda, and the atomic number of carbon. Nothing wrong with six. She knew a lot of things about a lot of different subjects as a six-year-old!

She shouldn't have taken Dr. Ramey into Liam's office that day during their tour. That was all there was to it. He didn't even really like *her* looking at his art, like the rock collection imprints and the painting. No wonder he'd acted like Dr. Ramey bugged him after that. He'd never said anything to Molly about it, but she'd known as soon as he'd come in the office while they were talking that day that she shouldn't have been there, brought a guest inside. The heat had crept up her neck to her cheeks the same way it did anytime she went in his office to look at the artwork when he wasn't in there. The very first day she'd noticed the artwork, stood to admire it, Liam had come over and talked to her about the painting the same way she had discussed it with Dr. Ramey. But after that time, he hadn't been happy to have her visit the office and look at the art. She guessed she didn't blame him. She wouldn't want other people staring at her stuff when she wasn't there, either. It just felt creepy.

"Mr. Tyler, we believe Molly can answer certain questions for us based on where she was located inside the building at the time the shooting occurred," the unfamiliar female said.

Her stepfather let out an audible sigh.

One. Two. Three.

"Fine. I'll call her down. But let's keep it short this time. Okay, ladies?"

Molly jerked her head back through the rails and sprinted the few steps down the hallway back to her room.

"Molly? Hon? Can you come down for a few minutes?"

She closed her door as she came out so it would sound like she'd been in her room all the time. She took the stairs one by one at a hop, all twelve. *Twelve in a dozen, twelve dozen in a gross. Twelve months in a year. Twelve edges on a cube, like her Rubik's cube. Force twelve, the maximum wind speed possible for a hurricane.*

She landed on both feet at the bottom. "What's going on, Liam?"

"Dr. Ramey and Agent Ovarez came by to talk to you. Is that all right?"

She glanced past him to the foyer, where she saw Dr. Ramey smile and wave as well as the lady with darker skin and almost-black hair pulled into a ponytail who stood beside her. "Sure."

"You know you don't have to if you don't want to, right?" Liam asked.

Molly nodded. Never mind that he didn't think she could help. "I know. I want to."

Liam turned and gestured for the two agents to come over. Molly followed as he led them into the kitchen, poured them both a cup of coffee and Molly a glass of juice.

"Well, you ladies let me know if I'm needed. I'll be in the living room," he said.

Dr. Ramey thanked Liam, and he left.

Molly did like Dr. Ramey. The doctor was fun to talk to, mainly because Molly could tell Dr. Ramey thought of her as any other person. Not like a lot of adults.

"So, Molly, how have you been doing?" Dr. Ramey asked.

"I'm okay," she said truthfully. Everyone had been worried she would have bad dreams after the grocery store or be really upset over the ordeal, but really, the only things about it she'd given much thought were Mr. Beasley, the man in the cereal aisle, and how much she missed seeing G-Ma almost every day. She really did miss G-Ma. A whole, whole lot.

"I'm glad. This is Agent Ovarez. She's working with me on this case," Dr. Ramey said, nodding to the darker-skinned lady, who flashed a smile and put out her hand.

Molly let go of where her own hand lingered on her juice cup and stretched it across the table to shake Agent Ovarez's brown hand. She liked that the new lady wanted to shake hands. Maybe she was a lot like Dr. Ramey.

"Hi," Molly said.

"Nice to meet you, Molly," the agent replied.

"Molly, we need to ask you a few more questions about the day of the grocery store," Dr. Ramey said. "Anything you happened to notice is important, so tell us whatever pops into your mind. Sound good?"

Molly nodded.

"All righty, then. Molly, I need you to think about being in the store *before* the bad stuff started to happen. What you and G-Ma were doing right before the loud noises and yelling started, before you called nine-one-one. Okay?"

"I can do that," Molly said, sure of herself. She had a good memory.

"Great. Now, I brought some pictures with me. Some of the people in the pictures were in the grocery store while you were. Other ones weren't there at all. I need you to look at the people in the pictures and tell me if you recognize any of them, and if you do, anything you might've noticed about them while you were there."

"Like what color shirt they were wearing?" Molly said, her heart beating faster. She couldn't tell why, but she was almost excited about this responsibility. She didn't know what made it such an important job, but if they came all the way out here to ask her to tell them things she noticed, it had to be. She needed to do it right.

"Let me explain a little more," Dr. Ramey said.

Molly leaned in, elbows on the table. *Concentrate. This is big.*

Jenna leaned forward, mimicking Molly. She could tell the little girl was eager to please, but explaining what it was they wanted her to detail to them without leading her in any way would prove tricky.

"We'd love for you to describe what they were wearing. Sure, that could be something you'd notice. You could talk about clothing or anything else about the way they looked that day that the picture doesn't show. But this can include anything you noticed about them in addition to how they looked, too. You could tell us if you saw an item you remember being in their grocery cart or if you heard them talking at all, what their voice sounded like, the topic they were talking about . . . anything like that. You can tell us if you felt a certain way near them, or if they seemed friendly, reminded you of someone you knew . . . made another person nearby laugh, walked faster than you did . . . anything," Jenna continued.

"Or if they had lots of groceries in a cart or were carrying a full basket and lots of stuff in their arms, too? Or if they had a basket, but it only had a few small things in it, probably not even enough to need a basket. That's one thing I noticed about Mr. Beasley. That's the reason I knew he was missing from the back room where they kept the witnesses that day. Because I'd looked at him and his basket, talked to him."

Jenna had to suppress the urge to snicker so she wouldn't interrupt or insult the little detective in the making, but it wasn't easy. Molly's stepfather might be trying with everything he had to keep Molly from any further involvement with the case, but the kid had different ideas, as the team had found out recently. After Eldred Beasley's call to Jenna, Teva had followed up with Eldred's daughter, who at first couldn't tell them much if anything—her dad hadn't told her he remembered being at Lowman's at all, and she said she couldn't imagine why he'd had the seemingly random, isolated moment of clarity regarding the incident that he must have had the night he'd called Jenna.

But this morning, the daughter had called Teva back. She'd been at her father's apartment to drop off some takeout for him to have for lunch when he'd mumbled something about talking to "that little girl" on the phone.

It hadn't taken much digging after that to find out that Molly's interest in numbers had given her a leg up in her amateur-sleuthing pursuits. Somehow, Molly had managed to obtain Eldred's phone number despite not even knowing his name. Apparently, she'd been concerned when she realized he hadn't been in the back room of the grocery store where the witnesses who'd seen the shooter were held until the police could talk to them. So she decided to make sure to get the involved parties in touch with each other since they were all very busy doing other important things and consequently it might get put off without their realizing.

What else did you see in Eldred Beasley that we haven't yet? But they'd get to that later. First, a control question.

"What was the first thing you noticed about the first person you saw when you and G-Ma entered Lowman's that day?"

"It was more crowded than on other days we'd been to that store at the same time of afternoon. G-Ma told me it was senior citizens' discount day, and we started produce shopping. One old man who was older than G-Ma seemed almost shorter than me, but he wasn't really. He was just hunched over. I noticed he didn't have many things in his cart, but by how slowly he walked, I wondered if he got a cart instead of a basket so he could lean on it for support walking."

Jenna's stomach flip-flopped. She *knew* this kid had instincts. The team was driving the stepfather crazy and probably seemed to be talking to the child in his home more than the other witnesses combined, but call it whatever he liked, this little girl might be their most valuable witness. She seemed to be the only person able to sift through lots of information without thinking solely about the crime.

"Perfect, Molly. That's just the kind of thing I want to know. You ready?"

Molly nodded. "Uh-huh."

Saleda slid the flip-book of pictures they'd compiled across the table. It contained photos of patrons from the grocery store, a few random mug shots, a few pictures of police officers in street clothes. They needed those controls so they could be sure Molly was remembering the right people and for the right reasons, rather than pointing to every photo and telling them things about the person that she may or may not remember simply because she knew they wanted to hear information. Such a fine line to walk with kids: leading them versus not, determining which of their observations constituted magical thinking about people versus solid thoughts based in reality.

Molly opened the book and glanced at the pictures one at a time, her gaze scanning the page slowly from left to right.

She pointed to a picture of a female with a short brunette bob. "This lady was there. She walked like she was hurt."

Jenna looked to the picture. Indeed, it was one of the witnesses in the store. "Why do you say that?"

"She limped," Molly said. "And she was slow. G-Ma wanted to pass her in the fruit section when we were behind her but felt bad, so we just walked slow awhile."

The girl went silent again, taking in the photos. She turned a page.

Her finger landed on the first picture on the next page: another grocery store patron.

"He was on his cell phone. He talked loud."

Jenna felt rather than saw Saleda making a note on her legal pad next to her. Good. Mr. Too Loud on Cell Phone *was* a possibility. It was rude to talk on your cell phone in public. But he was also a man, and other than what she now thought to be bystanders in the grocery store at the wrong time during the massacre, the Triple Shooter had only killed women.

She ignored the voice in the back of her head trying to tell her that this was a total shot in the dark. Sure, even if Molly remembered a lot of these things and they could check the potential victims more in depth, it didn't narrow down the target pool entirely. The girl couldn't have seen every person in the store or gotten a bead on their habits. But still, something told Jenna that Molly could help. A lot.

Molly had moved on to a photo on the third line of that same page, which happened to be a photo of Eldred Beasley. She tapped it with her pointer finger. "Mr. Beasley is probably the one you need to be talking to. He has trouble remembering stuff, but doesn't that maybe mean he's the one person from the store that day who hasn't gotten a chance to tell you everything he saw?"

"We're in touch with him, Molly. We'll be interviewing him soon. Thank you for that," Saleda replied.

Jenna leaned in, brushed Molly's shoulder with hers, then winked. "Though, for future reference, it's always best to either tell your mom or Liam and they'll contact us or for you to contact us yourself when you remember something like that instead of contacting a stranger. You did a great job, but it helps us do our jobs better if we're in the loop, and even though Mr. Beasley is a nice man, not everyone involved in cases we tend to lurk around is, you know?"

Molly smiled sheepishly but nodded her assent. "I'll call you next time."

"Good deal," Jenna replied. "But back to Mr. Beasley. What do you know about him?"

The little girl nodded. "He's a nice man. When he told me he remembered some things, I told him he really needed to call you. I'm glad he did before he forgot to again," she said thoughtfully, maybe even a little proud of herself in the aftermath of Jenna's previous slight scolding.

"Me, too," Jenna said. For someone so young who probably didn't yet understand all the ways Alzheimer's disease could ravage someone's mind, Molly was quite astute about the effects. No wonder kids and animals were good for people like Eldred Beasley. They were the few with the patience to treat them like they weren't different. Still, she needed to bring Molly back to the task at hand. "What other pictures on this page?"

"This man dropped his glasses on the floor. I picked them up for him, and he said thank you."

Jenna noted the elderly man with salt and pepper hair Molly had pointed to. Yep. Also in the store. If nothing else, she was consistent.

They went through the same tedious process for the entire picture book, and Molly never once identified a picture of someone who hadn't actually been in the grocery store the day of the killings. Armed with a list of about ten people to look at closer—and a lot more of Molly's thoughts on Eldred Beasley—she and Saleda walked Molly back to the living room.

Liam and Raine were there, watching some nature show on TV. Liam held the remote control idly in his right hand, a can of soda in his left. His feet were propped on the coffee table. Raine sat on the love seat across from him, both feet on the floor, back straight, hands folded in her lap. Her eyes were on the screen, but her gaze was far away.

Poor lady. Jenna knew that look all too well. She had the same one anytime she pretended to do something else while she thought of Hank, she was sure.

"All done," she said, giving Molly a little push in the small of her back to send her toward her family.

Molly scampered over and crawled onto the love seat with her mother, eyes on the television. "Is this the cheetah one?"

"Nope, the crocodiles this time. It's a good episode, though," Liam answered, standing. "May I see you ladies out?"

"Sure, thanks," Jenna replied. When they reached the door, she turned to shake his hand.

He obliged, giving a curt smile. "Happy to help."

Orange—a lie—flashed in. *I'll bet.*

"Good evening," Saleda said, also shaking the man's hand.

Then they were out the door, and it closed behind them. Since they'd been in the Tylers' home, the temperature had dropped with the setting sun. Jenna rubbed the goosebumps popping up on her arms.

"Thoughts?" Jenna asked.

"Yeah. My thoughts are I need a drink," Saleda replied.

31

The next morning, Jenna rolled over and reached for her cell phone. She did it every morning she wasn't with Yancy these days, but this time, it was different.

When she and Saleda left Molly Keegan's house last night, they'd decided they could both use some rest. With nothing particularly time sensitive on the line, they called it a day and went home. But unlike most other nights, Jenna hadn't talked to Yancy at all, and she was starting to get worried.

She breathed out relief when she saw the text message from him.

Coming over first thing. Need to talk.

Who cared how he knew she was home. He was okay, and he hadn't been taken hostage by any psychopathic mothers named Claudia in the last forty-eight hours. That was what mattered.

Besides, Jenna had this feeling she knew exactly what local *Ramey Enquirer* field office had informed Yancy of her movements, and it was called Charley.

She crawled out of bed and threw on a pair of wrinkled black slacks from her dresser and a light blue button-down. The last time she ironed had to have been before they'd moved into the house from the apartment in Florida. She wouldn't even know where to find an iron if she wanted to. Oh, well. Good thing catching killers wasn't dependent on a tidy appearance.

After Jenna had combed her hair into a neat low ponytail, she swiped on some mascara to look a little more awake and headed for the kitchen. As she walked down the hallway, she passed Charley's room. He was sitting on his bed, restringing his guitar. She poked her head in. "Traitor."

He didn't look up. "One of the pitfalls of living with your little bro all your life."

The cameo pink Jenna had seen when she was around eight flashed in. It had been the day her grandmother had told her that she always wanted Jenna to remember to follow her dreams, and something had tickled Jenna's gut. A sick, worried sense that her grandmother was trying to prepare her for something. A few weeks later, she'd told the whole family she had cancer.

Jenna blinked. "What is that supposed to mean?"

Charley's fingers worked at the instrument, but something sparkled in his eyes. "Oh, nothin'. I guess matchmaking's just part of my charm . . . one of the many services I offer, that sort of thing. Or in this case, maybe I should say making you make up with your match is just one of the many services I offer. I don't know. Which do you think would sound better in the commercial jingle?"

Neon lime green flashed in. Mischief.

"That did not sound anything like an everyday Charley-assesses-his-own-greatness statement, for the record," Jenna said, ignoring his joke about advertising his own services and instead honing in on the tone of his voice when he'd mentioned the downside of the two of them living in the same house as adults. Despite the playful, devilish green she'd seen following the cameo pink of preparation, the skepticism and foreboding of the pink were the associations that resonated with her most in conjunction with his tone. If she hadn't known better, she'd think Charley was gearing up to tell her he had plans to move out.

Surely not. No matter how overbearing and paranoid Charley might think Jenna was or how many speeches he might give her about being overly fearful and not enjoying life to its fullest, he'd always seemed okay with Dad and him living with her and A. Not just okay; he'd been *happy*. Could he have met someone? Be thinking of moving in with a girl?

No. Right? She'd have met her. Wouldn't she have?

"Color coding's failing you, Rain Man. I'm not going anywhere," Charley said, strumming a note on the guitar to check it. He looked up. "And yes, I know you're doing it. You give off some kind of pheromone when it happens . . ."

"Oh, shut up," Jenna said, though she smiled. Maybe she *was* paranoid. After all, he'd moved all the way to Virginia with her and Dad when she'd been offered her job back at the BAU. He wouldn't have come all this way to just walk away from them without a serious reason, and he'd always been honest with her—almost to a fault. Even if he'd been trying to keep something cryptic from her before now, he'd just reassured her that her random fear based on nothing but a throwaway sentence was unfounded. He didn't have a reason to keep anything secret from her.

"Love you," she said, grinning as she left his room.

"I know you do. I'm too awesome for you not to," he called after her in a loud whisper.

Jenna entered the kitchen to see Yancy, the only outside party in the world who was *supposed* to be able to find this place. He sat at the table with a strawberry Pop-Tart. Jenna glanced at the clock. Charley must've let him in, too. Too early for her dad to be up.

"Hey, you," she said as she reached for the coffeepot.

"Hey," Yancy said.

Something about the little side smile he always did looked different today. It was slower to develop, and his eyebrows didn't lift the same way. But mostly, it was the defeated way his greeting sounded that let her know he was still low from their fight.

She sat down across from him with her coffee, this time shaking a packet of sugar to its bottom before opening it and dumping it in.

"Listen, I'm sorry for the other day. I know how bad it sucks for us to have to be so separate when I'm on the job, particularly after working so closely on the case last year. It sucks for me, too," she said.

Wow, his eyes looked tired. Bags underneath them, bloodshot. She did miss him. So much.

"Don't worry about it," Yancy said. "I need to talk to you about—"

"But I *am* worried," she cut in. He wasn't weaseling away from the issue that easily. She'd been a psychiatrist too long to stay silent when she knew something was bothering him. If they didn't discuss it, they would both let their feelings fester so long they wouldn't be able to talk about it if they tried.

"I know, but . . ."

"But nothing. I want us on the same team again. Bad," she said. *I want you to never go a whole two days without letting me know you're okay again. Ever.*

"Jenna, I know you think you know what this is about, but . . ."

Yancy stared down at his Pop-Tart, his fingers working steadily at pulling off the frosting-less edges.

"I know I can't possibly understand how you feel. I'm not ever going to insult you enough to think I can."

He was quiet, just looking at the pastry. He half smiled again, though his eyes stayed on his plate.

Body language says shame. But you don't have to be ashamed of missing me . . . Maybe you think I'm hearing your words and taking them as you being too clingy? Not even close. I'd give anything to cling to you on every step of this case.

"I *want* you to understand. I'm just afraid you won't," Yancy said, still staring at his food.

She reached across the table and covered his right hand with her left. "I love you, Yance."

He looked up at her, met her eyes. His were watering, his face pained.

"I love you, too, Jenna. More than you know." He stared into her face a long minute, then smiled, this time brighter. "Your last few days been okay? How many monsters have you saved the world from since my last update?"

So, that's how we're playing this, huh?

But if he didn't want to talk in depth, she couldn't make him, no matter how convinced she was it would be best. Staying close was the next best thing, and she still hadn't had a chance to catch him up about Hank's brother, Victor.

"Well, now that you mention it, it was weird. You'll never believe who was here yesterday."

After Yancy left for work, Jenna tiptoed through the hallway. She eased the knob of the door on the left until it pushed open into the room swimming in fairies and flowers. The morning sun spilled in from the window, leaving a bright, lined pattern across Ayana's face and white-blond hair. It was no wonder that Hank's mother wasn't convinced Ayana was his. The platinum hair, the porcelain skin. She hardly looked mixed.

Jenna knelt down beside the bed and smoothed her hand over Ayana's locks. As she gazed at her little girl's closed eyelids, she smiled. Behind them, Hank's eyes. If his mother saw those, how could she ever doubt?

"You're gonna wake her up, Rain Man. Might not matter to you, but I was kinda looking forward to watching a little MTV *before* the twelve back-to-back viewings of *My Little Pony: The Movie*."

Jenna turned to see Charley standing in the doorway, crunching a mouthful of cereal, the hand not holding the spoon cradling the bowl. "The *My Little Pony* movie hasn't been on the table since the last VHS player died, and you know it. And I'm not going to wake her up."

Ayana stirred.

Shit.

"He shoots, he scores!" Charley said.

Her daughter blinked sleepily, yawned. She rolled her eyes at the way Charley was now pretending he was a radio announcer and making a weird hiss come from the back of his throat to mimic a roaring crowd. "Mommy?"

Jenna smiled and shook her head. "Don't worry about Uncle Charley. You know how werewolves change into wolves on full moons? Well, this is kind of Charley's werewolf thing, only it's less predictable and way less cool."

"Hey!" he cut in. "I'm offended by that."

"Well, I'm offended that you think I don't know my own daughter well enough to peek in on her and not disturb her," Jenna said.

"But you did disturb her."

"And you're a towel," Jenna said, turning back to Ayana.

"Hey, sweet A. Go back to sleep, sweet girl. I just came in to give you a kiss."

Ayana blinked more as if trying to get her eyes to focus. "Did you kiss Yancy, too?"

What the hell?

"Huh?"

She didn't mean for it to come out, but the surprise was so great, she couldn't control it.

"Yancy was here, right?"

How on earth . . .

"I saw . . ." Ayana yawned again. "Out the window. Then fell 'sleep 'gain."

That explains a lot.

Ayana stared up at her. "You know what Yancy's like to me?"

Jenna grinned at her daughter. Whenever Ayana said something like this about a person, something silly that Ayana approved of was sure to follow. *I sense the word "marshmallows" or "kittens" coming up.* "What's that, baby girl?"

Ayana sat straight up in bed and stretched her arms wide, yawning again. She finished and slapped the pink-and-yellow, unicorn-covered comforter with her palms. "Lime beans!"

"Lime beans? You mean lima beans? I thought you liked Yancy. You can't stand lima beans."

"No, not the veg-able. The *color.*"

Behind her, Jenna heard Charley coughing loudly and on purpose. Well, this was a first.

"We've always known it might be genetic," Charley said smugly.

Jenna shot him a look. It was true, they'd all wondered if Ayana would be a synesthete like Jenna, since the phenomenon was hereditary and more common in females. But even though she'd known it was a heavy possibility, experiencing actual signs of it felt just plain weird.

"What's Unk-a Charley talkin' 'bout?" Ayana asked, looking confused.

She patted Ayana's hand. Even if her daughter was a synesthete, she was too young to be in touch with her color associations anyway. "Oh, he's just being goofy as usual. You ready for breakfast? How about pancakes?"

"Mmm!" Ayana said, kicking her feet excitedly.

"Okay. You hop up and make your bed, and I'll get 'em started. Sound good?"

"M'kay!" Ayana said with enthusiasm.

Jenna closed Ayana's door behind her as she left, then glared at Charley, who'd adopted an innocent expression. "Charley Padgett, you know better."

"I didn't do anything! She has no clue what I'm talking about, and even if she did, it's not like it's a bad thing." He shrugged. "Unless you don't enjoy nicknames like 'Rain Man.' "

"You know what I mean. I don't want her to know much about synesthesia—"

"You're not going to have her be that girl whose parents don't tell her what condoms are until she comes home one day as a teenager and tells you about a boy she fooled around with who happened to have a balloon in his pocket, are you?"

Jenna ignored the comment. "Because if she does have it, I want her to find out for real. Kids can think they have a certain characteristic and 'try to' have it—"

"Little hypochondriacs," Charley murmured.

"It's the same reason we can't ask leading questions to children in police work. Keep your mouth shut."

Charley mimed zipping his lips. "I won't say another word."

"You just did," Jenna said.

"But if I *was* going to say another word, I'd ask what lime bean color means to you."

Jenna kept walking into the kitchen and removed a frying pan from the cabinet. "It doesn't matter. Even if Ayana *is* a synesthete, she'd probably have different associations from me, anyway."

But no matter how true that argument was, Jenna couldn't help but think how the dull, pale green of lima beans happened to echo the color of moss in her mind. A color she associated with doubt.

32

Yancy slid into his seat, his heart heavy. He hated lying to Jenna, even by omission. But he couldn't involve her in this, *especially* not now that Hank's brother had warned her a dispute over whether or not Ayana would get the money Hank left to her in his will was coming. Hank's mother would have a field day if somehow this thing with CiCi and Denny went badly and Yancy was caught for *killing* a cop. And then the only way news of Ayana's gold-digging mother's cop-killing boyfriend could get worse would be if it was discovered that Jenna knew about the whole thing and had helped him cover it up.

No. It was better—and safer—if Jenna stayed blissfully ignorant.

Even if it meant the openness and honesty their relationship was built on was now about as transparent as Jenna's alarm code system. *Fuck.*

He inserted his earpieces and hit the button to signal he was ready for calls, though taking other people's emergencies was the last thing he wanted to do today. God only knew he'd feel better wallowing in his own self-pity at home, with only Oboe's incessant scratching to keep him company. Sure, worrying wouldn't do any good, but at least he'd know he was sitting there obsessing properly over this complete screw-up of his, rather than moving on with his everyday life as if he was just some common, conscienceless sociopath. *Shit, cool guy. Way to mess up everything.*

Yancy took a call from an elderly woman whose Chihuahua was barking, which had her convinced prowlers were lurking in her backyard. He dispatched a car to check on her, but he had a feeling all they'd find would be a nosy squirrel or stray cat taunting the little dog through the glassed-in door. He sent a cop to investigate a suspicious person loitering outside a female dorm at one of the local colleges, then clicked to answer the next call.

"Nine-one-one, what is your emergency?"

"I . . . I'm stuck here."

"What is your name, sir?"

"Armond Hester," the man said, sounding agitated.

"Sir, can you tell me your location?"

"Yeah, I'm . . . I'm at the corner of, uh, Bentley and Cramer."

Yancy typed the location into his computer. Now to assess who he needed to send. "And what seems to be the trouble, sir?"

"I'm stuck! I just told you!"

"What do you mean by 'stuck,' sir?"

"I can't get off the street!" the man said again, the frustration in his voice heightening.

Yancy sucked in a deep breath. Sometimes when people were panicked, they found it hard to elaborate. He needed to ask the right questions. "Why can't you move from where you are, sir?"

"There ain't no taxis on the road!"

Yancy closed his eyes. *One, two, three . . .*

"Sir, not being able to hail a taxi is *not* an emergency unless you have a medical emergency, in which case I can send an ambulance. But since you didn't tell me any immediate medical crises when I asked your problem, I suggest you dial information and call a cab company rather than clog this line. That way people with real emergencies can get through. Have a safe day now."

He pressed the button to release the call. People were insane.

His red light came on again. Maybe this time it would be someone who couldn't find a porta-potty at an outdoor event, or someone at a deli who ordered a sandwich with no lettuce but received a lettuce-loaded nightmare that might or might not contain bread or meat at all underneath the many layers of the green bunny food. They happened every day, but they never got any less strange . . . or stupid.

"Nine-one-one, what is your emergency?"

"Yancy! It's me. I . . . I need help."

Yancy's heart thudded like raindrops on a tin roof. He'd *told* CiCi they couldn't ever act like they knew each other, for her own safety, yet here she was, calling him by name on a recorded 911 dispatch call, having recognized him by voice. He couldn't scold her, of course, lest he give them away even more, but damn, he wanted to chew her out from here to Timbuktu.

"What seems to be the problem, ma'am?" he asked, trying to sound neutral despite his pulse racing so fast it seemed as if his blood might shoot right out of his veins. He knew the pimp couldn't be there . . . He was dead! Had the other dirty cops found her?

"It's not . . . well," she hesitated, seeming to think better of what she almost said. "It's my dad. Yancy, he's been attacked!"

"Ma'am, I need you to remain calm," Yancy said, willing CiCi to listen to his words but also to read between them and follow his lead. To help her, he had to get them out of this current situation, which unfortunately for them was being recorded and could be legally referenced. This call had to be wrapped up in a way that didn't end with cops at CiCi's. "You sound *panicked*," he said, emphasizing the word and hoping she'd catch on to what he was doing, letting it be a signal to her that while he knew she was upset, she shouldn't blurt out everything in her mind on this call. "You said your dad was attacked. *Why do you believe this?*" Yancy asked, each word slow, deliberate.

"Um . . ." CiCi's shaky voice stalled, her breath rattling as she tried to compose herself. "I guess he might've fallen . . . now that I look closer at everything."

"Okay. And is he alert?"

"Yes."

"Does he appear to be physically injured?"

She hesitated. "I . . . don't think so, no. Actually . . ."

Relief flooded to every muscle in Yancy's body as her tone told him she was catching on.

"I actually think he must've just taken a spill. I came in and saw him on the floor and just overreacted. He seems completely fine now. But thank you, and I'll call back if there's any change. I'll hang around and watch him awhile just to make sure."

Yancy quickly rattled off the signs of a concussion and encouraged her to call if she suspected her father's condition changed or became more concerning. Then he shoved back from the table and grabbed his satchel, already heading toward the main office. Yancy told his supervisor he had a family emergency, and he hightailed it out of the dispatch building. He floored the Prius toward CiCi's home. If her father had been attacked, the police needed to be brought in. But given what had happened two days ago, they needed cops at her home dusting for fingerprints and conducting an investigation about as much as Yancy needed to see a front-page photo of the Ramey house after its location was leaked to the media. Christ, what a disaster.

He pulled into a parking spot in the little lot down the street reserved for the neighborhood pool, and jogged the rest of the way to CiCi's. He didn't want his Prius parked in front of her house any more than it had to be, even if their "we don't know each other" cover *was* already blown.

The door flew open before he could knock, and CiCi threw her arms around him. "Oh, thank God you're here! I don't know what to do. Someone broke in . . . hit Dad over the head. He swears he's fine, but when I got here . . . oh, God, Yancy. I thought he was dead. I came in and scared whoever. They ran out the back, and I was too busy tending to Dad to try to get a look . . . He was laying there, still and everything. Jesus. Who would do something like this?"

Cops who are seeking retribution for killing one of their own come to mind. "I don't know, CiCi. Are you *sure* he doesn't need to be checked out by a doctor, though? I know we don't want or need police at this house right now, but we could take him to the ER, tell them he fell or something. I don't know."

She shook her head. "I know, I know. He probably does need to be checked. But . . . police would get involved anyway after him being at that grocery store and everything. They're already after him for more interviews even though he can hardly remember yesterday from today, and if they hear something happened to him . . . My God! They might think it was related, want to put him in protective custody. Oh, God, Yancy, I can't let them take him—"

Yancy's head spun. "Whoa, whoa. Slow down. What do you mean he was at the grocery store? You're not talking about the mass shooting at Lowman's?"

Rocks seemed to drop into the pit of his stomach even before she nodded. He'd wanted so badly to keep Jenna from being involved, but little did he know, she was *already* involved. Fate always *was* a cruel bastard.

"What do we do?" CiCi squeaked.

"*You* don't do anything. Stay with your dad a minute. I have to make a phone call."

33

Jenna reached headquarters at about the same time Dodd did. He held the door of the office open for her.

"You look like you got run over by a lawnmower," he commented.

"Thanks. You look pretty zombie-like yourself," she replied. The truth was, she might've slept the night before, but it had been the sort of sleep where somehow her brain had seemed to still be working and worrying even while she wasn't cognizant of it. Combine that with how obviously upset Yancy had been this morning, and she was in no mood to spar with Dodd. She'd thought seeing Yancy would make everything feel better, but instead, his palpable feelings had only clouded her thoughts. And she couldn't blame him. She could kick herself for even letting the thought cross her mind when Ayana had said what she had about "lime beans" green. It was just plain silly.

"I did box a couple rounds with my kangaroo before coming in to work. Gets the blood pumping, ensures the day can only get better from here."

"Sounds exhilarating," Jenna replied, plopping down in one of the chairs in the briefing room.

"Nah, I jest. I was on the phone with the Chicago crew about the nightmare in the Cobbler case. Looks like this guy is going to get sent to a padded room. I still can't believe it. The sheer stomach it takes to saw off feet . . . damn. And based on bleeding and bruising, several were still alive when he did it. A lifetime supply of thorazine? It's too good for him."

Jenna sighed. She could empathize for sure. She'd seen one too many cases where a mental institution could never do justice to the pain and terror some bastard had dealt. Hell, knowing Claudia had spent most of her time incarcerated in a cushy institution was enough to cause Jenna's liver to produce bile at rapid rates and send it up her esophagus just to say hello.

But now, the mental institution seemed like the lottery compared to knowing her mother was out there somewhere—anywhere—able to go out for a steak dinner and maybe even make a new man a nice morning cup of joe with three sugars, one half and half, and two arsenics just for good measure.

"It's already done?" she asked.

"Might as well be," Dodd said, his voice weary. "Everything approved, rubber stamp only thing missing. Then he's on a transport."

"Shit."

Dodd nodded his agreement. "Shit indeed."

The others spilled into the room, and Saleda began tacking up pictures on the front board. Jenna recognized the people in the photos as the "candidates" Molly Keegan had identified last night: people who might have attracted the Triple Shooter's—or the Furies'—ire. *Let Operation Needle in a Haystack begin.*

But before Saleda finished, Jenna's phone vibrated. She glanced at its face. Yancy.

Guilt washed over her as she clicked the button to send the call to voice mail. The daily briefing was about to start, and even if they were on the rocks, she couldn't talk right now.

A second later, though, the phone vibrated again. This time a text.

Call me NOW. Is relevant to your case. Alzheimer's guy attacked.

Jenna's heart sped up as she reread the message quickly, then a third time just to be sure. "Alzheimer's guy" had to be Eldred Beasley. He was the only person she was aware of in conjunction with the case who had the medical condition. But how did Yancy know about him? He could've taken the 911 call about the attack, but that didn't make sense. If it had gone through police, she'd be getting a call from someone at the crime scene who'd realized this might be related . . . not from Yancy, who as far as she knew until now, hadn't known a thing about Eldred Beasley's name, medical condition, involvement in the case, or anything else. Even if Yancy *had* taken a call about Eldred Beasley, in theory, he should know as much about the man's golf score or Internet search history as his being at Lowman's that day.

What the hell . . .

"Be right back," Jenna muttered, standing and stepping into the hall. She hit Yancy's number on her speed dial.

When he answered, she didn't waste time asking how he knew about Eldred Beasley. If the man had been attacked, the chances of it being unrelated were slimmer than the chance she might let Ayana go to senior prom without a bodyguard.

"Where are you? Where's he?"

"One Ninety-two Peake. But, Jenna . . ."

Something in Yancy's voice sounded strange. Strained.

"What's going on, Yance?"

A sharp breath.

"Jenna, come. But if you have to call cops in . . . look, just don't ask me why right now. I need you to trust me and not make me explain until later. If cops need to come, call the *state* cops. No locals."

The quality of his tone made a shiver ripple up Jenna's back. She'd never heard him sound this way before. Ever.

She swallowed hard. "Okay."

Jenna hung up the phone and headed back into the briefing room.

Her thoughts ran, her heart prodding her to go to Yancy alone, to find out why he was so afraid. To protect him.

Nevertheless, if something had happened to Eldred Beasley, the team needed to go. Even Yancy, for whatever reason, knew an attack on a man who was a witness at Lowman's—even if he couldn't remember jack shit about it—was no coincidence.

"Folks, we need to head to the Kelly Garden neighborhood. Our Alzheimer's patient who witnessed the shooting at Lowman's has been attacked."

Jenna climbed out of the SUV at the home of Nancy Winthrop on Peake Road. The place was already buzzing with police, but she knew it would be. Despite the fact that she had no clue why Yancy didn't want the local cops involved, she'd pushed away her wildest guesses at how Yancy could be mixed up in this and her desire to find out just that before calling *any* police. Instead she just did what he'd asked: trusted him. She called the staties since she had no choice but to take the team, but if she'd taken the team and *no* cops were at the home, everyone in the BAU would be suspicious of Yancy's tie to the case before she had a chance to figure out what it was and what to do about it. They might still figure out something was awry, but hopefully they'd just think a trooper was closest when a 911 call came in. At least until she could come up with another plan, anyway.

Just because she'd trusted him didn't mean she couldn't kill him when this was over if it turned out to be crazy.

Saleda led her and Porter toward the house. They'd left Teva and Dodd at Quantico to go through some of the profiles of the "candidates" Molly had identified, looking for rudeness or immoralities that might anger a Fury, and Irv was working overtime to churn out even more intimate life details for each.

A cop stood guard at the door, apparently there to determine the looky-loos and reporters from the legitimate experts. Saleda flashed her badge, and Jenna and Porter followed suit.

"Right through to the kitchen," the officer said. "Officer Ellis is already inside and can catch you up, though I'm 'fraid there's not much to go on at this point."

Jenna followed Saleda through the halls, Porter trailing her. *Officer Ellis?*

But she saw him before she had a chance to wonder too much. Victor Ellis was in uniform. He looked both like Hank and so different at the same time. He carried that same official air, but something about him was less cocky, cooler.

Softer.

Jenna tore her gaze away from Victor and looked across the kitchen table. An aging man she guessed to be Eldred Beasley, a brunette she assumed was Nancy Winthrop . . . and Yancy.

God help me, Yancy, when I get you alone, I'm going to grill you like a cheese sandwich . . .

"Officer Ellis, pardon the interruption. I'm Special Agent in Charge, Saleda Ovarez. May I have a word?"

Victor nodded to her. "Excuse me, folks."

The little group meandered into the hallway they'd just come through. Victor turned around.

"Well, well, well. If it isn't Hardass," he said.

So much for professionalism.

Saleda's head whipped in Jenna's direction. "You two know each other?"

Jenna had never been one to share a lot of personal details at work, even with her own team, so she hadn't mentioned Victor's visit to any of them yet. "Um, we're acquainted."

Saleda's eyes narrowed a second as she studied Jenna, but finally, she relaxed and let it go. Jenna would probably hear about this later, but for now, the case was more important.

"What happened here tonight?" Saleda asked.

"Looks like an attempted robbery. Perpetrator saw no cars in the driveway, assumed the place was empty. The father, Mr. Beasley, was here on a signed-out visit from the assisted living home where he lives and surprised the robber. Robber knocked him in the head, but Ms. Winthrop came home during the break-in and spooked him. Ran away through the screened back porch, it seems. No sign," Victor replied. "Now, this would be a normal, everyday case, excepting for the fact that this call didn't come from first responders or the victim or even the next-door neighbor's poodle. It came from the FBI BAU. Anyone care to fill me in on the details of why the hell I'm standing here right now when there's no reason I can tell that this falls into my jurisdiction whatsoever?"

Saleda glanced at Jenna, eyes wide. Might've been good to fill Saleda in on that so she could explain, but Jenna didn't even know the damned answer herself. So Jenna did the only thing she could: she told half the truth.

"Victor, we believe this isn't your cut-and-dry robbery. Eldred Beasley was a witness to the recent shooting rampage at Lowman's Wholesale a few days ago, and we believe he may have knowledge that could lead us to our UNSUB. The problem is, he has severe dementia in the form of Alzheimer's disease, so he, uh, can't remember it all."

"And this has *what* to do with a robbery in the house, exactly?" Victor asked.

Hell if I know.

"You're telling me *you* wouldn't look closer at an assault that *happens* to involve a key witness in a mass murder?" Jenna countered. "What'd the guy steal?"

Victor's mouth set in a line. "Nothing."

"Uh-huh."

Jenna felt Saleda's tap on her arm. Her superior was right. Whatever she felt about the fact that Hank's brother had been following her for months, had found her house, and had delivered the news that Hank's mother was Satan's spawn, this wasn't the place.

"I'm sorry. It's just that to be honest, I have no idea how the UNSUB would've known to find Eldred Beasley here, but if he did, it makes me more sure than ever that he has key information in this case someone doesn't want us to have access to," Jenna said.

Victor nodded, understanding. "That still doesn't explain what this has to do with me and the state cops."

Jesus.

"There's a leak," Jenna blurted. She felt Saleda's stare on the back of her head burning through her. "Someone in the local department leaked sensitive information we were holding on to to help identify the UNSUB to the media, and I don't want them anywhere near this. This man obviously has some memory locked in his mind somewhere, and I don't want anyone else knowing it but us, him, and the UNSUB."

Victor was quiet a moment, seeming to let the words digest. He gave a curt nod. "Fair enough. So, what can we do for you other than take the report? FBI's obviously in on this . . . Why do you need us?"

Saleda spoke up.

"We don't know the cases are related. We're operating on a hunch. We need someone to treat this like any other attempted robbery and assault, collect evidence, and put it on the books as an open investigation. Our asses are grass for being here without proper cause. We just need the cops investigating this cute little scene to cooperate and give us some room."

"Done," Victor said. "I questioned the man, but like you said, his memory's like sand running through fingers. He's shaken up, but EMTs checked him over and gave him a clean bill. If this is what you think, though, he got *damned* lucky."

"Yeah he did," Jenna agreed. It was one thing she couldn't quite understand. If this was the Triple Shooter, and their profile of the Triple Shooter was correct, why would he leave him? In fact, why had he left Eldred Beasley alone this long? Something had to have triggered him to come back for the guy, and then, if the UNSUB was schizophrenic and not operating as a stable individual, he wouldn't have been too spooked by Nancy coming home to flee without finishing what he came to do. He'd have just finished off Beasley and killed her, too. And the blunt object was a whole different story in itself. No gun . . .

"Though I do think it's only fair to tell you we found out pretty quickly that this home isn't a stranger to law enforcement visits. Locals have dropped by the house several times just in the past couple months for domestic disturbance calls," Victor said.

Jenna controlled her breathing, tried not to show what she was feeling outwardly. But here it was, why Yancy was involved. Nancy. CiCi. This was the domestic abuse victim he'd gotten so hung up about.

Apparently, considering he was here in her home, even more hung up than she'd realized.

Her neck burned, whether from embarrassment, nervousness, jealousy, or anxiety, she couldn't tell. Maybe a combination of all of them. *Shit, Yancy.*

"Where's the husband?" Saleda asked.

Damn. Good question. Why hadn't she thought of that?

Because you were too busy imagining your boyfriend coming to the rescue of another damsel in distress.

"On a business trip, it looks like," Victor replied.

"So no chance the break-in could've had anything to do with him and or the domestic abuse calls?" Porter ventured.

Victor shook his head. "Unlikely. Guy's checked in at a hotel in Detroit right now. Hotel staff confirmed with one of my guys about twenty minutes ago. If he was here to break into his own place, he had to have hopped a flight and snuck back, but I'm guessing whoever he's meeting for business would miss him if he didn't hightail it back fast."

"Let's double-check it to be sure, but sounds pretty cut-and-dry," Saleda replied. She turned to Jenna. "Shall we take a crack at Eldred?"

Jenna rubbed the sweat from her palms on her slacks. Saleda hadn't asked about Yancy's involvement yet, but she knew she would. Any opportunity to delay *that* awful moment, she'd take. And talking to Eldred might be cake compared to talking to *Yancy.* Or finding out what the heck he had to do with this to make him not want the locals here.

"Ready when you are," Jenna said.

35

Eldred's head felt swimmy, his thoughts bleeding into each other so he couldn't tell where one started and another began. He glanced around the room. A kitchen. So many people. He didn't know them. His head hurt so, so much, and he just wanted to sleep.

Now a young lady sat across from him in the place the black policeman had sat moments before. He didn't know her . . . did he? She might be familiar. Or maybe he was just trying to force her to be.

"Mr. Beasley, my name is Dr. Jenna Ramey. You called me yesterday to tell me what you knew about the shooting at the Lowman's grocery store. Do you remember that?" she asked.

It was as if he was hearing her through a tunnel. A phone call? He'd called this woman? He'd never even seen her before! Had he? No. Surely he hadn't. That was nonsense.

"Miss, I think you're confused. If you received a phone call, it didn't come from me . . ."

She nodded, but something about the tightness in her face told him she didn't believe him. He knew whether he'd made a phone call or not, damn it!

His cheeks tingled. He didn't like this. He wanted her out.

"Can you tell me how you got that bump on your head, Mr. Beasley?" she asked.

Bump . . . ?

Eldred reached up and touched the side of his head where the woman's gaze rested. Immediately, he winced. The skin there was tender, raised. *But how . . .*

"Must've fallen," he muttered. Yes. That was it. He'd taken a spill. This floor always *was* slippery. He'd told Sarah over and over she needed to dry it with a rag after she mopped, but she *never* listened to him!

"Is everything all right, Mr. Beasley?" the woman asked.

He followed her eyes to his hands, which were fisted on the table. He must have banged them down. He didn't recall doing it, but somehow, he knew he had.

He unfolded them and placed them in his lap. "Oh, yes. Yes. Just lost in thought is all."

"Mr. Beasley, a man was in this house earlier. We think he could've been the same man who hurt those people in the grocery store. We also believe he might've hit you in the head," the woman said. She'd called herself doctor, hadn't she? If she was a doctor, maybe she could make his head stop hurting . . .

"Man? Nonsense . . ."

But even as he said the words, something prickled in Eldred's mind, an itch he couldn't quite locate to scratch. The kitchen table still smelled of sandwiches, the cold cuts they'd eaten for early lunch. He was used to eating lunch early at the home.

"They eat lunch almost right after breakfast," he said out loud, chuckling. Those fools!

"Pardon me?" the woman doctor said.

He glared at her, the cold-cut smell and how it was helping him scratch his itch, lost all because she'd interrupted him. "I wasn't talking to you. You *never* listen to me! You don't understand! How come you do this *every single time*?"

The woman doctor had stood up and taken a step back when he felt a hand on his arm.

"Dad, it's okay. Dr. Ramey is just trying to help us, all right?" Nancy said.

It was only then that he realized he, too, was standing, and his hands had gripped and lifted the kitchen chair in front of him slightly off the ground. He let it drop back down. What had come over him?

"I'm sorry," Nancy said. "He gets a bit frustrated sometimes."

"No problem at all," the doctor woman replied.

No problem, his left arse-cheek. The two of them, standing here with him in the room, talking about him as though he weren't present. Or worse, as though he was a child. He wasn't a child! Hadn't been for some time. If he was still a child, he'd eat peanut butter for lunch instead of the ham and cheese.

Again, the smell of the deli meat and cheese took hold of him, sending his thoughts back the way they had come. *The grocery store. An itch. Can't scratch.*

"Mr. Beasley, I think it's best if you get some rest, but do please call—or tell your daughter to call—if you remember anything else, all right?" the woman doctor said.

He nodded as the smell and the thought again slipped away.

36

Jenna followed Saleda out of the kitchen toward where Porter was chatting with Yancy. Her boyfriend looked awful. Somehow, she hadn't noticed this morning that he hadn't shaved, nor did he look like he'd taken a shower. He had to have gone straight to work from her house. What could've been going on with him that he went to work like that? Was it their fight or more?

"Porter and I will talk to the daughter. I'm going to give you five minutes alone with him to find out what in the fresh ninth circle of hell he has to do with this before I come in there and gouge out his eyeballs myself," Saleda whispered.

"Your generosity knows no ends," Jenna replied. Her boss wouldn't have to gouge any eyeballs; if Yancy didn't tell her everything—and fast—she'd be removing a few other choice parts herself.

She gestured for him to walk outside with her. "Walk and talk."

Yancy trudged toward her, hanging his head. She didn't blame him. She'd be dreading this, too, if she was him. It was bad enough on her end.

When he'd shut the front door behind them, Jenna turned on the stoop to face him. "Spill it."

. . .

H alf-truths were still lies, weren't they?

Yancy bit his lip, looking into the eyes of the woman he hoped to marry. He shoved his hands in his pockets. The cool circle that was the engagement ring brushed against his right fingers, and he immediately removed his hands again.

Telling her would be bad. Not telling her would be worse. Or was it vice versa? *Shit, cool guy. How ya gonna worm your way out of this one?*

If he told her about the dead guy, he'd be asking her to cover up what amounted to a homicide, no matter how you sliced it. She'd have to turn him in to stay out of trouble, and no matter how mad she'd be, she wouldn't do it. He didn't have to see people as colors to know things about them, and Jenna loved him. Snitching wasn't her style. Protecting was.

"The husband on the business trip? He's involved in some heavy stuff," Yancy said, conveniently leaving out the fact that even if the husband *didn't* happen to be on a business trip when the cops checked in on him, he wouldn't have been in the house anyway. The only way Yancy could keep Jenna safe was to twist all the details he had available to him to try to make it make sense without her getting too involved.

"What kind of stuff?"

"He's a pimp," Yancy said.

Lie number one. Fuck. *Make a man you don't even know out to be a pimp. Great idea.* Poor bastard was already being painted as an abusive ass by his estranged wife for God knew what reason, and now he was a pimp in rumor, too. For him to walk out on CiCi *and* for her to throw him under the bus and say he abused her every time a pimp beat her up meant he couldn't be a prince, but damn. Yancy'd hate to be him and ever find out the stories flying about all the shit he *hadn't* done. So far, all Yancy knew he was guilty of was being in an obviously fucked-up marriage.

"Okay," Jenna said slowly.

Yancy held his breath as he watched her. He could tell by the way her forehead scrunched and she cocked her head that she was weighing what he'd said.

"So what does that have to do with not calling the local cops?" she asked.

Yancy blew the giant breath out. His heart thundered under his shirt so hard he was surprised the fabric wasn't fluttering with the beats. "He's involved in a prostitution ring that is run by some local cops."

He paused. Fuck. *And why, if there's no evidence of a dead body in that house, would it matter if they dropped by? Hell, if anything, they'd be more protective of someone they knew was in their circle than ready to arrest him, you moron.* As if mixing truths with giant lies wasn't enough, he was doing it and still digging himself deeper.

"He's been holding out on them money-wise, though, to pay for CiCi's dad's medical bills and everything. So far, they haven't found where he lives since he does all his dealings with them, uh, elsewhere. The home, car, all their registrations, are in CiCi's name. But if they come here . . ."

"Their cover's blown," Jenna filled in.

You could say that.

"Yes," Yancy mumbled, ashamed of how easy the lies had come out.

Lying to Jenna wasn't like lying to anybody else in the world. First of all, she didn't deserve it, and second of all, he loved her. But third, he never knew when she was going to pull her weird human trick and call him on it because she saw a festival of tangerine or whatever exact shade of orange she associated with untruths.

But the moment passed, and apparently no color clues had de-camouflaged him. The relief he expected to come didn't. Instead, a painful clenching wrapped his chest.

"You need to talk to . . . CiCi," Jenna said slowly. "She's not gonna like it, but we almost have no other option besides putting her father into protective custody. The killer is aware he knows something, and this guy is desperate and dangerous. He'll come back."

Yancy was already shaking his head. Sooner or later, the cops involved with the pimp cop Yancy'd killed were going to notice he was gone. Hopefully they'd never realize CiCi's house was the last place he was, but if they did, and her father was in protective custody, it would be the *least* safe place for him. Alzheimer's might be what Jenna was thinking, but all Yancy could consider were the ways they could use Eldred against CiCi if anything went wrong.

"You can't do that, Jenna. You just can't. It'd kill her," he said.

Jenna looked taken aback. "You must know her pretty well . . ."

Yancy sighed. "It's not like that . . ." *Yeah, you tell her as she finds you at the woman's house and knows you've walked by it before. How can you expect this vibrant, intelligent woman to buy your crap when you don't even believe your bullshit?* "He's a weak guy, Jenna. Even you can see that. He's confused enough around people he's known for decades. How terrifying would it be for him to wake up in, what, a jail cell?"

"There are lots of ways to keep someone in protective custody that don't involve jail cells," Jenna said.

"Still. He won't understand where he is, and these might be the last years . . . hell, months of his life he'll recognize his own daughter. Do you really think it's fair to deprive him of that?"

"Are you sure you don't mean 'her of that'?"

Yancy swallowed hard. "I deserved that. But I'm serious. Plus, if he *does* know something, from what I've heard of this disease, Alzheimer's patients tend to have the most access to their memories when surrounded with familiar environments and people to jog them. If you want to find out what information about the shooting he's got locked in that head of his as bad as the killer *doesn't* want you to, wouldn't it be more beneficial to keep him in a place conducive to making that happen?" Yancy begged.

Jenna scratched her cheek absentmindedly as she sometimes did when she thought about something hard. God, he loved her. He should really just pull the ring out right now. Right here. After all, a crime scene would be appropriate as a proposal spot for them, right? If only things were like last year and they were working side by side, they'd never have drifted so far apart that he would have gotten so wrapped up in his own stupid, fucking self-pity. He'd never have tried to play Superman with CiCi, and he wouldn't be lying to the woman he loved.

"Hey," he said, something snapping in his brain. "I could stay with them."

Jenna's gaze jerked toward his face, an eyebrow raised.

Way to go, buddy. That sounded right. "Hey, how about I hang out at the home of this girl you found me with who you're clearly threatened by if for no other reason than that I'm a douche . . ."

"Look, I'm doing a really awesome job of shoving my foot in my mouth, which blows, because I *really* can't stand the taste of metal, but I'm being serious. Remember when I stuck around at Zane's last year because you couldn't leave a cop, since it would spook the bad guy we wanted to lure? It could be like that again. You know me. I can handle myself, and I can handle protecting these two. It'd be a way for you to make sure Eldred stays safe and sound while you work your magic to abracadabra the memories out of him, and at the same time, he won't be scared shitless or too confused to try to remember."

"And you think her husband will be all right with that when he comes back from his business trip?"

Shit. Hadn't thought of that one, had you, buster? Care to explain why you're not even worried about the dude coming back?

Yancy shook it off. "Let me worry about that."

Jenna swayed back and forth on her feet, staring at the cement of the door stoop. Finally, she looked up. "Okay, but *only* if Saleda gives the go-ahead, and *only* if you swear you're not going to yank the secret gun out of your leg unless the killer is on the porch trying to slip in under the guise of selling Girl Scout cookies or something. You won't make a move like that unless there is real, *confirmed* danger."

Her words bit at him like a cool breeze. If only she knew how close she was to the truth. God, if only he could tell her he *had* perceived a real danger. That he *had* shot when he was sure he needed to.

Instead, he forced a weak smile. "How many times a year do you think most FBI agents get to say, 'swear you're not going to yank the secret gun out of your leg' and really mean it?"

She smiled back, leaned forward, and brushed her lips against his. She smelled perfect, like honeysuckles and pancake batter.

"Not enough, I'd guess," she said as she pulled away from him. "Now come on. I've got a really awful plan to sell to a superior."

Yancy followed her through the door. "Use the leg line. Gets 'em every time."

After Saleda grudgingly agreed that the best thing for Eldred Beasley's memory was to remain home—with Yancy as an impromptu bodyguard—she, Jenna, and Porter left the Winthrop home and headed back to Quantico. When they arrived, Jenna shoved aside the buzzing in her head about Yancy's predicament, him being in the line of danger, and CiCi's role in said danger to focus on the files strewn across the table.

"Welcome back," Teva muttered, not looking up from the folder she was perusing.

Dodd, however, stood. He pushed his way past two chairs turned sideways to hold a slew of papers the two of them had apparently categorized in some way, and he thrust a folder into Jenna's hand. "Pictures from the surveillance footage at the college. These are the few shots taken during the timeframe Diana described that happen to be from angles that caught others present. When she and Brooklyn were in the Student Life Center forecourt with the homeless guy, I mean. I'm not gonna lie . . . it's not too helpful."

Jenna opened it, but only half looked at the grainy images inside. She knew Irv had done his best to catch these frames, but these pictures looked like they were taken from cameras made the same year surveillance equipment was invented.

"What about the homeless dude himself?" she asked.

Dodd shook his head. "We talked to him, but he's more burned out than a rock star at his retirement party. He couldn't tell us a thing."

"Damn. So any luck judging the books by their covers?" Saleda asked.

Dodd let out a sigh. "I wish. We haven't found anything damning about Donalyn Greer other than that she teaches elementary Sunday school and volunteers at a pet shelter."

"Which one was she again?" Saleda asked.

"The woman who ate the grapes she wasn't buying from out of the bag on the shelf," Jenna supplied.

"I guess she was just late for lunch that day," Porter said.

Jenna smirked. Trying to weed out potentially "immoral" people present on a random day in a grocery store based on statements made by a six-year-old was never going to be the perfect scientific method. But it was all they had, so she'd resigned herself to the fact that some silliness would accompany anything functional. Plus there was every chance that whatever had caused the Triple Shooter to go after whichever of the potential targets was something that wouldn't be obvious in the profiles Irv dug up, something they couldn't possibly find by looking through employment histories or socioeconomic backgrounds. The things Molly had told them were details Irv couldn't hunt down in any online search. After all, Brooklyn Satterhorne probably looked fine on paper, but the killer watched her intentionally mind-fuck a homeless man. That was all it took.

"So grape lady is probably a no. Next?" Jenna said.

Teva pushed a folder across the table at Dodd. "Connie Ehrenhaft isn't a princess by any means. She's the one Molly saw rushing and rolling her eyes at her nineteen-hundred-year-old father in the toilet paper row. She said the woman had seemed frustrated and in a hurry.

Well, it was probably because she *was* in a hurry. Her license is suspended right now because she missed a court appearance for a speeding ticket. Still, do Furies hate speeding?"

"Speeding *is* against the law," Dodd said.

"Poor old guy. Getting ratted on for taking his time in the toilet paper row. I mean, when you lose the dignity to take as long as you want making an ass-wiping decision, what do you have left to lose?" Porter chuckled.

The cardinal red Jenna associated with stupid cockiness flashed in. Porter wasn't a jerk, but the joke was the kind she'd have expected from the guys at her high school who thought it was hilarious to chase and slap each other with wet towels in the locker room.

"Grandpa Ehrenhaft's ass isn't the only thing shitty in this room," Dodd interjected.

At this, Jenna laughed. She was starting to enjoy Dodd's presence more and more, especially any time he proved he had a drop or two of human DNA in him.

The biggest problem with this entire method was that even if Connie "Fast and Furious" Ehrenhaft had enough speeding tickets to supply her father with rough toilet paper for a year, there was no guarantee the shooter knew about and was offended by them. All they were doing here seemed to be taking some good guesses at which person on their short list was a more likely target than the others. But even then, the real target could be missing from the short list altogether. Molly couldn't have seen every action of every single person in the store, and even if she had, surely some people went to a grocery store, bought their items, and left without ever giving away that they were banging their pool boy while their husband played golf. She just had to trust that Irv could cross-reference the names they narrowed it to and that they'd get lucky.

"Didn't Calliope Jones mention dishonor of parents as one of the Furies' pet offenses?" Saleda asked.

Jenna nodded. That did sound familiar. "Okay, so we put a gold star by Connie Ehrenhaft's name and don't exclude her yet. What about the guy Molly saw demanding that the employee fetch some detergent he couldn't reach from the top shelf?"

"You mean Mr. 'I Like To Treat Lowly Store Employees Like Dirt' Stevens? He's also a resident of Carmine Manor. Came on the bus that day. Other than that he's a World War II vet who enjoys checkers and long walks on the beach—and also likes the toilet paper row. I can't find anything that makes him undesirable on paper," Dodd answered.

They ran through the remaining list of potentials, including the woman who spanked her screaming child right in front of the salad dressing, the man who bumped into someone and didn't say "excuse me," and the guy who wouldn't surrender the last box of graham crackers to the mother who requested them because they were the only brand her toddler wasn't allergic to. None of them presented promising leads.

"We never talked about the man who didn't tip the bagger," Jenna said, remembering Molly's short rant about feeling as though it was unfair that the store's official policy required employees to refuse tips. "Even when employees at a place like that comply with the rules and try to turn down tips, it's more common than not that customers at least try to give them a little something even if they ultimately don't shove it in their pocket and insist they keep it. So common that a child noticed it and mentioned it, anyway. Regardless of the fact that any rational adult probably wouldn't think of failing to offer a tip as a slight given the store policy, the Triple Shooter's profile says he's not necessarily rational. He might have his own logic, but his rules are most likely like a child's in the way that his concepts of fair might be more based on instinct and feeling than technicality."

"You're right. We don't know for sure he's schizophrenic, but we all know we believe it. If hearing goddesses has shaped the skewed social reality his cognitive bias suggests, the real rules are irrelevant. His perception of events is all that matters. The Furies *do* have a thing for protecting poor people, as we well know," Saleda replied.

Dodd yawned. "That may be, but unless the UNSUB followed Vince Zolfer on a spree of stiffing the working poor of America or observed as the guy screamed in the bagger's face all the reasons he would never tip him even if he could, the simple act of doing nothing probably didn't trigger any outbursts. And on paper, the guy is a paragon of virtue. He probably didn't tip the bagger because he's out of money after the three thousand he donated to charity last year alone."

"Yipes," Teva said.

"I know what you mean. *Three* dollars is my limit," Dodd said.

Jenna glanced over her list again. "The employee Molly overheard blowing off the coworker she was supposed to cover for?"

Dodd shook his head again. "Oath-breaker-in-chief's records didn't send up any red flags."

Jenna groaned. They were getting nowhere, and fast. Game plan number two would've looked better and better, only she had no clue what it was.

"What about Beasley himself?" Saleda ventured.

Jenna looked up at her. Blinked.

Saleda was right. Eldred Beasley might be a harmless old man, but he *did* have a temper, even if it was out of frustration with his failing memory.

But as soon as the thought had intrigued her, she felt herself shake her head. "It doesn't make sense, though. If Beasley was the target, why would the Triple Shooter—"

"UNSUB," Dodd interjected.

"UNSUB! If Beasley was the target, why would the UNSUB go to his place to silence him and knock him in the head instead of putting three bullets in his chest?"

Plus Jenna couldn't get past the fact that every previous Triple Shooter victim was female, even if the profile didn't dictate that as a necessary victimology for him, other than it had happened up to this point. Well, until the grocery store killings, anyway.

"He ran out of bullets?" Teva suggested.

"If Beasley was the target, he'd have killed him when he went back for him in the style he kills all his victims. MO doesn't change *that* much. If it's the Triple Shooter, even if the grocery store shooting *was* different, the weapon wouldn't change that dramatically, would it?" Dodd asked.

The last bit of the statement had been directed at her.

"I don't think so. There's still just so much we're missing somewhere. Something we're missing about the grocery store massacre that doesn't add up. Beasley is somehow involved, but he wasn't the target. I'm sure of it. He's still alive, and if the Triple Shooter—"

"UNSUB," Dodd cut in.

Jenna groaned. "If the UNSUB has proven anything, it's that he's good at not leaving people that way," Jenna said. As she said it, something nagged at her. Not a female. The Triple Shooter kills easily.

"Whoa, wait. That's one thing that keeps bugging me. The Triple Shooter—and yes I mean the Triple Shooter," Jenna said, shooting Dodd a glare, "is really good at swooping in, carrying out his little chores for the Furies, and leaving without anyone being the wiser, even in places like the Target parking lot during business hours. The grocery store shooting doesn't follow his normal protocol, but the break-in at the Winthrop house doesn't fit his MO, either. And I don't just mean that he didn't shoot anyone."

"You mean because most of his kills were in broad daylight and in public? Don't forget he killed victim three in her apartment," Teva reminded her.

"Maybe, but there's just something about the style that's different that I can't put my finger on. Both are audacious . . . reckless, even," Jenna said as a shade of blue flashed in with the word "reckless," alongside thought of the break-in. Not quite the cornflower she associated with disorganization. This one was more confident, a little mixed with some sort of red or pink, though it definitely wasn't the purple of impulse, either. Periwinkle. Reckless blue. The break-in at CiCi's house, the blunt trauma to Eldred, the running away . . . it was reckless, for sure. She blew out a breath, relaxing for the color she associated with the spirit behind the other Triple Shooter crimes to wash over her, something that would mix the reckless periwinkle with the pomegranate red of confidence. A shocking pink flashed in that seemed to mix recklessness, impulse, and confidence combined. Daring. Bold. "He does what he wants when the Furies dictate it. He's bold. He doesn't have it in him to ignore it when he thinks someone needs to die or to wait until the circumstance is absolutely perfect. Three of his victims, not counting the grocery store fiasco, were killed and left in public places in the daylight. This guy just doesn't feel like the stealth break-in type. Sure, he killed Ainsley Nickerson in her apartment, but I have this feeling it was only because it was where she happened to go right before he was ready to strike."

"You mean if Ainsley had, say, gone to the mall, he'd have killed her there because he was ready to kill her?" Porter asked.

"Yes."

"So what exactly are you thinking accounts for the difference here?" Saleda asked.

Jenna didn't speak at first. After all, it was she who'd said all along that this grocery store massacre was the work of the Triple Shooter. Her opinion hadn't changed. The colors matched . . . mostly. The times, date. The Triple was their maniac with the gun.

Only now she'd seen those other colors mixing in with his attitude toward the crimes, colors that didn't belong to him alone. Somehow they were being influenced, and suddenly she was no longer sure who was pulling his strings.

Yancy got off the phone with his supervisor. He'd called to let work know he would be taking a few personal days while he stayed with a friend after an attempted break-in at her house. They didn't need to know he was staying just in case a murderous nutjob came back for CiCi's father. He also texted Jenna to remind her about feeding Oboe.

When he hung up the phone, CiCi stood in front of him, carrying a stack of sheets, a pillow, and a folded blanket. At some point she'd changed into a pair of fluffy pink pajama pants after the attack. *Some days all that's left is to give up and hole up until it's over and the next day finally comes around.* "I'll go get Oboe and bring him over in the morning. Jenna said she could stop by and feed him later this evening," he said.

She nodded. "So now that the pooch is taken care of, right this way, knight in shining armor," she said. "I'll get you set up in your room."

He followed her up the winding staircase and into the guest bedroom off to the left. The oak bed had four posts, and each was draped with willowy, whitish-gray chiffon. In stark contrast to the fancy bed, the mattress was bare. CiCi lay the stack of sheets and blankets on the bed.

"I usually keep the sheets and comforter from the other bedroom Dad's using on this bed, but he wanted them in there. They were his and Mom's. Bed was, too, actually, but he can't sleep in it anymore because it's too high for him to climb into," she said. "If you get cold, there are more blankets in the linen closet at the end of the hallway, so just help yourself. There are quite a few books in the corner cabinet down in the living room, along with the TV, though you might have to fight Dad for it around now. *Andy Griffith*'s on. If you get really bored, you're welcome to explore the basement. There is some neat stuff down there. Mom and Dad used to love to travel together, and Dad collected stuff from everywhere he went. The more bizarre, the better. It's where he used to spend most of his free time. Said each thing represented a good memory. He doesn't go down anymore, though."

As she turned and walked out the door, he couldn't help but notice the way her waist curved into her hips, how those loose pink pajama pants didn't quite manage to hide the perfect, round shape of her ass.

He shook his head hard.

You're in a relationship, cool guy. There's a ring in your pocket, and *this woman is still technically married, even if her husband isn't living here or abusing her. And she's a prostitute. Don't forget that part, cool guy. You feel me?*

When CiCi was out of sight, he closed the bedroom door. He made the bed using the sheets CiCi had supplied. When he'd finally managed to get the fitted sheet, regular sheet, blanket, and comforter onto the queen size bed, he sat down on the edge. This bed was softer than his . . . or Jenna's, for that matter. He removed his gun from its secret compartment and laid the piece on the nightstand for easy reach should he need it. Then he leaned back.

He practically sank into the lush bedding. God, he could sleep for years in this thing. He'd better hope if Eldred *did* need protecting while Yancy was here that he wouldn't be in too much of a comfortable stupor to help him.

Yancy stared at the ceiling. Tired as he was, he wasn't *sleepy* at all. Too much on his mind. He'd killed a man, hidden his body. They might never find it, but if they did, there'd be hell to pay. And Jenna. He was lying to her over and over again. How was he supposed to ask a woman to be his wife if he couldn't even tell her about one simple little act of manslaughter? But he wanted Jenna so much, and if she got pulled into his screwups, she stood to lose way more than him.

He couldn't take Ayana's mom from her. He wouldn't.

A light knock on the door.

"Come in," Yancy said softy.

The door opened, and there stood CiCi, this time wearing a satin pink bathrobe over the too-big pajama pants from before. "I just wanted to make sure you didn't need anything," she said.

Her dark hair spilled around her shoulders, still damp from a midday shower. A droplet or two of water had fallen from her locks to her neck, where it lay sparkling against her fair skin.

"Nah, I'm great. But hey, um, would you want to come sit for a little while? Just talk? It's been kind of a long day for all of us . . . I figured you could use the ear or the company," Yancy replied.

She glanced back toward the other guest room where they had gotten Eldred settled, then back to him. "Yeah. That might be nice. God knows I'm not going to get any sleep anyway. That's for sure."

Once CiCi'd stepped in and closed the door behind her, she walked over to the wicker chair in the corner. She tugged the pink satin ribbon around her robe, and the robe loosened. She took it off, revealing the same solid white cotton T-shirt she'd been wearing with her pajamas earlier. She flung the robe onto the chair, then sat on top of it.

"So you never told me. Why did you come that day? To take me to coffee? It's not like all nine-one-one dispatchers make coffee dates with callers," CiCi said.

"It's not? I thought that was the thing now. In fact, I've heard it's going to totally replace Match.com and eHarmony in the dating market. All the emergency dispatchers make dates with their callers these days. You're just behind the times," Yancy said, smiling.

Did you really just make a date reference, cool guy? You're the moron who kept rationalizing how getting coffee wasn't a date.

"You're a real innovator, huh?"

"Franklin, Edison, and me," Yancy said; his chest felt heavy but he managed a halfhearted smile.

A shadow crossed CiCi's face, and she looked down at her pink-polished toes. "Are you ever going to tell me what happened when you left that day?"

The anxiety in her voice took over the worry in his own mind. She didn't need this, either. She had enough problems to dwell on, what with owing a bunch of dirty cops money and the sick dad. The burden of knowing everything that had happened that night would be enough to break anybody.

Yancy shook his head. "Nope."

"But . . ."

He sat up and scooted to the foot of the bed until he was directly across from her. He held a finger to her lips.

"You're only safe if you *don't* know anything. I've got you, CiCi. I've taken care of it, but you have to let me, okay?"

CiCi nodded hard, tears welling in her eyes. Yancy could tell she wanted to protest but at the same time, wanted to do as he wished. She reached out and took both of his hands in hers, squeezed.

"You know, I never knew someone . . . anyone . . . in the world would protect me just because it was, well, because they thought it was the right thing to do. Usually I'm all I have. I know I'd better take care of myself, because if I don't . . ." She choked as a sob came out, and tears streamed her cheeks. "Well, nobody will."

Watching CiCi's tears fall made something inside Yancy ache. He couldn't stop himself. Before he knew it, he'd leaned forward and enveloped her in his arms. He rubbed her back through the soft material of her T-shirt, and she laid her head on his shoulder, his neck a cradle for her tear-stained cheeks.

He inhaled deeply as he gathered her closer to him. She felt so small in his embrace, so unbelievably soft. "Well, somebody's here to take care of you now." He leaned into her more, squeezed her tighter. He gently kissed the top of her head.

Strands of her long brown hair brushed his lips as he whispered, "I've got you, CiCi. I've got you."

39

J ustice watched the woman he'd been following most of the day slam the door of her red Toyota Camry, the same one with chipping paint he'd followed from midtown, where she'd run errands, all the way here.

Her dark ponytail bobbed with her stride as she walked toward the Harford Suites. If she knew she'd been watched going into the hotel several times now, she might've bothered to put on those detestable giant sunglasses that made her look like a praying mantis–human hybrid. But the girl was blissfully ignorant of her audience.

Justice rubbed his palm on the rough fabric of the truck seat beneath him. When that didn't staunch the itch, he brought his palm to his mouth and moved his hand back and forth across his front teeth, the only thing that even remotely helped. This had to be over soon. He couldn't wait any longer than today. If the itch stayed, he was going to go crazy.

He'd known *they* were angry with him for waiting this long, but the itch had gotten worse just since morning. *No more! Not another minute!*

Luckily, it was at that very moment the man burst through the double doors of the hotel. He made his way down the parking lot aisle to his silver Lexus, climbed in, and pulled out of the space. Now was the time to act.

Justice jumped out of the truck and pumped his legs as fast as he could toward the building, turning sharply where, normally, a visitor would've gone through the doors. Instead he went to the back employee entrance he'd noticed, one he'd learned had no special requirements for entry other than knowing it was there.

Once inside, he moved swiftly toward the elevator, but second-guessed himself at the last moment and took the stairs. Elevators were videotaped.

He scratched his arm as hard as he could as he opened the door leading to the third-floor corridor. *Sick.* All he wanted to do was stop and writhe on the ground, let his body graze the industrial carpet until it rubbed his prickly skin clean off.

Can't get sidetracked. He'll be back soon.

It was the same every day. The woman arrived at her married lover's hotel a short thirty minutes after her husband left for his own job. She went in, and the lover came out. He would climb into his Lexus, drive to his child's school, pick up the child, transfer the child to hockey practice, then return to his mistress's arms. The whole process usually took all of twenty minutes, so no time to waste.

He strode through the hallway, stopping briefly as he passed a room-service cart set outside someone's door after they'd finished their meal. *Maybe so.*

Cart in tow, he continued toward room 354. He rapped on the door. "Room service," he said. She'd never know that the man hadn't ordered a bottle of wine or some fruit before he left. She wasn't careful anymore; she didn't worry it was someone she wouldn't want to find her. He knew, because he'd watched.

Sure enough, the doorknob turned. The door opened. Justice shoved the cart hard into the exotic-looking beauty. She fell backward, and he pushed into the room, closing the door behind him.

Before she had a chance to recover from the wind being knocked out of her and scream, he drew his gun, silencer in place. He pulled the trigger once, twice, a third time.

The itching, for one glorious moment, stopped.

40

"So let me wrap my head around this," Saleda said. "You're saying the Triple Shooter isn't acting alone?"

Jenna shook her head, pushing away the green color that flashed in every time she talked about the Triple Shooter's list of conquests. "Not exactly. I think his *triple shooting* crimes . . . you know, the ones that involve triple shots . . . are his and his alone. But if someone else was involved, it would explain why the grocery store killings were such a divergence."

Saleda leaned back and folded her arms. "I'll buy it. Maybe. But if someone else is involved and *knows* the UNSUB is the Triple Shooter and just sort of *lets him be*, then—"

"Then we're dealing with a really sick fuck," Dodd cut in.

Jenna conjured up red in her mind, a red she recognized as the dominant color that appeared any time she dealt with a case involving a dominant team killer and a submissive one, just to see how it felt. And yet, it didn't match. Not quite. The Triple Shooter wasn't a classic subordinate in that he had his own reasons for his kills, his own style, and his own course. In the classic team formulation, the submissive of the two killers was usually goaded into the kills somehow, be it for fear of losing or disappointing their dominant teammate or having a violent streak the more violent, dominant person had cultivated in them. The Triple Shooter, she was sure, had acted alone up until the grocery store. So what changed?

"The target *has* to be the way we're going to blow this thing open," Jenna mumbled.

"Back to square one then?" Teva asked.

Dodd grunted. "Back to 'Who's That Sinner' is more like it."

The phone in the middle of the conference room table rang, its little red light flashing with the promise of news. Jenna's heart skittered as Yancy's face came to mind. If Eldred *was* attacked again, at any moment that phone could tell her Yancy was hurt. Or worse.

"BAU," Teva answered.

Jenna watched Teva nod, her heart slowing. From the side of the conversation Jenna could hear, it just sounded like the local cops calling in a status report on their roadblocks, more or less notifying the BAU that there wasn't anything to notify them about.

"Sure thing. So if we need any further information about the manhunt as far as the roadblocks, we'll call Hoskings instead of Officer Mullins," Teva said.

As Jenna watched Teva grab a pen and scribble a phone number on a white pad at the end of the conference table, her own cell vibrated in her pocket. Her pulse quickened as she pulled it out and pressed the button.

A text from an unknown number.

Jenna. Victor. Come to Harford Suites Hotel in lower Peabody.
We've got a body, and let's just say it has your number on it.

Jenna crossed under the crime-scene tape in front of the doorway of room 354 at the Harford Suites Hotel after showing her badge to the cop on duty. Dodd ducked under behind her. The two of them had been nominated for this glorious turn of events while the rest hung back and scheduled interviews with some of the potential targets still on the "Sinner List," as Dodd called it.

A man in a striped tie and gray trousers sat on the couch of the two-room suite, head in his hands. Cops bustled around the room, dusting for prints, and a clerk snapped photos of every nook and cranny.

Feet away, the body of thirty-two-year-old Pesha Josephy lay wide-eyed on the dark carpet. She'd been shot in the chest three times, and the killer couldn't have been more than a couple of feet away from her. Based on the placement of the bullet holes, it had probably been fast. All were right at the heart.

Dodd was already kneeling next to the body. He didn't touch it, but instead, pulled an ink pen from his pocket and held it across from the gunshot wounds, conducting some strange assessment that only made sense to him.

"The UNSUB's getting better at shooting these days. Maybe you should check for recent frequenters of the gun range," a new voice said.

Jenna looked up from the body to see Victor Ellis stepping through the bedroom door.

"What brings you staties here?" she asked.

"Eh, just in the neighborhood, tired of playing with my radar gun. You know . . ."

"You say that like you're joking," Jenna sparred.

"Well, only partly. Call came in, we were closest. Bam." He tilted his head toward Pesha Josephy's body. "She's yours, isn't she?"

Well, that's one way to put it.

"Yeah, it would seem." Jenna glanced over at the man in the power tie who was slowly rocking himself on the couch. She took a step toward Victor so she could speak more softly. "What about him?"

"Her partner. An affair. He's scared shitless. He'll tell you anything you want to know," he said. "You can look closer at him if you're worried this might be a crime of passion and copycatted to look like a Triple Shooter victim, but it's not. First of all, this guy has as much stomach to shoot anyone as I did when I was four. Second, check this out."

Victor led Jenna toward the table where the TV stood. He picked up a pair of evidence bags. "Already bagged and tagged, though it's a little tainted since Power Tie over there ripped them off during his distraught attempt at figuring out whether or not his lovable little mistress might still be breathing, but I knew you'd want to see them. Over the eyes."

Jenna held the bag up so she could better identify the objects inside. One was a price tag off of a knit skirt that had cost Pesha forty of the last dollars she'd spent.

She squinted into the second bag, trying to identify the contents. It was another tag, one cut out of a garment. She pushed away the purple color trying to flash in, mostly because she wasn't ready to make sense of it. *Not yet.*

"I don't get it," she said. "Where are the threes?"

"Good question. Come look at this," Victor said.

Jenna followed him into the bedroom. On the nightstand lay a coral-colored clutch purse. Its clasp was silver—a straight bar that curved gently at the edges, three bars beneath it arranged in such a way that the shape formed was clearly some sort of an emblem, even if she'd never seen it before.

"The skirt those tags were pulled from was draped over the chair here," Victor said, gesturing toward the corner armchair. "Prince Charming in there says Pesha brought in some packages the day before yesterday. She'd done some online shopping, and she'd picked up her purchases from the post office box they were shipped to. He claims she opened the packages and gave the items the once-over. She switched everything from her old purse to that new clutch immediately and started using her new one, but the skirt she laid there on the chair, and she hadn't touched it since. She apparently couldn't take it home because she was planning to wear it for a heavy date of theirs, and it was supposed to be just for Mr. Man-on-the-Side. Sweet, huh?"

"How long have they had this room?"

"For about a week," Victor said. "And it would seem they use it, um, *regularly*."

Jenna glanced to the unmade bed, the sheets twisted and furled like they'd had a fight with a gorilla.

"I'll say. So just the purse and the skirt, then?" she replied. "Usually there are three . . ."

"You didn't look real close at those tags, did you, Hardass?"

Jenna pictured the tags in their little plastic baggies again, held them in her mind. She couldn't place what he was talking about though. The price tag had definitely been $39.99.

"What am I missing, Hotshot?" she said, humoring him.

"The skirt. It was from Trinity Place Department Store."

Whoa.

"I've never heard of it. Where is it?"

"New York City," Victor replied.

"You're kidding."

He grinned. "I never kid about fashion."

When he smiled, the same little lines around his eyes appeared as they had on Hank. Whatever she and Hank had been through, she missed him. Way more than she'd realized she would.

And if she missed him, she could only imagine how his absence would affect Ayana's whole life. It wasn't fair how the world picked and chose who to take away and who to leave and let live. Jenna had seen some of the worst monsters imaginable make it from day to day, but kids like Ayana and Molly didn't have birth fathers in their lives at all. Whatever else was true about her and Hank's relationship, kids deserved a chance to know their fathers as long as they weren't just like Claudia.

Victor shrugged. "You can order from anywhere online these days, I guess."

But Jenna was only half listening, a thought of her own taking shape. If the items that caused the three alignment had been purchased online, the Triple Shooter couldn't have seen Pesha Josephy buy them in the store of threes—Trinity Place—then followed her to see if she'd committed some immoral act. This time, the MO seemed *backward.*

"Did he know these two were playing married hanky-panky on the side and then *look* for the threes?" Jenna muttered to herself, pacing the room. So far it seemed the only way to explain this, but the change in process was so huge that she had no idea what to make of it. *Surely not . . .*

"She didn't open the packages that gave the alignment of threes until she was here. The skirt—and its two tags that seemingly made up two of the triggering grouping of threes that caused the UNSUB to unleash on her—never left this room. So even though the purse did, we don't have the right batch of threes. They might fit incidentally, and he might've noticed this and used the tags because he had them on hand, but the threes that never left this hotel room aren't the ones that set him off," Jenna said, still pacing.

Her eyes roved every inch of the room as she begged them to hone in on the real culprit that had acted as a flag to bring the monster to this place. Industrial sheets, white towels. None of this had been outside the hotel, either.

Jenna's gaze again landed on the coral purse with the three bars—three bars that could very well have acted as one of the group of threes that led the Triple Shooter here. She turned to look at the nervous businessman still whimpering and rocking himself on the small couch.

"You said she carried that purse places, right?" she asked.

He nodded hard.

"Okay," Jenna said, and she grabbed a pair of latex gloves from the box CSI had set on the nightstand. She snapped them on, then picked up the coral clutch, popped it open. She sifted through its contents: driver's license, debit card, more credit cards than any human should have, a tube of mauve lipstick, a lambskin condom, a vial of eye drops. A circular birth control pill pack. A few dollar bills.

Then she saw a crumpled paper wedged along with a couple of empty gum wrappers under a fine-tooth comb. Jenna snagged it and straightened it out. A deposit slip. A deposit slip dated only a few days ago.

Jenna's head snapped toward the late Pesha Josephy's married lover. "What bank did she use?"

"Huh?" the guy said, mouth gaping like she'd just asked him to subtract Ringo Starr from Blue and then multiply the answer by cats.

"Pesha. Your girlfriend, Pesha. What bank did she go to?"

He pressed both palms over his face, squeezing the sides of his head like he was in pain. "Gah, oh man. I know this. I know this . . . ah! It was the All Trust."

Jenna's pulse quickened. "Which branch?"

The guy grimaced again as he forced his brain to try to extract the information. He snapped his fingers. "Third Street. I'm pretty sure it was on Third Street."

Three-bar purse at a bank on Third Street. That's two.

Jenna whipped out her cell phone and dialed Irv.

"And what can I do for my Crayola Wonder today?" the tech analyst answered.

"Get me all security footage from the All Trust Bank on Third Street, inside and out. I'm texting you a picture of, I'm sorry, a dead girl—"

"Aw, come on! You know I stay in this computer room because the bad guys scare me," Irv cut in.

"Irv, you stay in there because it's air-conditioned and you can play computer games during your downtime," Jenna sniped.

"That, too, but I do like it here better. Okay, send me the girl's last headshot and I'll find any shots of her in the security footage. Anything else?"

Jenna paused a second, bit her lip. It was worth a try anyway. "Yeah. See if anyone around her seems suspicious—watching her or anything like that. Then cross-reference those images with the ones from the Student Life Center surveillance footage from the college and let me know if you happen to notice if we have any characters who just happen to haunt both areas."

"Long shot," Irv replied.

"Everything is in this case," she said.

"In *every* case," Irv said, and he hung up.

"I'm guessing we'll find another three at that bank," Jenna said to Dodd. "But if he saw the threes at the bank, why the tags over the eyes?"

The bizarre purple that kept trying to crop up throughout the case—here, at the grocery store—flashed in again, and the picture of the tags as she'd just imagined them burned in her mind. Suddenly the purple clicked into place. "Victor. The tags. I need to see them again."

"Sure thing," he said, and he extended a hand as if to say "After you."

She rushed back into the sitting room and snatched up the first evidence bag. Sure enough, there on the tag it said SIZE SEVEN.

Before she even reexamined the other tag, she was already sure what it would say. But, there it was, as plain as could be. Seven.

Without explaining, she yanked out her phone and speed-dialed Irv. Her veins filled with ice, and for the first time in a long time, she was genuinely afraid.

"Yellow, Jell-O, mellow. What *else* dost thou have for me?" Irv answered.

"Irv, when you're done with the other stuff I need you to look into the other Triple Shooter victims, and pass along word to Saleda, Teva, and Porter to start digging, too. Find out if the other victims—the single victims, not the grocery store—had a seven involved with their deaths anywhere. The number seven."

She only half listened to his assent, too busy paying attention to the drumming of her own heartbeat in her ears. She didn't know what the third three the Triple Shooter had seen was, but now that the purple she'd been seeing for so many days without recognizing it had finally manifested into a clear-cut association, none of that mattered.

Seven. Jenna associated the number seven with this very purple she'd seen. There'd been seven victims at the grocery store. The Triple Shooter had deliberately stopped at the seventh, but he hadn't killed his intended target. Now here were sevens again, and she was almost sure that when the team dug into his past victims, they'd find sevens hidden in the scenes or circumstances there, too. This killer wasn't only preoccupied with the number three. He was seven-obsessed, too.

But it wasn't the number that had Jenna's blood down to the same temperature Pesha Josephy's was now. It was the other thing she kept associating with that same shade of violet. Until now, she'd not only failed to place the color association, but she had somehow managed to overlook that the same color had appeared in connection with this case over and over again. Her gut usually put puzzle pieces like this together *for* her, but this time her internal assembly line had malfunctioned disastrously.

Maybe she'd missed it. Maybe the oversight was the result of fatigue or the confusion of the case as a whole before they'd realized that another perp was somehow in play. That alone was probably skewing her perceptions, even those of her oh-so-reliable color dictionary.

But as Jenna hung up with Irv, she knew that none of those reasons were why she'd not seen the connection. She held the phone in her hand, staring at it. Another phone call might be in order, but to whom and for what, she wasn't sure. It had to happen, but the situation would have to be handled with care. Right now, she didn't have any idea of the best way to protect, the best way to explain . . . the best way to *move*.

She hadn't seen this connection because it was too hard to fathom. And she hadn't wanted to.

The gunman fired at the seventh victim. Seven. Purple.

The same color she had seen every single time she'd been in the presence of little Molly Keegan.

After updating Dodd and then calling Saleda to fill her in on the development, they all decided that as much as Jenna's heart might be telling her to run, snap up Molly Keegan, and put her into witness protection, that course of action wasn't the way to go. Yet, anyway.

Still, as Jenna dialed her next contact, her stomach clenched painfully. The thought that that sweet, precocious little girl could've been the target of a mass shooting cut straight through her.

No time to think like a mom. Be a cop. Figure out who did this.

The phone rang four times without answer, and Jenna left a quick message and hung up. She dialed Yancy.

That was the problem, though. All of the Triple Shooter's victims had been adults. First, they needed to figure out how Molly lined up with threes and sevens—or they with her. Another big question that needed answering: who else was involved in the grocery store massacre to make the shooter change MO? That led to maybe the most important question of all: if they were right, and the shooter changed MO because someone else was involved, then why was that mystery person involved? There were only a handful of reasons for being associated with a mass killing, and the most likely among them happened to be that you wanted someone dead. They'd been trying to identify the Triple Shooter's true target inside the grocery store, but what if another of the patrons was a target, too? What if another patron was the target of the mystery person involved with the Triple Shooter? Which patron were *they*? Even though the mama bear in Jenna was coming out, the truth was, if Molly was the Triple Shooter's target, she was most likely safe. His pathology made it highly unlikely that he would come back to finish off a victim. She wouldn't have known this right after the grocery store shootings, since if he was frustrated enough and killing a particular target was his first priority, it was possible he would obsess over it and not move on until he'd succeeded. And yet he'd clearly moved on. Brooklyn Satterhorne was dead, signifying one specific regarding the way he determined his targets and carried out his rituals in killing them, and that was that even if they were preordained to die by higher beings in his mind, his ritual did not include the need to complete one before moving to another.

In certain types of pathologies, killers might hold a grudge against an escaped target, but this pathology just didn't ring true of the Triple Shooter against the rest of his profile. That disorganized cornflower blue. Brooklyn Satterhorne hadn't been part of some large-scale plan that also still involved Molly. Brooklyn became a victim because the Triple Shooter was finished with the grocery store and had seen his next set of threes. He would then become fixated on that set of threes, the last completely out of mind. After all, he wouldn't live up to being the obsessive that his profile suggested if he was still thinking of Molly. Stalking and killing Brooklyn because of her threes was passionate. It showed commitment that required unbroken attention.

Eldred Beasley's face popped to mind, his confusion as he rubbed the knot on the side of his head from where the intruder had bashed him.

The accomplice, on the other hand . . .

Yancy's voicemail picked up.

"Shit," Jenna muttered.

At the beep, she left a message for him to call, but as soon as she hung up, she composed a text message:

Need to meet with Eldred. When?

"Any word?" Dodd asked, stepping back into the bedroom from where he'd been questioning the ill-fated Pesha's married squeeze.

"Left two messages, sent Yancy a text. I still say Eldred wasn't the accomplice's prime target, because if he was, how hard could it be to kill a weak old man in an assisted living home any time you wanted?"

"Maybe he doesn't like getting his hands dirty. He couldn't even finish the job when he broke in to silence the guy," Dodd answered.

"But then why involve the Triple Shooter and wait for a grocery store? If Eldred is the man the accomplice wanted dead, and the accomplice clearly didn't want to kill Eldred him- or herself, why not hire someone to kill him? Or hell, if convincing the Triple Shooter to go on a homicidal rampage is his thing, convince him Eldred Beasley . . . I don't know . . . double dipped his tortilla chip in the communal salsa and needs to be punished for breaking that unwritten rule of society," Jenna said.

Dodd laughed. "I'm not sure Eldred has enough teeth for tortilla chips. Besides, I always double dip. It's stupid to only get to enjoy dip on a third of the damned chip. Germs boost immune systems."

"He must have needed to use the grocery store for some reason. The numbers *did* line up, so easy enough to lure the UNSUB to the place. The Triple had to have had a target there, too, or else UNSUB B could've talked the Triple Shooter—"

"UNSUB," Dodd said.

"—the UNSUB into thinking the person UNSUB B wanted dead . . . well, it's like what we were saying about Eldred. If UNSUB B wanted the other UNSUB to kill Eldred, it wouldn't be too tough. Just make the maybe-the-Triple-Shooter-UNSUB think Eldred didn't have a copy of *Emily Post's Etiquette* in his book collection. If maybe-not-but-probably-the-Triple-Shooter didn't have a target at the store, too, UNSUB B could've convinced him he did."

Dodd smirked. "What, like he said, 'Hey, that god-awful kid over there just picked her nose, rubbed the booger on the white shoes she was wearing after Labor Day, then passed gas while chomping loudly on her gum as she stands blocking the entrance to the escalator. Why don't you go kill her on this day of threes . . .' "

Jenna rolled her eyes. "Something like that. But point is, if the most-likely-the-Triple-Shooter-UNSUB didn't have a target at the store in *addition* to the target of UNSUB B, yes, UNSUB B could've planted the seeds to suggest his *own* target so that the UNSUB would believe UNSUB B's target was simply his all along. If that happened, UNSUB B could've just let the very-clearly-the-Triple-Shooter-UNSUB kill the target any time, any place, no instructions necessary," Jenna said.

Dodd nodded. "The MO would've looked slightly different upon investigation since up to then the Triple Shooter had only killed adults. But single, female victims and similar rituals would probably be plenty proof it was just another sad victim of the Triple Shooter, not too many extra questions asked."

"Exactly!" Jenna replied. "But that's *not* how it was done, so the Triple Shooter must've had a target, too. And if he did, then two bodies would've been left in the attack, a shocking change of MO *sure* to draw attention. So UNSUB B needed something else . . ."

Fuchsia flashed in as she said the words, the color she'd realized meant "misleading" in her color dictionary one day when she was around eight or nine. Her dad had been planning to take Charley and her to the go-cart tracks that afternoon but said they had to clean their rooms first. But while Dad had run to the pharmacy to buy some bug repellant for them, Jenna had gotten distracted by a show on TV. Lucky for her, about halfway through the program, Claudia had come into the living room to start dusting and told her she'd picked up Jenna's room, but that if it ever looked like a tornado had ripped through again, it'd be Jenna's business. Later, while putting on her shoes to go to the go-cart tracks, her dad had asked if she'd cleaned her room. "Spick-and-span," she'd said, feeling only slightly guilty. After all, it hadn't been a lie. Just a little cleverly worded was all. Misrepresentation, at most.

"I'm guessing the drastic shift in the MO was UNSUB B's—the manipulating UNSUB's—brilliant idea. He somehow uses the alignment of threes to talk the Triple Shooter into attacking—"

"The UNSUB," Dodd cut in.

"He somehow uses the alignment of threes to talk the *UNSUB* into attacking a place at a time when his *own* target will be there, but he's smart enough to know the ideal way for this plan to go down without leading back to him—something he's clearly desperate to do considering he's already manipulating another killer into committing his murder *for* him—is to make it look like a crazy, isolated incident perpetrated by a gunman no police would be familiar with. UNSUB B knows that if the Triple Shooter goes in and kills just two targets— the Triple-Shooter-*like* UNSUB's and UNSUB B's—that two things will happen. First, the Triple Shooter, assuming he's our UNSUB, is connected to another body. Already a diversion in MO enough to spark questions about a famous serial killer suddenly changing habits that might lead to theories of another person's involvement. And second, when those questions crop up, UNSUB B knows he is connected to the Triple Shooter. It might be a close affiliation, might be vague, but he's far safer and less likely to be caught if he's never linked to a serial killer who is probably crazy, a factor that means being linked to a serial killer that, at some juncture, will probably be caught. I'm guessing UNSUB B told the first UNSUB during planning to just go in and run amok as long as he got the jobs done, and I'd bet, in the UNSUB's number-obsessed mind, he just ended up taking down seven bodies because the number was a soothing one because of whatever it is about the numbers he's fixated on."

"You're on the same page as me. Somehow UNSUB B knew the first UNSUB, whom we believe to be the Triple Shooter, and convinced him to be at the grocery store for whatever reason. UNSUB B somehow knew our presumed-to-be-the-Triple UNSUB's next target already, or—"

"Or he set him up at the grocery store without a target," Jenna blurted. The thought was a brand new one, and she wasn't sure of it by any means. More just trying it on for size.

"How so?"

"The date, time. Maybe UNSUB B knew *his* target would be at the grocery store, so somehow influenced the Triple based on the date and times lining up in threes. There's a seven we haven't found yet, other than the number of victims, but maybe it was enough to draw the Triple to the spot if the manipulator was clever enough and knew what to say. The Triple is paranoid. It probably wouldn't have been hard, given that lineup of threes," Jenna said.

The beginnings of a headache throbbed behind her eyes. They were still missing something. For every piece of this thing that made sense, one stubborn detail wouldn't fall into place. It was like Molly Keegan's Rubik's Cube. If Jenna had tried to fiddle with that thing, the same thing would happen that always did when she got one of them in her hands: she'd be able to line up all but one square within a row, but when she'd try to correct it, even more would be thrown out of whack.

"That's a theory," Dodd said. "But no matter how you slice it, unless we get a new lead, to find UNSUB B, we still need to know who the first UNSUB, allegedly the Triple Shooter, is. We can't figure out who the hell knew the Triple Shooter *well enough* to manipulate him without knowing *him* first."

If only Dodd wasn't as right as he was. The Triple Shooter was the key to the second UNSUB, who was the key to the Triple Shooter. It was the most annoying sort of case, and right now they were chasing their tails. "Though if we find UNSUB B's target, we might have a chance of figuring out who wanted them dead. Even if Eldred Beasley wasn't UNSUB B's big show, I do think he has some knowledge UNSUB B doesn't want us to have."

Jenna glanced toward Victor, who was talking with the coroner. Pesha Josephy had been loaded into a body bag and was about to be on her way to the ME's office. With any luck, the autopsy would magically show someone's DNA besides her married "friend's" latest deposit.

She nodded toward Mr. Power Tie Boyfriend, who still sat on the couch, now tapping his fingers nervously on the side table. His leg bounced in time with the whir of the ceiling fan. "Anything new from lover boy?"

Dodd shook his head. "Swears he didn't see anyone different, notice anyone keeping an eye on them, or anything like that. I'm inclined to believe him, too. People having affairs are pretty reliable when it comes to noticing whether or not someone's watching too close. You know what they say about paranoia, and there are all those great private eye, share-the-awful-pain-of-your-two-timing-spouse-with-the-world reality shows now to remind cheaters to keep their guard up."

"True," Jenna replied. "That's another weird thing, though. Up to now, we've been sure the Triple Shooter was punishing people for things the Furies in his head were telling him needed avenging. Even if UNSUB B's target—Molly—wasn't the presumed-to-be-the-Triple-Shooter-UNSUB's target, in order for UNSUB B to sic the Fury-hearing freak on her, UNSUB B would've had to have at least made the Triple Shooter think she deserved to be punished by the Furies, too, right? What does a six-year-old do that's up there with adultery and kicking over a homeless guy's life savings?"

"You ever seen *The Exorcist*?" Dodd asked, smirking.

"I'm not joking here, Dodd. This kid . . . you've met her. She's pleasant, smart. Do we seriously think she's done anything UNSUB B could use to convince the Triple Shooter that she invoked the wrath of some Greek goddesses of vengeance?"

He shrugged. "So are you thinking our profile is off base? That we need to go back to square one?"

Jenna closed her eyes, letting the purple color that had connected all of the things only moments before wash over her again, hoping something new would surface. It didn't.

"No. I'm just saying that even though I'm sure about this, it feels like jamming that one puzzle piece you have left into the only open slot, trying to force it in because you don't want to admit that somewhere in there, you've got another piece jammed in, too," Jenna said.

"Deep," Dodd replied.

Jenna's phone buzzed.

We dropped by Carmine. Eldred needed some clothes. We're headed back to the house now. We'll see you there.

Jenna typed a quick thanks back to Yancy, deciding this wasn't the time to lash out at him for not answering his phone when he was staying with people who were apparently on a murderer's to-do list. That was a job for in person.

"Got Eldred waiting. If this is what he keeps trying to remember and we can jog that for him, maybe he can clue us in to even more."

Her phone buzzed again. She opened the text from Yancy.

Do me a favor: go get Oboe.

Despite her irritation at Yancy for having freaked her out by not answering, she smiled. "We better get a move on. We've gotta make a stop on the way."

42

The woman looked familiar to Eldred, but even when she said her name, he wasn't sure where he knew her from. For that matter, he didn't know the young man staying at Nancy's house.

Wait. Yes, he did. But only because they rhymed. Nancy and Yancy.

Dr. Jenna Ramey said they'd met before, but clearly she was mistaking him for someone else. He forgot a thing or two occasionally, but not a name and not so quickly as she claimed.

He sat across from her at the dining room table, unable to stop thinking of how much he missed his little two-person table in his apartment at the home. They'd gone over, him and Nancy and the young man, but he wasn't sure why. Maybe they just wanted a change of scenery. Been cooped up in the house all day, after all. He visited Nancy a lot, even stayed overnight sometimes, but he did like the cozy little place there. A little place of his own. Sometimes he didn't like it *as* much, but today, it wasn't so bad. But they had rushed him out almost as soon as they'd gotten there, and now they were back in the big dining room, the one too big for him.

"Mr. Beasley, I need to talk to you about the phone call. The one you made to me a few nights ago. You told me you had remembered something about the shooting that happened at the grocery store," the woman doctor said.

"Someone was shot at a grocery store? That's awful!" Probably one of those gang members. Kids nowadays didn't have morals. Or maybe someone was upset they lost their job. People could get desperate nowadays, for sure.

"Mr. Beasley, someone shot some people at the grocery store several days ago while you were there. You called me about something you saw. You called me after you talked to a little girl. Molly was her name. Do you remember Molly?"

Pictures coursed through Eldred's head, mental Polaroids his brain occasionally took of things he saw but then filed away without showing him what compartment they'd been placed in. Dark hair, chubby cheeks. Boxes of breakfast cereal. Cheerios scattering over the tile floor. The view of the aisle from where he was hiding behind a display of boxes.

The little girl diving between the rows.

"Yes," he croaked, his throat dry.

"Mr. Beasley, we need you to tell us anything you can about Molly on the day of the shooting at the grocery store. Where you saw her, things you might've seen near her . . ."

Eldred blinked. The snapshots playing a slideshow in his brain had evaporated, and try as he might to fish for one, hook it, and retrieve it, they had dipped into a sea he couldn't see the bottom of, sunk just beyond his reach.

"I don't know . . ."

The young woman leaned forward, her elbows propped on the big table. She couldn't have any idea that even bent forward, she wasn't close to bridging the expanse between them.

"Do you remember talking to Molly on the telephone?" she asked.

Chubby cheeks. Dark hair. Voice soft, but easy, like a flute.

"Her voice was steady. Direct. She talked like . . ."

He could hear her even now. She hadn't spoken with him like so many people did, unsure of him, afraid. She wasn't annoyed, and she hadn't made him feel nervous or embarrassed. He hadn't felt foolish talking at his own speed.

"Like what, Mr. Beasley?"

He smiled at the memory, pleased with his brain for releasing it. "Like a grown-up."

Jenna ran through a series of questions, attempted different imagery and sensory wording to try to elicit thoughts and memories from Eldred, but she was getting nowhere with new details from him. The only times he seemed at all responsive were when their conversation turned to Molly's phone call. An idea she didn't like in the least was beginning to take hold of her, and the more time went by, the more she was sure it was the only answer.

"I'm sorry, Mr. Beasley, I just remembered that I need to make a quick phone call if you don't mind. Will you excuse me?" Jenna said.

"Of course," Eldred replied, staring down at where he was twiddling his thumbs.

Jenna stood and caught Saleda's eye, cocking her head toward the front door. Saleda took the cue and moved toward her. She'd been standing in the doorway between the dining room and the living room where CiCi and Yancy sat, just in earshot of Eldred and Jenna's conversation but out of the way enough not to be a distraction to the Alzheimer's patient.

When they were outside, Saleda pulled the door closed. "What's up?"

"I think we're going to have to bring him to Molly or her to him," Jenna said, hating every single word that came out of her mouth. Not only was Saleda going to loathe the idea, but Jenna didn't feel too swell about bringing Molly into this any more than she already was, either.

"May I ask *why* this is a good idea?"

"Look, I know Molly's being a target of this shooting puts her at the center of this nightmare far more than any six-year-old ever should be, so I get why also making her a miniature BAU consultant might not be ideal. But you were listening in there. The *only* moments he comes even remotely close to a vivid memory is when Molly comes into play, the most definite times being him remembering her voice. Talking to her is what triggered his memory before, after all," Jenna replied. "I don't like it any more than you do, but let's face it. It might be our best shot."

Saleda frowned as she leaned against the wall. "Well, there are plenty of studies that suggest children are therapeutic for the elderly, but even if I *were* to agree to this, I don't know how on earth we'd get her family to give it the okay."

Jenna let the amber orange she'd come to associate with Liam Tyler crash over her. Molly's stepfather had been cooperative until now, albeit maybe not *happily*. But still, she could imagine a scenario in which the more Molly continued to be involved in the investigation without a good reason, the more and more protective he'd become. Not that she could blame him. If it were Ayana, she'd want her family and little girl to be allowed to let normalcy reign again, too.

Would knowing Molly was the target make him more or less likely to lend a hand? It could go either way. He might see the need to find the killer at any cost, or he might throw down the roadblock and refuse to allow her to be involved with the case any longer in fear of putting her in more danger.

Robin's egg blue flashed in.

"Raine. We go to Raine."

Saleda raised her eyebrows. "You think it wouldn't go *through* Liam first? He kind of runs the show there . . ."

Didn't she know it. She rarely spouted her synesthetic relationships to other members of the team, but Liam was definitely the dominant personality in the group. The cool, gentle blue she had just realized she saw in conjunction with Molly's mother attested to Raine's meek temperament, as Jenna nearly always saw submissive individuals in cooler tones, often blues. The colors were never something she could explain to anyone entirely, and while she could discern certain characteristics and feelings from them, other parts of the existence of a color surrounding a person or feeling were somewhat incidental. The feelings she got from the colors came from a base part of her gut instinct, and that was something no one she knew seemed to ever understand. Yancy had come closest, but even he might not entirely get it.

It was that sort of feeling—the one she got from the robin's egg blue of Raine Tyler—that made her feel sure that while Raine let Liam call the shots in almost all cases, in this case she would handle it with discretion. The blue wasn't like some others Jenna had associated with submissives in the past; those submissive blues held positions closer to violet on the color spectrum. She often associated shades of those blues with tenderness, compliance, devotion.

And while Raine's color fell in that family, it swung further toward the greens on the scale. Greens tended to be more calculating. It was a distinction she'd have trouble conveying to others, because any time she put forth observations like this, people she was explaining to tended to then put colors into that box going forward. There was no hard and fast rule that said someone who showed as a shade of green would be calculating or those closer to the violet spectrum wouldn't be. It was simply like anything else in profiling: certain behaviors, demographics, and environmental factors gave the team a good spot to start guessing, since they were often indicative of specific personality types. Raine might be a teary, docile type most of the time, but Jenna hadn't forgotten the way she had taken the phone from Liam that first day, told them to come over. She was a follower, but the shade of blue confirmed for Jenna that the woman could think for herself. Especially when her mother's death was involved.

"It might get back to him," Jenna conceded, "but if it does, trust me. She'll hold her own."

Saleda shrugged. "I'll make the call."

J enna didn't get much satisfaction out of being right in this case.
Raine had agreed to let them borrow Molly, but she couldn't
arrange it when Liam wasn't around until the next day. So they
wrapped things up with Eldred, who insisted he needed to get to
bed. They thanked him and CiCi and started to leave.

"Hey, Jenna," Yancy called just before she shut the door. "Do
you . . . can you stay? I have some stuff I, uh, wanted to talk to you
about."

Jenna glanced at Saleda. "You go ahead. I can call a cab."

Saleda nodded, doing a great job of holding in the smirk threatening to cross her face. Such a good acting job, Jenna was sure it
would fool maybe one person on earth. Wow.

Jenna shut the door behind Saleda and was suddenly standing
awkwardly in front of Yancy and CiCi. Based on their respective
positions in the room, if Jenna hadn't known better, the way Yancy
and CiCi stood on one side facing her, opposing her, seemed like the
couple who lived in this home, greeting a visitor.

CiCi glanced back and forth from Jenna to Yancy, something stir-
ring in her eyes. Comprehension? *Apprehension*? She couldn't place
it. Maybe she was tired, too.

"Well, I think I should probably get some rest, too," CiCi said hesitantly.

CiCi stared at Yancy for a strange, never-ending moment that seemed to hang in the air. Yancy's gaze remained fixed on Jenna, but the unsettled feeling of the few seconds made Jenna almost sure he knew CiCi was trying to get him to glance over.

Jenna shifted on her feet uncomfortably, the conversation with Ayana about lima bean colors and her thoughts of how, to her, it meant doubt surging forward. She couldn't help it. For two people with nothing between them, Yancy and CiCi had been found in an odd situation already, with Yancy at her home after Eldred's attack. And now, that look . . .

Trust him.

Finally CiCi tore her gaze from Yancy and turned and climbed the stairs where Eldred had disappeared minutes before.

Now Jenna stood facing Yancy, and what was usually the place she felt most comfortable—alone with the person who knew her best—suddenly seemed foreign and distressing.

As though he sensed what she was feeling, he took a step toward her, closing the ocean between them ever so slightly. "I'm glad you stayed."

A surge of affection rushed her as she caught that familiar look in his eyes. It was the same one she saw there every time he dropped his corny leg jokes that were his go-to whenever he felt self-conscious. He probably didn't even realize when he let down that guard, but when he didn't crack the jokes was when she knew she was with just him at his most honest. His most comfortable.

"Me, too," she said.

He gave her a sad smile. "Not to mention, you're stranded. Maybe you should stay-stay." He wiggled his eyebrows feebly. "I can push Oboe over in the bed so you'd have some room . . ."

"I really shouldn't," she said, though every fiber in her wanted to. She missed Ayana and her dad and Charley, but she missed Yancy, too. Ayana would already be in bed, and Jenna would have to leave the house before she was awake in the morning. Charley would be up just in time to give her grief about it, and even if Dad didn't say anything to her face, she'd see his silent disapproval.

"What if I promise to let you sleep on the non-nub side?" Yancy said.

She grinned. "You know, what you lack in tibias, you make up for in sense of humor."

His halfhearted smile turned to an actual beam. "What can I say? Adversity gives you a leg up."

Jenna laughed. This was the very thing she'd first fallen in love with. "Well played, sir. How could a girl say no?"

Yancy fought to set the water dish he'd just filled in front of Oboe, the dachshund's sharp little nails scratching his good leg as the dog jumped on him. "Cool it, dude. This'll be infinitely easier if you let me put it *down* first. Jenna, you didn't happen to throw his nail clippers in that bag while you were at it, did you?"

"Nope," Jenna said from where she was busy rifling through the bag of essentials she'd been thoughtful enough to pick up for him while she was retrieving the little wiener. "I didn't bring any pajama pants for you, either. I must've forgotten them in my hurry. I know, because I was planning to steal them."

Stealing is a petty crime compared to what your awesome boyfriend's been up to.

"Boxers?" he asked.

"Oh, don't worry," she said. "Those were my next option."

The sound of Oboe's lapping filled the room as Yancy sat on the bed and watched Jenna shuck the black slacks she wore, her plain white bikini briefs peeking from underneath where her previously tucked-in shirt fell long over her hips. In the seconds between then and her pulling on the green plaid boxers, he could just glimpse the smooth curves of where her thigh rounded into her butt. God, he'd been lucky enough to see this every day for months now, a common little moment so ordinary and so private at the same time.

You've really fucked up this time.

He'd asked her to stay with every intention of telling her everything—about the pimp, about the gunshot . . . about getting rid of a body. As much as he wanted to protect her, when he'd seen her face tonight all he'd been able to think was how he just couldn't keep something from her. Not this.

And yet, every time he'd tried to start, something had come up. Important shit, like suddenly noticing that bald patch on Oboe's butt he needed to check out, or Oboe's near-fatal thirst. It was all that little asshole's fault.

Just man up and tell her, cool guy.

Now Jenna's fingers moved down her blouse, unfastening buttons one by one. The mounds of her breasts over her sensible bra peeked out of the slit that opened at the third button. Damn, this woman could rock some boring undergarments . . .

No, sir. You will not be thinking about doing this in a house where you fucking killed someone, then accidentally checked out another woman. You're already going to hell. If you do anything but tell her this shit in this house, you're going to hell in place of *a certain dead pimp.*

Jenna, however, was oblivious to the personal purgatory he was going through, because she was now picking up the line of conversation she'd been on when his previous guilt trip had culminated in an urgent trip to find Oboe a water bowl.

"Even if Molly's our only hope for unclogging Eldred's memory, and even if she's well-adjusted enough that she'll handle it perfectly, I can't help but feel sick that I keep exposing her to reminders of something as violent and evil as the grocery store shooting," she said.

Yancy ripped his gaze from where the shirt now fell open to reveal her chest and stomach. "I know what you mean, but you've gotta think the kid's gonna be seeing mental images of that scene the rest of her life either way. Bad as it sounds, might as well let her reminisce with other people and help. Better than doing it alone in her room at night."

His distraction lapsed, and he turned back toward her. She was now in just the bra and boxers and was combing her long chestnut hair into a messy ponytail.

He'd been wrong. Lying to her wasn't the torture. Not being able to walk over and pull her onto the bed with him *because* he was lying was.

God, he needed to think. Clear his head.

Get up his nerve.

He jumped up. "I'm gonna hop in the shower while you're here to keep watch. If anybody comes while I'm gone, just throw Oboe at 'em to buy time."

Sure, tough guy. Sell out your best friend. Why not? You're already on a roll. It's the next logical step.

"Sure thing," Jenna said, too concerned with locating a T-shirt in his bag to look his way.

He moved into the bathroom and, without looking back at Jenna, disrobed and carefully stepped into the shower. As he turned to run the water, he caught a glimpse of Jenna slipping a second arm out of the remaining bra strap and rotating the lace toward her front the way she always did to unfasten it. Her bare back was so perfect he could just feel his fingertips running down her spine, brushing where the small of her back curved gently at the waistband of his own boxers.

Shit, son.

He pulled the shower curtain closed.

Jenna held the soft, worn T-shirt bearing +1 SHIRT OF SMITING. Yancy hadn't played his computer role-playing games nearly as much since they'd started seeing each other, she knew. But now, as she stood half-naked in another woman's guest room and looked down at the shirt, a nagging thought bit the back of her mind.

What if when he said he was RPing, he wasn't?

She blinked rapidly, forcing away the tear forming in the corner of her eye.

Ridiculous. He works and sees you and Oboe. That's it.

Jenna clenched the shirt in her fists.

"Hey, Yance?"

The running water of the shower pelted the bottom of the tub, pausing and restarting presumably depending on Yancy's movements.

"Yeah?" he replied.

She closed her eyes. "Why were you at her house?"

Her heart sped up as she waited for the reply, every inch of her body tensing. *Please, let him have a good reason.*

An eternal pause.

"It's a long story," he called from the shower.

Red anger flashed in. "You do realize that's a cop-out, don't you?"

Silence again.

She perched on the end of the bed and watched Oboe continue to lick at the long-empty bowl. She waited, listening to the water run.

Just when Jenna thought her entire head might explode, Yancy spoke again.

"Jenna, I know there's a lot that looks so wrong about all of this, but it's one reason I wanted you to stay tonight. I . . ."

Water.

"I got too involved, I know. It's just . . . with us being apart so much and you starting back at the Bureau, I've . . . well, I've been . . . God, it's so fucked up," he said, pain oozing from his tone.

Jenna looked down at her bare knees. She'd neglected a lot lately, and apparently picking up a new pack of disposable razors was included on the list of those things she'd put off. If she'd gotten so busy with her job that she had let her prickly knees languish, she could only begin to imagine how Yancy was feeling. Their argument over the phone that day he was at work flooded back to her, her harsh words reaming him for not having self-control echoing in her mind.

"I . . . I wanted to be useful, Jenna. I know how that sounds, believe me, but . . . oh, God, this is hard to explain . . ."

She hung her head, memories of her own lack of self-control

pummeling her. She'd once driven to a prosecutor's home to do nothing but tell him off, and Yancy had sat in the car, waiting for her. Not judging her, but *waiting* for her. She'd already taken this man who'd helped her so much and ripped him from his place as her teammate in the field, and now, she was making him feel guilty for being the very thing she was when her emotions reeled.

Hypocrite.

"I didn't mean to . . . I just sort of found myself wandering over here that day after the nine-one-one call, and after that, things . . . oh, God . . . I just felt like she needed me for some reason, you know? Not in any way like *that* . . . God, please don't think that . . . but I just . . . I needed to *do* something . . ."

Without thinking, Jenna stood up. *Claudia screwed up so much of my life. Because of her, I haven't trusted people who don't happen to share blood with me and aren't named Claudia. For so long. I've lived my whole life without trusting anyone, damn it!*

Until Yancy.

"Me being here, Jenna . . . it's never been about anything like what it must look like, I swear . . . but then, she called into work so many times, and things just got confused. And I felt like it was my job . . . oh man . . ."

Fuck you, Claudia.

Jenna brushed the shower curtain back. Yancy turned from the spray, surprised by the noise.

"What're you—"

Jenna cut him off by leaning into the shower and pressing her lips hard into his. She drank greedily, relishing in their softness. He tasted so good.

He tasted like home.

Yancy kissed her back furiously, something in him just as needy as she was. His arms wrapped around her waist, a current pulling her in the direction it had already felt so easy to go. She stepped into him, into the shower, boxers and all.

She pressed her hands into his chest, pushing him away so she could slip the underwear off. He gave in to the pressure reluctantly, but the pause didn't last long. She slid the boxers from her ankle just in time for his lips to dip to the base of her neck. She tossed the shorts onto the bathroom floor, then pulled his head to her.

His hands roved her body, and in the next instant, he'd whirled them around so she was under the spray. Her balance thrown, she took in a sharp breath as her shin knocked his leg.

He lifted his head, met her eyes.

"Sorry," he said. "Reflex. You were cold. Androids are immune to cool air."

She held his face in both hands, staring into him. "You know, if you didn't mention the leg so much, I wouldn't even notice anymore," she said truthfully.

He gazed back at her, hands by his sides, his breathing heavy. His face was so serious, she couldn't tell if the statement about that thing they never talked about except in joking had been right or wrong.

"Except that I bruise easy, and I think I have shrapnel lodged in some weird places from times like this," she threw in, feeling tears springing to her eyes.

Please, don't be over. I need this. I need you.

Yancy's jaw set in a line, his chest heaving for a long ten seconds as the water beat down on them. Jenna was vaguely aware of the beads forming on his face and chest as she held his eyes, willing him not to look away.

Then his hands gripped her thighs, hard, right under her butt, and she felt her feet leave the floor. Instinctively, she wrapped her legs around his waist, clung to his neck for dear life as they rotated sideways. Her back met the tile, and she pushed against it to give leverage as she let go with one arm.

She reached down, taking him into her hand, and guided him inside her. With one delicious thrust, she gasped as she felt every bit of him. He kissed her as he bucked his hips into her, water streaming on the left side of her face and into her mouth, mingling with their kisses. Her hand dug into his shoulders to push herself harder against the wall as he filled her over and over.

She pulled back from his hungry kisses, her climax building closer and closer, so intense she could barely catch her breath without more air. The steam had expanded to nearly suffocating, but air was a small price to pay for the surge of pleasure swelling inside her.

Yancy clutched her legs tighter as he thrust faster, moaning louder and louder with every push. "Jenna . . ."

Every muscle tensed, and she squeezed his frame with her legs. The wave of bliss crashed over her, ripples coursing through her body. "Yance . . . I'm so . . . sorry . . ."

His thrusts grew more urgent, his breaths becoming grunts as they varied in depth with what she could tell was his own desire, his sensitive places, everywhere he wanted to touch inside her. With a final thrust that smacked her tailbone into the wall, he climaxed, a loud groan to echo his release.

It was only after both of their gasps had slowed that Jenna realized the previously scalding water had turned lukewarm. Her legs shook from maintaining the position, and she was suddenly just very, very tired.

Yancy's head dropped to his chest, showing her he was equally spent, but he seemed to be jarred back to the reality of their super-human stance at almost the same moment. He looked up at her and blinked water out of his eyes.

"I would brush it away for you, but if I let go, we'd probably be in trouble," she said, grinning.

"Yeah," he breathed. "We better disengage. I might rust."

He lowered her to the floor, and she felt him slip out of her. Disappointment washed over her as she felt the sudden, stark reality of being a separate person from him once more.

Why the hell had she ever thought Ayana's green could've meant doubt?

44

The next morning, Jenna rolled over onto her other side, the feather pillow beneath her head squishing and making her head sink. It took her a minute to remember she was at CiCi Winthrop's house—with Yancy.

Yancy sat in a straight-backed chair across the room and was staring out the window. She wondered if he was thinking about their sex in the shower last night the way she was at the moment, and if he, too, was hoping for a replay.

Jenna's phone vibrated on the nightstand. She groaned and reached for it. Saleda.

"Time to hit the trail, I'm guessing?" she said, all hopes of an encore performance for her and Yancy dissolving in the air around her.

"Yeah. Raine Tyler just called. Liam left for work, so you can drop by in about an hour. I have some things to tie up here, but I'm sending backup just in case," Saleda replied.

"Please not Dodd," she blurted before she could think. It wasn't that he was an awful guy, but his last run-in with the Tyler family had gone less than stellar. Jenna's life would be easier if they could avoid any unnecessary temper flares or sparring matches.

"Couldn't send him if I wanted to," Saleda said. "He had to catch an early flight to Chicago. Let's just say this might very well turn out to be *the* worst day of Dodd's damned life."

Jenna drew her neck back. "Ooh, that sounds bad. What's going on?"

"Agent's worst nightmare. You know how they were moving the guy Dodd caught and saw convicted for the Cobbler murders to a mental institution?"

"Yeah. Dodd was less than thrilled, but that doesn't exactly seem like an agent's nastiest moment. We've all had stuff like that get turned over on us—"

Saleda cut Jenna off. "Not quite like this one, Doc. The Cobbler made it to his new home with the padded walls all right, but when he got there, one of the orderlies recognized Feagin McKye from *another* facility she used to work at."

"Oh, boy," Jenna said. "I feel a headache coming on."

"Yep. I could give you a few guesses, but you're only gonna need one. So I'll spoil it for you," Saleda replied. "According to this orderly, Feagin McKye was held as an inpatient under twenty-four/seven suicide watch in the famous fish bowl they used to house and observe schizophrenics off their meds. He was there for three days. The same three days the kidnapping, killing, and dismemberment of the third Cobbler victim took place."

"Holy shit," Jenna mumbled. "How the hell is this just *now* coming to light? Shouldn't this have been found out during the trial?"

"Heh. That's the best part. Apparently, at this hospital where the orderly saw him, he was checked into the psych ward involuntarily through the emergency room. He was in the emergency room because he'd been found sitting outside a 7-Eleven literally ripping out chunks of his own hair and screaming about being on fire. Somebody called nine-one-one, and he was taken to the ER to be evaluated. He went through triage and signed in as Bunky Ross. Had an ID for Bunky Ross, too. So no one had any reason to think he wasn't Bunky Ross."

"Well, now that we *do* have reason to think he *isn't* Bunky Ross . . . well, who the hell is Bunky Ross?" Jenna shot back.

"His younger brother. Stepdad adopted him, so his last name's different," Saleda said. She chuckled. "If that nurse hadn't transferred when she did and seen him today, the staff at that hospital would've probably gone on forever not knowing it wasn't Bunky Ross they had over there all that time."

"Good grief." Jenna sighed. "That's just not even . . . Ugh! I don't know what to say, but the idea of the whole thing gives me the chills. Shit!"

If the third victim was killed while Feagin McKye was in lockdown as Bunky Ross, there was no way he was the Cobbler.

"Shit's right," Saleda replied. "Dodd's been called up there to do a lot of explaining and clean up some really serious messes, not to mention probably grieve the loss of what he thought was an open and shut case."

Jenna shook her head in disbelief. "Should've been. They had evidence. Feet, for Christ's sake."

"What they had was a really fucked up framing," Saleda said. "But as much as we might want to help Dodd, we have to keep our eye on the prize. Porter'll meet you about quarter 'til nine to talk to Molly Keegan. Let's see what you can get out of ol' Eldred today, shall we? Good luck."

With that, Jenna hung up the phone. Time to put her game face on.

"I take it that means no breakfast?" Yancy said as Jenna stood and grabbed her dirty slacks from the previous night.

"Nope, though if CiCi has a coffeemaker, I wouldn't say no to a cup."

"We're going to them and not bringing her here? Don't you think Eldred would be more likely to remember things in a place where he's familiar with the surroundings?" Yancy said.

"True," Jenna answered, hesitant. She wasn't a fan of the thought of taking an Alzheimer's patient to a brand new place he didn't know to try to jog his memory, either, but she knew that ethically, it was safer for Molly. "Normally I'd bring her here in a heartbeat, given Eldred's circumstances, but if the UNSUBs know where he is or has been, I'd rather be cautious about taking Molly anywhere she might be seen in connection with this case. Someone could follow us to her home, maybe, but it's likely we'd see that coming and react. If this house or Eldred's place is already being watched somehow, having Molly show up here would be like waving a sign telling the UNSUBs we have a theory that she was the target for some reason. I need to use Molly, but I don't want to flash it around any more than I have to."

Yancy nodded. "Makes sense, though I seriously hope no one's watching this place. You really think this little girl can help Eldred tell us something about the shootings?" he asked.

Jenna buttoned her pants, unable to stop thinking about how CiCi probably didn't yet know she'd spent the night in her home. Maybe CiCi would surprise her and be totally cool about the whole thing, but if it were Jenna's house, the realization a stranger was there would feel like some sort of violation. Never mind what they'd done in her shower . . .

Then again, Jenna was more sensitive than most about things like that.

Liam Tyler's face the day he'd walked into his office while she and Molly had been chatting flashed into her mind. Maybe it *wasn't* just her.

She smiled, remembering the strange conversation full of numbers and facts about numbers that Molly had stuffed up in her head. So many details for someone so small. Jenna had only fleetingly considered what it was inside Molly's head that caused the little girl's intense preoccupation with numbers. After all, Jenna was all too used to people trying to label what it was she did, too. When everything had first come out about how her color associations helped expose Claudia's crimes, scientists had seemed to come out of the woodwork to give interviews to news show talking heads about their theories on the brain mechanisms that might cause synesthesia. None had proven certainties even today. Molly's interest and propensity for number memory offered a few suggestions that might be more tangible, but without brain scans and lots of other gratuitous testing, they'd probably never know. Jenna was just fine with that. In her mind, why Molly did what she did didn't matter. The only label Jenna needed for her was "amazing"; after all, Molly could do things she'd never been able to. Jenna had associated colors with feelings and people since she could remember, but at Molly's age, she probably couldn't have explained to anyone how her brain worked to process the associations. She still couldn't most of the time. Heck, at that point in her life, she wasn't even sure she'd noticed she made the associations in the first place.

Molly knew a lot of numbers, but she also somehow possessed a gift for putting people at ease. She wondered if Molly was aware yet of how unique she was.

The royal purple she had seen in conjunction with Molly flashed in. Seven, always considered the most magical number. Seven Wonders of the World. Triple sevens in slots made a winner. A lucky number. The seventh day finished off the week, a sacred number.

Maybe one day, when the danger had passed and the little girl's color association with a number was no longer quite so scary because the Triple Shooter had long since been caught and thrown in jail, she could have this conversation with Molly. For whatever reason, she knew Molly would like it.

Seven pillars of wisdom in Proverbs made it a number of understanding. Sevens in numerology were the thinkers . . . seekers of the truth. She'd always seen seven in the same family as problem-solving Tyrian purple, a shade fixed in Jenna's mind as one close to ripe red grapes. It was a number of solutions.

Purple, the seventh color of the rainbow. A number of completion.

"All I know is, I think somehow she'll put something together for Eldred we can't."

45

Molly was excited. She couldn't help it. She'd been trusted with a mission, and she knew she could do it.

She sat with the crayons and paper Dr. Ramey had laid in front of her on the kitchen table, next to Mr. Beasley, the man from the grocery store. She'd asked him to color with her, just like Dr. Ramey said. She chose a dark golden yellow, and she drew tiny circles on the bottom of the sheet, thinking of the secret Dr. Ramey had told her and what she needed her to help with. Dr. Ramey hadn't told her how to help, other than giving her the paper, but she knew it was because Dr. Ramey trusted her. Way more than other people trusted kids. That was why she wouldn't let Dr. Ramey down.

Next to her, Mr. Beasley used a gray crayon to color in a very good cat he'd done. Maybe he was an artist before he forgot how to be. She'd have to ask him later. But for now, she needed to focus on her own picture.

She picked up a brown and drew a big rectangle. The one Mr. Beasley had sat behind in the grocery store.

"Mr. Beasley, do you remember when we were at the grocery store and all the loud noises happened?" she asked.

She didn't stop coloring, but only because she felt like she shouldn't. It would make him nervous, she thought. She didn't like it when other people looked at her drawings before they were finished, either.

"Grocery store," he muttered. "Yes, I think I remember that."

She doodled different boxes on the shelves. She wrote "Fruit Loops" on one, even though her words didn't fit inside the lines. "When you saw me there, were you afraid?"

It was a personal question, she knew, and she was a little sorry for asking it out loud with other people watching. She wasn't sure what to say. So she just decided to talk to him about it, and it was what she really did wonder. But she'd been afraid, so it was okay with her if he was.

He put down the gray crayon and selected a pink. He drew in the cat's nose. "I was a bit. Yes."

Despite knowing she shouldn't, she pointed to where the cat's tail should be. "He doesn't have a tail yet."

Mr. Beasley looked at her and nodded. "My cat Mobley didn't have a tail, either."

Molly cocked her head. She'd never seen a cat without a tail.

"Was he born that way?"

Mr. Beasley shrugged. "Dunno. He took up at our house. He was like that since I knew him, though."

Molly nodded. That made sense.

"Was he a nice cat?"

Mr. Beasley drew in red curtains on the window Mobley sat in front of. "I liked him."

"Where is he now?" Molly asked.

"Oh, he died. Long time ago. He was mine when I was little," he said.

Feeling like she'd intruded a lot, Molly picked up a red and drew some splotches on the floor. "Like the people in the grocery store?"

Mr. Beasley shook his head, now drawing a chair beside Mobley. "No. He just died one day. By himself."

"Yeah," Molly said, sadness pooling up in her stomach in a way that made her feel a little like throwing up. G-Ma hadn't died by herself at all. That was why Dr. Ramey wanted her to talk to Mr. Beasley. Because when she had talked to him before, he'd remembered something that might help catch who hurt G-Ma, but now he'd forgotten it again. "That was scary. I remember when I heard the pops and went to hide. Then it got quiet again, and I came to your aisle."

Mr. Beasley stopped coloring. He scrunched his forehead, looking confused. Then he looked up, and his eyes stared far away.

"Yes," he mumbled.

He picked up a black crayon, and in the middle of the picture of his living room with his cat, he started to sketch something that didn't make sense in the rest of the drawing to Molly. She didn't know if she had upset him, because his coloring had gotten faster, but her stomach tickled. The look on his face reminded her of Pop-Pop's when he couldn't find his keys but needed to in a hurry.

And somehow she knew right now that she should be very, very quiet.

Eldred scribbled as fast as he could, so afraid of the thought slipping away again. The picture, the one that had nudged him so many times but slid away before he could grab hold of it, was finally there again.

The little girl had been in the row, and the man in the mask had arrived. He had raised his gun to shoot . . . her.

Eldred hadn't been able to look away. The big black weapon had pointed past him, and as he'd stared, too frozen and terrified to do anything else, the man's shirt had lifted with the raising of his arms.

The man's side had been white, like the rest of his own skin, but something strange and black snaked there. Eldred's picture wouldn't be nearly as ornate and detailed as the image was in real life, but he needed to tell people about it before it went away.

He drew, faster and faster, muttering under his breath. "Looked like it was real, almost like an extra body part . . ."

Eldred pointed at the sides of his sketch, and the little girl leaned in to look closer.

"See here?" he said, hoping she'd understand. She would. He knew she would. "The edges around here were so light it somehow made it look like it grew out of his skin . . . then it got darker here, and the further in, the more it was like a picture on TV or in a movie. So clear. Lots of different colors really close to each other, but all dark and nearly the same."

Why did he know that? He'd been too far away to see that kind of detail, and yet . . .

"Looked like it grew from him," he repeated, trying to think of even better words that matched what he'd seen, since that didn't quite describe it. "Or like it had ripped through his skin and was what was underneath all along."

He picked up the red crayon, added some gentle streaks around the picture the way they had been, then some pinks of different colors, all the while lamenting his inability to draw it just so.

Eldred closed his eyes, trying to access any other specifics he could about the picture. Tears stung his eyes, the image slipping.

He felt something warm close over his hand, and he opened his eyes again.

Tiny fingers clasped around his hand where he still held the crayon poised to the paper.

"It's okay, Mr. Beasley. You did a good job."

J enna stared wide-eyed as Molly took the paper from Eldred Beasley and sauntered over from the kitchen table. She'd arranged to have Eldred brought to Molly to do this, but even she hadn't been sure how the little girl would manage it or what they were trying to get from Eldred's memory. But lo and behold, they'd watched as she'd brilliantly extracted a drawing of the three-headed dragon tattoo, the piece of the puzzle Eldred had seemed to lose over and over again.

"Can we give this kid a job?" Porter said out of the corner of his mouth so Raine Tyler, who was folding laundry a few feet away, wouldn't hear.

"I wish," Jenna said truthfully. Who knew? Maybe the kid had a career in psychology one day.

"Unreal," Yancy echoed.

CiCi stood next to him, silent, her mouth hanging open.

"Here you go," Molly said, handing the paper over to Jenna. She repeated everything to them Eldred had told her, though they'd been close enough to listen in.

"Molly, you're amazing," Jenna said, accepting the picture. No truer words had ever been spoken. "Thank you."

"No problem," Molly said. "I like coloring."

"Me, too," Jenna replied.

Molly shifted from side to side, and it seemed like she wanted to say something else. Weird. Usually, the little girl spat out whatever came into her head.

"What's up, Molly?" Jenna asked.

"Um, it's just . . ." She looked at CiCi. "Would you mind if maybe Eldred came over sometimes? I think . . . I think he needs it."

Jenna couldn't help the smile that stretched over her face. The kid had it. Whatever "it" was.

"I'll talk to your mom about it, okay?" CiCi said.

Molly nodded, then scampered back over to the table to color some more.

"So, random tattoo. Where do we go next?" Jenna wondered out loud.

"Case the tattoo parlors in town? Though he could've gotten it anywhere," Yancy said.

"Surely there's a better place to start than the Yellow Pages," Jenna said. "People with ink are really into their art. From what Eldred described, this thing is pretty intricate. Surely we know someone with tats who can tell us some of the best artists in town we could run this by. The Triple Shooter's murders are all within a certain radius. He wouldn't go states away just for the tattoo, right?"

"Not a clue. Irv might have one, though," Porter filled in. "Irv has tattoos."

Porter was right. Their technical analyst had a sleeve of them, and he was back at the next stop they needed to make anyway.

"Yancy, will you guys be okay to head home without us?" Jenna asked, catching her boyfriend's eye. She knew he would be fine, but she wanted to acknowledge how much she hated leaving him. She wished he could come with them, just be a part of the team.

He nodded, and something mischievous flashed in his eyes. "Get back to headquarters, Dr. Ramey. You've got a tattoo artist to find."

. . .

The second they walked in the door, Saleda didn't give Jenna a chance to speak.

"You were right. Sevens in all of the other Triple Shooter murders. Based on the time she left the restaurant where the takeout receipt came from, the shooter saw the threes line up around Wendy Ulrich right around seven p.m. Victim two, Maitlyn O'Meara, was found off of Exit 7B. Ainsley Nickerson's birthdate was, get this, seven, seven, nineteen seventy-seven."

The news of the tattoo died on Jenna's lips with the surprise. "How would he know her birthday if he just happened to see threes align by chance?"

Saleda shook her head. "We're working on that. But he had to have either known her or come across it. Too big a coincidence. Still haven't found the seven connection with Brooklyn Satterhorne, but I'm guessing it's only a matter of time. And no luck with finding anyone or anything that appears in both the Student Life Center courtyard surveillance *and* the bank surveillance, unfortunately. No creepers stalking Pesha Josephy in the bank footage, either. Though we did find Pesha's other three. She made her deposit that day with the teller at station number three."

Of course she had. Good grief. Before this case, Jenna wouldn't have thought the ways a trio of the number three could manifest in everyday life would be this numerous *or* this varied. But then again, before this case, why would she? The Triple Shooter was set off by a combination of variables that most people wouldn't even ever notice.

"Is it just me, or do you guys now find yourselves intentionally avoiding that integer in all facets of life, too?" Teva said. "I almost jumped out of my skin this morning when I got out of my car to fill up my gas tank and noticed I was parked at pump three. Jumped in the car and moved one over. Stupid, but I couldn't help myself."

Saleda laughed. "Not just you. I added an extra topping to the pizza I ordered yesterday solely to make sure the toppings didn't add up to the bastard's favorite number, because God knows I've got plenty of sins under my belt for him to punish me for if I catch his eye." She looked to Jenna. "How'd it go with half-pint and Methuselah?"

Jenna glanced around the room. "Where's Irv?"

Teva pointed toward the door to the side office Irv often inhabited. "In his Irv Cave."

Without answering Saleda, Jenna pushed past and into the office.

Irv looked up from where he was frantically pecking away at the keyboard in front of several monitors. "I'm looking for seventh heaven around Brooklyn as fast as my fingers can fly, but unfortunately she was born in May—"

"I don't need Brooklyn's birthday or astrological sign or bingo score—"

"She was a college student. I doubt she played bingo," Irv cut in.

"Whatever," Jenna replied. "I need to pick your brain about a tattoo."

"Better than my nose."

She took the picture Eldred drew out of her pocket and unfolded it. She laid it in front of the tech analyst.

"Whoever did this tattoo charged too much—"

"This was drawn by the Alzheimer's patient who witnessed the grocery store killings," Jenna said. She gave all of the details Eldred had conveyed that he couldn't show in the drawing, like the tiny variances in colors and the appearance of the dragon ripping through the man's skin on his side. "The Triple Shooter lives or at least spends a lot of his time around here. Granted, he might've grown up thousands of miles away, but unless his parents were into finding tattoo parlors that liked to illegally ink minors, I'm pretty sure he didn't get that massive dragon tat until his adult years."

"Yeah and it had to be pretty recent to still come across so well. If he'd had it done when he was super young, his skin would've changed, even if just slightly, enough to affect the look of a tat designed to have that kind of 3-D effect," Irv said, swirling in his chair.

"Right. So where around here would he have had something of that caliber done?"

Irv frowned. "He wouldn't have, necessarily. People will go way out of their way to get a tat they want, or if he needed privacy, there are some people who will travel to them. No hard and fast rules . . ."

"And no one who specializes in dragons?" Jenna asked.

Irv leaned back and crossed his arms. "I wouldn't bark up the specific graphic preferences tree. It more often depends on what the client is looking for in quality or fine points of the design they're seeking. I'd focus in more on the detailing. The shading skill involved in the effect you're describing gives you a loose profile of the artist who had to have done it. I know I'm the guy behind the desk and not the biggest profiling professional in this room, but I know enough about the world to tell you that much. If you're looking in this area for who could've done something that takes that sort of skill, there's only one place anywhere near us that could. I'd go to Glory."

47

Yancy sat in Raine Tyler's living room with CiCi and the very quiet Raine. They'd decided to wait a little longer before dragging Eldred home. He didn't get out much as it was, and he seemed to be enjoying himself in the kitchen with Molly, so they'd left them to it for now. Raine was okay with it, she said. She seemed happy enough with just having some company. Yancy wondered if her mother had lived with them before she died.

They sat around in silence, watching the television play through an old episode of *The Andy Griffith Show* that none of them laughed at. God, what it must be like to be a child in this home . . .

As the familiar whistle of the theme song sent them into the credits, Molly meandered into the living room. She stopped as she came closer to the couch and stared at them all, confused.

"Where's Mr. Beasley?" she asked idly.

Yancy looked at CiCi, then jumped up, his body in overdrive. *Oh, no . . . oh, no, no, no . . .*

He ran into the kitchen. Eldred's chair was painfully empty, the coloring paper still at its place where Eldred had been working on it moments before. He ran back to the living room.

"Molly, where did he go?"

Molly blinked at him like he was stupid. "I don't know," she shrugged. "That's why I asked. I went to the bathroom, and when I came back, he was gone. I thought he came in here."

Shit.

Yancy ran back to the kitchen, CiCi on his heels and cussing.

He glanced around the room. Nothing. He went to all the doors to the other rooms inside the house, looked out the windows. No sign.

Something caught his vision at the front door.

A smear of blood on the doorframe.

Oh, God, please no . . .

He reached to his leg and in a second had the gun out. He'd promised Jenna not to use it unless someone tried to take Eldred. The hairs on Yancy's arms prickled. What if this was that moment . . .

"CiCi, call nine-one-one," he said, pushing the door open. He realized uncomfortably that it was loose, like it hadn't quite been pushed closed all the way.

"Oh, my God, Yancy . . ."

"Do it!"

He rushed out the door.

"Whoa, whoa. Slow down," Jenna said. She could hardly understand Yancy's frantic words. It sounded like he was running.

"Eldred is gone. Jenna, I . . . I think someone took him," he panted.

"What? Why do you think that?"

He huffed harder. Yes, he was running.

"Molly went to the bathroom, and when she came back, he was gone. There's blood on the doorjamb. It looks like he might've been dragged . . ."

Jenna's mind reeled like the spin of the SUV's tires on the freeway. "Did you see a car?"

If this was UNSUB B coming back for Eldred, he couldn't have made it far lugging an unconscious grown man anywhere on foot.

"No, no, I didn't," he said.

Through the phone she could make out the sounds of cars in the background, sirens.

"Which door?"

"Front," he said. "It was ajar. I didn't see a vehicle, but I have no idea how long Molly was in the bathroom. They could've made off before we even knew they were gone."

"Ask her," Jenna blurted, frustrated.

"I can't," he said. "She's at the house. I'm . . . well, I'm looking . . ."

"Yancy, I doubt someone came in and took him without you guys hearing *anything*," she said.

The whoosh of air that had been passing over his phone as he moved around stopped. *He must be standing still.*

"Jenna, stealth exists. I mean, what if this person has some kind of training . . ."

His voice trailed off, hesitant.

A salmon color she couldn't readily place flashed in, but she shoved it back. She'd worry about that later.

"I hear sirens, so I'm guessing you already called help. Right?" she asked, just making sure.

"Yeah, yeah, but, Jenna, we have to find him!" he said, panicked.

The salmon flashed in again.

"We're going to. Stay put, and tell the cops everything you can when they show up. I'll call Victor in case there's anything you *can't* tell them," she said, thinking vaguely of Yancy previously not wanting the local cops involved where Eldred was concerned. "He might've just wandered off. Not that we don't need to find him either way, but people with Alzheimer's do that, you know."

"But, Jenna, the blood—"

"I know," she said, her heart racing. If UNSUB B knew to come and *get* Eldred at Molly Keegan's house, it would mean UNSUB B had been following them all along . . .

None of this made sense. God, what she'd give to be able to run this by Dodd. When the hell would he get back from Chicago anyway?

Surely they wouldn't keep him away from this important of a case indefinitely. His being gone left the team shorthanded *and* short-minded. In the BAU, minds were everything.

Jenna's brain tried to tease out what reason the second UNSUB could possibly have for going after Eldred. He couldn't exactly silence him. Not anymore. They already had what they needed from Eldred.

Then again, UNSUB B wouldn't know that. They had to find the second UNSUB, and fast.

And to do that, they had to find the first UNSUB.

"Keep looking. Whatever you do, make the responders understand this is no normal missing person, and they have to search even if he hasn't been gone long. If UNSUB B took Eldred from the house, he couldn't have gone far. As long as they close the net, they'll keep both Eldred and UNSUB B in it," Jenna said, feeling the looks from the other team members.

"Jenna, what if I've screwed this up worse than anything I've ever done—"

"Don't," she cut him off. Then, before she could stop herself, "I know you, Yance. You can find him." She should let the other cops handle it, but right now, she knew Yancy was there and she wasn't.

"Jenna—"

"Go. I'm sending Victor. I have to find the Triple Shooter."

48

Walking into Glory was like entering a strange combination of an art gallery and a dentist's office. The dark brick walls of the open, cement-floored space were plastered with abstract paintings, and some of the countertops could pass for wet bars in a different context. As it was, they were covered in spray bottles and canisters of cotton balls. Black lounge-style chairs were set every few feet like stations in a hair salon, but the buzzes of the equipment sounded more like dental drills than blow-dryers.

"Welcome to Glory," a brunette with streaks of dark burgundy through her pigtails said. "Do you have an appointment?"

Jenna glanced around at the bustle throughout the studio. A girl with the strap of her tank top pulled down sat smiling as a guy with a shaved head inked her shoulder. A middle-aged man lay back perspiring as a girl with a messy blond ponytail worked at his wrist.

"Um, not exactly."

She pulled out her badge and she felt Porter do the same behind her. "We need some information about a certain tattoo. Specifically, whether or not someone here might've inked it."

The girl blinked, wide-eyed, at the badges. "Sure thing. Let me get Wren."

She walked away and disappeared behind a back curtain. Porter stepped toward the counter, flipped a page of the book of designs set out for perusal. "Did she say 'Wren'?"

Before Jenna could answer, a guy who could've passed for The Rock's brother stepped from behind the back curtain, the pigtailed girl following him.

"I'm Wren," he said, stretching out a hand. "I own the joint. How can I help?"

A little ashamed in the face of the brilliant work in the flip book in front of them, Jenna held out the modest drawing of Eldred's. She quickly explained the story behind it, then filled in the other specifics that weren't in the sketch, just as she had for Irv.

"We were told this was probably the only place around with artists who could pull off those sorts of colors and details," she said, hopeful.

He held the drawing, studying it. "As much as I hate to say this, no one around here did this. We do mostly black-and-white stuff here. We're boss at cool shading. But while we do keep some colors on hand, like I said, we're almost only black-and-white. Any color access we keep is strictly to complement those black and whites in a very limited capacity. The variation you're talking about wouldn't be something we could pull off with our supplies."

"Color access?" Jenna repeated.

"Yeah. It's not particularly sanitary to mix ink colors, so a studio like this one is limited in color ink we have available. If the tat had a lot of subtle differences in colors like this guy said, the person commissioning it would need someone with skill *and* a massive assortment of colors."

The parlor owner's brow furrowed again. The raspberry color Jenna associated with recognition flashed in.

Wren gestured to the red and pink streaking Eldred had drawn to indicate the ripping effect the artist had tried to achieve. "I've seen this somewhere. A guy a couple towns over who does some specialty work turns out a lot of 3-D effects. I've sent people to him who've come in here wanting something in colors we didn't have. He's done some things like this."

Jenna's pulse picked up. They had to find the Triple Shooter now so that they could find the second UNSUB who was after Eldred. If UNSUB B had tried a second time to quiet the old man, at this point, he wouldn't stop.

"How do we find the guy?"

Jenna had called Saleda the second she and Porter had left Glory and Wren to tell her team leader they needed to get to Richmond. They could drive it, but flying would be quicker. The team had also sent field agents to Molly's house, despite Yancy's protests that he had it under control. She should've done it all along, damn it. Something about this whole thing didn't sit right. A pink-tinged orange color kept creeping into Jenna's psyche, but she pushed it away each time. It'd have to wait until after they talked to this tattoo artist.

As the chopper clipped high above the city, Jenna and Porter filled Saleda and Teva in on any details about Glory they hadn't heard yet. Jenna couldn't explain why, but she suddenly wanted to keep Saleda close by and up to speed. Her gut said this thing was about to break wide open, and when it did, her team leader needed to be on hand and ready to roll.

Once they were on the ground and had power walked the few blocks to the joint owned by the tattoo artist Wren had mentioned, Saleda pushed open the door. Jenna followed her in while Porter and Teva waited outside. Jax Hallenbrand's studio looked a lot less modern than Glory, and a lot less clean to boot.

The mohawked Jax looked at Eldred's picture for about ten seconds. "Yeah, I remember this. Guy was here for a good twelve hours. Normally I'd break that up into a few sessions, but he was traveling, so I told him I'd do it in a sitting."

Yes.

"Do you remember his name?" Saleda asked.

"Oh, God, no," Jax said, scratching the back of his neck. "That was a good while back. I don't forget a tattoo, but I can forget names plenty. As long as he paid me, I probably wouldn't have ever thought about him again if you hadn't come in."

Normal guy with nothing particularly extraordinary about him to make him stand out. Everyday customer, other than the out-of-town part.

Out of town.

"Did he drive here?" Jenna asked.

Jax stared at her for a moment like she was speaking a foreign language. Then he cocked his head.

"Come to think, yeah, I do remember that. It was the reason he couldn't come back for multiple sessions. Didn't have access to his own vehicle. He was on company time. Drove a big delivery truck. Some furniture place or something."

That'd explain how the Triple Shooter saw Ainsley Nickerson's address.

"Jax, we need the name of the company. Did you see the truck?"

The guy rubbed the nape of his neck again, a thinking tic. "Nah. I can't remember it. I'm sorry. It was so long ago . . . I'm talking months . . . maybe a year."

Fuck.

Saleda thanked him for his time. Jenna followed her toward the door, disappointment taking her over.

It's not over. It's just not easy.

She stopped just short of the glass door where she could see Porter and Teva lingering outside. "We know somewhere he's parked recently," Jenna muttered to Saleda.

Phone out, Jenna texted Irv:

Need video surveillance footage from Harford Suites the day of and leading up to Pesha Josephy's death. We're looking for a delivery truck.

She stuffed the phone back in her pocket, returning Saleda's nod of a job well done. Saleda pushed the door open, the bell on it jingling.

From behind them, Jax called out.

"By the way, if it makes a difference, it wasn't a dragon, exactly. It was more specific than that. He wanted a three-headed hydra."

49

The clip of the helicopter blades filled Jenna's ears, drowning out whatever it was her brain was trying to piece together. Something about the second UNSUB knowing where to find Eldred. The salmon in conjunction with the knowledge. She'd seen that color before, but it wasn't coming to her.

She'd called Victor to send him to the house of Molly Keegan and the Tylers, hoping he could sort out any mess there. She didn't know why she trusted him. For all the fighting she'd done with herself to realize she should trust Yancy, somehow the newfound confidence in the police officer had slipped in, unnoticed. Maybe it was because he was Hank's brother. Maybe it was because he was protective of Ayana. Either way, she couldn't question it right now. She wasn't on the ground, and he was all the help she had to send Yancy at the moment.

Her cell blinked.

"Aren't you supposed to turn that thing off in the air?" Porter yelled sarcastically.

"You know me. I'm a rebel," she called back, opening the text she'd left the phone on to receive.

It was from Irv, as expected.

Surveillance shows truck for Furniture Fast in the Harford Suites
parking lot the day of Pesha Josephy's murder. Cross-reference of
victims' names shows Ainsley Nickerson bought a living room set
there the week before she died.

Jenna wasn't shocked. She typed back:

Save the fanfare and give me a location so I can turn this bird around.

She alerted Saleda and the pilot to the current situation as she
awaited more from Irv.

"A furniture delivery? Why didn't we notice this until now? That
reeks of stranger danger," Saleda said.

Jenna wondered the same. She texted Irv to ask, her curiosity
getting the better of her.

He replied in about twenty seconds.

Knew you'd ask. We checked the employees on the delivery and
the sale. Squeaky clean. Guy wasn't listed anywhere near Ainsley
Nickerson, though he had to have seen her order somehow. But he
was the one driving the truck a few days ago when it was at the
Harford Suites. Tobias Gray. Oak Pointe subdivision, not too far
from our first victim's location.

Jenna typed a quick thank you, then called to the pilot.
"We're going to Alexandria."

H e heard them coming.
    Justice ran to the middle room, hands clapped over his ears.
He'd always expected them, and yet, he'd worked so hard to appease
them he'd hoped he'd never have to see them.

Now the itching bit through him so intensely he couldn't even
begin to try to scratch. He knew it was futile.

Instead he picked up his gun. Whether or not guns would work against them, he wouldn't know until he tried. Until this moment, he'd never dared oppose them, but now they'd come for him. It was the only way.

He sat in the middle of the room amidst the plethora of equipment he'd amassed for just this moment, fear gripping him. He had failed to do what the angel had said. Now he would pay.

They'd been cleared to land in a football field a street over from the house—practically in its backyard. No way he wouldn't hear them coming. So much for the element of surprise.

Backup from the locals was meeting them there. By the time they'd trekked through the fence of the school toward Tobias Gray's home, the barricade was already set up outside, and guns were drawn, trained on the single most bizarre picture Jenna had ever laid eyes on.

A small white house in the middle of a suburban block, completely lit up with Christmas lights covering every inch possible. The sun would still be up for hours, and yet the house glowed like a small planet plopped down in the center of the street.

"Well, that's something you don't see every day," Porter said.

"You know what they say about hiding in plain sight," Saleda replied.

"*That's* hiding?" Teva ventured.

Jenna moved faster. "Neighbors probably chalk him up to being that crazy guy next door and don't bother wondering if he really *is* crazy or not . . ."

What the hell?

They reached the barricade and were updated by the locals that the man inside had been screaming at them from the window. "Incoherent babble," said the officer in charge.

"What *kind* of incoherent babble?" Jenna asked. *It's probably not as incoherent as you think.*

"Something about creatures of darkness not taking him without a fight, begging 'them' for mercy, whoever *they* are . . . shit like that."

So Tobias Gray thought the Furies had come for him. Made sense now, the lights. Calliope Jones's words echoed in Jenna's mind: *"The three goddesses of vengeance, sometimes known as the Daughters of Night. It's a misnomer though. They were the children of Mother Earth, Gaea, and Uranus."*

The creatures were supposedly children of Night, and they were from Hades itself. Wouldn't be the first time this guy had believed whatever information he'd randomly learned about mythology. They'd established a while ago that he was an amateur enthusiast at best. In other words, the son of a bitch was scared out of his mind.

And more important, he wouldn't let them take him without a final battle. A problem, seeing as how they needed him alive in order to learn more about the other UNSUB.

"Let me go in and talk to him," Jenna blurted.

"Absolutely not," Saleda said. "He's barricaded himself inside his house while he's hearing voices, and he thinks we're them. He'll blow anyone coming within a few feet of him sky high. Reasoning with this guy isn't going to work, Jenna. You know that."

"Oh, come on. You *know* I'm the most qualified to talk to him, and the fastest way to the other UNSUB is through him. Besides, he believes what he's hearing is real. Law enforcement end up using force against mentally ill people all the time because they think they're more violent than they are. Most of them aren't."

"Jenna, with all due respect, we *know* this one's violent," Saleda said.

Touché.

"Okay, so let's use his own idea against him. Let's blind him from taking shots long enough for me to talk to him."

This had to be the worst idea she'd ever had.

Kevlar in place, Jenna walked toward the Triple Shooter's window, knowing explosives that would mean Ayana didn't have a father *or* a mother anymore might come next. This was stupid, but she had to do it. She had to find out who had put Molly Keegan's life in jeopardy.

It had taken about twenty minutes to get the strobe light here. If Tobias Gray was epileptic, this would go downhill fast.

She crouched beneath the windowsill and nodded to Porter at the switch. He hit it.

Electric lights flew through the afternoon air.

"Tobias, it's not who you're afraid of. Look at the window."

Silence.

Then a soft sound, like he was moving around inside.

"Who are you?"

The voice was right beside the window. *Shit.*

"I'm a friend, and I know about the Furies."

"You . . . *know?*"

Bingo.

Most people tried to talk schizophrenics out of their delusions. She'd rather talk him into them.

"Yes. I know, because they talk to me, too. They told me about . . . a little girl. In a grocery store not long ago. Did they tell you about her?"

Nothing.

Jenna hesitated, not wanting to push him too hard. She needed to say more though. Had to. "I haven't found her, but I'm looking for her. I'm afraid they won't be satisfied until I find her . . ."

When he spoke again, his voice was low, afraid. "That's why they're still mad at me. Why the itching won't stop, no matter how many heads I cut off of the evil. I didn't stop her, either."

Jenna took a deep breath. *Heads I cut off.* The hydra tattoo.

"Maybe I can stop her for both of us. The thing is . . ." Jenna said, thinking of the way Tobias had taken the visual cues from all of his victims to let him know they were bad. "I still haven't seen her do anything to confirm she's the one. Did you?"

Quiet again.

"I need to be sure I have the right person," Jenna said, trying to shove confidence through her tone even though she was shaking like a bikini-clad woman in the Arctic.

"I . . . I didn't, either," he said, nervousness seeping from his voice.

"But you tried to find her, right? How did you know it was her?" Jenna asked.

Moving again, maybe shifting in place. "An angel told me."

An angel? This was a curveball Jenna wasn't ready to respond to, but she had to keep talking. But what to say? The wrong thing could make this take a bad turn fast.

"What did the angel tell you?"

"You already know!" the Triple Shooter yelled, suddenly sounding angry. "Bad things happen then. The threes . . . and seven . . . and that day. Bad things happen that day."

"Which day?" Jenna asked, racking her brain for a connection.

"You . . . you told me you knew . . ."

Oh, fuck.

A fist smashed the glass from the other side of the window, and sharp shards rained down on Jenna. She covered her head, knowing what came next. *Please. Ayana.*

Shots from all directions popped loud in her ears as she planted herself as flat as she could get against the porch, arms wrapping around her head. Deafening, everything. Screaming. Yelling. Her name.

Something dropped above her. Warm liquid, a weight.

Then it was over.

She peeked from under her arms and saw Porter, gun drawn, cops running from the lawn toward them. Saleda reached her first, lifted the heaviness from her. A thud as something solid dropped. A gun.

Dear God . . .

Jenna rolled over just in time to see Saleda and another local police officer pull the body of the Triple Shooter, crumpled at the waist over the windowsill, out toward them. Paramedics pushed through the crowd, but it wasn't going to matter. Porter's bullet had hit him directly in the head.

As glad as she was to be alive, she was equally sorry to see Tobias

Gray dead, whatever he'd done. The quickest way to find the person who had told him, for whatever reason, to kill Molly was the Triple Shooter's connection to them, and now they'd need to do it the hard way.

You'd think being almost shot was the hard way.

"Are you okay?" Saleda asked, now helping Jenna brush glass off herself.

"I'm fine, but Eldred might not be. We have to find the second UNSUB."

Porter had joined them. "Thoughts on how we do that?"

Jenna shook her head. "Retrace his steps, I guess. And as much as I hate to say it, find out what the hell day he was talking about."

"Who would know that except the dead man in there?" Porter asked.

Jenna blew out another breath, wishing the tightness in her chest would let up.

"The only person I can imagine who'd know would be Molly."

50

A dults were really bad at keeping secrets. So bad, in fact, Molly sometimes wondered if their hearts were really in it.

She'd listened at the door while Dr. Ramey told Mom they needed to talk to her. Lucky for Dr. Ramey that Liam wasn't home from work yet. He'd told her mom a while back that he thought it best for them to stay out of the investigation as much as they could from then on. He felt strongly that it was time for their family to move past the day at the grocery store.

Boy, *this* probably wasn't what he'd had in mind. Lots of policemen had been around this afternoon, looking for Mr. Beasley. She wouldn't mind going out and helping them look for him if they'd let her. But they wouldn't. Said she was too little. Dr. Ramey would've let her help look.

Come to think of it, Molly wondered why Dr. Ramey and the agent with her were stopping to talk to her at all, but then again, Dr. Ramey hadn't been one of the policemen out searching. Maybe Dr. Ramey was trying to track down something else. She didn't want to ask too many questions. She liked helping Dr. Ramey too much.

Now they sat in the living room, and Molly let her legs dangle off the recliner chair. One day, her feet would touch the ground, and that wouldn't be nearly as fun as swinging them.

"So how are you, Molly?" Dr. Ramey asked.

"I'm good," Molly said, watching the glitter on her new pair of shoes glisten in the living room lights as they moved.

"I wanted to come by and check on you. See how you were doing . . ."

"That's not what you said to Mom," Molly said. Dr. Ramey hadn't treated her like a baby before, and she wasn't about to let her now.

Dr. Ramey bit her lip, then frowned. "You're right. I shouldn't tell you something like that. You're a big girl, and you've helped us a lot. You deserve to be treated like you can handle the situation."

Molly smiled. That was better.

"Thank you," she said.

"Molly, I need to ask you something, and I can't tell you a lot about the question because it has to do with our case. You know how I told you before some things about the case have to stay secret, right?" Dr. Ramey asked.

"Sure," Molly said.

"Okay, good. I just need to ask you one important thing. It might seem confusing, but you're the person I know who can help. You're really good at numbers, and I think this could tell me something I need to know."

Molly nodded. "I'll try."

"Okay. Sounds good," Dr. Ramey said. "If I were to ask you the first day of the year that came to mind, what would it be?"

"Christmas Day," Molly said without thinking.

Dr. Ramey nodded. "That's a good one. What would you tell me about that day, in numbers?"

Molly cocked her head. What a weird question.

"Um . . . twelve twenty-five. Twelve days of Christmas, which *is* twelve twenty-five, so that's funny. Twelve signs in the zodiac. Twelve knights in King Arthur's Court, but it was thirteen if you counted King Arthur, kinda like Jesus in the *Last Supper* painting . . ."

Dr. Ramey looked almost disappointed for a second, but the minute Molly tried to figure out why, the face was gone.

"What other days are special?"

"I like Halloween. Ten thirty-one," Molly said. This time she didn't wait for Dr. Ramey to ask. She wanted her to know she caught on. "The numbers thirty-one, three hundred thirty-one, three thousand three hundred thirty-one, thirty-three thousand three hundred thirty-one, three hundred and thirty-three thousand three hundred and thirty-one, three million, three hundred and thirty-three thousand three hundred and thirty-one are all prime. Isn't that weird? Thirty-one flavors at Baskin-Robbins ice cream. Ten cents in a dime. Ten pins in bowling, ten frames in each game. My favorite thing about ten is that it comes between nine and eleven, my birthday."

Dr. Ramey's head jerked slightly.

"Your birthday?"

"Mm-hm. Nine eleven oh-seven."

"How old will you be on your birthday this year?"

Dr. Ramey really sounded weird now.

"Seven," Molly answered, worried she'd said something wrong. "Dr. Ramey, are you okay?"

"Fine, Molly. Hang tight right here, okay? I need to talk to your mom a minute."

Jenna nodded to Porter to stand guard in the living room. No one in this house would be alone until whoever had taken Eldred was found, so she'd leave Molly under his eye for the moment. She had to speak to Raine.

The second Molly said nine eleven oh-seven, the jungle green she associated with puzzle pieces had flashed in. She wasn't sure exactly how any of this fit into the Triple Shooter case, his obsession with threes, or his weird connection to Greek mythology, but her gut said it did.

Plus Molly was turning seven and was born in the year two thousand seven. The sevens were there, and she was supposed to be the seventh victim. Something about this added up. Jenna just had to figure out how. God, trying to put this together was making her head hurt.

In fact, this case and the way none of its colors matched up neatly gave her a downright migraine.

Raine was sitting at the top of the stairs, waiting. It seemed like a strange place to park and think, but Jenna was no one to judge. Besides, if she were Raine, she'd stand within earshot of the people talking to her daughter, too.

Jenna sat on a step a few below Raine.

"We've called Liam at his office to let him know what's going on," she said quietly.

Raine stared at her feet, smirked. "He was thrilled, I bet."

Jenna patted the woman's clasped hands where she was currently wringing them in her lap. "He'll be all right. We all know he wanted to keep Molly out of the middle of this for the best of reasons, but it was important we talk to her. You made the right decision."

Raine looked up, and her eyes met Jenna's. "You think? Even if I might've put her in danger?"

Jenna took a deep breath. How could you tell a mother that her child already *was* in danger? "Raine, do you know anyone who would want to hurt Molly?"

Raine cocked her head, confused. "What?"

Jenna sighed. This wouldn't be easy.

"I'm concerned that someone tried to hurt Molly that day in the grocery store. It's hard to explain, but I think someone told the shooter to aim for her the day your mother died. I'm not sure why anyone would do that, but I need to know if you can think of anyone who might have a reason to want to harm your daughter."

Raine stared at her, eyes blank.

Then she shook her head. "I can't imagine anyone who . . . my God! Are you sure?"

It was the most animated Jenna had seen the woman yet.

"I'm trying my hardest to learn more so I can tell you what exactly is going on, but yes, I'm fairly certain."

Raine shook her head again, touching the gold charm on her necklace. "No, I don't know anyone who'd want to do . . . oh my God. Is she . . . are they . . . are they coming back?"

A color tried to jut in as Raine's moving fingers drew Jenna's eyes, but she pushed it back in favor of holding on to her current train of thought.

If someone had wanted to hurt Molly, they could've done it at any time since the shooting. The only thing she could figure was whoever *they* were, they didn't realize the FBI had determined that Molly was the intended victim, and so for now, had left her alone. But if they'd wanted her dead for some reason—whatever reason a person could want a child dead—they would eventually target her again.

Jenna forced herself to ignore the pesky voice in her head trying to make sense of why, if Molly was the target, they wouldn't have just gotten rid of her when they had the chance. The pain in her temple throbbed harder.

"I don't know. No one's going to leave you alone in the house while the search for Mr. Beasley is on in the neighborhood, but even after that, I'd like to station some agents outside for your family's protection. In the meantime, I need to ask you to keep this information completely confidential. No one needs to know that Molly was a target. Letting anyone know that we're aware of this could put Molly in jeopardy," Jenna said.

Raine nodded hard, still fiddling with her necklace. "I understand."

"If you think of anyone who might have a reason to want to hurt Molly, call me. No matter how small the information may seem," Jenna said. So many times in these situations, the mother would be a suspect, but in this case Jenna had dismissed Raine as a potential suspect as much as Molly herself. First of all, Raine couldn't have kidnapped Eldred and be in the room with CiCi and Yancy at the same time. Second, unlike classic cases of parents wanting to be rid of their kids, the child hadn't disappeared one day at random, the parents issuing vague claims about the kidnapper's looks that could fit half the general criminal population. Molly had been shot at by a serial killer.

And third, Raine's color just didn't add up. That robin's egg blue had nothing to do with the crimes so far. And while this information wouldn't ever hold up as official evidence or in court, for Jenna it was good enough.

"I will," Raine said.

Jenna climbed back down the stairs only to see Yancy standing at the bottom just past the curve where the foyer moved to the staircase. He'd been out looking for Eldred Beasley. Jenna hadn't seen him since they'd left this very house hours ago, when the old man was still safe and sound.

Yancy's hair was dark with sweat, his shirt damp as well. He looked so tired, but something else lingered in his eyes. Something she'd seen before. Failure?

"Heard anything else?" he asked, hopeful and resigned at the same time.

"No, unfortunately. They're going house to house asking if anyone's seen anything, but so far, no luck. Where's CiCi?" Jenna replied.

He gestured toward the door. "She's riding with Victor. He let her go along with him to drive around the neighborhood and look for places Eldred might've gotten interested in if he wandered off. I honestly think Victor's just trying to give her a way to feel like she's doing something."

His face fell at the mention, and the salmon color she'd seen when he'd called to tell her Eldred was missing flashed in again. This time, she recognized it: holding back.

"What aren't you telling me, Yance?"

He looked down, was silent a long moment. "Let's walk. We might need some air for this."

51

Yancy put one foot in front of the other, with every step his dread growing. How do you tell someone you love that you've screwed up something so badly they might never forgive you?

"Jenna, I can't keep this from you anymore, not just for my sake, but because of Eldred . . ."

Shit, this was hard. What would happen to Oboe if he went to prison? Jenna probably wouldn't take him. Not after his owner had been such a douchebag, screwup failure.

"Yancy, what are you talking about?"

A police car passed, one of the many out looking for CiCi's father. God, if something had happened to him . . .

"I didn't tell you everything about why I didn't want the local cops called in," he said quickly, afraid of losing his nerve.

He couldn't tell if the sudden chill in the air had to do with the sun setting or his own nerves.

"Okay," she said.

He walked on, the familiar thud of his leg as it clicked the pavement the only sound between them while neither spoke. Jenna hadn't even noticed the metal leg the other night in the shower when their shins hit, and he'd worried he might've ruined the moment.

The longer you don't tell her, the more you're putting Eldred at risk. Your little lies by omission and switching a few details could be the reason he's gone, cool guy.

"The husband isn't exactly what I said. She . . ."

Jenna stopped at the cross of the road that intersected with the end of the Tylers' block. "Spit it."

Yancy glanced around. Cops everywhere, all of them capable of swooping in after he said this if she called them. But for the moment they were out of earshot.

Tell her, you coward.

"I was meeting CiCi for coffee. I know I shouldn't have gotten personally involved, but at the time, you didn't need me on this case . . . and she . . . well, I felt needed."

Pathetic.

"When I got to her house to pick her up, someone else was there. He was threatening her. I thought it was her husband. I tried to scare him off with my gun, because he—Jenna, he was strangling her . . ."

Jenna's face darkened. "What did you do, Yance?"

His eyes stung in the breeze. "Jenna, he pulled a gun on me."

Her hair blew in the wind, and she rubbed the chill bumps forming on her arms. He wanted to put his arm around her, but the straight line of her mouth, the attack posture, said he couldn't go to her.

"What. Did. You. Do?"

"I shot him, Jenna. Okay? I fucking shot a man," Yancy blurted, throwing up his arms.

Tears glistened in her eyes, which were wide in disbelief and anger at the same time.

"I don't . . . I don't understand. What . . . you're still not telling me . . . something . . . God, Yancy, what the hell . . ."

"He wasn't her husband. Her husband doesn't even live with her anymore. They're separated. The guy was a pimp. That part was true.

He wasn't her husband, though. She was making money on the side to support her father's medical needs, and this guy was threatening her, hassling her for the money she owed him."

"You didn't call the cops? What the hell *did* you do?" she practically screamed.

"Jenna, I couldn't. The pimp and the people running the prostitution ring were dirty cops. That part was true. I did some digging." He leaned in, whispered, "You know, Yancy kind of digging . . ."

Jenna nodded, still pissed. She folded her arms.

"Well, I looked into it, and she wasn't lying about that. They'd have killed her *and* me if they found out I'd killed one of their own, and . . . oh, fuck . . . I was scared they'd come after you, too. And A . . ."

Jenna's glare turned even colder. "Don't you *dare* bring Ayana into this."

Yancy closed his eyes, unable to look into hers anymore. He turned his back, hands clasping his head. He opened his eyes again. With Jenna's disappointed expression no longer glaring at his face and instead just searing his back, he tried to steady his breathing. "I'm not just saying that, Jenna. I swear."

"So what are you saying? He's dead, and you called no one? What did you *do*?"

The way she said it, he realized she already knew the answer. He couldn't bring himself to say the words.

"It could be them. Who took Eldred," he said instead. "The way they came in and got out without us hearing. Cops could manage that, right?"

She said nothing.

He spun around, needing desperately to read her body language. Her gaze was fixed on her feet, and she was just shaking her head back and forth.

"I didn't tell you before, because I don't think it's likely. They wouldn't know . . . there's no way they *could* know what happened. But what if they do?"

Her head snapped back up. "Why wouldn't they know? Tell me, Yancy. Say it!"

He stared into those eyes, the ones he'd looked into in the hot, sensual shower just the night before. So loving, satisfied with him. So *his*.

"I got rid of him," he said, unable to believe he was hearing himself saying the words out loud. "They couldn't know, because I made sure no one could, damn it."

Jenna looked back at her feet. She was quiet a long moment.

Then she stepped toward him, swift. Purposeful. Past him. Back toward Molly Keegan's house.

He moved to catch up to her, and she spun around.

"Just stay away from me right now, Yancy. Just get the fuck away."

He watched her go, not sure what she'd do next or when he'd talk to her again. But he had no right to defy her wishes. Not anymore.

"I'm sorry," he mumbled, but he knew he was saying it only for him to hear.

52

Jenna slammed the door and furiously bolted one lock after the other, muttering. "What was he thinking? How could he have . . . ugh! This changes everything. How could he . . ."

"Whoa, now, El Tigre." Her dad's voice met her ears. "You okay?"

She hung her head, breathed slowly and evenly for a moment. No way could she tell him about this. Not now. Maybe not ever.

"I'm fine," she said, turning around and putting on her most composed face.

"Clearly," Vern replied, smirking. "You and Steampunk have a fight?"

Jenna passed him and opened the fridge, not really hungry but unwilling to lie to her dad's face, even by omission. "Not exactly."

"You know, if our lives are any indication, change isn't *always* a bad thing," Vern said.

So he'd been listening to her angry rant as she was coming in the door, when she'd thought she was alone. Great. *Mental note: When Ayana is an adult and she has a boyfriend—or girlfriend—don't think you know exactly what's going on, even if you've come to like Prince or Princess Charming.*

"Dad, I know you and Yancy get along, but it'd be great if you didn't jump to take his side. I'm still your daughter, you know. He's still an outsider coming in," she spat, fighting to control the violent reaction.

"Ouch," he said. "That's kinda harsh, isn't it?"

The deep, rich red of the Japanese maple leaves in the fall outside her and Hank's apartment so many years ago flashed in, the one she'd so long associated with a kindness, an inherent good-hearted nature. She shook it away. "I'm just saying he's not your flesh and blood. Don't be so quick to think he's got it all figured out."

Vern let out a loud laugh. "*You* of all people are suddenly using the old 'blood's thicker than water' cliché? I hate to remind you of this since you rarely forget it for a millisecond of any day when I wish you would, but if blood was any indication of a person's character, I should probably be the one locking *you* out of this house. Then again, by that definition, I'd need to lock myself into a house away from you, Ayana, *and* Charley . . ."

Jenna's face burned. "You don't understand."

"So make me," Vern replied. "And close the refrigerator door. You could've eaten every piece of old cheese pizza and drank the entire pitcher of Sharkleberry Fin Kool-Aid in there by now if you were actually looking for a snack."

Jenna's jaw clenched, and she slammed the door of the fridge. She turned to face her father. "I can't. You wouldn't get it."

"Try me."

She stared into her dad's face, the face that had smiled back at her from the bottom of the slide as he'd waited to catch her, that had been slack and pale as Yancy had carried him out of the safe house just the year before, after Claudia's latest attempt to take him from her. He'd probably understand far better than anyone else what she was feeling at the moment. The problem was, she didn't want to rip that rug of trusting Yancy out from under him like it had been ripped from her. Losing what had been so hard to gain hurt too bad.

But despite the thought, she couldn't help what came out of her mouth. "I'm just not sure I . . . What if we don't know him as well as we think we do?"

Vern frowned. Something in his face changed, a cloud crossing it, like what she'd just said had thrown him. What could be so damned confusing? She'd come in fuming, after all.

"What's that look for?" she demanded, this time unable to keep the frustration out of her voice.

He stayed quiet a long moment, then said, "No one ever knows someone quite as well as they think they do, Jenna. But I'd say your gut has served you well. Wouldn't you?"

Tears bit Jenna's eyes as she thought about the color she'd always seen Yancy as, the salmon of him holding back the truth, and then the moss green lima bean conversation with Ayana that morning. Doubt.

"The colors aren't clear-cut anymore, Dad," she whispered. "My gut doesn't know what to think."

A small whine came from the direction of Ayana's room. She must've woken from her nap.

"That's my cue," Vern said, smiling. "Duty calls. I'll get her up, we'll have a little dinner. Maybe some time with your shortest fan will clear your head some."

He started toward the hall, but stopped at the kitchen doorway, turned, and looked back at her. "For the record, though, I think you're confusing your gut feeling with your special little superpower. I know they're tied together, but just make sure you don't get so wrapped up in reading colors that you forget to read people, Jenna. The distinction might be subtle, but of everyone I know on earth, you're the one I trust most to separate the nuances."

And he left to go bring in her daughter.

Jenna handed one of her own plastic, sectioned plates to Ayana, who enthusiastically dried it with the towel Jenna had given her. One day she'd be old enough to realize that this was not a privilege, washing dishes. But for now drying seemed great to her. A pleasure, so simple.

Must be nice.

She looked out the window above the sink and jumped, then relaxed. Victor.

She wasn't sure Ayana was ready to meet her uncle. Not yet. Or maybe it was that with Victor having Hank's eyes, Jenna wasn't ready for it. Either way.

"A, go in and see if Uncle Charley wants to read *Fox in Socks*. Tell him I'll come in after I talk to someone," she said.

"Okeydoke," Ayana replied. She put the towel and plate on the counter over her head, then skipped off.

Jenna rested both hands on the edge of the sink, breathing. Then she turned to open the door. After she'd gone through the lock series, she cracked it.

"Hey," Victor said. "I asked for you when I got back to the scene. They said you'd gone home in a hurry. I was . . . well, can I come in?"

Jenna nodded, opening the door wider.

Victor stepped past her, and she closed the door, taking her time relocking every bolt in the series. She had no clue how to explain her absence from the scene of Eldred's disappearance, particularly since she'd called Victor into it in the first place. Not to mention her reason for calling him in was because she had a personal stake in the case. He knew he was there because of Yancy. How could she excuse her own disappearing act without telling the whole story when he was already aware Yancy was involved? Burning guilt crept up her spine.

I'm not the liar.

"I just couldn't stay anymore," she said truthfully.

Despite her best efforts, the tears came. Fast. Hot. Painful.

"Jenna, what on earth happened?"

The concern in his voice, its steadiness, pulled at her. She could confide in him. She could ask advice from someone.

For whatever reason, she trusted him.

"Why do you care?" she blurted despite the thought, pushing past him to tackle the remainder of the dishes.

She turned on the water, snatched up a plate. Harder and harder she scrubbed, throwing plates onto the drying rack as she finished them.

"Maybe because if I don't speak up for those dishes, no one will? Seriously, Jenna. They don't deserve to be treated like common criminals . . ."

Her hands slowed at the cup she was now scouring with a brush. *Gut instinct. You trust it everywhere else.*

"Victor, if I told you something, would you swear never to tell another soul?" she whispered, closing her eyes.

"Of course," his voice came back.

A soft melon flashed in. Sincerity.

She reopened her eyes, set the cup back into the sink unfinished, and faced him. "Even if it was the worst thing you'd ever heard, and your conscience told you to tell?"

He studied her, calculating. "What are we talking about here?"

"Would you?" she pressed.

Those eyes of Jenna's ex's met hers, though the lines of his face, his build, and his color were all different. Fixed on her, he nodded.

"I swear."

"The reason Yancy couldn't call the locals in. I want you to know up front, when I involved you, I didn't know this . . ."

"Point taken," Victor said. "Mind if I sit?"

She shook her head. "Go ahead. Mind if I wash while I talk?"

"Only if you promise the plates a fair trial."

She reached for the cup again, this time washing more slowly. Deliberately.

"Victor, Yancy told me tonight that he killed someone."

"What? When?"

Dear God. A nightmare.

And Jenna told Victor everything. What Yancy told her about shooting the cop, why he'd done what he had, the color she'd seen to know he wasn't telling her everything, how there was a chance this could have something to do with Eldred going missing. How even if she knew it was wrong, she couldn't tell the cops or her team, because no matter how mad she was at Yancy, she wasn't willing to throw him to the wolves. How she didn't know what to do now.

When she finally finished, she turned off the faucet and faced Victor, ready for judgment. Hell, if she were him, she'd judge her, too. She should've told Saleda the moment she found out.

Instead of judgment, however, she got only a grim, set jaw. "Where's the body?"

Jenna blinked. "I . . . uh . . . I don't know."

In her anger, she'd left without forcing Yancy to tell her the details. She hadn't acted like a cop, but a girlfriend. A pissed one, and for good reason.

Victor held her gaze, a fierce look in his eye. "I need you to be really frank with me here, Jenna. Do you believe what he said? About the people who did this maybe coming after you and Ayana if they were to find out?"

She licked her lips nervously, tried to picture Yancy's face and voice as he'd said it. She'd been fuming when he'd mentioned Ayana, and yet . . .

Yancy's personal genuine yellow flashed in. It wasn't the color she saw in anyone else for sincerity, of course, but it didn't have to be. It was the color she saw as *him*. He'd been himself in that moment. No salmon of holding back or burnt orange of lies. Just him.

"Yes," she said.

The ding of a text on her phone cut the thick air between them. She tore her eyes away from Victor and picked up her cell from the counter. With the team still working overtime on this case, anything new that came through would come to her. She couldn't afford to ignore the phone, as much as she needed the night off.

Sure enough, the message was from Saleda.

Got hold of the Triple Shooter's old psych and have some leads.
Need your brain. You on the way?

She hadn't exactly told Saleda she was coming home, and apparently Porter hadn't, either. As much as she'd love to tell everyone to back off, whoever tried to manipulate the Triple Shooter into killing

Molly Keegan was still out there, and Eldred Beasley was still missing.

She typed back.

Be there in twenty.

Jenna looked back at Victor. "They need me at Quantico."

She wanted to plead with him to help her, to tell her what to do about Yancy and this situation. She needed someone, for once, to save *her*.

He stood. "I can see myself out. Go give the fam good-bye kisses."

Jenna undid the lock series despite what he'd said. He couldn't see himself out if he wanted to. She opened the door, her heart dropping as what felt like her only ally walked away.

Victor turned just past the stoop.

"Don't tell another person what you told me. I'll talk to Yancy and make sure he doesn't. Don't let on to a single person that anything strange went on tonight or that night," he said.

"Victor—"

He grabbed her hand, squeezed it.

His hand was so warm.

"Don't think about it again. I'll take care of it," he said.

And he left, without another word.

53

Jenna was in the back of the unfamiliar conference room next to Saleda, munching a donut and listening. When she'd gotten to headquarters Saleda had filled her in on the conversation with the psychiatrist Tobias Gray had stopped seeing a year ago. Now that Tobias was dead, it was a lot easier to ask his old doctor questions and actually have him answer. Less worries about doctor–patient confidentiality. Saleda had questioned him about who might've had any sort of influence over Tobias Gray, about anyone who would've known about his mental state. He'd pointed the team to an AA meeting he knew the Triple Shooter had started attending. Tobias hadn't been a drinker, but the principles of self-control and self-forgiveness in AA could apply to schizophrenia recovery. The psychiatrist himself had suggested the idea. It was the only thing he could point them to. Tobias's family had cut him off, no longer sure how to deal with his illness, and his former patient had had trouble making real friends because of that illness.

Lucky for them, that very AA group had a meeting in Alexandria tonight, and Saleda and Jenna had made it in time to slip in the back.

When the current speaker stepped down and the leader asked who'd like to share next, Jenna stood. This wasn't going to be pleasant, but they didn't have time for the normal routes of inquiry. A man was missing, and he might've been taken by someone who told the Triple Shooter to kill a six-year-old.

She made it to the podium and held up her badge. "I'm Dr. Jenna Ramey, part of the Behavioral Analysis Unit of the FBI. I'm here to find out what anyone here knows about this man, or anybody who might be associated with him."

Jenna held up a picture of Tobias Gray's driver's license photo, blown up for just this purpose. "This is Tobias Gray. He used to come to this very meeting, and in recent months or days became involved with a very dangerous person. We don't know who that person is, but we hope someone here can point us in the right direction. We need to know who he was around or what he was doing in the days leading up to now. We have no more leads, and in order to pursue him, we need something—anything you can give us."

Silence met her, the blank stares of the meeting participants echoing surprise, concern, and a plethora of other emotions. Some even had fear written on their faces.

She'd known this would be difficult, especially since some people here had already faced run-ins with the law they weren't keen to dredge up again. Not to mention, the whole point of these meetings was to remain anonymous, though she knew they all were aware of each others' names, occupations, and more.

"No one?" she asked. "Okay, let me put this another way. I can have some answers here, or I can bring each and every one of you in for questioning. But trust me, this man has done some awful things, and a lot of what he might do from here on depends on us finding out who he was involved with recently. Every law enforcement agency from here to the North Pole would be all right with me dragging in twenty people for questioning if it meant getting the information we need."

Victor's nickname of "Hardass" popped into Jenna's mind. She hated doing this, because it was always better to win trust. But in some cases, there just wasn't time for that.

A woman in her thirties raised her hand, then stood. She shook slightly.

"He . . . Tobias stopped coming here almost a year ago. Might be doing something totally different by now, but back then, he'd started going to another meeting. A Celebrate Recovery assembly at a church somewhere a town over, I think."

"Okay. I have Celebrate Recovery. Anybody care to share anything else about that? Someone's gotta know . . ."

No one spoke for a long minute. Then the group's leader stood up.

"I don't know where he went, but I can provide a list of the Celebrate Recovery meetings within a hundred mile radius," he said.

"Great. Come with us, sir. The rest of you, thanks for your time."

After the group leader had given them the list and thoroughly berated them for interrupting the room full of fragile, healing minds and bodies, they left the conference hall. Jenna searched online for the nearest FedEx store, and they set out for the print shop to send the list to Irv. Jenna had tried to take a picture of the papers and send them, but between the tiny print and number of pages the list stretched across, faxing the sheets would be easier and faster. It would take her and Saleda days to comb through all these meetings, and time was something they didn't have. They had no idea what Irv might be able to do with the list, but hopefully he could give them a place to start.

"What's he going to do?" Jenna asked as they waited to receive confirmation that their fax had gone through. "Cross-reference Tobias's name with his ass crack? We gave him a list of anonymous meetings in a hundred mile radius. It's not like there's some ritual all alcoholics perform prior to meetings that would show up on electronic records, like depositing checks at the bank next door to the church where they get together."

"I've never been a drinker, so I wouldn't know. Let's hope there is something like that, though. We're screwed for tonight and maybe all week if not, and Eldred doesn't have that long," Saleda replied.

Jenna picked up the list again. Maybe they weren't screwed. Not yet, anyway.

"What if we thought like him? The group leader said he asked for this same list, and that's how he found his own meeting when he started turning more religious. If you were the Triple Shooter, how would you use this list to find the one place *you'd* like to go?" Jenna said, not sure if she was talking to Saleda or herself.

"The place with the best donuts?" Saleda ventured.

"Okay, but if you were *Tobias Gray* . . ."

Jenna was already scanning the list for things that might jump out at her if she were him. Maybe a Celebrate Recovery meeting at the Church of the Hydra or something Greek . . .

Then, she saw it, the green of the Triple Shooter burning bright in front of her eyes.

Three Thirty-three Claxton Street. St. Ignatius Holy Church of the Sabbath.

Sabbath. *Seven.*

Jenna pointed to the listing. "It's this one."

Saleda didn't ask, but instead said, "No meeting until tomorrow."

"Well, we'll just have to wait then . . ." Jenna said, sarcasm dripping from her tone. Then, "What are you, nuts? We're the FBI! We'll get Irv on the horn, he'll fetch the staff listings, and we'll call up every employee until their phones ring so much they feel crazy enough to answer. When they do, we'll ask for the name and contact information of whoever is in charge of those meetings."

Saleda stared at her, and Jenna immediately felt herself blushing. Telling your Agent in Charge what to do wasn't just crossing the line. It was downright rude.

"Sorry," Jenna mumbled.

Saleda nodded. "Me, too. This case has my head in a twist."

She pulled out her phone and called Irv, and in a short few minutes, they had the name, phone number, and home address of the person responsible for the Celebrate Recovery meetings at St. Ignatius. But from what the church secretary told them before she'd given it to them, they wouldn't need it. The church was only a few blocks away, and the leader of the meetings, "Brother Ozzie," was there now, volunteering during a drop-in communion and prayer candle lighting.

"Hope God's okay with wrinkled slacks," Jenna said as they left the FedEx store's parking lot.

"Slacks are the least of my worries. I have a bunch of unpaid parking tickets."

Jenna's heart panged with the thought of Yancy and what he'd done. Was the situation even fixable? Victor said he'd take care of it, but what the hell could he take care *of*?

"Parking tickets. Right," Jenna breathed. Best not to think about it right now. "Brother Ozzie, here we come."

54

Eldred didn't know this place. Where was he?

The room was dark, but with a glow from somewhere he couldn't quite see. He stepped farther inside the place. Strange things. He didn't recognize any of this.

He ran his hand along a canvas on the wall. It seemed somehow familiar, but he wasn't sure why. He'd seen it, though. Maybe somewhere with Sarah once? He couldn't be certain.

The glow beckoned him. He was curious now, and he had to see where it came from.

He opened something that looked like a closet, but no clothes hung inside. No light switch. Was he indoors or out? Was this a place with electricity?

The glow he'd seen from behind the canvas now seemed to come from a tiny door near the bottom corner of the closet-like area. How could that be? The canvas was outside this closet, and this closet on another wall entirely.

That made no sense to Eldred.

He crouched at the tiny door. After he turned the two small screws—one in the tiny door's center top, the other opposite the first at its bottom—the door came off to reveal a space inside just big enough for a person. The floor inside was boarded over. Seemed safe enough . . .

Eldred squatted, then gingerly sank down to his knees. He crawled inside.

Down the short tunnel from the entrance, a new room opened up. This was the glow.

Even stranger things here, but this time, he could see them in the light.

Eldred could see another person already here, too.

The man held up his hands amidst all of the strange things. "Mr. Beasley? It's Mr. Beasley, correct? Please don't be alarmed. I'm a police officer. I'm Special Agent Gabriel Dodd."

M olly sat in front of the television, pretending to watch the National Geographic special on the blue whale. Really, she was listening to her mother and Liam arguing in the corner in hushed voices.

Even though the police had called Liam to let him know he was about to come home to a giant police hunt for a man involved with the grocery store investigation, she didn't blame her stepdad for being surprised. He'd told her mother a bunch of times that he'd rather her not be involved in the case, that they all needed to move on. Molly knew he just wanted what was best, but it did hurt her feelings a little that Liam of all people wasn't able to see how much she could help.

"You specifically went behind my back and told them they could come?" he was saying in a harsh whisper.

"I didn't do *anything* behind your back. She's *my* daughter, Liam. I make the decisions about her," her mom hissed.

Molly gulped. She'd never heard her mom say anything like that before. They were always telling her that Liam was as good as a real dad and better than some, that she should respect him like he was her own. And she did. They were her family.

But now her mom was telling Liam she wasn't his daughter? This case had made everyone frustrated. Not just her or Mr. Beasley or Dr. Ramey . . . everyone felt bad. If only she could fix everything. She just wanted to go back to normal.

"Eldred Beasley leads some nutcase to our doorstep, and you want to tell me *I* don't have Molly's best interests at heart? Raine, you're delusional!"

"I never said you didn't have her best interests at heart. I'm just saying your mother didn't die, and the decision to involve Molly isn't yours to make."

This time, Molly let her eyes drift toward the argument and away from the TV. Liam's face was blank, and he looked like he'd been slapped.

"Well, it used to be," he said.

Molly jerked her head back to the TV as Liam stood and stormed away.

55

Jenna stepped into the foyer of St. Ignatius Holy Church of the Sabbath behind Saleda. The church had a formal feeling about it, like the congregation had to be very serious about itself to attend. It didn't feel like an only-Sundays sort of a place, that was for sure.

Saleda headed into the sanctuary, but as Jenna made to follow, she stopped at the foyer table right outside the sanctuary doors. A book on the top of a stack on the table had caught her eye. The book bore the words "A Christian Celebration" on the cover, and it was adorned with a design of curlicues around a lozenge shape.

An olive green flashed in. She'd seen that color before. *Strange . . .*

"Jenna . . ."

Her head shot up from the book. Saleda was beckoning her with a hand. She'd spotted someone.

She followed Saleda toward the fifty-something man at the front of the church lighting candles.

"Excuse me. We're looking for Ozzie Quay," Saleda said.

The man turned and smiled warmly, his forehead wrinkling with lines from showing the expression so often. "Look no further. What may I do for you ladies?"

Saleda displayed her badge and introduced Jenna, then launched into the reason for their visit. She told Brother Ozzie all about the Triple Shooter, how they came to find him, and why it was imperative they know more about him. That was when she told Brother Ozzie his name.

"Tobias? A killer? That's . . . terrible," he said, though somehow he didn't sound as surprised as some people did when told a friend or acquaintance of theirs had committed despicable crimes ending with the deaths of other human beings. Traditionally, people were dumbfounded and horrified at the revelation, and their shock was understandable. They had known and been associated with cold-blooded sociopaths who were fantastic actors. However, in Tobias Gray's case, with his Christmas-lit house and probably unusual phys-ical tics, Jenna doubted those around him had had to worry about being fooled by an accomplished, highly functioning performer.

"You don't seem stunned," Saleda said.

The minister looked down, shook his head. "I'm not, unfortunately. I haven't seen Tobias in several months, but he did attend church with us here a while after starting the Celebrate Recovery program. He seemed to like it here, felt he fit. At the same time, he was . . . unusual. He was a disturbed person, very upset by many things. Sensitive, easily perturbed. For example, I recall a conversation about the Sep-tember eleventh tragedy that came up at a potluck dinner once, and the sheer mention of the date made Tobias excessively nervous. We all have horrid memories of that day, of course, but for Tobias, it seemed to hit a particular nerve, to the point where I wondered if someone he knew and loved had been harmed in the attacks."

Jenna was sure her face gave away her surprise, but right now, she didn't care. September eleventh . . . the infamous date of the ter-ror attacks. Molly's birthday. "Nine eleven, did you say? What did he do when the date was mentioned?"

Brother Ozzie looked up and to the right, a common direction to glance for those trying to remember a past event. That particular orientation of the gaze usually indicated visual memory, as opposed to how someone making something up would look in a different direction. If Claudia had been "remembering" something she hadn't

really done or seen—before she got good at fooling people, anyway—
she'd have looked up and to the left, a standard habit of those taking
on visual *construction*.

"He didn't do anything, really, just talked strangely. He would
mutter repeatedly about how bad things happened on that date . . .
how things always went wrong then. He also mentioned something
about how the tail number of one of the planes was N-three-three-
something-or-other, and Flight Ninety-three . . . this or that about
those numbers combined with the date had always been bad news,
had always meant nothing would end well, or something to that
effect. I can't remember what all he said that night. But it was clearly
a subject that had bothered him enough to file away those facts and
memories," Brother Ozzie said, shaking his head sadly.

Three threes combined with the date. That had to be the reason for
Molly, though how he knew her birthday remained to be seen.

"Do you know of anyone in the congregation who is"—Jenna
stopped and thought *was*—"well acquainted with Mr. Gray? Someone
who might know more specifics about why the date September eleventh or these numbers upset him so?" She left off the "because that
person could be our other killer" part. September 11, 2001, troubled
nearly everyone in the country, as did its subsequent anniversaries,
and for good reason. But had the date bothered the Triple Shooter
because he'd lost someone that day or been traumatized himself in
the attacks, or was he already obsessed with those numbers for some
other reason, like he was threes and sevens, and the tragedy that
Tuesday morning only gave him more evidence that the numbers
could surround nothing good?

Brother Ozzie nodded slowly. "If anyone would know, it'd be another minister who worked here for about a year and a half, and was
here while Tobias was attending. Really took him under his wing,
worked to keep him involved, give him someone to talk to. Funny
really, since the minister was somewhat new to our church himself.
Superintendent had just brought him to us from Raleigh, but before
that, the conference had sent him to North Carolina from Kentucky.

I think he was actually in Illinois and Indiana prior to that. Sheesh. So is the way of the council, though. You must go where you're needed and sent. Anyway, that minister left to take on another church a few towns over about six months ago, but he definitely knew Tobias better than anyone. Haven't seen Tobias since he left, either. I guess after he was gone, Tobias didn't feel like he fit anymore. Liam was like a security blanket to him here in a lot of ways."

The hair on Jenna's neck stood on end, her breathing fast and shallow as the unthinkable swarmed her mind. "Did you say Liam?"

Brother Ozzie nodded. "Uh-huh. Liam Tyler. Great fellow, for sure. Can I get you his contact information? Maybe he can help."

But now Brother Ozzie's voice was nothing but white noise in the background, Jenna's pulse thundering in her own ears. "Oh my God," she muttered.

The olive color she'd seen when looking at the book in the foyer flashed in. Images flew through her head at a rapid pace: Liam Tyler, his office, Molly Keegan in his office, showing her the painting of *The Last Supper*. The symbol from the foyer . . . it leapt out at her from her memory of the painting. The symbol was the same design repeated over and over on the wall tapestries in the painting, the restored-color version in Liam's office. The tapestry, an olive green.

That symbol . . . in the painting, the foyer . . . Jenna had seen it somewhere else, too. The curious charm hanging from the necklace Molly's mother, Raine, always fiddled with at the base of her throat. As the symbol glowed in Jenna's mind, the tiny diamond inside the curlicues of it seemed to radiate off of the green background.

Liam's discomfort the day he found Molly with Jenna in his office at their home. It hadn't been protectiveness of Molly. It was defensiveness because of their proximity to the painting. As Molly had counted items in the painting, Liam had become increasingly agitated, particularly when Molly had counted the feet shown in the painting. She'd pointed out that there were only fourteen feet visible in the picture, but there were thirteen people, so there should've been twenty-six feet.

Molly had pointed out that there were twelve people other than

Jesus in the painting. Heck, just the other day . . . *"Twelve knights in King Arthur's Court, but it was thirteen if you counted King Arthur, kinda like Jesus in the* Last Supper *painting . . ."*

Sixteen feet in *The Last Supper,* and two of those were Jesus's. So the twelve apostles should've had twenty-four feet between them. But they didn't. If you didn't count Jesus's feet, there were only fourteen feet for all twelve apostles. Ten feet were missing.

The Cobbler hadn't *always* cut off the victims' feet. It had seemed at random. Depending on the victim, he'd removed one, none, or both.

The Cobbler had been caught and imprisoned after an anonymous tip sent police straight to his door. They'd found ten feet in the mentally ill man's freezer. *Ten.*

For twelve victims.

And that mentally ill man, as they'd just realized, had been framed.

Liam Tyler had known the Triple Shooter, and he'd known his buttons. He wanted Molly out of the way, because she knew his secret, even if she hadn't realized she did.

At any moment, she could figure out all by herself that her stepfather was the Cobbler, and he was going to make for damned sure she didn't and no one else did.

"We have to get to Molly and Raine fast. We have to warn everyone there," Jenna sputtered. Yancy was at the house, too. And CiCi. It was Liam's house. He could've known Eldred was there even if they thought he had no way to or even if they thought Liam was gone. Unlike Tobias, Liam was exactly the person who *would* surprise someone like Brother Ozzie with what he was capable of. A coldblooded psychopath who could act like someone he wasn't, be a different person if it served his ends . . .

"Oh, God help us," Jenna said, running toward the door without explaining anything more. "We have to get to them *now!*"

56

L iam had moved toward the stairs. Molly could only guess he was headed to his office. He probably wanted to be alone.

Which was why she had no idea why she decided to sneak away from the living room while her mother had gone to the bathroom to blow her nose, and follow him.

Now she stood with her back pressed to the wall outside Liam's office, her breaths catching nervously. Her stepfather didn't like her here when she wasn't supposed to be, and if he found her right now when he was already angry with Mommy, he wouldn't be happy. But now that she'd seen him doing something strange, her curiosity had gotten the better of her. She had to know.

After all, when Liam went into his office, he always sat down behind his desk. He never went into the closet.

She could hear her stepfather cursing under his breath. Then nothing.

Was he still in there? *Of course he is. He can't come out without me seeing him.*

Still, Molly couldn't help wondering if he wasn't. The movement *and* the muttering inside the closet had stopped. Dare she glance inside?

Stupid, she knew, but she couldn't stop herself. She peeked around the corner carefully, ready to jerk back to attention beside the door at the first hint she'd made a mistake. Maybe run up the stairs.

But she didn't have to. The office was empty.

Except . . .

A weird glow was coming from behind *The Last Supper*. The skin on Molly's neck tickled, and suddenly, her forearms were covered with goosebumps. Something about the eyes in the pictures looked almost like the figures had cats' eyes. That eerie glow behind them made her feel nervous. More nervous than that day at the grocery store when she knew something might really hurt her.

Don't be silly. You're in your own house.

Molly glanced toward the double doors of the closet where Liam had disappeared. How had he gotten out of this room? In the whole time she'd lived here, she'd never known there was any other way except through the door she'd just used to come inside. Her mom had shown her all of the exits, she'd thought, in case of things like fires or a burglary.

But now, here she was, and somehow her stepfather had left the office without her seeing.

And that light . . .

She pushed the closet doors open, half expecting Liam to be hiding in there and to jump out and scare her. He'd want to teach her a lesson about not being nosy. But he didn't.

Molly's eyes were drawn to the corner of the closet, where another light peeked from an opening near the floor, a little door that had been covering it set aside on the closet carpet. The same kind of light, in fact. Eerie, glowing. It came from somewhere beyond the portion of the open hole she could see.

Molly looked back toward the office. She should tell Mommy about this. Maybe they could go in together . . .

But Molly knew how upset Mommy had been since G-Ma, and maybe she should check it out and know what it was for sure before she brought her mom.

With a deep breath, Molly crawled into the little hole.

. . .

Yancy stood right outside the closet in Liam Tyler's weird-ass office.

After Jenna left, he should've walked out the door behind her and rejoined the search for Eldred. Jenna might hate him, but going home wouldn't help anything. In fact, it'd just evoke more misery, trying to think of what to do or whether or not he should do *anything* in case Jenna might turn him in to the cops for Denny's murder. Besides, at some point, he'd have to break the news to CiCi that their secret wasn't so secret anymore. But he couldn't do it until her father was found. He didn't have the heart.

So he'd been at the Tyler place when Victor had come looking for him. The cop had demanded a lot of things from him, and the worst part was Victor had *known* about Denny. He'd also told Yancy not to say a word about any of it to another person. The cop had been a complete asshole, but in the end, he'd said he was going to make the whole thing go away . . . however the hell he thought he could manage that.

Mad as hell after their conversation, Yancy had come inside for a breather, maybe a glass of water, and to see if CiCi was in the house, when he'd noticed Molly sneaking off after her mother stepped away. Liam had come home, but Yancy saw no sign of him, either. This wasn't a good time for a six-year-old to be alone, so he'd gone after Molly.

Now she had stepped into the closet in this creepy, glowing place, and she hadn't come back out. Something didn't feel right. Not at all. Yancy crouched next to the glowing hole in the wall that led to some kind of crawl space.

Voices.

"What's going on?"

Eldred.

Yancy whipped out his cell phone, his stomach turning nervous flips. He texted Jenna as fast as he could, their fight forgotten. God, he hoped she'd open the text even when she saw it was him.

I know where they are. Inside. Liam Tyler's office. In a closet . . . a
crawl space. I'm outside it now.

"Shut up, old geezer," a man's voice Yancy recognized as Liam
Tyler's said. "I need to figure out what to do."

A text pinged back, the phone silently blinking the red light to
Yancy.

He opened it.

Who is they?

Yancy plucked out the letters:

Eldred, Liam Tyler, and Molly, that I know of . . .

He took a deep breath in and held it, trying to catch the muttering
at the other end of the crawl space, but the sound was muffled by
distance. If he wanted to hear better, he'd have to go inside.

The red light flashed again, and Yancy opened the text.

God. Yancy, Liam's dangerous. He's the Cobbler. Get Molly away.
He wants her dead.

What the hell?

"Oh my. What have we here?" Liam Tyler said. "Oh, Molly, you
really shouldn't have come. You'd have been just fine if you hadn't."

Oh, shit. It was too late. Liam had noticed her . . .

Yancy's pulse pounded. He'd go upstairs, get Victor and the other
cops. They could storm the place.

On instinct, though, his hand moved toward his leg, took out his
gun. If he waited, Molly could be a goner by the time he brought
them all back with him.

"You really should learn to leave things be, you know," Liam said.
His voice came from a distinct direction inside the crawl space. "I'll

deal with you, but they'll all know. They'll be here soon. You, I'll hang onto for when I need you . . . I could lie, but it might not be the best course . . ."

Now Liam seemed to be muttering more to himself than to the others. Was this nutjob saying what Yancy thought he was?

Yancy glanced in the direction of where the weird, glowing painting of *The Last Supper* would be in Liam's office if he could see through the closet wall, then back toward the crawl space. He pulled his phone back out and shot a text back to Jenna.

> Don't take his word for Molly being okay until you see her or talk to her yourself. Trust me.

His breathing quickened as he readied himself to dart into the crawl space. Jesus. How did he always get himself into these positions?

I love you, Jenna.

He pushed through the doorway right as he heard the gunshot.

"Oh, God! Yancy, no . . ."

Jenna's fingers flew over her phone, typing, begging him not to go in after Molly, to notify the cops at the house. But even as she pressed send, she knew it would be too late. Yancy wasn't one to sit by while someone was in danger, be it his loved one or a person he barely knew. And *she'd* told him to get Molly away from Liam.

"ETA five minutes," Saleda called over the whir of the helicopter's blades. "The head officers there are on their way down to the office now. They'll control the situation."

The hell they will. Somehow, they hadn't even thought to look *inside* the Tyler *home*, yet Eldred was in there. How could that be? Not that she could blame the search teams. She hadn't taken a thorough look through the house, either. The blood on the doorjamb, the open door . . . she'd been so sure Eldred had been taken or had wandered outside . . .

And Liam had walked right past them all without them knowing. The guy was smart. He'd framed a mentally ill person for his previous crime spree almost without flaw, and then he'd persuaded another mentally ill person to do his dirty work for him, even though the latter didn't finish the job. Liam Tyler had controlled them all with such ease, weaved seamlessly in and out of a police investigation without so much as a thought drawn to him other than the consensus that he was a protective stepfather who loved his family. And right under the nose of the man who'd investigated the case that happened to be his own serial murders. No wonder he'd hated Dodd so much at their first interview with Molly at the house.

"Have you called Dodd?" Jenna yelled back.

Saleda nodded. "He didn't pick up. The office he was at earlier said he was already en route back, so he must be in a dead zone."

Shit. "What about the state cops? They're still here, right?"

"On the ground, briefed, and waiting for instruction," Saleda said.

She opened a new text and composed one to Victor. Liam wasn't stupid. If they stormed that room or wherever they were inside the crawl space, Liam would be an animal backed into a corner. For the moment, the evil stepfather needed to think he had the upper hand, or else everyone in there—including Yancy—would be in big trouble.

If they weren't already.

She reread her message:

Stand down and negotiate. He'll know you know where they are. He'll know you're coming. You don't have the element of surprise, even if it feels that way.

She hit send.

A moment later, his reply.

He couldn't know anyone saw him down there. We can find a way in. They pulled the house plans. It's an unfinished storage space. Like an attic, but instead of above, it's behind a basement office. The office closet in the basement has one corner giving access to an unfinished crawl space. That crawl space leads to a large unfinished storage room directly behind the office. We can end this with minimal damage.

Then, a long few seconds later, another text from Victor:

Gunshots fired. Regrouping.

Jenna held back tears, tried not to imagine the worst. She typed furiously, her heart beating faster as the message grew so long it might be sent in multiple parts. He had to listen!

She sent her next message.

He knows others are in the house who would've heard the gunshot. He's got two choices: kill everyone down there then try to frame one as the gunman and explain why he lived, or be smart and realize his jig is up. Even if he *could* frame one of the people in there, which he can't because of who they are, for all he knows others followed them and were just smart enough to stay outside and listen to the dirty laundry air. He's been a step ahead the whole time. You can bet that won't change. He thought like us the whole time. It's how he almost got away with it.

She squeezed her phone tighter, willing the spirit behind her pleas to transmit through to Victor. He couldn't try to overtake Liam. She had no idea what that bastard would do, but he wouldn't go quietly. He was down there now, having been followed and found out, and he was plotting his way out.

Claudia flashed in, images from last year bright in Jenna's mind.

If she knew one thing about psychopaths, it was that they wouldn't do what the cops expected. They were wise to the cops, could anticipate their next moves. Heck, they could anticipate *most* people's next moves, cop or not. It was why they could blend.

The phone vibrated, and Jenna opened the text.

What do you suggest then?

Jenna exhaled, but her relief lasted only seconds before she was panicking again. She'd told him to stand down and not do what Liam would see coming, but it didn't mean she had a plan to get Eldred, Molly, and Yancy out of that space alive.

Yet.

She turned her phone over in her flat palm, thinking. There had to be a way . . .

The jungle green of masterful plotting, the puzzle piece of calculation, flashed in. Liam was calculated. He plotted every move. To catch him off guard, they needed the opposite.

What was the opposite of jungle green?

Your colors don't work that way, Jenna . . .

But somehow, even as she consciously knew they didn't always, that her brain picked colors for associations at random most of the time, her gut said that this time, it *would* work. She closed her eyes and pictured the color wheel.

Red-violet hues occupied the positions across from the large slice of the color pie made up of, among its many other shades, jungle green.

The hue of ripe red grapes flashed in, the Tyrian purplish color of problem solving. Plotting answers, laying down framework for well-designed puzzles happened to be directly across from the color she'd associated for such a long time with figuring out the most difficult complexities.

The same family of colors she'd been thinking of the day she figured out Molly's connection to the sevens in this case, as coincidence would have it.

She typed again as the helicopter drifted lower, landing zone in view.

I'm almost there. Announce your presence to him, but from a distance. Work on sending a phone in to establish contact. Treat it like any hostage negotiation situation.

Jenna stopped writing, afraid of what she had to say next. Even if she was right, it scared her. This could go wrong, and if it did, she'd never forgive herself.

She gulped in breaths, steeling her will. Building her confidence.

Reminding herself she was good at what she did.

She finished the message and sent it before she had a chance to overthink the words.

Jenna sat and stared at the screen, her last text to Victor still glowing on her phone's face:

In fact, escalate it TO a hostage situation if he doesn't realize it's one already. We need to do something he won't expect. He won't think we'd want a hostage crisis.

58

Yancy rushed the doorway of the small room behind Liam Tyler's office when the gunshot rang, his own gun at the ready to take on the enemy.

But what he saw took him off guard, and for a second, he was mesmerized. Another painting of *The Last Supper*, this one scrawled with names, pictures of dead bodies tacked underneath each apostle pictured in the painting. Though the men in the photos posted under figures in *The Last Supper*—one corresponding to each apostle—had already met their fate, if the blood, their crumpled positions, and staring eyes were indications, every one had feet in the pictures. All their feet. On the pictures of some of the dead, large, heavy black X's, seemingly drawn with permanent marker, had been scratched atop feet. Some bodies, two X's. Some one. A few didn't have any of the horrifying markings, but they were in the minority. Yancy's gut had flipped a somersault, threatening to send up his lunch at the sight of the black X's. Molds of plaster hung on the wall that looked similar to those hanging in Liam's office, only these were quite obviously upside-down footprints of . . . God only knew who. The people tacked under the painting, he supposed.

"You like my little display?" a voice said.

Yancy whirled to see Liam Tyler holding Molly in front of him with one arm, the other holding a gun to her temple.

Yancy's heart skipped a beat, and his hand trembled.

"Oh, put the gun down, hero. We both know all it'll take is me giving you a countdown to when I put one in her skull if you don't, and you'll do it anyway. So let's make this simple and save little Molly the anxiety."

Yancy's hand lowered by instinct. Then he dropped his weapon. What else could he do? With Molly in front of the evil fuck, even he wasn't reckless enough to take a shot.

"That's a good lad. Now backpedal toward the wall there and join our other friend," Liam said, gesturing to a wall behind Yancy and to the right. "That is, if backing up won't *trip* you up . . ."

Liam chortled at his own joke.

Yeah, yeah. Very funny, psycho.

"Ah," Liam sighed, finishing a good chuckle. "Now, now. You're right, I probably shouldn't be rude. After all, you *were* admiring my work."

How can I be right if I didn't say anything to you? And admiring is one way to describe what I was thinking. One wrong *way . . .*

Something hard collided with Yancy's back. The wall he'd been commanded to back toward.

"Right, now. Have a seat, will you? Now, Molly, go sit with Mr. Hero over there," Liam commanded.

Molly half trudged, half ran to where Yancy was lowering himself to the floor near a confused Eldred Beasley. Meanwhile, Liam took a step toward his awful canvas.

But Yancy didn't watch him for long. A still mound near the back corner caught his eye.

A man lay unmoving on the loose earth, and from here, Yancy couldn't tell how bad he was wounded, whether or not he was breathing, anything.

Molly, who had taken a seat between him and Eldred Beasley, leaned over and whispered, "That's Special Agent Dodd."

Yancy gave her a nod so she'd know he'd heard her, but no more, hoping their quiet would keep Liam's attention off of them as long as possible. Right now, Liam was gazing at his own handiwork, turned sideways so he could see both them and it.

"Most people would probably attribute my . . . spree, they'd probably call it. Yes, they'd say my *spree* was prompted by religious radicalism, some brand of insane preoccupation with beliefs, all because what I did was inspired by one of the most famous Bible-based paintings, a piece of artwork most known by Christians. Fools. Just because I'm a minister, the rank and file assume so readily I'm a man of God," Liam said. He laughed. "God is for the weak, but more than that, he's for those who need him to exist because he gives them a *purpose*." Liam snickered again. "Well, then again, like I said. The weak."

Yancy's gaze followed Liam as he strolled beside the painting with its gruesome addendums. If this twisted asshole thought it was strong to kill people and chop off their feet for some reason, then he had to think he was a damned fortress . . .

Wait. That's it.

Yancy glanced at the painting again, this time ignoring the pictures of dead bodies and looking at the one figure without a companion photo. Jesus.

Two feet showed from under the robe of the depiction of the Son of God, resting on the floor beneath the table. Yancy bit his lip, let his eyes roam the rest of the pictures again. He had to suppress a mirthless laugh as the new glance at the photos confirmed his suspicion. If he'd been looking at this in any other context, he'd not only find it fascinating, but he'd be flying high from solving the case.

As it was, all he could do now was stare at the lifeless men, their bodies contorted in what had to have seemed meaningless ways to most, including those who had previously investigated the case. Yancy chanced a quick look at Dodd, but still saw no movement or signs of life. He turned back to the photos of the dead, who he now realized had not only lost feet according to whether or not those of their corresponding apostle were visible in the painting, but who had been positioned in ways similar to those matching their apostle partner as well. One closely groomed dark-haired man had been rolled partway onto his left shoulder. His head looked to his left, his left arm draped across his body, hand open in what might be a gesture toward something at his back or side. His right arm stretched straight out to the right, palm up and open in a gesture that complemented the one implied by his other hand. On the opposite side of the painting, on the left-hand side of Jesus from Yancy's viewpoint, another dark-headed man, this time with facial hair and a bushier mane atop his head, had been lain diagonally with his feet closest to the camera. His chin was tilted up, his head looking in the direction of his left shoulder. His right arm was bent at the elbow, and his fisted hand lay on his chest. The other hand was outstretched to the right and forward, palm down, almost as if it were waiting to clasp something.

Christ. They even look like the apostles, too . . .

Suddenly, Yancy realized Liam was staring straight at him, wearing a close-lipped grin. He nodded. "You've noticed it, haven't you?"

Yancy gave a silent nod. *I've found Jesus. I wish I hadn't.*

Liam nodded, too, smiling wider. "Yes, for the strong don't need a god to give us goals and ambitions. We can find our own purpose, our own passions to occupy time. If there were more of us, maybe there wouldn't be so much pointless war and pathetic religious squabbling to begin with. People go to church and war for the same reasons: they're bored and they need a reason for being. I suppose when you're easily bored it's hard to find one. So, they congregate with people who will tell them that reason, then give them cause to fight when it's 'threatened' by vague, shadowy people and concepts. They're off fighting for what they've been told to believe, and all the while, here I am," Liam said, chuckling again and using his gun to gesture toward the painting. "An artist with my *own* ambition—nobody needed to tell me which direction to go—creating my masterpiece, the only real danger to any of them. And they'd never even know it. They're too busy hunting illusions to realize the threat to them is their own blind eye."

Yancy squirmed as his gaze drifted again toward where Agent

Dodd lay still in the corner. Everything in him urged him to move toward the man, check his pulse . . . start CPR. But the man with the gun holding them all at bay had other ideas.

What now, superhero? How are you getting yourself out of this mess? Haven't you had enough of putting yourself in places you can't get out of? Like elevator shafts?

And yet, he couldn't help but listen to that other little voice. The one the bigger, derogatory voice in his head usually bitch-slapped into silence. The voice that, deep down, told him his being in these situations—last year, Denny, this—wasn't a coincidence. He was here because he was supposed to be, for whatever reason. He was here for the same reason he showed up at the shelter the day Oboe had been scheduled to be put down.

Because he should do some good.

A rustling from the hole in the crawl space. From the way the other heads in the room turned, Yancy knew they'd all heard it.

Liam took aim and fired, but his shots were met only by a voice.

"Mr. Tyler, my name is Officer Victor Ellis with the Virginia State Police. You're surrounded by a SWAT team, sir. We don't want anyone hurt here today. We just want to get us all out of here, everyone okay. That includes you. We have a negotiator on the way, but we want to send in a phone so you can talk to us at a distance without us needing to yell in this manner. Can we do that?"

Liam Tyler's bemused face from moments before had changed to pissed, confused, and enthralled all at the same time. More than anything, the energy in his body said one thing: wired. He aimed the gun he held at the three of them, letting it drift back and forth over them all as if to say "Make a move. I dare you."

"Prepaid cell phone *still* in the packaging *only*," he called. "The kind in plastic packaging. No boxes. Anything else, and I won't talk."

A moment of silence, then, "Okay."

And with that the conversation—and the presence of help—was gone.

Yancy wiped his palms on his pants, but it did no good. They immediately soaked with nervous sweat again. *Think.*

They were sending a negotiator. It would *have* to be Jenna. She was the one on the BAU team involved in this case who was trained in depth in that sort of thing. If Jenna was coming in, that could be his greatest advantage, because he knew how she thought. In some ways, anyhow. It was why he'd known after his 911 call with Molly at the grocery store to tell Jenna to look for Molly. He'd just known she'd find the little girl useful.

Next to him, Molly patted Eldred Beasley's leg, her own head lying on her knees, probably to keep from having to look at the disturbing shit in this room. Yancy couldn't save her from that, but maybe he could get her out of this mess alive.

Again, he studied the "evil twin" painting of *The Last Supper* in the room where they now sat. He squinted, chewed harder on his lip.

Victor's voice had come from the tunnel back to the left behind him. The painting in Liam's office was behind the desk, which he'd crossed in front of to enter the closet. When he'd come in, the tunnel in the closet had opened up in the corner and snaked right, but the closet's actual end put its edge several feet deeper into the room than the desk. And the *painting* was behind the desk.

Oh, now, cool guy. Maybe you have something here.

The glowing in the office before he'd stepped into the closet. The glow from the hole at the tiny space's base. He'd known to follow Molly.

His own text popped into his head. After he'd heard Liam muttering about lying to the police, Yancy had told Jenna not to believe Liam if he said Molly was all right without seeing or talking to her. The phone was coming.

Liam stood off by himself, too close for them to try to move at all, but in his own world, talking to himself again. Dare he chance it?

"Molly," he whispered. "Don't look at me, and don't say anything back. Just listen, then nod once if you understand. Jenna—I mean,

Dr. Ramey—is going to be on the phone soon. There's something really important I need you to do . . ."

Yancy talked fast out of the corner of his mouth, explaining his plan. When he was done, he watched her in his periphery for affirmation.

She gave a barely visible nod.

Please, God. Let this work.

59

They put down the chopper on a high school baseball field a few blocks down from where the action was currently taking place. Jenna exited the chopper and jogged down the street toward the Tyler home just in time to see Victor coming out the door of the SWAT command center. He stretched his hand toward her, and she realized it held a cell phone. She took it from him as she and Saleda ran in his direction, away from the helicopter.

As soon as they could hear again, Victor said, "He'd only bite for prepaid, still in plastic. So that's what he got. I'm good at following instructions."

Jenna nodded as she climbed the steps, following Victor into the armored vehicle that was serving as the current SWAT command center. Inside, she could see views of several places in the house on computer monitors, and one showed Liam Tyler's office. Two SWAT team members stationed there, two more in the closet, ready for action.

She looked to Saleda. "Any last minute thoughts?"

Saleda just gave her a nod. "Go get 'em."

Victor had already dialed the prepaid phone's number, so Jenna pressed send. *If there's a God in heaven, he wouldn't let a little girl die at the hand of her stepfather. Even if he is a cold-blooded, murdering sociopath.*

The ringing at her ear stopped. Breathing.

"To whom am I speaking?" Liam Tyler's voice asked.

"This is Dr. Jenna Ramey, FBI. We've met before," she said, heart thumping in her chest.

"Oh! Dr. Ramey. So good of you to call. I'm glad you weren't with Special Agent Dodd this time around. It didn't turn out so well for him, so better for you to be out than in."

Jenna held back her gasp, but wildly gestured to Saleda for a pen and paper. The items were passed to her, and she scribbled as she talked. "What is Special Agent Dodd's current condition, Liam?"

She finished writing, "Dodd down there," and pointed emphatically at her note as if Victor and Saleda weren't already angling for position, trying to read.

"Maybe dead," Liam said matter-of-factly, his voice ambivalent. "Either is or will be. Shot was good. Sorry about that, Doctor. I do know how you folks hate to lose your own."

Jenna took in a calming breath. She couldn't let him get to her. Not now. Too much was riding on what she did next. Too many people needed her to keep cool.

"And you have other folks down there," she said, her best attempt at pretending his statements about Dodd didn't affect her. "What will it take for us to get them out in better condition?"

This time her question was met with a laugh. "Oh, Doctor. You know as well as I do that this won't end well for me."

So why are you holding hostages instead of popping them and then trying to take as many of us down with you as you can when we come for you?

But Jenna already knew the answer, and so did Liam, even if he said one thing to her and thought another. He was a narcissist. So while he was smart and maybe even realistic at times, he hadn't given up on finding a way out. He was holding the hostages to guarantee some time to think and some leverage if he came up with a plan.

"If you'd decided that already, we wouldn't be talking, would we?" she asked, even though it wasn't a question. *Talk to him as though you're on his level. He'll underestimate. What* he'd be underestimating, exactly, Jenna wasn't sure. She didn't have a plan, either. Yet. "So now that we've cleared that up, any ideas so far?"

Quiet met her ears.

Then Liam spoke again. This time, the mocking in his tone from before had evaporated. "I want complete and total immunity."

Jenna couldn't stifle a laugh. "Oh, yeah? And onion rings on the side?"

Liam Tyler clicked his tongue. "Actually, Doctor, this is pretty straightforward, and everyone makes it out happy. We both know I can't escape without it getting messy, and the messy half of the equation is the part you don't want. Stepping over bodies of friends and children is never fun. However, we can avoid that altogether. You find me a nice DA, introduce us. He makes me a little deal. I cooperate and give you everything you need to know about the Triple Shooter— he is, after all, a very bad boy. You'll put away an unstable killer who has wreaked havoc in this area for months, your friends will walk away from this crawl space room without bullet wounds, and we can all call an end to the day. In exchange for all of my help, I'm presented with my stay-out-of-jail-free card. I mosey on my way, and none of you have to hear from me again. Now doesn't that sound lovely?"

Jenna tightened her grip on the phone. The fact that she hated his scheme and the thought of him securing immunity was irrelevant. No DA on the planet would go for a deal like that even if she *did* like the idea. But maybe there was something in there she could use. Anything that would buy her more time—or information—to swoop in and whisk Yancy, Molly, and everyone else out of that room un-harmed.

"And if I can't sweet-talk this magical DA who would have to be high on ecstasy into offering such a deal to a spree killer?" she asked.

Liam grunted a laugh. "Well, then I'll give you the courtesy of picking which of my guests down here takes the first bullet to the temple before you call Mr. DA back. Hopefully he'll have enough time while that's happening to down a few more Scooby snacks and be high enough to keep the second bullet recipient in the on-deck circle. How does that sound?"

"Not nearly as lovely as all of them coming out still breathing," she admitted.

Her heart beat harder as she imagined Yancy, Eldred, and Molly somewhere behind the office where the SWAT team members waited, holding for orders. God, if only she had a camera on the inside of that room so she could know exactly where everyone was positioned. But she'd already asked on the way in: no point of entry existed other than the crawl space in the closet. No doors, windows, air ducts . . . nothing. Even though a sniper's bullet could get through that wall, they couldn't just strafe the room with gunfire in hopes of hitting Liam. They didn't have a bead on where their target was, where the hostages were in relation, or any other possible obstacles they might encounter. There was no way to *get* a clue, either. The good guys on the outside were in the dark for the foreseeable future.

Get a clue. Problem-solving. Ripe red grapes.

The day she'd put together the sevens with Molly in this case, she'd done a mental rundown of all of the things different shades of purple represented to her. The Tyrian purple shade of ripe grapes that meant problem-solving had been one of them, but the whole reason her brain had been on that track at the time had been because she'd realized she'd seen Molly herself as purple.

The memory of Yancy's text flashed in. *"Don't take his word for Molly being okay until you see her or talk to her yourself. Trust me."*

She couldn't be sure, but something in the pit of her stomach flipped the same way it had last year when Yancy had given her a piece of information so shrewdly disguised it had been what had allowed her to fight Claudia. Maybe he hadn't been giving her instructions when he'd texted earlier. He wasn't yet in danger, so if he'd meant it to be a plan, he'd have just flat told her what he was thinking.

But as misleading fuchsia flashed in, Jenna knew that now that Yancy was behind that wall and himself a hostage, he would be racking his brain for what to do. He could and did think under pressure. He'd be sitting in there trying to figure out a way to send her information, when and if he could.

The yellow she associated with Yancy flashed in. It didn't mean anything specific and yet everything specific at the same time. It embodied everything he was to her and everything she knew about him.

He would remember the text. She knew it.

Asparagus green flashed in as details of a plan took shape in the depths of her mind, the fuchsia of misleading she'd seen moments before driving it. Play it right, and this might actually work . . .

It was a normal request, after all. Most negotiators did ask to speak to the hostages at some point before considering giving into terrorist demands. He wouldn't suspect.

"Liam, before I can get *any* ball rolling, I'll need to talk to my supervisors. Then I'll have to find a DA who's willing to hear me out or high or both. But first, I have to make sure that everyone is all right and unharmed. None of those people I just mentioned will budge an inch unless I can offer them that guarantee," she said, concentrating on keeping her voice from shaking.

Another laugh, and this time the mocking voice returned. "Would you like pictures of everyone holding today's newspaper?"

Jenna forced out a sardonic chuckle. "I think two minutes on the phone with each will suffice."

"Two *whole* minutes, Doctor? That seems excessive . . ."

"Okay, maybe not two whole minutes. But long enough for me to determine that each is the correct person, you haven't yet harmed them . . . and haven't assured them you're going to."

"Smart girl," Liam answered. "All right. Sounds like a fair enough arrangement I can give you. Except for Agent Dodd, of course. He's . . . unable to come to the phone right now. You get the okay from your higher-ups, Doctor. Find that DA, but find him fast, and call me back in twenty. Don't make it any longer than twenty, Doctor. I'm a busy man."

They hung up. Saleda immediately launched in, throwing her hands in the air.

"What the *hell* do you think you're doing? Even if there was a DA on earth who would grant immunity to a known serial killer, which there's *not*, the Triple Shooter is dead. If we go in there offering this guy a fake deal, it could blow up in our faces in too many ways to count."

"Would you relax?" Jenna said, but Saleda cut her off.

"If Liam Tyler smells a rat or gets so much as a whiff that the Triple Shooter's already fertilizer, he'll kill every single person in that room, *including* your boyfriend and a six-year-old girl. Or just as good, we promise him a fake plea bargain. He lets the hostages go, hires a lawyer to make O.J. Simpson's legal team look incompetent, and gets off for every single crime he's committed, scot-free, all because we handed him the perfect technicality to use against us."

Jenna grabbed Saleda by the shoulders and forced her to look into her eyes. "Saleda. I know what I'm doing. Trust me."

She cut her glance over Saleda's shoulders to check who else was listening. The others in the SWAT vehicle were talking among themselves, each group a few feet away. Jenna lowered her voice. "I have no intention of offering him any deal, Saleda. I just need him to *think* I'm going to offer it so we can get what we need."

Saleda bit her lip as Jenna outlined what she planned to do. They took the next moments prepping those around them for what was to come. Orders were issued, and Jenna dialed a third prepaid phone— one held by one of the SWAT team snipers in Liam's office. Now she would three-way dial Liam's prepaid cell.

Let this work. It has to work.

"That wasn't even fifteen minutes, Doctor. You're an overachiever," Liam said.

"I aim to please," she said, smirking.

"So," he said, and she couldn't tell whether his voice sounded confident or just steady, "what's the word?"

"We're go," she replied.

He laughed into the phone. "Wow! Ask and ye shall receive, huh? I knew you people could get things done fast, but I never knew you'd let a monster like me run away and disappear that easily."

"We're here to serve and protect, Liam. Right now, that means protecting the innocents you have in there with you. We can worry about what that means where you're concerned later, though I'm sure you'd already thought of that or you wouldn't have requested what you did," Jenna said. *Make him believe the bureaucracy really would value those lives over his, even if you're not positive it would've. Right now, it's all about selling what you've got.*

"So what's the ol' district attorney's ETA, hm?" Liam asked.

Jenna took a deep breath. "He's standing by awaiting my call, which he'll receive as soon as I have the evidence I requested from you showing me everything is intact."

He chuckled again. Damn, she was growing to hate that snicker.

"Don't you mean every*one*, Doctor?"

"I'd like to speak to Mr. Beasley first," she said, ignoring his jibe.

She could tell he'd extended the phone, because she could hear his voice from a ways away saying, "Paging Eldred Beasley, paging Eldred Beasley."

A shaky voice came on the line, and Jenna began talking to the man. She asked him a few questions, tried to calm his nerves with her words. He sounded so confused, but she couldn't let him go prematurely. The length of each call needed to be similar, lest Liam grow suspicious.

She heard Liam say, "Time's up. Pass the phone to your right, will you, old man?"

A crackling as the cell phone was transferred between people.

"Hello?" a small voice said.

Molly. This is it.

"Molly, I need you to do something for me, but don't move much to do it. Tell me the first numbers that come to your head to do with that room, okay?"

Jenna could picture Molly's pigtails bobbing with her nod as she spoke.

"Yes, I know what that is. That's the same thing they told me to do when I called nine-one-one. To be brave."

Jesus. This kid was brilliant. She was confirming they were on the same page—that Yancy had told her what to do.

"Okay. Give me as much as you can, but do exactly what you just did and disguise it as much as possible," Jenna encouraged. She held her breath.

"Oh, there are lots of happy thoughts I can think about. Like kittens! Mom even says if I pass my spelling test on the thirteenth, she'll let me get a kitten. But not a black one, because a black cat on Friday the thirteenth is supposed to be unlucky, but maybe a nice . . . I don't know. I don't like just plain gray, but if I could find a gray *and* orange one, it'd be *perfect* . . ."

A color tried to crowd in at the last word as Jenna's eyes flitted over the painting of *The Last Supper*, but she ignored it for the moment. She knew Molly's reference the moment she'd said the number thirteen was to do with the central figure in the painting. Jesus, the "add-on" to the apostles. Liam had to be right there, behind Jesus on the other side of the painting. But something about the little girl's tone when she'd kept talking about the kitten . . .

Amethyst flashed in again, the same color that had butted in when Molly said the word "perfect" just now. The color of the gemstone was fairly rare in Jenna's color lexicon in the way it registered not as the stone's classic purple pigmentation alone, but as though the color included certain properties of the stone itself. She couldn't help it. It all played into the color's meaning for her. The luster drawing the eye, a sheen causing it to glow. A hard, crystalline shell to protect its inner intricacies. Opaque in some places that hid select secrets, but completely clear in others so that light could be reflected through those existing transparencies, projecting the stone's color out into the world from its many facets. Looking back, the origins of the association with the color—even if at the time she didn't realize she had made it—

happened the day she'd gone to the mall with her best friend and her friend's mom as a ten-year-old. They'd gone into one of those costume jewelry stores, each picking out a ring. Her friend had chosen sapphire, and she'd bought the amethyst ring. When she'd come home later that day, too scared to go to Claudia, she'd admitted to her dad she'd spent twenty dollars on the ring even though she wasn't supposed to buy anything. Her dad had told her he understood, then lifted her hand and kissed it right on top of the ring. He winked, their private signal that let each other know that when it came to where they stood as a pair, they were okay.

Then it jumped out at Jenna. The word "perfect" was emphasized, the amethyst further proof Molly had used it to alert her to something important, a beacon to guide her. Her breath was fast and shallow as she scanned the painting of *The Last Supper* again. The mountains in the distance outside the window behind Jesus. They were gray. *Only* gray on one side . . .

And gray *and* orange on the other.

"Molly, I want you to grab Mr. Beasley and move far away from what you just told me. Shut your eyes tight and don't open them until we talk again. Now tell me . . ."

"Time's up. Pass it along," Liam's voice said.

Jenna jotted the instructions on the paper in front of her, underlining the specific point behind Jesus three times.

Saleda took the paper and, with another cell phone at her ear—this one a direct line to the SWAT teams—moved away from Jenna to give the order.

"Hello," Yancy's voice said, so on edge.

God, let him be okay.

"Yancy, if you're not sitting or crouching, do it now!"

A shot. Then another. Jenna watched on the monitor as the sniper in the office took one more kill shot right past Jesus's right ear.

"Move in! Move in!" she heard Saleda command the closet SWAT team.

Jenna held the phone to her ear, but Yancy wasn't on the other end anymore. From the commotion she heard through the receiver, it sounded like his phone had been dropped. She heard the scuffle of the SWAT team entering, their voices yelling the clear for different parts of the room as they swept it. Tears stung her eyes as she waited, hoping. Praying, even. She had to have made the right call.

A sound met her ears, this time over the speaker on the cell Saleda held.

"Target is down. Four packages are wrapped. One package wounded. We need EMTs for officer down."

After word came that everyone else was okay, Jenna ripped herself away from the monitors and headed for the front of the house. She'd nearly reached the porch when a SWAT team member burst through the door, leading Yancy with a hand on his elbow.

Jenna bolted forward, grabbed Yancy hard around the torso. He wrapped her in his arms and squeezed back.

"So you got the message, huh?" he whispered, his breath hot on her ear.

Memories flooded her of Claudia last year, the final struggle that had ended with her mother running and being on the loose once again. The thought made her tense, but she pushed it back. They hadn't seen a sign of her in almost a year, and the only person who'd tried to find them at all was Hank's brother, who was trying to keep them safe *from* Claudia. And right now all she wanted to think of was this man's—*her man's*—arms. Not what he'd done to some dirty cop prostitution-ring leader, not how they had an uphill battle if they were going to deal with whatever the fallout might be or what Victor had done to postpone or keep that fallout from happening, and definitely not her evil mother who, by now, had to be states and maybe even countries away.

Nope, just this man, and just this moment.

Except, of course, for answering his question about getting his message.

"I always do, don't I?" she whispered back into the soft flesh of his neck.

"Dr. Ramey!"

Jenna opened her eyes to see another SWAT member carrying Molly. "Oh, thank God," she said.

She let go of Yancy and stepped toward this brilliant, wonderful little girl. The SWAT guy carrying Molly set her down in front of Jenna. She crouched and hugged Molly as tightly as she would her own daughter. Without this kid, none of this might've ever happened. But it had, and it wasn't her fault. More important, though, without her, nothing could've turned out this well, ended this clean.

Jenna leaned back from Molly and smiled at her. "Way to go, girl. Perfect ten."

"I know you told me not to open my eyes until I heard your voice again, but I opened them when the policeman said I could. That's okay, right?" Molly said.

Jenna grinned. "Like I said. Perfect ten."

"Molly!" Jenna heard from back near the command center.

She tilted her head toward the holler. "I think I'd better move out of the way. Someone more important needs a word with you."

Molly smiled and scampered past Jenna toward her own mother, who was running across the grass, having finally been turned loose by the policemen who'd forced her to sit with them during the negotiations.

Jenna watched Raine scoop Molly into her arms and clutch her like a life raft. She knew that feeling all too well.

To the right of the porch, Jenna saw CiCi Winthrop touch her hand to her father's confused face, like she could hardly believe he was alive in front of her. She recognized that one, too.

Dodd.

"I'll be right back," Jenna said to Yancy.

She trotted toward the ambulance, where medics were loading Dodd into the back on a stretcher.

To her surprise, the agent opened his eyes wearily. He blinked. "Dodd!"

He managed a weak grin. "I'm all right. Not as bad . . ." He winced. "As he thought. I was playing possum."

"Sounds like you," Jenna said. "Just letting us think you were a goner, I mean."

"Had to. He'd have shot me again. I'm crazy and old, but I'm not entirely stupid." He frowned as he said the words. "Well, not always entirely stupid, anyway. I figured it out in the end. Got some records while I was away that uncovered a relationship between a person who might've been Liam Tyler and the man we'd . . . well . . . convicted. I wasn't sure, so I came back to check. Remembered you telling me about those rock molds in his office . . . thought they might be the footprints . . ."

Jenna moved toward the ambulance as the paramedic started to close the doors, and she put one hand up to stop them. She leaned far in and took one of Dodd's hands, gave it a squeeze.

"We can't always be superhuman, you know," she said.

He choked out a scratchy laugh. "Not *all* of us anyway. But I'll take closure."

She let go of his hand. "Speaking of, better get that bullet removed and that hole sewn up. That's the best kind of closure for *you* right now. I'll come see you soon."

He nodded, and the paramedic shut one door of the ambulance.

As he reached to shut the second, Dodd gave her a wave. "Thanks, Doc."

Jenna watched as the paramedic slammed the other back door, then climbed in the passenger's side of the ambulance. Lights swirling, siren on, the emergency unit sped away.

"All's well that ends well, huh?"

Jenna turned to see Victor striding toward her across the lawn. She nodded and grinned. "I can think of a lot of ways it could've gone worse, for sure."

He smiled back.

"We make a pretty good team, Hardass. When that court date for Hank's will does come around, I have this feeling we'll see the situation is under control. Ayana has nothing to worry about. Her grandmother will know it, too," he said seriously.

Jenna looked at her feet, the knowledge that she *should* find out where they stood regarding Yancy's predicament heavy on her shoulders.

Fingertips, soft against her chin, urged her face upward. Her eyes met Victor's—Hank's. The resemblance was so striking it was just unheard of.

"Hey," he said softly. "No worrying about that right now. I told you I'd take care of it, and for now, that's all you need to know. We can talk more tomorrow. Or next week. Yeah. I think next week sounds good."

She bit her lip. Why in the hell was this man treating her so well? He had absolutely no reason to, other than that she used to be in a relationship with his brother long before said relationship got his brother killed.

"I don't know how to thank you," she said.

With a smile, Jenna remembered making a similar statement to Yancy last year, and he'd told her he charged a tall fee. She'd bit, and he'd asked to know his color—the one she associated with him. He'd been the first person she'd actually told his own color.

Victor laughed. "Just don't shoot me next time I drop by to say hello. That's thanks enough."

As a venetian red flashed in, the color she realized Victor had now claimed in her mind, she gave Hank's brother a nod. "I think I can manage that."

Victor stared at her, not letting go of her gaze for a long few seconds. Then he cocked his head toward the porch. With a hitchhiker's thumb, he gestured toward Yancy. "You better get back. Even if lover boy dug himself a pretty deep one this time, I'd say it's a good day to keep making up." Victor wandered past her, back toward the command center. A few steps away, he turned, backpedaled. "But you know how they say forgive and forget? Don't forget, because I still wanna have lunch with you next week."

She caught herself laughing. "You've got it," she called.

Then she turned and headed for Yancy, who'd been checking on CiCi and Eldred. When Yancy saw Jenna coming back over, he wrapped up his conversation with CiCi and strode her way.

Jenna waited for him on the bottom porch step. "How's Eldred?"

"Shaken up. Disoriented. I think CiCi's planning to take him back to Carmine Manor, let him sleep in his own bed so maybe he'll manage a full night's rest," Yancy replied. "I could use one myself. Miss my own lumpy, saggy excuse for a mattress. Might not come from a high-end furniture store, but man, it's comfy."

Jenna felt the raise in her eyebrows. It made sense that Yancy wouldn't stay at CiCi's now that the person after Eldred had bled out by sniper bullet in the house behind them, but somehow, she hadn't expected he'd leave yet. At least not while CiCi was still in danger of Denny the dirty cop/pimp's friends coming after her.

"She's okay with being alone at her house so soon?" Jenna asked.

Yancy shook his head. "She's not going back. Checking into a hotel for now while she gets a real estate agent and looks for an apartment. Putting it up for sale. It turns out—" He glanced toward CiCi, then stared at the ground, almost like he didn't want to see Jenna's reaction. "It turns out she'd stayed so long because it was her parents' old house. She kept it in hopes she could bring him to visit, help him keep his memories longer. It ended up ruining her marriage. You know how we assumed all those nine-one-one calls she claimed domestic violence for were the pimp? Turns out what I walked into was a one-time thing. Makes sense, too, since she didn't call dispatch that day at all. I'd been right in thinking she didn't want to get caught involved in a prostitution ring, only I was wrong in thinking she lied about her husband beating her to avoid it. The nine-one-one calls were about Eldred. Every time, she'd checked her father out of Carmine Manor for overnight visits. He turns violent when he's really confused sometimes, and more than once, she was on the receiving end of his temper. Husband used to pull him off of her when he was in a rage. Her husband left after a skirmish that resulted in her miscarriage because she refused to put Eldred in a nursing home even after that."

"Guess that explains why she never called nine-one-one before those first hospitalizations," Jenna replied. But damn. She couldn't blame the husband. Granted, Jenna's calls involving a parent had been a little more clear-cut. Arsenic pretty much disqualified Claudia from birthdays and Christmases. But still. Loving a parent was one thing, but losing a child to that parent's temper? That seemed another thing entirely. "I know it's a hard decision, but I still can't imagine."

Yancy sighed. "She knows Alzheimer's is always going to be a downhill disease, but she thought the longer she could keep him in a home where he was watched but allowed to be checked out, taken to familiar places, she'd keep him *him* longer. Then, after the husband left, she started having to call nine-one-one when Eldred's temper flared. She never told the truth about it when she called nine-one-one, because if she had, the police would've notified a social worker, and the social worker would've contacted Carmine Manor. The assisted living place doesn't allow residents with those sorts of tendencies. They aren't staffed or trained to deal with them. CiCi would've had to move him to a full-time nursing home. She still couldn't stand the thought of it, so she pinned the domestic disputes on her husband. It definitely explains why she wouldn't press charges any of those times."

Jenna frowned. She couldn't believe it. It made so much sense, and yet she hadn't put it together at all. And while she understood CiCi's reasoning, her blood ran hot at the thought. If that woman hadn't lied to Yancy on her emergency calls, he'd have never seen the pimp at her house and mistaken him for an abusive husband. The danger he'd seen had been real, and anything still could've happened, but this changed things.

If CiCi hadn't called and lied about an abusive spouse, chances were that Yancy would've never gone to her house that day at all. Whatever would've happened would've happened. Her father would've been moved to a nursing home, the calls to emergency dispatch ended.

Jenna swallowed hard, hot guilt washing over her as she realized the full implications of what she was wishing. If Yancy hadn't been at CiCi's house that day, Denny probably would've killed CiCi. If not that time, then another.

She shot a look at CiCi. The woman stood on the porch with her elderly father, watching him with worried eyes as she held a Styrofoam cup of water the paramedics had given him so he could sip it through a straw.

Eldred wasn't Claudia. He hadn't caused CiCi to lose her unborn child on purpose or in cold blood. The woman was losing her father, but he was losing himself, too. That was the difference. Everything that had happened with Claudia had happened because of who Claudia was. Eldred's temper flared when he wasn't himself at all.

An image of her own dad's face flashed in Jenna's mind, the times she'd fought to save him. For CiCi, things had gone so wrong because she was fighting to save her dad, too. It might not have been a living, breathing psychopath trying to take him from her, but the reality was as terrifying in its own right. In a way, maybe it was easier to fight a separate, physical demon. At least then, it's easy to tell the good from the evil.

You do what you have to for people you love.

She turned back to Yancy. "I guess every family has their dark little secrets then."

He nodded. "Yep, unfortunately. And mine is—" Yancy stopped and frowned. "I'm sorry. I guess I shouldn't even start to make that joke under the circumstances. My real dark secret is fucking awful enough."

Victor's words echoed in Jenna's head. Jenna grabbed Yancy's hand, twined her fingers with his.

"No worrying about that right now," she repeated Victor's advice to her. "Let's talk about it next week. Besides, we both know your dark secret. You trick people you don't like into strolling with you during storms, then use your natural conduit to draw lightning to them."

She grinned as he stared back at her, surprised.

Then his face broke into a smile all his own. "Only works if I stand on my head, but they always get so suspicious."

Jenna pulled him toward her, and she kissed him on the lips. Short, but so sweet.

"Come on, Magneto. Let's go home."

"Home?" he asked. "Whose home?"

She gave him another quick peck. "Either, as long as I can have a few good hours with you to test out that electric current of yours . . ."

"Is that what they're calling it these days?" Yancy said, wiggling his eyebrows.

Jenna urged him to walk with her, and side-by-side, they made their way toward the command center to check in and verify they were cleared to leave.

"I brought CiCi and Eldred in my car, but surely one of the cops can give them a ri—oh, shit. I just remembered. We'll have to go by CiCi's place anyway. I have to pick up Oboe. So we might as well drop them off."

Jenna was so happy just knowing Yancy wouldn't be at CiCi's tonight that not even the little wiener dog's inconvenient needs could bother her. "Sounds good to me. Besides, if we're gonna have to ride all the way home without stopping every few miles for me to touch you to make sure you're really still here and okay, we might need a chaperone."

"If Oboe's good at one thing, it's badgering people. Get it? Badgering?" Yancy looked expectantly at her.

"Um . . ."

"You know, because dachshunds were bred to hunt badgers . . ."

Jenna swatted Yancy's rear end with her free hand. "Stick to the leg jokes, Tin Man. You're better at those."

He leapt away from her, squeezing his butt in and arching his back to keep it away from her as if the spank had hurt more than it did. "Hey! I thought you said you never notice my leg anymore."

She caught up to him, re-clasped his hand. "I said I *didn't* think about it, not that I *couldn't* think about it. Come on. Let's get cleared so we can pick up Toto and head back to Oz."

Jenna and Yancy helped CiCi settle Eldred into CiCi's car for the drive back to Carmine Manor before they were finally alone. The assisted living home had agreed to allow Eldred to stay a few more days while CiCi arranged care for him at a more appropriate facility.

After watching them drive away, Jenna followed Yancy to the front door of CiCi's house and watched him unlock it with the key she'd left him. Between Jenna and Yancy, they'd been able to talk her into taking her father straight back to his own home rather than waiting around. It wouldn't get any easier, and Eldred had had a long day. If he got frustrated, he'd be prone to more outbursts like the ones they now knew, and the less encounters with cops that CiCi could manage in her life right now, the better off they'd all be. Plus this way they could both get some rest—Eldred where he could be watched by professionals.

The second Yancy opened the door, Oboe darted outside. Jenna, closer to the steps, gave chase as Yancy stepped inside the house to flip on the porch lights. The dog wouldn't get far. Every other time he'd made a bid for escape, it only took a few steps before he gave up, lay down, and rolled over for a tummy rub from his pursuer.

"Oboe, you ass! I could've sworn I closed him in the bedroom," Yancy muttered.

Jenna, however, had honed in on something about the dachshund. Something looked different. His collar. Something bulky protruded from behind his neck . . .

She bent down and scooped up Oboe, kissed the top of his head, then reached for his collar. A folded piece of paper.

She handed the dog to Yancy, who was already scolding him.

"Oboe, you know, one of these days I should just *let* you go. You know? You'll run outside, and I'll just be like, 'Peace, fucker. See you later, dude.' "

But as he yammered on behind her, his words were drowned out by the blood pounding in her ears as she read the piece of paper that had been tucked under the dog's collar. The grass under her feet seemed to tilt, her eyes twitching like she hadn't slept in weeks.

I know I haven't written the way that I should. In the coming days, I hope I can make up for it, but for now, just dropping by to let you know that even if I forget to write, I'm always with you in spirit. With your boy toy Yancy, too. Even when he's being quite naughty. Not to worry, though. We'll just let what I watched him do be our little secret . . .
   For now.
   Give Ayana my love.

Your favorite mother,
Claudia

Jenna stared at the words, unblinking, adrenaline pumping through her veins. Finally, she tore her gaze from the paper, her eyes darting from house to house in her view, cars, people . . .

Nothing but darkness.

"Jenna?" Yancy said from the porch. "What is it?"

Jenna's breathing caught in her throat. She couldn't swallow. Fear engulfed her.

"We have to call Victor *tonight*. We can't wait anymore. It's Claudia, Yancy," she said, her voice sounding foreign in her own ears, like she was inside a tunnel in her own head. "Yancy . . . she knows."

ACKNOWLEDGMENTS

This book may be titled *Double Vision*, but just like with any book, so many different people bringing different points of view to the table were vital in this book's "birth." But whether I have four books out or four hundred, I'm sure one of my biggest fears will always be leaving out someone extremely important. So, if you happen to be the one I've left out of these pages this time, this entitles you to this blanket but sincere thank-you for your role in this book's creation, as well as one coupon for a free small coffee between the hours of 11 a.m. and 4 a.m. at participating locations while supplies last.

To the fantastic crew at Penguin Random House and Berkley: I have to start with my phenomenal original editor, Faith Black, for believing in, loving, and just plain "getting" the Jenna series. For taking it to new places and pushing for it to have a place in the world of thrillers. Thank you for knowing and understanding me as a writer so well that you could guide me to grow. For not only being the driving force behind this dream come true of mine, but also being a friend, thank you. To my outstanding current editor, Amanda Ng: Thank you for your leadership and enthusiasm in taking on *Double Vision*, full speed ahead, with grace, passion, and skill. I'm looking forward to many more words and successes with my new "partner in crime." To my staggeringly good-looking and brilliant publicist, the unparalleled Loren Jaggers: I can't thank you enough for your (always superhuman) efforts in getting these books seen and heard about. Thank you for answering my questions, aiming for the stars, and changing at least part of my name when talking about my craziness to your colleagues at parties so that I don't have to wear a bag over my head if ever I'm in the building. Making your author adore you: nailed it! To my cover designer, Jason Gill, and the entire design team: I'm so grateful for the unique vision for my work you turned into an eye-catching concept I'm proud to have represent the book. Thank you to every person at Penguin/Berkley who had a hand in this book's development—so much goes into a book making it out into the world. Your roles came together to give my novel a place on the shelves, and for that, I am grateful. And to Leslie Gelbman, my publisher, president of Berkley: Thank you for making *Double Vision* the book a reality. I am honored and humbled to be a part of Berkley's line.

To the absolute force of nature that is my agent, Rachel Ekstrom: my advocate, my superhero, my friend. Knowing you're always in my corner, watching my back, and at the same time, taking the lead and constantly moving, shaking, and fighting for my work in every way it needs is a security that simply can't be bought or replaced. Thank you not just for loving my work as much as I do, but for championing it every step of the way, for nurturing me as an author, and for cultivating the trust and teamwork in our partnership. I'm thankful and honored to call myself your client. To Irene Goodman and everyone at IGLA, thank you for all of the hard work you do day in and day out to help books like mine become something more than a stack of printer paper held together with a rubber band. To my foreign rights agents, the elite team of Danny Baror and Heather Baror-Shapiro of Baror International, thank you for your tireless pursuits to bring my books to new countries and for such an unprecedented opportunity to reach a wider audience.

As always, thank you to others in the industry who have stood by me and helped my books make their long, winding journey that is this industry. To Pat Shaw, for digging me out of the slush pile and fighting for my honor. To Stairway Press, my first publishing family. To Matt Stine, Paul Stoffer, and 27 Sound Entertainment for keeping my Internet home spiffy.

For every book I write, I spend at least as much time on research as I do actually penning the story. "Getting it right" is important to me, so it's a good thing I'm fortunate enough to be surrounded by many intelligent people from all different walks of life, and that occasionally, they're kind enough to indulge my questions. As always, a massive thank-you to Dr. Richard Elliot for providing expert analysis of fictional crimes and your consulting services for all questions in the area of forensic psychiatry. To Doug and Margeaux, for being my phone-a-cop contacts. To Zach Broome and Todd Meador, for your contributions to Molly's number facts. To Kate Crumbley, for her help with the Triple Shooter's "serial killer name." Thank you to Mark Ballard and Brian Woods for your expertise in art and color theory. To Amelia Garrett, for your knowledge of and experience with the tattoo industry and schooling me in the ins and outs of getting ink. To Flint Dollar and Jim Penndorf, for your ideas on music for a child prodigy.

To the Central Georgia Alzheimer's Association, specifically Karen Kinsler, Linda Thornbury, Mott Smith, and Kristie Touchton: I can't thank you all enough for doing what so many people need you to and what you did for me, which is raising awareness about Alzheimer's disease. I appreciate your role in bringing Eldred to life. He's written for you and the community of patients and caregivers you work so tirelessly to support. I hope you'll love him as much as I love all of you!

One thing I learned quickly in this profession was finding kindred spirits is important. Thank you to my Purgies, Pitizens, and Y-Nots for your support, advice, fresh eyes, and pep talks. Please never get off my lawn.

There aren't words to thank special friends who lent serious moral support to my writing process and career: Emily Rose Brunner, Nikki Vincent, and Sasha Penndorf. Thank you a million times over for giving me time and sanity to work as well as a willing ear if needed. To my theatre families who give me a place to be somewhere OTHER than work for a while, but who also are always ready to step up and support my work, too, I love you all. To Will Crews, Danielle Thuen, Meg Abney, and Brian Woods, who are always ready to jump in two-feet-first if I need help or a laugh when I'm overwhelmed—you guys are probably the reason I'm not in a padded room yet.

To Courtney: You'll never know quite how much your support really means to me. The fact that you believe in me is a support special to me in ways I can't quite describe. Maybe it's because as siblings, we tended to pit ourselves against each other. Maybe it's because I happen to know you have very selective tastes and hold said tastes to a high standard. But this year, you've supported me one hundred percent both in book writing and in a dark personal moment of my life, and it's something I will never forget. Thank you.

To Mom: Thank you for always believing in me, for being my sounding board, my cheerleader, my warm hug, my excited phone call, and my biggest fan. You will always be one of the people I'm most excited to hand over a book to read and hear what you think, because your opinion has always been so vital to me. I love you.

To Dad: I know you had a dream once that couldn't come to fruition for reasons outside your control. But you didn't let that stop you from having new goals and dreams and striving for them, and as I've grown up, I've become more and more aware that one of those new goals you decided you'd strive for was helping your daughters see *their* dreams come alive. But I'm here to tell you, they wouldn't have without you and Mom. You taught me the perseverance and passion, and you also gave me the push to go for them. I won't ever forget you did. I love you.

To Ashlee: Shit, son. What do I say here? You're the glitter that makes the darkest of my days go bright. You're the one I want to spend bright, sunny afternoons inside, sitting on the computer, with. You're the one there to tell me what I feel or think when I'm not sure where I am, because . . . how else am I gonna know? So to finish out this thank-you, a poem: The Thing shirts are red, the Things' hair is blue. Jesus holds dance parties and is awesome, and So. Are. You. (Yep. That's where your acknowledgments have gone . . .)

To the littlest members of my family: This time, I don't just want you to know when one day you read this that when I wrote it, I loved you. I want you to know that even back then, you were why. Your presences in my life put energy and hope and inspiration in my soul. Thank you both just for being who you are, because just the presence of those two sweet, amazing souls has put words into mine.

For David: I've always been ambitious and had this dream. I thought if I worked hard enough, I could persevere. And yet . . . it's no coincidence in my mind or heart that since "us," I've started writing novels again when I'd stopped because I just didn't have the passion anymore. It's no coincidence in my mind or heart that since "us," I've signed with a great agent, sold four books in the US and two in Germany while continuing to write others, when before, I'd practically given up. I guess it turns out that even if I've written the books and worked hard and persevered, before, there was a piece of the puzzle missing. A vital part absent, keeping things from working just enough that they wouldn't. Thank you for being my missing piece, but thank you even more for being found.

And last but certainly not least, to my readers for joining Jenna on her latest adventure: A lot of authors say that they write for themselves and that either other people will like it or they won't. For me, that is not true. I write for you, because you've trusted me with your time and energy. You've invested in me. You're the ones who love my characters as much as I do (if not more at times!), and you're the ones who deserve every bit of the story you opened this book hoping to get. So thank you all, for trusting me to entertain you. Thank you for jumping into my story and letting it take you away. I hope it has brought you much excitement, many surprises, and just enough thrill to keep your heart pounding at just the right pace. And as always, I hope it kept you reading late into the night!

WITHDRAWN

$15.00   6/15

LONGWOOD PUBLIC LIBRARY
800 Middle Country Road
Middle Island, NY 11953
(631) 924-6400
longwoodlibrary.org

LIBRARY HOURS

Monday-Friday	9:30 a.m. - 9:00 p.m.
Saturday	9:30 a.m. - 5:00 p.m.
Sunday (Sept-June)	1:00 p.m. - 5:00 p.m.